Praise for the incomparable romance
of *USA Today* bestselling author

SABRINA JEFFRIES

"Delightful."
Joan Johnston

"Humorous, sexy, and entertaining."
Romantic Times

"One of the best writers in romance today."
Rexanne Becnel

"Luscious romance filled with sensuous moments
that will make your heart beat a little faster."
Oakland Press

"Intriguing . . . lively . . . occasionally bawdy."
Library Journal

"Wit, charm, and burning sensuality . . .
an absolute pleasure . . . anyone who loves
romance must read Sabrina Jeffries."
Lisa Kleypas

Avon Books by
Sabrina Jeffries

MARRIED TO THE VISCOUNT
DANCE OF SEDUCTION
AFTER THE ABDUCTION
A NOTORIOUS LOVE
A DANGEROUS LOVE
THE DANGEROUS LORD
THE FORBIDDEN LORD
THE PIRATE LORD

SABRINA JEFFRIES

A Notorious Love

AVON BOOKS
An Imprint of HarperCollins*Publishers*

This is a work of fiction. Names, characters, places, and incidents are products of the author's imagination or are used fictitiously and are not to be construed as real. Any resemblance to actual events, locales, organizations, or persons, living or dead, is entirely coincidental.

AVON BOOKS
An Imprint of HarperCollins*Publishers*
10 East 53rd Street
New York, New York 10022-5299

ISBN-13: 978-0-380-81803-7
ISBN-10: 0-380-81803-5
www.avonromance.com

First Avon Books paperback printing: September 2001

Printed in the U.S.A.

10 9 8 7 6 5 4 3

To Liz and Debbie,
who keep me sane.
And to all the ladies at
The Romance Journal
(www.romancejournal.com),
who know how to show an author a good time.

Chapter 1

London
October 1815

The hero now I speak of, he was proper tall
and straight,
Like to the lofty poplar tree, his body was complete;
His growth was like the tufted fir that does ascend
the air,
And waving o'er his shoulders broad the locks of
yellow hair.

"Rody McCorley,"
anonymous Irish street ballad

The Well-bred Young Lady avoids the merest hint of scandalous behavior.

Helena Laverick couldn't help remembering that stricture as she surveyed the deserted hallway of the St. Giles lodging house. For she was about to break it most flagrantly.

Her sister Rosalind had always criticized their late mother's favorite instruction book, *Mrs. Nunley's Guide to Etiquette for Young Ladies*. Rosalind's philosophy was to follow Mrs. N's rules when possible, but ignore them when they were impractical. Helena usually considered that her excuse for disregarding any checks to her outrageous behavior.

But in this case she had a point. Their young sister Juliet's mad dash into trouble made it impossible for Helena *not* to break the rules. And by venturing into this strange lodging house, where rats scrabbled all around her and burning rushlights clogged the air with their scorched mutton scent, she was breaking quite a few.

The Well-bred Young Lady does not take long trips alone—she'd broken that one when she'd traveled alone to London from Warwickshire. Since Rosalind and her new husband, Griff Knighton, were honeymooning on the Continent and Papa was unable to leave his bed, *someone* had to handle this messy situation.

The Well-bred Young Lady never ventures outdoors without her maid—that one was laughable. The fewer servants involved in her secret mission, the better. Servants did have a tendency to talk.

Her grip tightened on her cane as she stared at the scarred oak door before her, the one that belonged to Mr. Daniel Brennan, her brother-in-law's unmarried man of affairs. Now she was about to violate one of Mrs. N's most serious strictures—*The Well-bred Young Lady does not call on a gentleman in his lodgings unchaperoned.*

And certainly not at dawn. Why, Mr. Brennan's own

landlady had refused to risk his ire by rousing him so early.

A shiver ran down Helena's spine as she remembered the last time she'd provoked Mr. Brennan's ire, when he and Griff had been guests at Swan Park this past summer. Not that he'd had any right to be angry. *He'd* been the one in the wrong. *He'd* been the one shamelessly taking money from Griff for misleading them all, for pretending to court them while undoubtedly laughing at them behind their backs for believing his kindnesses and compliments . . .

No, she mustn't think of that. All that mattered was saving Juliet. Which was why she must swallow her pride, rouse her courage, and awaken Mr. Brennan. And soon, too, because her bad leg pained her from the arduous climb up the steep stairs, and nothing would be more mortifying than having it give out in front of *him*. So before she could change her mind, she rapped sharply on the door.

At first she heard nothing. Merciful heavens, what if she had the wrong place? She'd wondered why Mr. Brennan would reside in a slum like St. Giles when he surely could afford better, but Griff's coachman had insisted that the man lived here.

She knocked again, this time more loudly. Nothing. Might he refuse to answer? Panic seized her at the thought, so she rapped the silver head of her cane on the door repeatedly, loud enough to raise the dead.

Success at last. Through the thin walls, she heard heavy steps and a male voice growling, "I'm coming, devil take you!" If not for her mission, she might well have fled. Instead she braced herself for whatever might happen.

But nothing could prepare her for her first sight of the burly giant. Bare-chested, clad only in his drawers.

Struck speechless, she gaped at him. Despite what her sisters thought, she did have *some* curiosity about men, especially half-naked ones of such impressive dimensions. Mr. Brennan was a veritable Samson, with the muscular shoulders of a pugilist and the broad, sculpted chest of a laborer, thickly sprinkled with dark blond hair. As for those arms swathed in sinew . . . she could easily imagine them pulling down a temple.

Just now, however, the Samson was staring at her, perplexed. "Lady Helena?" He shook his head as if to clear it. "It is you, isn't it?"

She kept her eyes trained on his face as a blush crept up her cheeks. "Good morning, Mr. Brennan. I'm sorry if I awakened you." Not that there was any question of it—his tousled sandy hair and lack of attire confirmed it.

"Is everything all right at Swan Park? Your father is well?"

"Yes . . . no . . . I mean, I . . ." Her lame attempt at coherent speech came crashing to a halt when he leaned one huge forearm against the doorframe, unwittingly causing all his muscles to shift and flex.

How in creation could a lady converse rationally when such a magnificent display of male flesh was before her? Despite his size, he hadn't an inch of fat on him—no hint of unwanted flesh on the chest and arms, no telltale thickness about the waist. Not a woman above the age of fifteen could miss that Mr. Brennan in his drawers was a fine figure of a man.

"M'lady, are you well?" he queried.

Only when her head snapped up did she realize her gaze had wandered down to his bulging drawers. "Yes!" she cried too loudly, then added in a more subdued tone, "I'm fine. Quite well. Yes."

He cocked an eyebrow, as if knowing precisely how much his appearance unnerved her. "Forgive my inappropriate dress, but I wasn't expecting company at dawn."

"No need to apologize. I hadn't even noticed your draw— I mean, your dress— I mean, your lack of—" Heavens, she was being a complete ninny. She started again, futilely attempting to regain some shred of composure. "I hadn't noticed a thing, I assure you."

"Nothing?" His gray eyes danced with mischief. "D'you mean to wound my pride, Lady Helena?"

"Of course not! That is . . . well . . ."

"It's all right." He idly rubbed his hairy chest, and her gaze greedily fixed there. "Why don't you tell me why you're in London calling on me at such an ungodly hour?"

"Certainly." She drew herself up, trying to recover her badly slipping ladylike demeanor. "You see, Mr. Brennan, I . . . er . . . require your assistance in a personal matter."

"*Require* it, do you?" His eyes narrowed. "Has your ladyship not heard that I'm no longer in your brother-in-law's employ? Although I'm running Knighton Trading until his return, I'm not his man of affairs anymore, so anything you want in *that* capacity—"

"No! It's nothing to do with Griff. Not exactly."

"Then p'raps you'd better tell me what it *does* have to do with." He pushed away from the doorframe, looking impatient.

"You see, I—" She broke off when another lodger emerged from the stairs. As soon as the unkempt man skulked past and shuffled into his own room, she lowered her voice. "Please, Mr. Brennan, I must keep this conversation private. May I come in?"

A devilish smile touched his lips. "In here? With me? Isn't your ladyship worried about your reputation? About being alone with a man of *my* reputation?"

Though he said it with a trace of sarcasm, his assumption was not entirely wrong. Mr. Brennan might be respectable these days, but he'd spent his youth with smugglers. The bastard son of a notorious highwayman, he was also known to live rather wildly—or so Rosalind said. And considering his scanty attire . . .

"I'd rather you put on some clothes, of course," she ventured.

"And I'd rather return to my bed. So why don't you go back to wherever you're staying in London, and I'll come 'round this afternoon. Then we can have all the private conversation you like."

"No, no," she protested, "I must speak to you now. It's urgent."

"Oh, Danny Bo-o-o-y," a melodious voice suddenly sang out from the inner recesses of his rooms. "Don't you want to see the nice surprise Sall's got for you?"

Helena froze. Lord, this was worse than she'd feared. He had a woman with him.

Mr. Brennan groaned. "Go back to sleep, Sall," he called out. "Be there in a bit."

But apparently his companion wasn't to be put off so easily. As Helena watched in horrified fascination, Sall emerged behind him. She was one of *those* women and fresh from his bedchamber, judging from her disheveled hair and brazen manner. Not to mention her state of undress, which exceeded Mr. Brennan's.

For Sall wore no clothes at all.

Helena found it incomprehensible that a woman could prance about in broad daylight entirely unclothed. She'd never, *ever* done so herself, and certainly she'd never been in the presence of another woman doing it—not even her sisters. Though she'd sometimes secretly wished to paint the naked human form, she'd never pursued it, knowing that flagrant displays of the nude body were outrageous and shameful.

Apparently no one had informed Sall of that fact, for

she strode boldly up to them. "H'lo." Planting her hands on her lush hips, the woman scrutinized Helena from the top of her modest bonnet to the end of the cane she could never hide. "Didn't know Danny called for more company. Haven't seen *you* around, luv. You one of those demi-reps what's kept by the gents? Here I been thinkin' Danny Boy's a gin man, when all along he's hankerin' for champagne. What a lark."

"Sall—" Daniel began in a warning tone as Helena gaped speechlessly.

"It's all right, Danny. I already know you like more than one tart sometimes, so just let the girl in. And if it's that leg of hers making you balk, you can be sure it won't make a bit of difference once we're all rollin' about—"

"Sall!" Mr. Brennan mercifully interrupted. "Before you go putting the lass in my bed, you should know that this is Griff's sister-in-law, Lady Helena. And I doubt she's here for entertainment."

A little gasp escaped Sall as she slid behind him and punched him in the back. "Then why did you let me rattle on like that to a proper la—" She suddenly burst into laughter. "Wait a minute—you're shammin' me, ain't you? A lady comin' to Buckeridge Street alone—you must think me a complete chucklehead!"

"I'm afraid, Miss . . . er . . . Sall," Helena sputtered, "that Mr. Brennan is not 'shamming' you. I am indeed Mr. Knighton's sister-in-law."

As an awkward silence descended, she kept her eyes focused on a chair across the room, utterly incapable of meeting Mr. Brennan's gaze. No doubt he found this situation amusing.

Meanwhile, Sall's words rang in her ears: *And if it's that leg of hers making you balk . . .* As if there would be any question of it. She'd learned the hard way that her bad leg always made men balk. Mr. Brennan wouldn't be any different.

"Sall, m'dear," he told the woman gently, "why don't you wait for me in the bedchamber? You're making m'lady a mite nervous."

"All right, but don't be long, luv," Sall responded without rancor, giving Helena a once-over that left her feeling utterly inadequate as a woman.

As Sall flounced back toward his bedchamber, hips wiggling, Helena felt a stab of envy. What would it be like to be the shameless woman waiting for Mr. Brennan in his bed, the one providing his "entertainment"?

Then she groaned. Whatever had given her such an indecent idea! She'd never in a million years wish to behave so scandalously. No, indeed. Never. Even if a man *would* want her in that way.

She forced herself to meet his gaze.

He was watching her with concern. "Please forgive Sall's . . . er . . . brazenness. I'm afraid she isn't used to seeing your sort around here."

Which sort is that? she wanted to ask. *The well-bred sort? Or the sort whose lameness renders her unable to jiggle her derriere in that provocative manner?*

She swallowed down her dreadful envy of the woman and muttered, "No, I don't imagine she is."

"P'raps it'd be best if I called on your ladyship at a more acceptable location later. If you'd just leave your direction with my landlady—"

"No, please, I assure you that this matter cannot wait." It galled her to have to beg him for help, but she had no choice. "I do not mean to intrude upon your—" Entertainment? Orgy? "I do not intend to keep you long, but if you'll give me a few minutes, I'd appreciate it beyond words."

She held her breath. He might be a libertine and God knew what else, but with Griff and Rosalind on the Continent, he was her best hope right now. Her only hope.

His gaze met hers, wary but clearly curious. He paused a moment longer, a moment that seemed like an eternity.

Then he released a sigh. "All right. Go downstairs and wait for me in the parlor. I'll be there soon as I dress."

Relief swamped her. "Oh, thank you, Mr. Brennan. I truly—"

"Go, before I change my mind," he said gruffly. When she turned away, he added, "And tell my landlady I said to put the tea on. Looks like we'll both be needing it."

Tea? She nearly laughed aloud. After he heard her request, he'd want something a good deal stronger than tea, and she would not blame him. Indeed, if it would ensure his cooperation, she'd give him anything he wanted.

Chapter 2

Sweet Una was the tightest,
Genteelest of the village dames;
Her eyes they were the brightest
That e'er set youthful heart in flames.

"Una's Lock,"
anonymous eighteenth-century Scottish ballad

Half an hour later, Daniel paused outside the lodging house parlor. From where he stood, an ancient mirror murkily reflected Lady Helena's image, though she wouldn't see him unless she looked up.

Hard to believe she was *here*, as out of place in the onion-scented lodging house as a swan in a swamp. She sat at his landlady's prized oak writing table, bent over a small sketch pad and laying pencil to paper with energetic slashes of her hand. He'd forgotten about her hobby, her sketching and the miniatures she liked to paint. What could she be sketching now with such enthusiasm?

Him, no doubt—setting a pair of horns on his head, a forked tail on his arse, and a pair of hooves on his legs. He could well guess what she thought of him after spying him in his drawers and naught else, with his pego half-stiff with morning.

He stifled a chuckle. Lady High-and-Mighty, flustered at seeing him in his drawers—that had been priceless. And the way she'd tried to act as if she hadn't looked. She hadn't gulled him. She might be a lady of quality, but she was still a virgin and they all had a bit of curiosity. He'd seen her sneaking a peek at his groin.

Making his damned pego go from half-stiff to full arousal—for her ladyship, of all people. It wasn't Sall, prancing naked about the room, who'd made him as randy as a stallion brought out to cover a mare. No, only Lady Helena had done that.

Not that he didn't have a sound reason for his lust. He slid into the doorway to get a better look at her.

Yes, she was miles above his station. Despite what Griff had uncovered about her da's title, the world still thought her an earl's daughter, and she had the breeding to match. And yes, she was lame.

But any man with an ounce of sense would desire her. Especially a man with a profound appreciation for all varieties of fine women.

He drank in every inch of her, glad to have the chance before she noticed him. What a perfect picture of a female. Aristocratic features and skin as smooth and creamy as new ivory. A slender figure swathed in white muslin with her swan's neck prettily yoked in a blue wisp of a scarf. Not to mention the feathery curls peeking out from under one of those annoying bonnets that hid all her hair.

He'd sure like a look at it. There must be oceans of silky mahogany wrapped up tight under there, just waiting for a man to unwind it so it could flow free over her naked body, so he could stroke it and bury his face in all that soft, woman-scented—

His pego roused in his trousers again, making him groan. Fool thing, to be angling after the likes of Lady Helena. What was he thinking? If any man came within ten feet of that fair swan, especially the bastard son of Wild Danny Brennan, she'd be squawking loud enough to wake the dead. That was the trouble with swans—they were pretty from a distance, but close up they were foul-tempered as the very devil.

Which made it all the more intriguing that she'd come to *him* for help. Nearly begged him for it, too. He was sure she'd always thought him coarse, and she probably thought him unscrupulous. So what could she possibly want with him now?

He shoved away from the doorframe. He'd made her wait long enough—might as well find out what daft notion had brought her to St. Giles.

"I see the tea is here," he said as he entered and noticed the tea tray sitting a few inches from her ladyship's sketch pad.

She started and closed her pad. "Yes. Do you want some?"

"All right. I'm parched this morning." Some wickedness made him add, "That's what happens when a man's spent half the night entertaining."

As he'd expected, she colored right up. Ah, he was a scoundrel to tease her so, but how could he resist making her blush so prettily?

Ducking her head, she daintily poured him a cup of tea. "Milk? Sugar?"

"Both, if you please."

The tiny smile on her lips as she added milk to his tea struck him as curious. Until she gave it to him and he drank some. "This tea's cold," he grumbled.

"What do you expect? Your landlady brought it in over twenty minutes ago."

The hint of reproof in her voice was unmistakable. Impudent wench.

"Didn't I rush down here fast enough to suit your ladyship?" He set his cup down on the table. "P'raps I shouldn't have bothered to dress. P'raps you would've preferred to have this conversation with me in my drawers."

To his satisfaction, her blush deepened to scarlet, and she drew the edges of her pelisse closer together. "Just because you enjoy cavorting naked in front of women doesn't mean the women take pleasure in it."

He rested his hand on the table and bent closer, feeling full of mischief. "Never had any complaints before."

"Given your choice of companion, that doesn't surprise me."

He laughed, which only seemed to annoy her further. The lass was still peeved over Sall and her boldness? And after he'd sent the shameless tart home without even a kiss, too. "I take it you disapprove of my 'choice of companion.'"

"I don't care in the least whom you consort with," she declared with an elegant little sniff.

"But I'll wager you have your own ideas about who it should be." Bent on devilment, he added, "P'raps a woman like your ladyship?"

"Certainly not!" Then, as if realizing too late the insult

behind her words, she stammered, "I-I mean . . . that is . . ."

"It's all right," he put in, annoyed by her answer, though he supposed he deserved it for teasing her. He straightened from the table. "You needn't worry I'll make improper advances to you, m'lady. I prefer the sort of woman who enjoys seeing a man in his drawers."

Just that quick, her embarrassment turned to frosty hauteur. She glanced away. "Then I suppose it's a good thing you live where such women abound."

He had the odd feeling that he'd insulted her, though he couldn't imagine how, and to his surprise, her distant air irritated him. "Ah, and where do *you* think I should live? Hidden away in the country like your ladyship? Where you can avoid the world and its troubles?" He dropped his voice to a thrum. "Where big nasty men like myself don't bother pretty women?"

She continued to stare woodenly beyond him at the cracked mantel. "I assure you, Mr. Brennan, we have our share of nasty men in Stratford-upon-Avon. And they have no compunction about making our lives a misery. Indeed, that's why I'm here."

That brought him up short. "What do you mean? Has somebody been causing you trouble?" Though it wouldn't surprise him. When she was vexed, the woman had a tongue that would strip bark from a tree and draw any man's ire.

"No, not me, not exactly." Focusing her gaze on her fingers, she toyed with her sketch pad. "I mean Juliet."

"Juliet?" Why, the little innocent was scarce out of the schoolroom. Would some wretch dare to hurt her?

Apparently Lady Helena mistook the reason for his

surprise. "You remember her, don't you?" Her gaze glittered bright with self-righteousness. "My youngest sister? The one you pretended to court while your employer seduced Rosalind?"

So she still hadn't forgiven him for that. "My *former* employer," he reminded her. "And yes, I remember your sister very well. She was the one who didn't hold my mistake against me. Come to think of it, you're the only one in your family who does."

"Because I'm the only one in my family not foolish enough to be taken in by every smooth-tongued rascal who lands on our doorstep."

That tore it. Leaning forward, he planted his hand on the table scarce inches from hers. "For a smooth-tongued rascal, I've been mighty accommodating of you this morning. And so far you haven't given me a single reason for being so."

She swallowed convulsively, then averted her gaze. "I'm sorry—you're right. You *have* been very obliging. I don't mean to be so ungrateful, but I'm worried sick."

"About *what*, damn it? What has happened to your sister?"

"Juliet's been kidnapped."

The second Helena spoke the words, she regretted them. They were a trifle misleading, and judging from Mr. Brennan's shock and fury, they were liable to send him off in the wrong direction.

"What?" he roared, straightening to his full height. "By who? What villains would dare? Have they sent a demand for ransom yet? Surely your father went to the authorities in Warwickshire—"

"No, no, I didn't mean to imply it was done against her will." She paused. "That is . . . well . . ."

His gaze narrowed ominously on her. "What the bloody hell *did* you mean?"

Her fingers curled into a knot. "Juliet has run off—has eloped—with a man."

He looked more astonished than alarmed. "Hold up now—are we speaking of the same lass? Your shy little sister, the one who jumped like a scared rabbit whenever I spoke to her this summer?"

"Yes." Her tone hardened. "But believe me, she didn't jump when that . . . that villain who carried her off spoke to her."

His expression altered, sharpening his features to flint. "Ah, I see. Lady Juliet has run off with an unsuitable sort, one beneath the touch of your family." His sarcasm made it only too clear that he thought any of them lucky to find husbands at all.

She shook off that lowering thought. "I'm almost certain he's a fortune hunter," she said defensively, "and I fear that he's worse."

There was a long pause. Then he crossed his arms over his chest with a belligerent air. "I'm not sure what any of this has to do with me."

"That should be obvious: I want you to help me find them before it's too late."

"Me? Why not hire a Bow Street runner?"

She looked blankly at him. "A Bow Street runner? What is that?"

He sighed. "I forgot you've spent most of your life in the country. Well, m'lady, Bow Street runners track down missing persons, among other things."

"Oh. Still, I wouldn't have the faintest idea how to find one."

"You found *me*," he put in dryly.

Was that unusual? Did he hide himself away in St.

Giles because he didn't want anyone to see his poverty? It was hard to believe he'd *prefer* it here. She could see soot-blackened, dilapidated buildings through the window and hear tenants arguing through the paper-thin walls. "Finding you was easy. I merely asked Griff's coachman to take me to where you lived."

"And he brought you to St. Giles, just like that?" He shook his head in obvious disgust. "I'll have the wretch turned off for that foolishness."

"You most certainly will not. I told him it was urgent, and I promised there would be no repercussions if he helped me."

"Oh, did you, now? Nice of you to appropriate Griff's servants like that. Why not ask one of *them* where to hire somebody to track Lady Juliet?"

"Because servants gossip. I'm certainly not going to let Griff's servants know what really happened, after taking such great pains to hide it from our own servants."

"What did you tell yours?"

"That Juliet had gone to London alone to visit Rosalind, and I was following after. Because if word got out that Juliet had run off with some unsavory character—"

"—your family's good name would be ruined," he finished for her.

"Don't be silly—I don't care one whit about *that*. What worries me most is Juliet's future. All she has ever wanted is a husband who will make her happy, and I am quite sure this man will *not*. And if anyone hears of the elopement, she'll be ruined, even if she is still . . . chaste . . . when we recover her. I know nothing about your Bow Street runners' skills or reliability, but I could not trust anyone to be discreet in this matter."

"Yet you trust me?" he said, clearly surprised.

"To be discreet? Certainly. And Griff trusts you to run

Knighton Trading while he's gone, so why shouldn't I trust you with this?"

"That's another thing. I'm s'posed to be helping Griff." He began to pace the room with quick, forceful strides. "And you may find this hard to believe, but I also have my own business to run. I advise gentlemen on how to invest their money, and I already have more clients than I can handle. I don't have time for chasing after foolish girls who elope with unsuitable men."

"I would have gone to Griff if he were here. I did send him and Rosalind an urgent message, but it won't reach them on the Continent for days, and this matter requires haste. So I came to you. You're the logical choice."

When he raised an eyebrow, she continued in a softer tone, "You know Juliet and seem to like her. I'm sure that if you heard the whole of it, you would understand why I consider this situation so dire."

That seemed to give him pause. Slowly he approached the table, then settled his hip on the edge, not far from her. "I'm listening."

Yes, and crowding in upon her with his giant's body that blocked the meager sunlight silting through the grimy window behind him. Must he loom like the great God of War poised to pounce? It was most unsettling.

She would have stood and moved away if she could, but she'd die before she let him watch her struggle to her feet with her usual awkwardness.

Instead, she concentrated on replacing his half-empty cup on the tray and tidying up the chipped tea things. "About a week after Griff and Rosalind were married, a man named Captain Will Morgan came to Stratford-upon-Avon. He claimed to be interested in seeing the sights in Shakespeare's birthplace while on leave from the regiment quartered in Evesham. But he stayed nearly three weeks, which I thought excessive. Indeed, although most people found him amiable, I distrusted him from the first."

He snorted. "That's hardly surprising, given your general distrust of my gender."

He fixed his too-perceptive eyes on her, making her flinch. He'd done that at Swan Park, too, studying her like a teacher searching out his pupil's weakness. She could easily guess what he saw—a woman whose lameness ought to make her grateful for any affection men might deign to bestow on her, who ought not to berate them for being untrustworthy. Who ought not to wish they could see beyond her deficiencies to the woman beneath.

She tilted her chin up proudly. Let him think what he wished. It didn't matter. "All the same, Will Morgan seemed far too interested in ascertaining the extent of Juliet's and my inheritance to suit me."

"Even a captain must think practically when it comes to marriage."

"Mr. Morgan is no captain." Now came the worst of it. "After I discovered him and Juliet gone, I went immediately to his supposed regiment. They'd never heard of him. He lied to us all from the moment he arrived."

Mr. Brennan rubbed his brow with slow, even strokes. She couldn't help noticing his blunt fingers and how surprisingly clean the nails were.

"Very strange, that," he muttered, half to himself. "Why would he pretend to be a military man? Did he think to impress people?"

"I don't know. He did ask a great many questions about Papa and his estate, his friends, etcetera."

"You'd expect that of a man intending to marry."

"Yes, but doesn't it seem rather calculated? Not to mention the alarming discovery I made as I came after them in Papa's coach."

He gaped at her. "You *came after* them? Alone?"

"Of course. Why do you think I'm in London?"

Mr. Brennan stood and began to pace again, like some magnificent golden bull. It gave her shivers just watching him, the dawn light streaking his long Samson hair with gilt and lighting his gray eyes to sparkling silver. How much power lay leashed in that massive chest and those wide, square shoulders, barely constrained by the simple linen shirt and serviceable fustian frock coat?

"What if you'd been accosted by highwaymen or footpads or any of the other unscrupulous wretches who prey on women traveling alone?" he growled. "What then? Did your father approve of this?"

"Certainly; he had no choice. He hasn't any more desire to see Juliet wed to a conscienceless fortune hunter than I." The fire had died down, and she shivered beneath her thin muslin pelisse.

Mr. Brennan caught sight of it, and his lips tightened into a grim line. Striding to the hearth, he scooped some coals into the hob grate and watched while they burst into flame. "You're not even sure the lad *is* a fortune hunter. Juliet's a fetching lass. P'raps he fell in love with her. I know you believe men don't marry for love, but young lads do sometimes lose their hearts to pretty women."

His reproof taxed her temper beyond her control. "Not in this case—or else he loses it with alarming frequency."

"What do you mean?"

"He tried courting *me* first. I rebuffed his advances, of course—"

"Of course," he echoed dryly.

She glared at his broad back. "But not before he waxed poetic about how he was 'drawn to me from the beginning' and how he 'could not resist my heavenly beauty.' Needless to say, I knew better than to fall for such false blandishments."

"Why assume they were false?"

"Because men have little use for cripples, sir."

She regretted her bald statement the moment he swung around to face her. A gaze deep with understanding bore right through to her soul. Then it darkened, edging slowly down her body, rousing a strange, unfamiliar heat wherever it lingered.

"Surely not all men are so foolish," he said huskily.

His look drove a shaft of need so deep into her that she ached with it. No man had looked at her like that since before the illness that had made her lame. Merciful heavens, she'd forgotten how some men could provoke a woman into wanting them with just a sensuous glance.

Why must he be one of them?

Because he was a libertine, of course. He handed out flatteries and flirtatious looks with the practiced ease of a vendor coaxing matrons to buy beauty aids. She, of all people, should know that.

She cleared her throat and attempted to regain her composure. "Not that I cared what Mr. Morgan thought of me one way or the other, you understand."

"Of course not."

The seeming gentleness in his voice made her scramble to hide her susceptibility. "He wasn't the kind of man I would find acceptable under any circumstances."

A beat of silence. Then Mr. Brennan said coolly, "No, I don't s'pose he was."

Gathering her dignity about her, she strengthened her

defenses against him. "Mr. Morgan's actions since then have proved I was right to distrust him."

"But your sister did not share your suspicions."

She sighed. "No, Juliet is young and naive. She dismissed my cautions with scarcely a thought. I'm afraid that my . . . er . . . viewpoint on men led her to assume I was unjustifiably biased."

"Can't imagine why she'd think that," he retorted. "You said you made 'an alarming discovery' while following them?"

She blinked. Lord, he'd been paying close attention. But then, he'd always been one to make a woman feel as if her every word was important. It was another of his little tricks. "On the road, I showed Mr. Morgan's picture to several people."

"You have a picture of him?"

"Yes. As soon as I found Juliet gone, I sketched an image as best I could from memory. With the aid of my sketch and a miniature of Juliet, I traced their steps and discovered they were headed south for London, not north to Gretna Green. If he intended to marry her, why did he bring her here?"

"A very good question," Mr. Brennan said, a frown knitting his brow.

"My alarm increased when I reached an inn in Aylesbury and found a maidservant who'd met Mr. Morgan *before* he'd come to Warwickshire." Her throat constricted. "On his journey from London, he'd stopped there with male companions, whom he'd left behind before heading off for Stratford. These friends of his were rather unsavory characters, however."

When she paused, remembering the maid's full recitation and the awful chill it had sent through her, Mr. Brennan approached the table. "Unsavory? How?"

"Well, they talked openly about their profession, and . . ." She lifted an earnest gaze to him. "She was almost certain that they and their friend Mr. Will Morgan are smugglers."

Chapter 3

Oh, it happened one evening at the playing of ball
That I first met lovely Willie, so proper and tall.
He was neat, fair, and handsome,
and straight in every limb;
There's a heart in this bosom lies breaking for him.

"Lovely Willie,"
anonymous Irish ballad

Daniel barely stifled his laughter. *Smugglers?* In Aylesbury, the heart of England? What a daft idea. It was miles from where smugglers worked and traded. And if this Will Morgan was one of them, why travel all the way to Warwickshire to carry off a girl with a moderate dowry, when there were plenty of rich heiresses in London?

But judging from Lady Helena's pale face, she believed it to be true. Some young fool eloped with her sister, and she decided at once he was a criminal.

Morgan did sound like a fortune hunter, however. He'd probably gone to Stratford on legitimate business, when Juliet—and her new dowry—had caught his eye. Perhaps he'd termed himself a captain to sound interesting.

But fortune hunters and smugglers were different sorts of scoundrel altogether. He fought to hide his amusement. "Why did this maid think all these men were smugglers?"

"They were rather free with their favors, giving away French goods to all the servants. One of them gave the maid a lace shawl from France and said he'd dodged the excisemen to bring it in."

This time Daniel didn't bother to suppress his laugh. "That's a young buck's foolish boast, is all. He probably bought the shawl in London, then spun that tale of adventure to win a warm bed with an easy wench. Men do it all the time."

"*You* would know more about that than I," she said, tilting her chin up so high he could see her lovely throat.

"Careful, m'lady, one of these days that tongue of yours will freeze solid and fall right off." That gained him a frigid glance. Perhaps he shouldn't tease her so, but God knew she provoked him to it. Smugglers, indeed. "Did this maid have any other reason for her suspicions?"

"She said the men sold the innkeeper some French brandy."

That was a bit more telling, but it didn't mean the fool had been a free trader. "Was she sure Morgan was one of them? P'raps he simply wanted drinking companions."

"Mr. Morgan did not strike me as the sort to require companionship. There was something heartless about him, despite his handsome looks and gentlemanly manner."

"Which of course means he's a criminal."

"I did not say that! Although he roused my suspicions from the first, I didn't think him a criminal until I heard of his companions."

"Who may not have been true companions at all."

"If you insist," she said crisply. "In any case, after I left Aylesbury I continued to London, but I lost them in the city yesterday."

Christ, he supposed he should be grateful she hadn't shown up here last night while he and Sall were drinking and prigging.

"I have no idea where to look," she went on. "So when I realized last night that I would not be able to find them, I thought of you."

"To track down Mr. Morgan and your sister."

"Yes. After all, you do have some experience with . . . well . . ."

The truth hit him like a well-placed blow, shattering his humor. "With smugglers."

She ducked her head to hide her face beneath the wide brim of her bonnet, and a long-buried anger twisted up his insides. He should've realized that all that business about trusting him was rubbish.

"You came to me because of my connection to free traders." Sarcasm weighted his words. "That's why you chose me, ain't it?" For once, he didn't watch his grammar. She thought him a villain, so he might as well play the part. "That's why, ain't it?"

She wouldn't look at him. "Not entirely. You're the only person I know in London. Though I did think perhaps . . . since you . . . I mean—"

"It's bloody clear what you mean. You've decided that since I used to be a criminal, I ought to be able to find a criminal."

"No!" Her head shot up. "Not at all. I—"

"I hate to disappoint you, Lady Helena, but there's no gentlemen's club for smugglers where we sit around cup-shot every night, jawing about old times." He leaned forward to plant his fists on the table in front of her. "I don't see those people anymore, so don't look to me if it's a criminal you need for tracking down this man."

"You misunderstand me," she protested, her cheeks paling. "I didn't mean to imply you were a criminal, for heaven's sake. I know perfectly well how young you were when you spent time with smugglers. You were only a boy—you could hardly have done much of a criminal nature."

He straightened, momentarily struck speechless. She didn't know? Perhaps he shouldn't be surprised—Griff wouldn't have told her, and Rosalind probably didn't know all that much herself.

He kept his voice carefully neutral. "What exactly is it that you think I did when I . . . er . . . spent time with the smugglers?"

"Why, I'm not sure." Her gloved finger idly traced the words on the cover of the sketch pad. "I suppose you held the horses. Watched for excisemen. Anything a boy might do."

A boy of seventeen, large for his age and with a quick mind, could do a damned sight more than hold horses and watch for excisemen.

"Anyone can tell you're no criminal. And Griff would hardly allow a real smuggler to work for him."

He stifled a smile at her naiveté. Before Griff had met Rosalind, he would've hired the devil himself if it furthered Knighton Trading. "Tell me, m'lady—what would you call a *real* smuggler?"

She waved her hand. "Oh, men who purchase spirits

and goods from abroad, run them into England, and then sell them. They have no scruples about firing on the Preventive Waterguard. They are rumored to be nasty, evil men who'd sell their own mothers for a profit." She leaned forward and lowered her voice confidentially. "I once read all about the Hawkhurst Gang in a pamphlet. Dreadful men, all of them."

He was torn between the urge to laugh and the urge to wring her neck. Yes, the Hawkhurst Gang had been ruthless and cruel, but not all smugglers resorted to violence. And why she thought a man of seventeen couldn't be a "real" smuggler was beyond him.

Still, he wasn't about to correct her misapprehension. "If you thought I wasn't a 'real' smuggler, why did you assume I could help you? Especially since I've been out of the free-trading business for years."

"Because at least you'd know what sort of man I'm dealing with. You'd know where they go and what they do. I thought that might help." When he remained silent, she added, "I truly would not have bothered you if not for the possibility that Juliet could be hurt. But the thought of her being . . . manhandled by a man like that, and my being unable to stop it . . ." She trailed off with a choked sigh so faint that a wiser man would have ignored it.

Daniel couldn't. Christ, the woman did know how to get at a man, didn't she? Gritting his teeth, he straightened from the table. "Do you have that sketch of Morgan with you now?"

Hope filled her face. "Yes." Picking up her sketch pad, she flipped to a page, then held it out.

He glanced at the well-rendered image of a handsome young man with dark hair and black eyes, then tore off the sheet and folded it. Stuffing it into his pocket, he handed her the sketch pad. This had to be the stupidest thing he'd ever considered doing. Between Knighton Trading and his own business, the last thing he needed was to involve himself with Lady Juliet's elopement.

"I'd best take the miniature of your sister, too." He held out his hand.

"Why?" she blurted out.

"Because I'll need to show it around while I'm asking questions about Will Morgan and Lady Juliet, won't I?"

Her eyes widened, but she fished around in her fancy velvet bag.

He doubted the chap was a smuggler, but that possibility should be eliminated first. Then he'd ask in the better inns and taverns. Perhaps luck would be on his side, and the two were still in London. If he acted quickly, he might track them down at once. Or not. London had a hundred rookeries and flash houses where a man could hide himself away without leaving a trace. Even the better inns could be discreet about their clientele, if they thought it would profit them.

And if the pair had already left London?

Bloody hell, he hoped they hadn't, because then he'd have to decide how far to carry this nonsense.

She handed him the miniature. "Does this mean you'll help me? You'll look for them?"

"That's what you wanted, isn't it?"

"Of course. But you've been decidedly unenthusiastic about the idea until now."

"Believe me, I'm not chomping at the bit, but I'll find out where they've gone." He only hoped it didn't take long. "Where was the last place you traced them to?"

"An inn named the Bear and Key on the outskirts of London. That was the final stop of the coach they took. They disappeared there."

"How long ago?"

"When I left Stratford three days ago, I was already a day behind. I lost time by going to his supposed regiment, and Papa's coachman refused to travel at night. He said it was too dangerous."

"At least there's one coachman around with some sense in him."

"That made me fall further behind, however, because they posted through the nights. So they've been gone from here two days now."

"Unless they're still in the city."

Horror filled her face. "Lord, you don't think they are, do you? That would mean that he . . . that they have no intention of eloping!"

He cursed himself for his quick tongue. "I'm sure they're gone—we just need to find out how they're traveling to Scotland. They may've come to the city to book passage on a ship."

She worried her lower lip with her fine white teeth. "Yes, but then it would have made more sense to go to the Bristol Channel. It's nearer to Warwickshire."

Which meant this mightn't be an elopement at all. He suppressed that ugly thought. Of course it was an elopement. "No point in speculating on where they went til I make some inquiries." He tucked the miniature into his coat pocket. "It sounds like you've had a tiring journey. Why don't you return to Griff's house while I take these 'round? As soon as I've got something to tell you, I'll let you know."

"I want to go with you."

"Not bloody likely." The very thought of the elegant Lady Helena trawling the flash houses with him made his belly churn.

"Why not?"

"Because some of the places I'm going aren't the sort you take a lady into."

"I don't care." She threw her shoulders back and stiffened her chin like the proud thing she was. "I'll go mad if I have to sit and do nothing."

"Better to go mad than find yourself in an alley with your throat slit."

Eyes widening, she clutched her fancy bag to her chest as if the flimsy bit of velvet would protect her from all those "nasty, evil" men. "You think it's that dangerous?"

All right, so he'd exaggerated a bit. He was known well enough that even in the rookeries, nobody would dare lay a hand on any companion of his. But he could move more quickly without her.

"Yes, it's that dangerous," he answered. "And one look at your ladyship will make all prospective informers keep their mouths shut. The sort of person to have information is also the sort that doesn't trust the upper ten thousand."

She chewed on that a minute. "I could change my clothing."

He snorted. "It'd make no difference, m'lady—you can't take the breeding out of your speech and walk and manner. It'd be like trying to hide a swan among the ducks."

"Be careful, Mr. Brennan," she said dryly, "you're coming very near to paying me a compliment, and I know you don't mean to do that."

Saucy wench. "What makes you think it was a compliment?"

Insulted, she tipped her dainty nose up. "I beg your pardon—I forgot that you prefer women with little breeding."

"Not true. I prefer women who know how to enjoy themselves—no matter what their breeding."

Her lovely eyes went round, and her lips parted on a gasp. He grinned. The bloody wench needed shaking up. She always thought she knew everything, but she might as well have been plunked down in Africa, for all she knew of him and the world she'd stumbled into.

"So you'll stay where you belong, and that's at Knighton House," he said with finality.

She looked as if she might argue, then sighed. "Very well. But you must tell me the minute you've found where they've gone."

"Of course."

"How long do you think it will take?"

"Don't you worry—I'll be quick as I can."

Thank God, that seemed to pacify her. Because the only thing that could ruin his day more than having to track down some foolish fortune-hunting rascal, was having to do it in the company of a winsome and maddening lady of quality.

He saw her out, stopping to chastise the coachman for bringing her to St. Giles. But he couldn't really blame the man, having given in to her wishes himself with alarming ease.

That thought plagued him as he strode off for the livery. What was it about the damned female that made him susceptible to her pleas? Yes, she was lovely, but he had his pick of the lightskirts, many of whom were prime articles themselves. And none of them was high in the instep or pricklier than a hawthorn hedge.

But none of them looked lost and vulnerable when fretting over their young sisters . . .

He ignored the tightening in his gut. His concern had

naught to do with Lady Helena; he was only thinking of poor Lady Juliet. This Morgan chap might be a bad sort. Daniel hated seeing any woman suffer, but especially an innocent lass like the youngest Laverick girl.

He'd seen enough innocents suffer during his childhood, first in the workhouse, where he'd been sent after his parents were hanged for highway robbery, and then among the smugglers. Like other men, smugglers treated their wives and children with varying degrees of courtesy—but a lifetime of ignoring the law led some to ignore common decency, and those were the men Daniel despised.

As a boy, he could only walk away from the troubling sight of a strapping man cuffing a wee lass. As a man, he didn't tolerate it. Many was the fight he'd got himself into because of it, which was why some smugglers had been as glad to see him leave Hastings at seventeen as he'd been to escape them.

If he'd ever entirely escaped them. As he passed a group of young scapegallows huddled together, probably planning their next crack lay, he thought about Lady Helena's assumptions concerning him. If she only knew the whole of it.

Not that he was ashamed of what he'd done in his youth; it was all he'd known until Griff had come along. Even now he rarely cared if somebody heard all about his free-trading past.

It's just that he didn't want *her* thinking of him as a "nasty, evil" man. Though he strove to deny it, he was pleased she'd come to *him* for help. That she'd trusted him at least a little.

A very little. After last summer's disaster, she thought him a true scoundrel. She'd made that damned clear. Still, he sometimes wondered what might've happened at

Swan Park if matters had been different and he hadn't been masquerading as Griff, if he'd truly been courting Lady Helena . . .

He shook off the thought. That was building castles in the clouds, to be sure. Men of his kind didn't sniff around well-born women if they knew what was good for them. Especially not ones as fractious and untrusting as her. If he so much as touched her, she was liable to blacken his name to every lord and lady she knew. His aristocratic clients cared naught about his past, but they'd care mightily about his insulting a lady. So Lady Helena was not for the likes of him, no matter what his pego thought.

After he left the livery, he rode toward the Bear and Key. Once he found out what he could there, he'd check other respectable inns. He doubted that Morgan was a smuggler, but he'd ask at the flash houses anyway, just to be sure. Blackman at the Black Horse would tell him if anybody unusual had been there, and would probably know if anybody had stayed at another rookery.

Twelve hours later, and after more silver had changed hands than he liked, he had nothing to show for his efforts—which relieved him. Nobody had seen Morgan or Juliet, aside from the proprietor at the Bear and Key, and then only long enough to sell them a mite to eat. So it was probably just an elopement after all.

And if Lady Juliet wanted to marry some low chap who was after her modest dowry, who was he to stop her? Besides, this Morgan might truly be in love with her. The only one to say otherwise was Lady Helena, and God knew he couldn't take her word for it.

As his horse trotted into St. Giles near midnight, he spotted Clancy's gin shop. He started to pass it by, but then hesitated. Clancy was a friend to smugglers and Daniel's only connection to the old crowd. If the Irishman hadn't heard anything about Will Morgan, there was naught to be heard, and Daniel could set Lady Helena's mind at ease with a clear conscience. Besides, a dram of gin would be just the thing now.

Daniel liked Clancy—everybody did. The Irishman was a swiller's favorite publican—jovial and generous with his pouring, not to mention a spinner of tales as tall as the Tower. His great belly and old-fashioned white wig made him look like a daft Father Christmas, but his eyes were sharp and his mind keen. Besides which, he had a soft spot for Daniel. Though Daniel was only half Irish, that was enough Irish for Clancy, who enjoyed jawing with him about the old country even though Daniel had never set foot in it his whole life.

Daniel paid a boy to keep an eye on his horse, then entered the ramshackle building that stank of tobacco, blue ruin, and stale piss.

"Well, if it ain't Danny Boy," Clancy called cheerily as Daniel sauntered past the six tables in the small room that served both as dram shop and public house. "You want me to send for Sall?"

"No. And don't tell the wench I came here, either." Daniel dropped onto a stool at the bar.

Without being asked, Clancy took a bottle of gin down from the shelf, poured a dram, and set the glass before Daniel. "She's in a pet, y'know. Says you tossed her out this morn for a fancier tart."

Daniel knocked back the dram quickly, relishing the burn. "Lady Helena is no tart, and Sall knows it."

"Oho, a lady of quality, eh? That explains it, then. Sall is probably jealous."

"Not a chance. Sall doesn't know the meaning of the word."

"All the same, you ain't been too friendly with the

girls of late, and they're all in a miff about it." The brandy-faced Irishman grinned. "They used to make a good bit of their blunt from you—even with giving it to you free sometimes. In the old days, you used to call for one or two of 'em every night. Now it's more like every week. Next thing you know, it'll be once a month."

Daniel hunched over his glass. "I'm getting too old for whoring."

"Too old! You ain't yet thirty! Besides, nobody's too old for whorin' or I'd have stopped going to Mrs. Beard's years ago. More likely you're gettin' as tightfisted as Knighton."

"P'raps," Daniel retorted with a chuckle, though that wasn't it, either. The truth was, Daniel didn't find it half so much fun anymore. In his youth, when the hot blood raged in him, he couldn't satisfy the needs of his John Thomas fast enough. But he was tiring of quick tumbles with women who wanted only his purse or his pego. Or the novelty of being bedded by the bastard son of the notorious Wild Danny Brennan.

Women like that weren't interested in giving a man true companionship. Strange, but even in the midst of all his female "companions," he felt lonely as the very devil. That was what came of watching Griff and Rosalind bill and coo. It made him ache for a lass of his own.

The trouble was, where to find one? Not in Griff's circles, where he still felt uncomfortable, and not with his old friends, either. He'd grown just civilized enough to chafe at his current surroundings, a fact that annoyed him.

"So what's the tale with this Lady Helena?" Clancy asked with a sly glance. "You thinkin' of gettin' married or somethin'?"

"To her?" He laughed. "Not bloody likely." He tapped

the counter with his empty glass, signaling he wanted another dram.

Clancy was more than eager to oblige. His wig curls bobbed as he reached for the bottle. "She must be ugly, then."

"No, she's beautiful. Not that it makes a whit of difference. The woman's favorite entertainment is sharpening her tongue on my tough hide."

"Surely you ain't gonna let a bit of shrew stop you from making a conquest, are you, Danny? I've seen you tame the fieriest tart with a handful of compliments."

"Fiery tarts are easy to tame. It's the self-righteous spinsters aiming to freeze a man's prick that cause difficulty. Besides, she's much too fine for my sort, and she knows it only too well."

Which was why he should get this business of Lady Juliet done with, so the Swan Queen could glide back to her fortress in Warwickshire and leave him be. Before he started thinking too much on Clancy's fool notion of taming her. "Clancy, I know you keep a room available for the old crowd when they come to the city. Has anybody unusual come asking to use it lately?"

"Unusual? How?"

"A couple? A man and a woman?"

Clancy shook his head. "Most of the free traders know it's small. If they've got a wife or ladylove with them, they go to Blackman's. He's got more room."

The tension ebbed in Daniel's body. "True."

"Wait, I forgot. There was a man asking about it a few nights ago. I had to turn him away because somebody else was using it. That's why it slipped my mind."

Daniel straightened. "He had a woman with him?"

Clancy nodded. "Pretty little thing, too. Young and

blond and dressed nice. Though the man dressed like a gent hisself."

"Not a free trader then?"

"Aye, a free trader, but with the fine manners and speech of a gentleman. Funny thing, that. He said Jolly Roger told him about my room. Crouch is about as far from being a gent as a smuggler can get—can't imagine why he even bothered to give this other chap the time of day."

Jolly Roger Crouch. Oh, bloody hell. "Does this man work for Crouch?"

"Don't believe so. You know the free traders; they all talk amongst themselves."

Daniel tamped down on his unease. All right, so Morgan was a smuggler who knew Crouch. A smuggler could elope with a woman same as anybody else. Half the smugglers in England did their free trading only part of the time and spent the rest in a respectable profession. There were vicars, for God's sake, who did a bit of clerking for free traders on the side. It didn't have to mean anything awful. "And the girl? What did this chap say about her?"

"Said she was his fiancée and they were going to be married. Pretty thing, she was. He treated her like she was made of glass, made her stay far away from me, like he was afraid I might hurt her." Clancy chortled at the thought.

That cheered Daniel enormously. "Did he give you his name?"

"Aye, he did. Let me think, what was it now?" Clancy pushed up his wig to scratch his forehead. "Mr. . . . Mr. . . . I think it was Pryce."

"Not Morgan?"

Clancy slapped his hand on the bar. "Morgan! That's it. Morgan Pryce."

"You sure his *surname* wasn't Morgan?" Daniel asked, though his stomach felt suddenly hollow. Why the alias?

"No, his name was Morgan Pryce. I remember it because it's so Welsh."

A Welshman named Morgan, and no doubt with dark hair and black eyes . . . Daniel drew out Helena's sketch, now stained and crumpled. He laid it on the counter, then set the miniature of Juliet beside it. "Was this them?"

Brow furrowing, Clancy pulled the candle nearer and peered down at the two. "Aye, near as I can tell." He lifted his gaze to Daniel. "What's all this about?"

"Nothing," Daniel said tersely, remembering Lady Helena's admonishment to be discreet. "And I hope you'll remember that if anybody else comes asking about them."

"If you like." Though there was no mistaking the curiosity in Clancy's eyes.

Daniel stuffed the sketch and the miniature back into his coat pocket. Very odd, this. An elopement, to be sure, but with a free trader traveling under a false name. Perhaps the man just wanted to make sure nobody could follow them. But still . . .

It worried him a bit. And the man knew Crouch, too. Did that mean anything?

No, how could it? Daniel hadn't seen Crouch in years. It was just a bloody coincidence, that's all.

Still, it bothered him enough that he discarded the idea of having Lady Helena hire a Bow Street runner. If this was an elopement—and everything pointed toward that being the case—then they needed discretion as well as speed.

He hated having to tell Lady Helena that she'd been

right about Morgan's profession. Thankfully, that could wait until he found out where the pair had headed. It had to be to Scotland, but how? By ship? Carriage?

Pulling out his purse, Daniel set it on the counter. "I'm looking for this couple, and don't ask me why, because I won't tell you. But I need to know where you sent them from here." He pushed the purse toward Clancy. "Name your price."

With an angry snort, Clancy pushed it back at him. "Your money ain't no good here, Danny Boy, and you know it. You think I'd take tuppence from you, after all you done for me and my son? Don't be makin' me come across this bar and throttle you for your impudence, you big lout."

The very thought of the portly publican attempting to thrash Daniel brought a smile to his lips. "You don't owe me anything, old man."

"The divil I don't. My boy's happy as a lark workin' as your clerk, and I'm right glad to have him out of this life. So don't be tryin' to pay me. I'll tell you what you need to know without all that."

"At least let me pay you for the gin."

Clancy broke into a smile. "Well, now, the gin you can pay me for. I ain't givin' that away to nobody for free."

With a chuckle, Daniel fished out a few coins. Clancy took them, threw them in the till, then leaned over the bar. "Now about that Morgan chap . . ."

Chapter 4

"There's a house in my father's garden,
lovely Willie," said she,
"Where lords, dukes, and earls they all wait upon me.
And when they are sleeping in their long silent rest
It's then I'll go with you; you're the boy I love best."

"Lovely Willie,"
anonymous Irish ballad

The next morning, Helena entered a small, neat building in the center of London. A written summons from Mr. Brennan had arrived at Knighton House: *Come to my office at noon.* It said nothing else, which she'd fretted over for hours.

At least he'd finally summoned her. Although she

chafed at his refusal to say more, at present he held all the cards in this delicate affair.

She halted in a modestly sized foyer sparsely furnished with elegant chairs and a tasteful Oriental carpet, and wondered if she'd stumbled into the wrong place. She would never have associated elegance with Mr. Brennan.

At one end of the room, the bespectacled clerk who sat behind an impressive oak desk looked up from what he was writing and spied her. He jumped to his feet. "Good morning! You must be Lady Helena." He showed a leg as if meeting the queen, so energetically that his spectacles dropped onto the floor.

"Yes, I am," she said, watching curiously as he picked up the spectacles and fixed them back on his nose. They looked odd. It took a second for her to realize why.

"Mr. Brennan said as how you'd be coming," the man was explaining, "though if he hadn't told me, I would've never guessed who you were, for you don't favor your sister a'tall, seeing as how her hair's not so dark and—"

"I beg your pardon, but I believe you dropped the glass out of your spectacles when they fell on the floor," she interrupted with concern. "Perhaps we should look for the pieces."

"Glass?" He looked bewildered. Then comprehension dawned. "Ah, I take your meaning, but there's no cause for concern. I haven't any glass in my spectacles."

"Then why wear them?" she blurted out.

The man drew himself up with a proud smile. "My da says they make me look more like a clerk, y'see. He's a clever man, my da. Clancy's his name. He owns his own gin shop. So if he says I ought to wear spectacles, then I wear spectacles." He lowered his voice confidentially. "I tried wearing the ones with glass in them, but they gave me the headache, and I was always falling over things. These are superior, don't you think?"

"Much superior," she agreed, fighting the urge to smile. What an odd little man. Leave it to Mr. Brennan to hire the son of a publican as a clerk. "And what does Mr. Brennan say about your spectacles?"

"He says as how I don't really need them. He says doing the work of a clerk will best make me look like one. But I expect he's only wanting to save me the trouble."

"I'm sure you're right," she said politely, then glanced around. "Is he here?"

"Oh! Yes, of course, I forgot to say, didn't I?" He jerked erect and spoke as if reciting a set speech. "At present Mr. Brennan is occupied with a client. If you would be so good as to take a seat, I assure you he will be with you shortly." Relaxing his stance, he added, "I expect he won't be long, milady."

"Thank you."

Occupied with a client. Obviously, Mr. Brennan did not share her sense of urgency. No doubt he kept her waiting on purpose after her prickly behavior yesterday. She couldn't blame him. Although she hadn't expected to interrupt an orgy when she knocked on his door, she should have been more "well-bred" about it.

Today she would do better. She would not criticize his habits or raise her voice. She would be the perfect lady. She would show him she appreciated his help, even if it meant sifting her remarks through gritted teeth.

The Well-bred Young Lady scents her breath with cloves and her words with honey, Helena reminded herself. A pity she'd grown a trifle unfamiliar of late with the language of honey.

Ignoring young Mr. Clancy's curious gaze on her, she

walked haltingly to the nearest chair. There was a certain advantage to spending all her time in Warwickshire. At home everyone knew of her bad leg; they'd had eight years to get used to it. So she was spared the pointed glances of others.

She sat down, and only then did Mr. Clancy take his seat. Opening her reticule, she took out a packet of cloves, removed one, then put it in her mouth to chew. The spice exploded in her mouth, as bitter as the knowledge that time was flying by, sending her sister and that wretched Mr. Morgan farther away with each fleeting second.

What if Mr. Brennan had found nothing and was abandoning the search? What would she do? Hire one of those Bow Street fellows? The very thought of hobbling into a succession of strangers' offices chilled her blood. But more chilling was the thought of what Mr. Morgan must be doing to sweet little Juliet . . .

She stiffened. It did no good to imagine the worst.

Yet that's all she'd done since yesterday. What a night she'd had—fraught with vague worries and portents of disaster. And dreams . . . Merciful heavens, the dreams that had plagued her! She still remembered the one where she stood fully clothed in a brothel of naked fancy women who were pulling on her, urging her to join them. She'd resisted until Mr. Brennan had appeared in his drawers and begun removing her clothes until all she wore was her blue scarf. And just as he'd leaned closer to untie it, she'd awakened, hot and restless, her hands touching—

Face flaming, she groaned. No, she wouldn't even *think* of that.

As if prompted by her groan, Mr. Clancy said, "Are you comfortable, milady? Is there anything I can get you? A cushion perhaps? We don't have any here, but I imagine I could pop round to a shop and—"

"I am perfectly comfortable, thank you," she put in, praying that her blush did not betray her indecent thoughts.

One thing she could say for Mr. Brennan's clerk—he was certainly friendly. He quickly launched into another subject. "We were all very happy when Mr. Knighton married your sister, y'know. She's a fine woman, a fine woman indeed."

She swallowed her shredded clove. "Thank you. I'm sure she's flattered by your regard." If Rosalind even noticed it, with Griff around. The stars in her eyes undoubtedly blinded her to anybody but him.

"It did seem like a good match. She and Mr. Knighton looked happy as larks."

"They are." What else did one say to that? *They're blissfully, annoyingly, maddeningly happy?*

She knew it was peevish, but Rosalind's connubial bliss made her ache with envy. And a bone-deep loneliness. Until this summer, the one consolation of being called a Swanlea Spinster, that dreadful nickname society had given them, was that she shared the title with Rosalind. She'd always assumed that Juliet would marry someday—the girl was too pretty to do otherwise—but Rosalind was to have been her companion in old age. Now she was alone once more.

"They ought to enjoy their stay on the continent," Mr. Clancy babbled on. "The weather's fine for travel this time of year." He leaned forward to wink at her—actually *wink* at her. "Besides, newly married couples never notice a drop of rain or two—"

"How long have you worked for Mr. Brennan?" she broke in before he could speculate on what newly married couples *did* notice.

The clerk adjusted to the abrupt change of subject

without blinking. "Nigh on two months now. Before that, I worked at Knighton Trading. But when Mr. Brennan set up his own office in August, I was awful proud he gave me the job as his clerk."

August? Directly after his disastrous visit at Swan Park? Surely Mr. Brennan hadn't parted ways with Griff over that. Yet she couldn't imagine his leaving Knighton Trading simply because Griff was marrying. That made no sense.

Mr. Clancy warmed to the subject of his employer. "Mr. Brennan has fine prospects ahead of him, fine prospects, to be sure. Long before he set up for himself, he increased the fortunes of many a man with his advice. Indeed, if your ladyship has funds to invest on the Exchange, you couldn't do better than Mr. Brennan for an adviser."

"I shall bear it in mind." She could well imagine where an unprincipled devil like Mr. Brennan had gained such knowledge and in what shady concerns he would invest her money. No, thank you.

Suddenly she heard voices in the hall, and Mr. Clancy leaped from his chair, hurrying around his desk and across the room to the coat rack, where he gathered up a gentleman's many-caped box coat and beaver hat. Seconds later, a well-dressed young man of obvious refinement entered the foyer, followed closely by Mr. Brennan.

Despite herself, Helena's pulse quickened at the sight of the burly Mr. Brennan. It was that wretched dream, of course, making her react to him like a silly girl. She must put it out of her mind at once.

She tried to guess from his expression if he'd found out anything, but he didn't even look at her. He was too busy playing the man of business with his client.

And looking very much the part. He'd replaced his

fustian coat and trousers from yesterday with a tailcoat of dark brown kerseymere, buff leather breeches, and a striped waistcoat, all of which were remarkably well-tailored. He looked attractive, even gentlemanly.

But none of the other attributes of a gentleman were in evidence. As always, the illusion of good breeding on Mr. Brennan was as thin as the veneer of oils on a painting; a mere scrape of a knife would expose raw canvas beneath.

And no canvas was rawer. His speech and manner proclaimed his true character, brash and ungoverned. Instead of tempering his opinions as a man in his position ought, he voiced them freely. Amazingly, his client did not seem to mind. Then again, Mr. Brennan's familiar manner did have a certain appeal. It always had.

A tiny part of her wished she could be like that—say and do as she pleased without thought to the consequences, without worrying about Mrs. N's rules. But look where such recklessness had led Juliet.

She would not make the same mistake. Besides, Mr. Brennan was reckless enough for both of them.

"I'll invest the funds this very day, Brennan," his client said as Mr. Clancy handed him his coat and hat. "Knighton must have been mad to let you go. But his loss is my gain, eh, old fellow?"

"Just be sure to look over that other proposal." Mr. Brennan spoke in a brusque and confident tone. "Your gain will be trebled if you invest in that coal mine in Wales, your grace."

A *duke*, for heaven's sake. One of his clients was a duke, and Mr. Brennan spoke to him like an equal? His investment advice must be valuable indeed.

"Don't worry," the duke was saying, "I'll consider it carefully. I've seen what your counsel has brought Dryden and Blackmore, and I don't intend to lose my chance at it. I'll be sure to make my decision before you return from your trip."

Trip? All her interest in the duke vanished. She searched Mr. Brennan's face. Then his gaze met hers, and she knew. He hadn't found Juliet or Mr. Morgan in London.

The two men continued to talk, but she just sat there numb, wishing she could shove the loquacious duke out the door. Now what? Did Mr. Brennan intend to go after them? But why would he do so after grumbling about her request for his assistance?

She was so distracted, she didn't notice the surreptitious glances the duke was paying her until he said, "I'd best depart now. I would not wish to keep you from your other visitor."

Startled, she glanced up to find him eyeing her with interest. No doubt he thought her one of Mr. Brennan's fancy women. The very idea made her blush.

Thankfully, Mr. Brennan had the good sense not to introduce her and hurried the man out. By the time he returned to her side, she'd already pushed herself to a stand.

"Sorry to keep you waiting, m'lady." He offered her his arm. "Shall we go back to my office?"

"Certainly." She took it, though holding on to him seemed incredibly intimate. But when his gloved hand covered hers, alarm bells of a different sort jangled in her head. He was being very kind and courteous. Had he discovered something he knew would alarm her? Cold fear turned even her good leg to lead.

"Have you been waiting long?" he asked as they made their slow way across the foyer to a hallway.

Her worry made her curt. "Yes—a whole day, if you'll recall. But I could not expect you to put aside a duke to attend to a mere annoyance like my sister's—"

He cleared his throat, and she looked up to see him glance meaningfully at the clerk. Merciful heavens, she must be more discreet. And less tart-tongued.

Honey, she reminded herself. *I must scent my words with honey.*

Glancing around, she forced a smile to her lips. "Your place of business is very pleasant. Very tastefully furnished."

"I claim no credit for that. Mrs. Knighton did it all."

"Rosalind did this?" Rosalind was many things, but tasteful wasn't one of them.

"Christ, no!" he exclaimed, then seemed to remember to whom he was speaking. "I meant Mrs. Leonard Knighton. Griff's mother."

"Oh, of course." That made more sense. Rosalind would have draped the walls in violet silk and gold tassels or something equally . . . provoking.

"Speaking of Griff's mother," he said, "is she still at Swan Park with your father?"

"Yes. I was thankful she could stay there with him while I came to London."

He made no answer. Having run out of innocuous conversation, they both kept silent until they reached the end of the dark hallway.

He led her into a cramped office piled high with newspapers and books. As he closed the door, she glanced around. This looked more like what she'd expect. Assorted documents littered his desk: snippings from newspapers, letters, and what were probably invoices and bills of lading. All were marked in ink—portions circled, notations scribbled in the margins. An odd device resembling beads on a loom lay atop one pile.

He caught her staring at it. "It's an abacus," he explained. "One of Griff's trader friends taught me how to use it for calculations." When she nodded absently, he added, "But you didn't come here to learn about the tools of a trader. Sit down, if you please. We have much to discuss."

Her pulse stuttered. "Why? Where are they? Have you found them?"

With a sigh, he circled to stand behind the desk. "No. They're not in London."

Though the news came as no surprise, it still struck her hard. She hadn't realized until just now how much she'd hoped that he'd find them quickly. "You're sure."

"Yes. They *were* here, mind you, but they're not here now. Half a dozen people remembered seeing them both at an inn called the Golden Lion three nights ago. And another several saw Juliet get into a hired carriage with Pryce the next morning."

"Pryce? Who's that?"

"It seems that Will Morgan is an alias. The man's real name is Morgan Pryce."

An alias. Lord, she couldn't breathe. The scoundrel was using an alias. "And I suppose he has some nefarious reason for changing his name."

"We don't know that. I expect all he wanted was to make it harder for somebody to follow them."

"But is he a smuggler?"

He hesitated. "It's . . . possible."

"Merciful heavens, I knew it! I knew he was a bad sort! What does he want with Juliet? No, I know what he wants, the wretch. He wants to ruin her, to hurt her—"

"Calm down, m'lady. He doesn't want any such thing. He called her his fiancée more than once, and nobody ever saw him lay a hand on her except in courtesy. From all I could gather, he truly wants to marry her."

"If he wants to marry her, it's only for her dowry—you know that!"

"We don't know yet what he's after." He spoke with an edge of impatience, even irritation. "Everybody I spoke to said he treated her very respectfully. You may be wrong about him. Free traders aren't all bad, y'know; he might only be eager to marry."

Her worry twisted into a fury most uncharacteristic of her. "Then he'll have to settle for marrying one of his fellow smuggler's sisters, because he is not getting mine!"

"He's already got her—that's the trouble."

"But not for long. You have to help me now. You must!"

"Of course. Why d'you think I spent last night in the taverns finding their direction and this morning preparing to leave?" Resignation laced his words. "Besides, I like Lady Juliet. She may fancy herself in love with the rascal, but she can't know what she's got herself into."

"Of course she doesn't! Juliet is the most naive, trusting girl in England. He probably spun her a romantic tale to sweep her off her feet." She stabbed her cane into the carpet viciously. "Well, he can just set her right back on them, because I shan't stand for this!" Her gaze fixed on his broad shoulders, the ones that seemed capable of bearing any burden. "When do we leave, Mr. Brennan? I can be ready very quickly, I assure you."

He cocked his eyebrow. "*We*? *We* aren't going anywhere. *You* are going back to Knighton House and staying there until I return with your sister."

"What? Not on your life! I shan't sit here and twiddle my thumbs while you race about the countryside. I'm going with you."

He drew himself up with all the stubbornness of a man

used to making his way alone in the world. "You've got no choice in this. I won't take you."

"Then I shall hire one of those Bow Street fellows to take me."

To her shock, he burst into laughter. "A runner? Not bloody likely. Yesterday you didn't even know what they were." He sobered. "Besides, you're too concerned about your sister's reputation for that. And with good reason."

Oh, the man could be so exasperating. "All right, then I'll follow you myself. Alone, if I must. You can't prevent me from traveling the same road as you if I wish."

That wiped the smug assurance right off his face. "You wouldn't be so foolish."

"Is it foolish to do all in my power to help Juliet?"

"Following me won't help her. You'd just get yourself into trouble, too. You'd be prey to every blackguard and varlet who trawls the highway. And what will you do if one of them tries to take your money or worse? Fight?"

"If I must. I'm not worried about myself, only Juliet."

Rounding his desk, he strode up to loom over her. As always, his sheer size roused a trifle apprehension in her chest. She feared no man, but Mr. Brennan was not just any man. For one thing, despite her height, her nose reached only to the top of his shoulder . . . his big, brawny shoulder attached to an arm that could fell her with one swipe.

He was so close now that his breath warmed her cheek. "See here, Helena, can't you trust me with this at least?" His tone was softer, laced with genuine concern. He'd never used her Christian name without her title, and it seemed shockingly intimate . . . and thrilling at the same time. "I'll bring her back safe as can be. There's no need for you to go."

"But there is. I know what he looks like. That sketch is not nearly good enough, but I can recognize him—"

"And I can recognize your sister, which is all that matters."

She went on the offensive. "What reason could you have for *not* taking me? Other than the stupid ones you've given so far?"

"Stupid?" He stepped back from her with a low oath. "To be concerned for your safety? Pryce might be a smuggler, remember? I'll have to go into seedy taverns and unsavory inns to ask after him, places you shouldn't even enter."

"I don't have to go into all those places with you. I'll simply stay out of your way while you do."

"You'll stay out of my way, all right," he growled, "here in London where you belong."

"You have no say in the matter, Mr. Brennan. Though I prefer to have your help, I refuse to take it if it means you travel without me. I followed them to London successfully, and I can follow them out entirely alone." She held out her hand. "If you will just return my sketch and miniature and tell me which direction they went—"

"Bloody hell, woman! What will you do once you catch up to them? Give Pryce one of your Lady High-and-Mighty stares and order him to release your sister? Lay him low with your contempt? The cut direct may make your kind quake in their boots, but it only angers mine. Act haughty in *my* world, and you'll find yourself knocked back on your elegant arse."

She pointedly ignored his insults, not to mention his coarse language. "I'll convince Juliet of her folly, and if that doesn't work, I'll . . . I'll summon a constable. Or pay Mr. Pryce off." When Mr. Brennan shook his head, she went on heatedly, "I don't know what I'll do, all right? But I'll stop him however I can."

What she wanted was to unman the wily Mr. Pryce, which would definitely break *some* rule in Mrs. N's guide. Besides which, she didn't have the faintest idea how to go about it. "I'm going after them, with or without you."

"What about your reputation?" he snapped.

That brought her up short. "What about it?"

"You travel alone with me, and you might as well throw it away. Such behavior isn't proper for a lady, and well you know it."

"I suppose bringing a maid along is out of the question?"

"It's *all* out of the question, damn it!" he roared. "It'll be difficult traveling with *one* woman under these circumstances, much less two!"

She sniffed. "Well, forgive my presumption, but I didn't think it would hurt to ask." When he drew himself up like a snorting bull about to charge, she added hastily, "In any case, I'm not concerned about my reputation." She thrust the point of her cane at him. "And since when do you care about what's proper? A man who greets his visitors half-clad is in no position to lecture on the proprieties."

"A lady who takes offense at it is in no position to flout them, either."

"Under the circumstances, I have no choice. Besides, it's not as if anyone need know we're traveling together."

He gaped at her as if she were insane. "What about the inns we'll have to frequent, the posting houses, even the road itself? You don't think anybody will notice a refined lady traveling with a low-born lout like me? You don't think they'll talk about it? Spread the tale from here to kingdom come?"

She swallowed. She hadn't actually considered that.

"Then we'll just . . . I don't know . . . invent a story about why we're together. We'll tell people you're my brother."

His laugh mocked her. "Oh, aye, they'll believe that. You and me are just two peas in a pod, aren't we? You might as well claim we're lovers, because that's what they'll think if you try to pass *me* off as your brother."

Lovers! The very idea! She ducked her head, striving to hide her blush beneath her bonnet's brim. "You could . . . pretend to be my servant."

"Oh, you'd have a fine time with that, wouldn't you?" he snapped. "You'd enjoy an excuse to whip me raw with your tongue whenever you take a notion to it. But I'm not putting myself in that position, so give up that idea right now, m'lady."

"I-I didn't mean—"

"There's only one explanation that anybody might believe—and I say *might* because it's as ridiculous as those others. You could pretend to be my wife. No one would question a woman traveling with her husband."

She lifted her gaze to his. Was he serious? She searched his face, the grim slant to his mouth, the hint of calculation in his gray eyes. Hard to tell. Yet the very idea turned her insides to jelly. "How does that differ from my pretending to be your sister?"

He shrugged. "Men of my kind don't have sisters born above themselves, do they? But they do marry above themselves—which is why Pryce can succeed at carrying off your sister."

"That's absurd." Yet she knew he was right. Still, was that satisfaction she glimpsed in his face?

He gave an exaggerated sigh as he strolled back behind his desk and began stuffing items into a small leather bag. "Well, then, there's no help for it. You'll have to stay here. If you travel with me unchaperoned you'll be ruined for sure, and we both agree you can't pretend to be my wife. A pity."

"I didn't say I can't," she hastened to correct him. "Or even that I won't."

His head shot up and his gaze burned into her. "You'd travel as my wife? Share a room with me if necessary? Because that's the only way I'll let you go. I'll not be responsible for ruining your future, and nobody'll ask questions if you travel as my wife."

Now she *knew* he wasn't serious. Share a room with her, hah! He didn't even like her. He was just trying to scare her off, the wretch.

She tossed her head back. "If that's the way it must be, then yes, I will."

"Like bloody hell, you will!" he exploded, proving her supposition correct. He raked his fingers through his hair, leaving the blond, rough-cut locks more unruly than before. "I've never met a woman as stubborn as you."

"You can't dissuade me from this, you know. I don't care about the dangers, I don't care about your dislike of me, and I certainly don't care if some strangers gossip about me afterward. I only care about Juliet."

Her hands trembled, but she went on even in the face of his black scowl. "Don't you understand? When you find her—*if* you find her—you'll need me, if only to convince her she can't marry this wretch. She certainly won't listen to you on such a matter. Besides which, I just can't . . . sit here and wait to find out what has happened. I have to do something."

When his frown softened the merest fraction, she pressed her advantage. "And I can be of use to you—I know I can. Surely there will be places where my rank or my sex can work in our favor. I could make things easier for you by ensuring that our lodgings furnish everything required for your comfort while you're making inquiries or—"

"Enough, m'lady. The last thing I need is you seeing to my comfort." His gaze played over her with an odd mix of emotion—exasperation tinged by something else, something shattering and dark and dangerous. He drew in a ragged sigh. "But if you go with me, there'll be conditions, d'you understand? You'll have to consent to all of them before I'll even consider it."

Hope filled her. "Of course. Whatever you say, whatever you want."

"Don't be so quick to agree. You won't like them." He crossed his arms over his barrel chest, looking for all the world like a powerful genie guarding the entrance to the treasure cave. His eyes assessed her coolly from bonnet to boots. "First, you'll have to dress different. Your pretty gowns will call attention to us, not to mention tempt every thief in three counties. You'll have to wear the plainest gowns you can manage—no lace, no fancy furbelows, no—"

"Done."

His scowl deepened. "Second, you do as I say without complaint. We eat when I say, stop when I say, and take lodgings when and where I say. Understood?"

She bobbed her head vigorously.

"You think I don't mean it, but I do. I promise to be the harshest of taskmasters."

"And I promise to be the meekest of servants."

He snorted. "That I'll have to see to believe. Third, and here's the rub, you keep quiet whenever we're around other people."

"Why?"

"Because every time you open your mouth, you make a man feel like he's two feet tall and missing his cods."

The vulgarity made her stiffen and his implication stung, but she guessed this was a test and so kept silent, despite having to gnaw on her tongue to manage it.

He gazed at her expectantly and when she said nothing, added bitingly, "We won't find out anything if you start talking to people like they're beneath your touch."

"I don't do that!" she retorted. When both his eyebrows arched high on his forehead, she added, "Well, only with men, anyway."

"Yes, and much of the time we'll be talking to men." He cocked his head. "Come to think of it, maybe you should always keep quiet. Then I won't be tempted to throttle you every mile or so."

At his glower, she shrank into herself. Perhaps this was not such a good idea after all. Would she have been better off hiring Bow Street runners? At least they wouldn't try to order her about.

Or would they? Men of that sort were bound to be just as arrogant. At least she was used to dealing with Mr. Brennan's arrogance. Besides, although he drove her insane and talked gruffly of throttling her, she didn't think he would actually harm her.

"I'll do whatever is necessary to make this endeavor a success," she vowed.

"Will you?" He surveyed her for a long moment, then let out an enormous sigh. "Very well. We've wasted enough precious time with this argument as it is. You've got one hour at Griff's to pack your things. Pack light, no more'n one bag. And if you're not ready to leave when I am, I'm leaving without you."

"So you're taking me?" she said, relief making her suddenly light-headed.

"Do you agree to my conditions?"

"I do, I do!"

"Well, then," he groused, "I s'pose we'll be traveling together, since you're likely to make a spectacle of yourself by trailing along behind if I don't take you."

"Oh, thank you! You won't regret it, I promise."

He gave a hard, self-mocking laugh. "I already regret it, believe me. I've never done a more foolish thing in my life." He picked up his leather purse, buttoned the flap, then stuffed it in his coat pocket and came around the desk. "Come along then, m'lady. It's time we got on the road."

Chapter 5

It's of a false knight from the North
Who came a-courting me
He promised he'd take me unto the North land
And there his bride would be.
"Lady Isobel and the Elf-Knight,"
anonymous Scottish ballad

Jarred from a deep sleep, Juliet Laverick opened her eyes to find herself sprawled across the seat of a moving coach with her face pressed to the window. What was she doing here?

"Had a nice nap?" asked a deep male voice. "Do you feel better now?"

Her gaze shot to the handsome man across from her,

and she remembered. She was running away with Captain Will Morgan, the man she loved.

"Much better, thank you." Dear me, her legs were stretched out on the seat like a schoolgirl's. Swiftly she swung her feet to the floor and flashed her companion an embarrassed smile.

But he didn't see it, having already turned his head to stare out the window. "Good. You needed to rest." A lock of coal-black hair dropped onto his forehead, making him look even more rakishly attractive. "We'll be in Hurst Green soon. We'll lunch there, and that should refresh you even more."

She relished the kind solicitude that he maintained even in the face of his concern that they might be followed. Of course, that would never happen, as she'd told him many times. The very thought was ridiculous. Helena hardly even left the house to go into Stratford, much less travel across England. Papa couldn't come after them even with Griff's mother helping him. So she and Will were quite safe.

Yet Will insisted on maintaining this punishing pace. They'd traveled so much in the past few days she'd forgotten what it was like not to have her body continually jostled, her sleep disrupted, and her meals bolted. He'd been a perfect gentleman throughout, taking a separate room for her in every inn out of "courtesy," but sometimes she wished he weren't quite so courteous. After they'd left Stratford, she'd expected him to become a bit more . . . well . . . passionate in his addresses.

But he was as much the gentleman as ever, and she found that distinctly annoying. Her love for him was so thrilling she often found herself wanting to cover his face with kisses, but she didn't dare. It would shock him—she just knew it. He was the kind of gentleman who kept his emotions in check. And though she ought to do the same, she found it harder every day they were alone together.

"How long before we reach Winchelsea?" she asked.

"This evening, most likely."

"And your friend's ship will be waiting for us?"

"It depends on when he docks in Rye Harbour nearby. We'll stay in his cottage in Winchelsea until then. It might be a couple of days, however."

"Perhaps if we'd taken passage in Bristol—"

"I told you—I don't have the funds for that. My friend from Winchelsea will carry us to Scotland for free." As if realizing how curt he sounded, he softened his voice and added, "You mustn't worry about it, my dear. It will all be fine."

She flinched at his typically indulgent tone. When they'd first met it hadn't bothered her, because he'd been so sweet otherwise, teasing her out of her shyness and delighting her with tales of war on the Continent. No other man his age had paid such attention to her, and with everyone else ignoring her, she'd basked in his approval.

He'd been completely sympathetic to her complaints about Helena's crossness. He'd agreed with her when she'd protested that Mrs. Knighton wasn't caring for Papa the way she ought, the way Juliet herself always had. He'd understood her listlessness after Rosalind had married, her disappointment in her own life and prospects.

She'd been sure that she and Will belonged together, like Rosalind and Griff. And when he'd warned that Papa would never approve the marriage and had suggested that they elope, she'd been eager to follow his lead, convinced that he loved her even though he never said it. Not in so many words. He spoke of "enjoying her company," "caring for her," and such things, but not love. It had seemed part of his natural reserve not to speak of it, so she'd squelched her concern, too full of her own love to do otherwise.

But more and more his reticence worried her. Sometimes it seemed as if he didn't see her as a lover at all, but rather as a child, the way Helena and Rosalind did.

Perhaps she shouldn't have been so hasty to dismiss Helena's concerns about him. What if she'd been mistaken in her impression of his character? What if Helena had been right after all?

No, how could she even *think* of agreeing with Helena on this matter? Helena's heart of ice made her suspect every man of villainy. And besides, Helena had barely spoken to Will, so what did she know of his kind nature and amiable character?

Indeed, there was only one thing that bothered Juliet about the way he was acting, and she couldn't keep quiet about it any longer. "Will?"

"What is it, sweeting?"

"Why haven't you kissed me?"

His gaze shot to her in surprise. Slowly it swept her, the way Papa's hounds eyed a joint of mutton cooking in the kitchen hearth. A little shiver snaked down her spine. He'd never looked at her with such hot, covetous hunger. It alarmed her.

It thrilled her.

"Do you want me to kiss you?" he finally rasped, as if the words were torn from him against his will.

"Of course!" When she realized how shamefully wicked that made her sound, she hastened to add, "I-I mean . . . well, we're to be married and yet you've done nothing more than kiss my hand. Even the boys in Stratford tried to—" Dear me, that sounded awful. "I didn't let them," she added hastily, "but they did *try*. One or two of them."

A smile tugged at his lips. "I imagine they did."

His gentlemanly façade was back in place, annoying her extremely. "You *do* find me pretty, don't you?"

He glanced away quickly. "You know perfectly well that I find you pretty."

"So why haven't . . . why won't—"

"I've got other things on my mind," he bit out. "There will be plenty of time for all of that once we're married. Right now, try to save your strength for the voyage ahead. It's sure to be tiring."

It won't be tiring as long as you hold me during it, she thought, bitterly disappointed by his answer. What had she expected? That he'd leap across the carriage and give her a passionate kiss like the ones she'd seen Griff give Rosalind?

Yes. That was what she'd expected, hoped for.

As if sensing her disappointment, he added kindly, "I'm only trying to treat you with the respect you deserve. Until we're married, I wouldn't dream of sullying your honor. I know you understand."

She didn't, though she dared not say it, for he'd think her the worst wanton imaginable. All the same, for once she wished he was not quite so much a gentleman.

For the hundredth time, Helena wished Daniel Brennan were more of a gentleman. A gentleman would wait upon her leisure. A gentleman would phrase his requests politely instead of barking orders.

A gentleman wouldn't give her so little time to pack.

Only an hour! How was any woman to pack in that time, especially when all her gowns were unacceptable? It had taken her half the time just to settle on two that might do, and she wore one of them now. Then there'd been decisions on what else to bring, what she could manage without, what Juliet might need once they found her.

One bag, the great tyrant had ordered. Obviously, it was another way to discourage her from going. As if they couldn't fit more than one bag in Griff's carriage.

Fine. She'd packed *one* bag. A very large bag.

She bent to close it for the waiting footman, then caught sight of Mrs. N's guide. Should she bring it?

Oh, why not? It wouldn't hurt to have a reminder of the rules of propriety—the ones she hadn't yet broken, that is. Mr. Brennan was the sort of man who made a woman wish to throw propriety to the winds, which would be terribly unwise.

Stuffing the book into her bag, she gestured for the footman to take it, then followed him out of her bedchamber on the second floor of Knighton House. She grew uneasy as they approached the grand staircase. It had been more than the allotted hour; she was sure of it. And Mr. Brennan was so *un*gentlemanly that he probably wouldn't even wait for her—the arrogant beast.

Even as she started down the stairs behind the footman, she caught sight of Mr. Brennan headed for the front door. "Wait, Mr. Brennan!" she called out, hurrying down the steps as quickly as her leg would allow. "I'm coming!"

He turned toward the staircase, his gaze falling on the footman hefting her bag. "I thought I told you to pack light."

"That's as light as I could manage."

He stopped the footman before he could pass. "Leave that here. I'll take care of it."

"Surely you will not be so wretched as to leave my bag behind," she snapped at her giant adversary. She reached the bottom of the stairs and halted a few feet from him. "It's far easier for a man to pack light than a woman, you know, and we're not sure how long we'll be gone."

"All the same—" he began, shifting his gaze to her face. Then he stopped short. "This isn't a good beginning a'tall, m'lady."

She refused to let him intimidate her. "If you mean to tell me I can't go along simply because my bag is too big—"

"I'm not talking about the bag. I'm talking about *that.*" He nodded at her neck. "I told you no lace."

Her hand instinctively went to her throat. The half-inch border of lace at her collar was the only lace on the entire gown, which was why she'd chosen the dress in the first place. "This gown is the simplest I own." Sarcasm crept into her tone. "I'm sorry if it has a trifle adornment. If I'd had time to remove it, I would have."

He quirked one eyebrow up. Reaching into his pocket, he pulled out a slender object and came toward her. Without warning, he reached up to grasp one end of her lace, but only when he lifted his hand did she see a flash of steel and realize what he intended.

"Don't you dare!" she hissed, but it was too late.

He'd already sliced the lace from her collar with a deft stroke of his pen knife. One quick pull and he tore it off as neatly as a milliner splits ribbon.

His eyes were sleet on slate. "There. That took no time a'tall." Then stuffing the sad little strip into his pocket, he lifted her bag and strode off toward the door.

She scowled as she followed him, her cane's staccato taps on the marble floor increasing in volume with her anger. "Even milkmaids occasionally wear lace, for heaven's sake," she grumbled.

He stopped short so quickly she nearly tripped over his

big riding boots. "Did you speak, m'lady? As I recall, one of my conditions was that you keep your opinions to yourself. You even agreed to it."

A pox on his "conditions"! They were almost as impossible to follow as Mrs. N's, and if the beast wasn't smirking at her as if to say, *I knew you'd never manage it*, she'd tell him so.

Jerking her gaze from his, she lifted her head high and walked right past him through the open door. "You misheard me just now, Mr. Brennan. I was merely complimenting you for your excellent knowledge of women's fashion."

"Were you indeed?" he drawled. "Then p'raps you should refrain from complimenting me lest I 'mishear' you change your mind about going along."

"You know perfectly well that I— Merciful heavens, what is that?"

She halted at the top of the entranceway stairs, frozen by the sight of a huge horse, saddled and waiting impatiently at the bottom for its rider. A groom held the creature's head, but even he looked wary of the gigantic bay mare.

"It's my horse," Mr. Brennan said from behind her. "What did you think a man my size would ride? A wee pony?"

Behind the mare stood a gelding bearing a sidesaddle. It was not quite so monstrous a horse, but still large enough to alarm her.

Mr. Brennan sauntered down the stairs to the groom holding that one. "Here you are." He handed the groom her bag. "Fit what you can of her things into the saddlebags, all right?"

"Very well, sir," the groom murmured and began his task.

"You can't mean to . . . we're not . . . where's the carriage?" she sputtered.

"We're not taking the carriage," Mr. Brennan said matter-of-factly as he climbed back up to her side. "Traveling by coach would slow us down, and you said yourself that this matter requires haste." He held out his arm to help her descend. When she didn't take it at once, he added, "Wait a minute, I nearly forgot—you don't ride, do you?"

She scowled at him. *Nearly forgot*, indeed. The devil. Well, his blatant tactics would not work. "Of course I ride."

He cocked his head. "That's not what your father said this summer."

"I thought you 'nearly forgot' that?" When his lips twitched, she tipped her nose up at him. "As it happens, Papa was mistaken. I can handle any horse you give me."

Well-bred Young Ladies do not tell falsehoods, she thought woefully. Though she used to ride every day when the weather was fine, she hadn't mounted a horse in the eight years since her illness had struck. She'd feared having everyone see her fail at it.

But as with the other things she'd had to tackle on her mad excursion, she'd do this, too. Because she refused to stay behind, no matter what Mr. Brennan sprang on her.

He eyed her skeptically. "Your leg won't give you trouble?"

Of course it would, but she'd never let him know it. She took the arm he offered. "Not in the least."

He said nothing more as they made their slow way to the gelding. Close up, her mount looked impossibly large. She swallowed hard. They would need a mounting block, and perhaps even two on top of each other, since she couldn't use her weak left leg at all to vault herself onto the horse.

Would her leg even serve well enough to ride? She tried to remember being in the saddle, how it had felt, how she'd supported her weight, if she'd needed that leg with the sidesaddle.

But memory was pointless. She'd been a different woman then, sure of her abilities. Her body had done the riding, not her mind, and how did one make the body remember anything? She couldn't even make her leg remember how to walk properly.

Mr. Brennan lowered his head. Concern flickered in his eyes. "Are you sure about this, lass? I don't want to see you hurt yourself."

Pride took over then, pride and a bit of the Laverick stubbornness. "I'm perfectly sure. I'll merely need help mounting."

"Of course." He took the cane from her hand and tucked it into the pack behind the cantle of the saddle. Then before she knew what was happening, he turned her to face him and placed his hands on her waist. "Tell me when you're ready."

"I was speaking of a mounting block!" she cried, seized by sudden fear. "You can't lift me so high!"

He chuckled. "Compliments upon compliments, eh? D'you doubt my strength?"

She stared up into his face uncertainly. He waited, expectant, sure of himself and his power. It wasn't *his* strength she doubted, but her own. If he lifted her and she did not maneuver her body into the saddle right, she might come crashing down on him. Or worse yet, fall onto the stone steps.

He bent close. "Trust me," he whispered, his breath

surprisingly sweet-scented as it drifted over her cheeks. "I can heft a slender thing like you with one hand. I won't let you fall, lass, I swear it."

Oddly enough, his words reassured her. His hands were heavy on her waist. She could feel their heat through her muslin gown. Their heat and, yes, their strength. She *had* seen his muscles for herself yesterday. If anyone could lift her into a saddle, he could.

Besides, the longer she hesitated, the more likely he was to guess she was lying about her ability to ride.

"All right," she said, taking a deep breath. "I'm ready."

The words had scarcely left her lips when she found herself soaring, held aloft by the sheer might of two brawny arms that set her upon the horse's back as easily as a swallow alights on a windowsill. To her vast surprise and satisfaction, old instincts took over, prodding her to complete the rest in one easy motion—hooking her right leg over the crutch at the knee and balancing her weight in the saddle.

When she had her limbs and skirts arranged and all that remained was to have him adjust the left stirrup so she could put her foot into it, she glanced down at him, shocked and elated. Triumphant.

He smiled approvingly up at her as he reached for the stirrup. "Well, well, how about that? You *do* ride. Or at the very least you sit a horse properly."

The compliment swirled about her like a heady fragrance. She did, didn't she? Why, she was seated as well as she'd ever been before she'd lost full use of her leg. As that realization sank in, Helena trembled from sheer exhilaration. She'd mounted a horse! With help, of course, and she didn't know what might happen once the gelding started to move, but nonetheless she'd done it! And she'd soon be riding, truly riding!

Her excitement was apparently infectious, for he smiled at her as he adjusted the stirrup. His eyes twinkled the way they had at Swan Park last summer whenever he'd teased her. Then he concentrated on fitting her booted foot into the stirrup and his smile faded, replaced by a dark intensity.

He clasped her ankle. "I s'pose I should have warned you about the riding so you could wear a proper skirt," he murmured in a husky tone. "This one's a mite short."

Indeed, she felt cool air creep through her wool stocking to chill her leg, which was partly exposed below her hiked-up gown. She tried futilely to jerk her skirt down, but it wouldn't cover all her calf. A good six inches showed above her boot.

Six inches that seemed enormously captivating to Mr. Brennan, who slid his hand slowly from her ankle to her calf as if measuring the strength in her leg. His rough hand encircled her lower calf.

"Are you sure about this, lass? Are you sure your leg won't be worked too hard?"

She cringed to think of what lay beneath his fingers—the withered muscles barely concealed beneath her thin stockings. Yet she was acutely aware of his intimate touch, the gentle, near caress he feathered over her lower calf.

His outspread fingers felt hot where they grazed her skin. What if he slid them higher, behind her knee and up her stocking under her skirts, the way he probably did with his strumpets? What if he brushed her thigh as tenderly as he did her calf now, all the way up to her garter and above, where he could curve his fingers around . . .

Her face flamed. Oh, dear, how could she even think of him in this scandalous manner! Mama was right. She'd always said that once a lady ignored one rule of propriety, the rest eroded away like the banks of a river.

"I'll . . . I'll be fine," she murmured. "And now if you will kindly release my leg and mount your horse, we can get on with this. You do know the matter requires haste."

His slow, sensual grin as he drew his hand back showed he took no offense at her admonishment. "I know too well. But even in a hurry, a man doesn't waste the chance to explore beneath a pretty woman's skirts."

With a wink, the bold wretch strode off toward his own giant mount. What a shocking thing to say! As if taunting her with her own wicked thoughts. He truly was the most outrageous rascal she'd ever met, and unrepentant besides.

Explore beneath a pretty woman's skirts, indeed!

And why must the phrase evoke such . . . interesting . . . pictures in her mind? Why must they grow more elaborate when he mounted his mare, the muscles in his buckskin breeches flexing as he threw his leg over? Her mouth went dry to watch him fit his bottom into the saddle as comfortably as he probably fit a fancy woman into his lap.

She must not think such things. It was ridiculous, unwise . . . naughty. Very naughty. The way he would be if he ever dared explore beneath *her* skirts.

Her skin still burned where he'd caressed it.

The groom approached Mr. Brennan and showed him some articles left over from her bag. From where she sat it looked like mostly inconsequential items. Still, it irritated her to see Mr. Brennan cast them a cursory glance and order the man to bring them into the house. He was such a tyrant.

Abruptly, he said, "Wait," took something from among them, and shoved it into his coat pocket. She couldn't see what it was, but her curiosity was piqued.

"Ready, m'lady?" he called back to her as he took up his reins.

That drove her curiosity right out of her head. She hurried to grasp her own reins, a new concern suddenly taking precedence.

Now she must prove she could ride. And she wasn't at all sure she could manage it.

Chapter 6

Then she got up on the noble brown
And he on the dappled gray
And they rode till they came to a broad waterside
Two long hours before it was day.

"Lady Isobel and the Elf-Knight,"
anonymous Scottish ballad

It took them an hour to escape London's tentacles. Midday the streets were choked with carts and carriages, vendors and victuallers. Daniel thanked God for the chaos that kept his attention on maneuvering his mare and away from the woman at his side.

But once they were cantering along the highway, he could no longer prevent his thoughts from settling on her. Lady Helena rode better than he'd expected. He'd have sworn she was lying about the riding just to bedevil him. That's why he'd set up that little test for her. He'd been sure she'd balk at the horses, and then he'd be rid of her. He'd even hoped she might see how outrageously improper the trip would be and refuse to go without a maid.

Only she hadn't balked or refused. He'd realized she truly meant to go on with it when she'd insisted on mounting the gelding.

Mad impulse, that—lifting her into that contraption they called a woman's saddle. He should've had a groom help her or sent one to fetch the mounting block she'd asked for. But the truth was, he'd been itching to lay his hands on her ever since they'd met.

He'd have thought a woman with her rigid ideas would wear a corset, but to his surprise, the delicate waist—which he'd easily spanned with his hands—had been all hers. And when she'd trembled, he'd wanted to do more than grasp her waist; he'd wanted to smooth out her anxious frown, whisper reassurances, hold her close enough to feel her heart pounding. Having her in his arms had been pure pleasure. Pure foolish pleasure.

Not to mention the delight of touching her leg. That was an enjoyment he wouldn't mind repeating.

Which was why when they stopped again, he'd best have somebody else help her mount and dismount. Many more encounters like that, and he'd have to find a cold stream to dunk his St. Peter in. Apparently there was a reason for all those tedious society rules: it wasn't at all wise for a man of his sort to travel alone with a woman, no matter what the circumstances. Especially when the woman turned him randy as the very devil.

A tin horn blared loudly behind them. They both slowed to a walk and pulled to the right as a mail coach thundered up. The wheels flashed scarlet as it passed in a clatter of hooves and jingle of harnesses, its black-and-maroon frame crammed full of parcels and passengers. After it left them in a cloud of dust, Lady Helena spurred her horse forward until she was abreast of Daniel.

"Why are we heading to Tunbridge?" she called over to him.

Ah, so she'd noticed the road they'd taken. "'Cause that's where Morgan and your sister were headed last time anybody saw them."

"But that's south."

He nodded. South, toward Sussex, which worried him. Sussex was where Crouch's band of smugglers dwelt. But that meant nothing—Sussex was lousy with free-trader gangs who led the excisemen a merry dance the whole year long.

"A good many free traders hide their cutters along the coasts of Sussex and Kent," he explained, "so Morgan may have one there. That might be why they headed south."

She looked unconvinced. Come to think of it, she looked downright ill, her cheeks pale and her lips pinched up tight.

"I don't think it's anything to worry yourself about," he added, trying to soften her distress. "It just means they're headed a different way than I'd expect."

"I know. It's not that." She flashed him a wan smile that was as false as a lady's bum roll. "I'm only a little hungry. I breakfasted early."

And he hadn't breakfasted at all. "I thought we'd stop to eat and rest the horses in Bromley, but that'll be another hour. Can you manage?"

If he hadn't been watching, he wouldn't have seen panic flit over her face. Then she covered it up and he wasn't sure he'd seen it after all.

"I'll be fine. But at this rate, it'll take us more than an hour."

He chuckled. Her and her tart reminders. She was right, however, they needed to get on more quickly. Clicking his tongue to his mare, he brought her back up to a trot, then a canter. A quick glance behind him showed that Lady Helena was keeping up.

The sun heated the road ahead, baking out the remnants of the last rain and warming him clear through to his insides. They passed a wheat field where threshers labored, rode along a thicket where they startled some quail, and then up a hill to where a windmill reigned over the rolling landscape.

Perhaps this fool's errand wasn't so bad. It cheered him to be in the open air, to see clear sky marred only by the swoop of a peregrine. Sometimes London's soot and fog dragged his spirits down, making him wish he didn't have to make his living there. It didn't happen often—he would get bloody bored in the country. But occasionally he tired of being boxed up with gentlemen who tolerated him only for his connection to Griff or for the money he made them.

From time to time he liked an adventure, and he suspected this would turn out to be one, provided Pryce and Juliet didn't outpace them. If the couple boarded a cutter as soon as they reached the coast, it would be nigh on impossible to do anything about it, but if they had to wait for a ship, he might catch them.

He certainly hoped so. Although Lady Helena annoyed him at times, he hated seeing her so distraught. If they reached the coast only to find that her sister was headed to Scotland aboard a cutter . . .

She'd probably swim after it, the plucky lass. A faint smile touched his lips. Much as he hated to admit it, he admired her perseverance. To come all the way to London on her own, stopping in inns and enduring the condescension of strangers, must have taxed her strength *and* her pride. One thing he had to say for her—the lass was determined to save her sister. A pity that Lady Juliet didn't seem to want saving.

Over an hour passed before they reached the thatched-roof cottages signaling the outskirts of Bromley. Lady Helena followed his lead as he slowed his mare to a walk, due to the village children playing quoits beside the road.

"Mr. Brennan?" she called over to him.

"Yes?"

"What am I to call you when we reach the inn?"

The question flummoxed him. "What's wrong with my name?"

At her prolonged silence, he glanced over. Her face was turned toward him, and he saw the creases about her eyes. She held her shoulders so rigidly straight he wondered how she didn't get the backache from it.

"I mean, are we . . . that is . . . how will you . . ." She gripped the reins in hands that trembled. "What will you tell them about why we're traveling together?"

Ah, so that's what was worrying her—his threat to have her pretend to be his wife. The proud wench looked bloody alarmed at the thought, too. He ought to let *her* invent an explanation, since she'd insisted on coming along. "What do you want me to tell them?"

"I don't know. I . . ." She trailed off, facing forward so he could no longer see her eyes behind the rim of her bonnet. "I suppose you don't have many choices, do you?"

"I'll think on it and let you know."

The trouble was, she was right—they had few plausible choices. The only men ladies of rank traveled with were their fathers, their brothers . . .

Or their husbands.

For a fleeting moment, he wondered what it would be like to be her real husband. He saw her slipping down onto a bed beside him, smiling for once, all soft and languid the way he suspected she could be if she wanted. And her hair . . .

He imagined her hair a thousand different ways, all more erotic than a bawdy painting. Hanging down loose about her bared shoulders. Twined about his fingers, the silk of it tickling his palm. Draped over one naked breast, with the strands teasing him to draw them aside and touch the pert fullness . . .

He swore under his breath. He had some imagination if he could put Lady Helena into any bed with him, and especially naked.

But it did tell him one thing—they couldn't share a room. No indeed. He wouldn't get an instant's sleep for thinking of how she'd look bare-breasted, with her hair her only gown.

Thankfully they reached the Blue Boar as the mail coach that had passed them earlier was leaving, which meant they could avoid the crowd in the common room and have a quiet meal. He could use a meal just now. Perhaps sating one hunger would make him forget the other.

Helena, too, was relieved to see the timber-framed building. Her bad leg throbbed from the hip joint down, and her good one ached only a trifle less. Her bottom was simply numb. It might as well have been made of leather, for all the feeling she had in it.

She desperately needed time off the horse to gather her

strength for the rest of the journey. Truth be told, she didn't know how she'd make it any farther.

As they pulled up in front, the stableboys and ostler came running. Although Mr. Brennan dismounted, he didn't come to her side at once, but instead spoke to the ostler about the horses. When a stableman approached and offered to help her dismount, she accepted eagerly, grateful that Mr. Brennan would not be putting his warm, unsettling hands on her again. Grateful . . . and a tiny bit disappointed.

She explained to the stableman about her leg and asked for a mounting block, but he was tall and rather broad, so he had no difficulty lifting her down. The moment her feet touched the ground, however, she realized she was in trouble, for her legs buckled. She had to grab the stableman to keep from collapsing. Dear Lord, she couldn't walk unaided, even with the cane that the man quickly withdrew from the saddle for her.

"You seem to be havin' trouble, miss," the stableman said. "You want I should carry you inside?"

"No!" She glanced over to Mr. Brennan, relieved he hadn't yet noticed her clinging to the stableman for dear life. "I merely need a little help."

"More than a little, I'd say," he responded.

She lowered her voice and jerked her head in Mr. Brennan's direction. "Please, I don't wish him to know I'm having a bad time of it. Do you mind letting me lean on you? There's a shilling in it for you if you keep him from finding out."

Merciful heavens, how far she'd strayed from Mrs. N's path. Now she was paying innocent servants to lie for her.

But the stableman didn't bat an eyelash, and clasped her tightly. Thankfully, between her cane and his arm she managed to stumble into the inn. The blessedly warm common room was deserted and Mr. Brennan was preoccupied with ordering them food, so by the time he joined her at the oak table, she was seated, confident that he hadn't guessed at her difficulties.

Still, she could hardly move without groaning, without feeling the impact in every muscle. And must the wretch look so utterly untaxed by their ride? Great lout of a man, she grumbled to herself. He probably had a bottom of iron.

Indeed, he looked quite cheerful as he dropped his heavy frame into the chair opposite her. "They've only a joint of beef and some boiled carrots, as well as bread and cheese and a pigeon pie. It isn't much, but it'll do until evening."

"Only two days' worth of food," she said dryly. "Couldn't they spare a ham and a leg of mutton? How will we ever survive?"

Looking faintly surprised, he cocked his head at her. "You laugh, but it takes a great deal to fill the belly of a man like me." His eyes twinkled. "Lots of good English beef is what gives me the strength to lift ladies like you onto sidesaddles."

His good humor when she ached from head to foot was too much to bear. "I suppose we have good English beef to thank for your bullish manners, too," she retorted.

"No, for that you can thank the lack of beef in the workhouse, or any kind of meat, for that matter. When a boy's hungry, he'll sell his mother for a bowl of good stew. He doesn't care about manners."

He said it matter-of-factly, as if boys raised in the workhouse who grew up to be successful men of business were commonplace.

"But surely you learned better once you were older and moving in . . . refined circles—"

"Refined circles?" He laughed. "The smugglers? Or after I left them, when Griff gave me the job as his man of affairs, when I acted as go-between for him and the smugglers?" His eyes narrowed. "Ah, but I think I know what you mean—my current business associates, men like the new Duke of Montfort at my office. Now, that's a refined circle for you—his grace and all his lightskirts. He likes them low and dirty, he does. Where the devil do you think I met him? He might have lordly manners when he's near a lass like you, but you can be sure they vanish when he's with Mrs. Beard's girls."

"Who is Mrs. Beard?" she asked, then realized what sort of woman she must be.

He flashed her a pained smile. "Let's just say she's not a woman you're likely ever to meet."

"I don't see why not. I've already met one of *your* 'lightskirts.' "

Lord, she could not believe she'd said that. The Well-bred Young Lady never alluded to women of ill repute, especially before a man.

His mocking eyebrow quirked up again, making him look more sinfully attractive than usual. He leaned to one side and draped his arm over the back of the chair with casual ease. "Your ladyship seems mighty interested in lightskirts. This is the second time you've mentioned Sall. Did she bother you that much?"

"Bother me? Why would she bother me?" But Sall did bother her, and a great deal, too. It made no sense. Why should she care if the wretch had a hundred shameless women strolling about naked in his rooms?

"P'raps because you're curious," he remarked.

"Curious about what?"

"What all the fuss is about."

"F-fuss? Whatever do you mean?"

"What those women do. With men. In private."

A slow heat filled her cheeks. "I would never in a million years speculate upon what those women do."

"Wouldn't you?"

"Certainly not."

But she would, and he knew it, judging from his unrepentant grin. He could read her so well, the beast. Somehow he'd guessed her secret thoughts, knew she was indeed . . . intrigued by those women's activities.

She always had been, ever since her first time in London. When Papa had brought her to the city for her coming out, they'd been in the carriage on the way to a ball when she'd seen a woman up ahead, standing beneath a street lamp talking to a gentleman. It was a seedy part of town, and Papa generally kept the curtains tightly closed as they passed through it, but he'd forgotten to do so that night, absorbed in some other matter.

So she'd seen the couple under the lamp. Though it was years ago, Helena remembered every detail as if it were yesterday.

The man had been handsome in a base sort of way, but it was the woman who'd arrested her attention. Smoky lamplight had spilled over her low-cut scarlet dress and the two mounds of flesh it exposed. Back then it had been the fashion to wear clinging gossamer fabrics, but the woman's fiery gown had nearly been a second skin. Like a loving flame it had licked the woman's body, tightening in the most indecent places, leaving little to the imagination.

Yet the gown had not been the most shocking part. Just as their coach neared the couple, the man bent to kiss the woman, then thrust his hand inside her bodice to fondle her breast. Right there in public.

And the woman let him. Not only let him, but plastered her body to him. Strangely enough, while the shameless couple was kissing and . . . and touching so outrageously, the woman's eyes remained open. And just as the coach had rumbled past, she had stared straight at Helena.

Helena had sprung back from the window, mortified and shocked. Fascinated. She'd never mentioned a word to Papa, who'd been staring absently out the other window. She'd never even told Rosalind or Juliet.

But she'd never forgotten it. Once in a while when she was alone, she dwelt on that woman's look—the smug glance that said, *I have a secret life you and your kind will never know. And I like it.*

That was absurd. What woman could . . . could *like* such a thing? Rosalind had said that what men and women did together was very pleasant, but Helena couldn't believe it after Rosalind had given her all the details. To have a man see you naked? Touch all of you, even your breasts? Put his . . . thing inside you? It was appalling!

Yet the way that woman had looked when the man touched her breast . . .

The Well-bred Young Lady does not think about men touching her breasts, Helena told herself sternly. Another stricture that did not appear in Mrs. N's guide. She had wandered so far from the rules of propriety that she was making up new ones just to keep from sinking into the abyss.

She shifted in her chair, then groaned unthinkingly as her muscles protested the small movement.

"You all right?" Daniel asked at once.

"I'm fine," she lied.

He started to say something else, but thankfully a servant girl brought the food then, accompanied by a scrawny, ferret-faced woman who was apparently the innkeeper's wife.

"I hope this'll be sufficient for you and your wife," the woman told Mr. Brennan in a decidedly hostile tone.

His wife? So he'd gone and done it, had he?

Mr. Brennan shot Helena a warning glance. "This will be fine, I'm sure. Won't it, m'la— er . . . m'dear?"

"Of course, my dear," she echoed, taking secret pleasure from his discomfiture.

The girl laying out the platters blanched when the woman cursed her and said, "Must you dawdle so, daughter? Back to the kitchen with you. There's work to be done."

When the girl fled and the innkeeper's wife started to leave as well, Mr. Brennan said, "Excuse me, madam, but they told me there'd be pie."

"We don't have no more pie," the woman growled as she stalked off. It sounded as if she added, under her breath, "Not for your sort, anyhow."

Judging from Mr. Brennan's frown, he'd heard it, too. Then they both heard the woman tell her daughter as she entered the kitchen to "keep an eye on those Irish around my silver. They're like to steal a body blind."

Mr. Brennan froze until he caught her gaze on him. Then he rolled his eyes and picked up a platter. "Hope you don't mind being a thieving Irishman's wife." He leaned forward to serve her a slice of beef. "Though I'll do my best not to steal you blind."

"You ought to steal *her* blind—it would serve her right," she retorted, outraged at the insult, even if he didn't seem to be. "And while you're at it, you could steal her deaf and dumb as well."

He chuckled. "You may not be Irish, but you do have a touch of the Irish wit."

"Thank you. I take that as a compliment."

Lifting his head, he shot her a warm glance. "I meant it as one."

Some understanding whispered between them, and a strange heat flared in her belly. The way he looked at her sometimes . . .

She jerked her gaze down and began sawing at her meat with a wholly inadequate knife.

He was silent a moment, then cleared his throat. "You needn't worry about this wife business, d'you hear? When we reach our lodgings tonight, I'll take separate rooms for us. Plenty of the gentry sleep apart, so nobody will think it odd."

What a relief. She suspected that sharing a room with Mr. Brennan would be quite . . . difficult. *The Well-bred Young Lady must not share a bedchamber—* There she went again, making up rules for what was not only ungovernable, but unthinkable.

One sniff of the food, however, and she forgot about strictures. She even forgot her aching legs, for she was quite hungry. She ate some beef, pleased to find it more palatable than she'd expected, though typical coaching inn fare. It was overcooked, but with a decent flavor.

Tearing off a piece of bread, she slathered it with butter and remarked, "Thank you for managing all this, Mr. Brennan."

A faint smile touched his lips as he ladled gravy over his beef. "If you're going to play my wife, you ought to call me Daniel. To strengthen the illusion."

"Daniel? Not 'Danny Boy'?" she quipped.

His smile faded. "No, m'lady—nor even Danny."

She suddenly remembered that his highwayman father's name had been Wild Danny Brennan. Heartily sorry for bringing it up, she said, "Well, you should not call me 'my lady' either. I give you leave to call me Helena."

"Do you? You'd allow a poor sod like me to use your Christian name?"

Though he coupled the comment with a teasing smile, his words still stung. She set down her fork. "I know what you're getting at. I am sorry, but I often forget that I no longer have any claim to the title of lady."

He paused in his eating to cast her a bemused look. "I didn't mean that at all."

"Didn't you? We both know that I'm not . . . that Papa is not—"

"For all intents and purposes you are. Griff would never reveal that your father's an impostor. He cares too much for your sister to do that. He's content to wait until your father passes on to take up the mantle of Earl of Swanlea."

"I know." Yet it bothered her. She didn't mind not truly being an earl's daughter; her rank had never brought her any great happiness. But she did mind being in this strange position—obligated to Griff Knighton for her dowry, painfully aware of how Papa had wronged him, and probably regarded as a fraud by Mr. Brennan . . . Daniel.

Why she should care what he thought of her, she didn't know. He *had* deceived them all last summer at Swan Park. And yet . . . he'd played the role of rich gentleman quite badly, as uncomfortable in it as Samson without his strength. Perhaps he'd actually disliked deceiving them.

She toyed with the carrot on her plate as he ate with the hearty appetite she'd expect of a Samson. "May I ask you something?"

He nodded and devoured another mouthful of bread.

"Was it *very* difficult for you? Pretending to be Griff?"

"You could say that. Playing heir to an earldom is not my cup o' tea, as you probably guessed." He shot her an earnest look. "I wasn't told what he was up to until too late, or I wouldn't have done it for any amount of money. I thought I was only helping him to what he deserved, and if it brought me a little something, then it wasn't so bad. But when I knew it all, I wanted out right away. Ask Griff—he'll tell you I did."

After what his clerk had said about when he'd set up for himself in business, she believed him, and his revelation warmed her. It made a difference, knowing that Daniel had felt as hoodwinked as the rest of them. "You do realize that none of us were aware that Papa was trying to blackmail Griff into marrying one of us. It came as quite a shock."

"I know." He paused to flash her a smile. "And I don't much blame him. He only wanted to protect his daughters. Any man would do the same."

"I suppose." But she suspected Daniel wouldn't. He seemed too forthright to do such a thing.

They ate in a companionable silence. For the first time since she'd left home, she felt less anxious about the future. Though her body ached more by the moment, everything else was going well. The stalwart Daniel seemed capable of anything, even tracking down her foolish sister. He'd succeeded thus far, after all, and surely now that they were on the right road, they'd be done with this soon.

They had nearly finished when the obnoxious innkeeper's wife approached. "Anything else you'll be needing, Mr. Brennan, or shall we settle the bill?"

What did the woman think—that they'd flee the premises before she got her money? Helena was sorely tempted to speak her mind, but before she could, Daniel did, and far more genially.

"Actually, there *is* something else." With an ingratiating smile, he drew out the miniature of Juliet and the sketch of Mr. Pryce. "If you'd be so kind as to look at these . . . my wife and I are searching for this couple. I thought they might've come this way. Have you seen them?"

Planting her reddened hands on bony hips, the woman cast the images a cursory glance. "Can't say as I have," she said belligerently.

"Are you sure? I realize that a woman who runs an inn so competently must be dreadful busy, but you might've noticed the young lass." He slid the miniature toward her. "It's my darling wife's sister, y'see, and the man in the sketch is a varlet who's stolen her off for her fortune."

"A fortune hunter, is it?" she asked, eyes narrowing.

"Yes. You seem to be a hardworking woman, so I know you wouldn't like to see your own daughter taken advantage of by a man who wants only to live off the work of others . . ." He trailed off meaningfully.

The woman unbent a little. "Aye." She regarded Daniel steadily. "Come from London, did you? You sound like a cit."

"That's where I live now, but I was raised in Sussex. My dear English mother ran an inn herself. You remind me of her a bit."

"Do I? What was her name?" the innkeeper's wife asked with clear interest.

"Molly. My father was an Irish soldier. They're together to this day."

"Molly Brennan of Sussex. I think I've heard of her. Good woman, as I recall."

"The best," Daniel said reverently, and the woman

softened still further. It was all Helena could do not to snort. Lord, could he spin a tale when it served him. Even she knew that his mother had been hanged alongside Wild Danny. And highwaymen's accomplices did not run inns.

The woman peered at the sketch once more. After a moment, she poked at it with one spindly finger. "There *was* a man like this in here two days ago. Handsome gent, but I could tell he was no good. He was in quite the rush."

"There was no woman with him?" Daniel prodded.

"If there was, I didn't see her. The fellow was in a coach, y'see. It stopped long enough to change horses, and this one ran in to fetch food from the kitchen, then run out. Never did see who else was in the coach. I don't think he was alone, howsomever, because he asked for two of everything to go with his loaf of bread—two apples, two hunks of cheese, two glasses. He paid for the glasses, too."

"You've been most helpful, madam." Daniel withdrew his heavy purse. "We might as well settle accounts now. You did say it would be ten shillings, nine pence, didn't you?"

"Yes." She watched with keen eyes as he removed several coins from his purse.

"Here's eleven shillings for the delicious dinner." He plunked down two crowns and a shilling, then added another crown. "And five more for the information." He dropped the purse onto the table beside the sketch, and the coins jingled loudly. "Did the man happen to say where they were headed?"

She scooped up the silver and dropped it into her apron pocket, eyeing the purse with a twinge of regret. "He didn't say. But the ostler might know."

Daniel fished out another shilling and gave it to her.

"Thank you all the same. I knew a fine Englishwoman like yourself would be happy to help me and my wife." Then he actually winked at the older woman.

To Helena's surprise, the harridan blushed as pink as a schoolgirl. "Oh, go on with you now, Mr. Brennan. It were nothing. You just let me know if you and your wife need anything else for your trip. And I'll go see if there mightn't be a bit of pie hiding somewhere in the kitchen after all."

Helena could hardly contain herself until the woman left. Then she leaned forward and hissed, "What a liar you are! Your poor sainted mother in Sussex indeed!"

"That wasn't a lie," he protested genially as he tucked the sketch and miniature back into his waistcoat pocket. "You notice I didn't say she managed an inn in *Sussex*. I said I was raised in Sussex, and that's true. My mother's name was indeed Molly, though it was Molly Blake, since Da never married her. And she did run her father's inn, but in Essex, before she met up with my da." He sighed. "He was a bad influence on her."

"I should say so. And what about *him*? Saying he was a soldier!"

He grinned. "Wild Danny did join up for a stint as a young man. Would you have preferred I'd mentioned his later profession?"

"God forbid. If she thought you were a thieving Irishman before, I can only imagine what she'd say if she knew your father was a highwayman."

"Y'see, lass, you don't have to tell everything, though it's best to stick as close to the truth as possible. I learned that from Griff when he made me masquerade for him. I didn't lie a bit—I just hid parts of the truth, is all."

Indeed he had. Daniel Brennan could charm the snakes

off the head of Medusa with winks and grins and half truths. Such a rascal, he was.

He slid his purse into his coat pocket, and it dawned on her that the rascal had also paid for everything. That would not do.

"Daniel, you must let me pay the costs of this trip. It should not be at your expense."

"It's not." He gave her the same quick wink he'd given the innkeeper's wife. "I plan to charge Griff for every penny."

"Oh." She hadn't thought of that. "Will he mind? Paying all this just to make sure Juliet doesn't . . . make a fool of herself?"

"Do you think Rosalind would *let* him mind?"

"I don't know. They're married now, and, well . . . men tend to be tyrannical once they become husbands, no matter how lenient they seemed during the courtship."

"Oh, they do, do they?" He finished the last of his meal and settled back against the chair. Tapping his fork on the plate with a faint pinging, he regarded her steadily. "Have you got a husband I don't know about?"

"Of course not."

"Then how can you know what one acts like?"

She drew her pelisse about her shoulders, the resultant pain in her back making her regret she had to mount a horse again. "One doesn't need experience to know these things. I do read. And people do marry in Stratford-upon-Avon."

"Ah, I see. From that, you've learnt exactly how every husband acts." There went that maddening eyebrow again.

"Oh, don't be so smug," she grumbled. "You've been my 'husband' for all of one day, and you've already proven quite tyrannical."

He leaned over the table with a wicked glint in his eyes. "That's only because I've had all the responsibilities of marriage and none of the fun. Now if I had a bit of the good part to soften my temper, so to speak—"

"*Not a chance*," she enunciated, but her insides flipped over at the very thought.

"Then I s'pose you'll just have to get used to my tyrannical ways, lass." He grinned. "Speaking of which, if you're done with your meal, we'd best be off."

She agreed hastily. As sore as she was, she preferred riding horseback—where she could hardly converse at all—to spending one more minute having such outrageous discussions with Daniel.

Leaning forward in her chair, she started to place weight on her legs, then froze. They were weaker than before. She wasn't even sure she could stand.

And the last thing she wanted was for Daniel to realize it.

She forced a smile to her lips. "You go on out and speak to the ostler. I . . . er . . . need to . . . make use of the necessary. I'll join you outside when I'm done."

"All right." With a scrape of his chair, he stood and waited for her to rise, so she made a show of drawing on her gloves, then removing her packet of cloves from her pocket. He finally shrugged and headed out of the common room.

As soon as he had gone, she popped a clove in her mouth and glanced furtively around. The room was still virtually deserted, with only the innkeeper's daughter cleaning tables. She scooted her chair back and reached for her cane. She could do this. What did it matter if her legs felt shaky? Or her joints throbbed? All she had to do was hobble to the horse. Then Daniel would lift her into the saddle and she'd be fine.

She chewed a moment longer on her clove, futilely hoping the bitter spice might steel her for the task at hand, then discarded it on her plate. Clasping her cane in one hand and the edge of the table in the other, she pushed herself to a stand. She managed to stay on her feet long enough to take one step away from the table.

Then her legs buckled and she collapsed.

Chapter 7

And if you dare to kiss my lips
Sure of your body I will be.
"Thomas the Rhymer,"
anonymous ballad

Daniel was talking to the ostler when the innkeeper's daughter ran out of the Blue Boar. "Sir, sir!" she called out. "Come at once! Your wife has fallen!"

Daniel's heart dropped into his stomach. "What happened?" he asked, immediately heading for the inn.

"I'm not sure, sir. I—I was cleaning the tables and then I heard a crash—"

"And you left her there?" he growled and stalked past her.

She hastened after him. "Mama is with her."

When they entered the common room, her mother was grumbling and futilely trying to lift Helena under the arms. Daniel took one look at the crooked position of Helena's legs on the polished oak floor and felt his insides lurch sickeningly.

"Let me be!" Helena protested to the other woman with a face flushed scarlet. "Truly, madam, if you will just leave me alone for a moment, I can—"

"I'll take care of her," Daniel told the blundering older woman, who was only too happy to relinquish her responsibility. Striding to Helena's side, Daniel bent and scooped her up in his arms.

"No, you can't . . . you must put me down . . . it's not prop—"

"Stubble it," he growled under his breath, "before you give everything away."

Though her blush crept to her ears, she hooked her arms about his neck and clung to him as he stalked toward the door to the common room.

"Have you a parlor where my wife and I can be private?" he threw back over his shoulder at the innkeeper's wife.

"Yes, sir. Second door to the right once you reach the hall."

"There's no need for this," Helena whimpered as he headed that way. "If you will just set me on my feet—"

"So you can fall again?" he muttered. "Not bloody likely."

He entered the parlor, kicked the door shut behind him, then strode to a settee and lowered her onto it. As soon as he released her, she tried to stand but couldn't manage it, and her pathetic attempt made him furious, as much at himself as at her.

"Don't you dare try to get up!" He glowered down at

her. "Tell me, Helena. When was the last time you rode a horse?"

"J-just a few weeks ago."

"Don't lie to me, or I swear to God I'll take you over my knee. You haven't yet seen me tyrannical. Now how long has it been? And this time try the truth!"

She blinked, then sank against the cushioned settee with a defeated sigh. "Eight years. Not since before my illness."

"Bloody hell." He should've known. He'd seen all the signs, but he'd ignored them. He should've realized that if he'd never seen her ride at Swan Park, and her own father said she didn't, then she couldn't. How could he have let it go this far?

Anger drove him to pace before the cold hearth. "I can guess why you lied to me in the first place, but once you were having difficulty, why didn't you say something? Why did you let me think you were managing all right?"

"Becausc I *was* managing all right."

He snorted. "I can see how well you managed." He stopped short in front of her. "Must you be so bloody proud about everything? Why not admit you can't ride?" He dragged his fingers through his hair in utter distraction. "You could've hurt yourself badly, y'know. You could've broken something when you fell. We don't know for sure that you didn't!" The very thought made him ill.

"I-I would have felt it—"

"The way you felt that you couldn't stand? You should have told me!"

"If I had, you would have sent me back!"

Her cry echoed stark and painfully simple in the cramped room.

Of course. Bloody stubborn woman. It was one thing

to be plucky; it was quite another to recklessly risk her own health.

"I still will," he said softly. "So your lack of regard for your own safety has gained you naught, d'you hear? When I think of how you looked—"

With a curse, he turned away before she could see his face. It made his gut knot to remember her crumpled on the floor, her legs twisted under her, her cane tangled in her skirts. "What the devil am I to do with you now? Going on by horseback is out of the question for you."

"If . . . if you'd just set me on the horse, I could probably manage to ride."

"You're either stupid or daft as a bedlamite! The only thing you'll be riding is a coach seat back to London, damn you!" He whirled back around. "And I swear—"

He halted at the sight of her face. She was crying, with delicate little tears that trembled on the tips of her eyelashes before falling oh so softly onto her cheeks. Like a swan, she made no sound. He wouldn't even have noticed if he hadn't looked at her, she was trying that hard to hold them back.

Bloody hell, he'd made her cry, and he'd never made a woman cry in his life, except to cry out during lovemaking. That showed how badly she'd shaken him, for he'd always been careful of women's feelings. Not to mention that bringing a lady as proud as her to tears took real effort.

When she caught him staring at her she ducked her head, but that only made it worse, for now he noticed her trembling shoulders, which rose and fell with her tears. Now he could hear her, too, the tiny gasps and starts of a woman weeping.

It tore him straight to the heart. "Christ, don't cry," he grumbled as he dropped his big frame onto the settee. "I didn't mean it. You're not stupid or daft. I . . ." He trailed off, helpless in the face of such pitiful female misery. "Shhh, lass, don't go on so." For lack of any better way to soothe her, he laid his hand on her shoulder.

She lifted her head to reveal red-rimmed eyes and a rosy nose. "You can't send me back. Please, Daniel, I promise not to make any more trouble. I'll hire a gig or something fast that I can drive myself."

"Helena—" he began, meaning to reason with her.

"I-I realize I should have told you about the riding, but I knew you wouldn't let me go if I did, and I truly thought I could manage it. It's only that my bad leg is so very weak and my good one was overtaxed and . . ." She trailed off with a choked sound, then mastered herself enough to mutter through gritted teeth, "I hate my leg! It won't do *anything* I need it to do!"

He squeezed her shoulder. "That's not true. But you can't expect it to get used to riding again all at once. Give it a chance."

"We don't have time for that." Her teary gaze fixed on him. "But I can go with you if we just make other arrangements."

He sighed, glancing beyond her to the whitewashed wall punctuated by oak beams. "Don't you trust me to find her?"

"It's not that. I *have* to go with you."

His gaze swung back to her. "Why, for God's sake?"

"Because it's my fault she's in this fix," she wailed as fresh tears coursed down her cheeks. "If I'd been more careful, if I'd only noticed how she—"

"Hush, lass, it's nobody's fault, and it's sure as hell not yours."

Settling against the hard-backed settee, he tugged her into his arms, wanting to comfort her. To his surprise, she accepted his embrace as if it were the most natural thing in the world. It felt natural, too, and sweet, making him want to hold her even closer.

She laid her cheek against his chest, her tears flowing like a damned spigot, dampening his coat, his shirt, his cravat. When he took out his handkerchief and handed it to her, she soaked that, too.

"I saw the way . . . he looked at her," she stammered through her sobs. "I even knew . . . Mr. Morgan . . . Mr. Pryce . . . was . . . up to no good. I should have . . . watched her more . . . carefully."

"You can't stop a grown woman from doing what she wants," he murmured. If he'd learned anything from this escapade, it was that. He pulled her closer, cursing himself for making her cry. Her bonnet poked him in the nose, so he tugged it off and tossed it to the floor. "Short of locking Juliet in her room, you couldn't have stopped her, even if you had guessed what she was planning."

Her sobs were petering out, but she still shook like a buffeted willow. He cradled her head against his chest just beneath his chin, trying to ignore the delicious scent of honey water in her hair as he crooned reassurances to settle her down.

"Besides," he murmured in a weak attempt at humor, "how do you know she wasn't trying to prod you out of Swan Park, and give you a bit of adventure?"

At least that dried up her tears. "That's not funny," she said in a small voice.

"Don't s'pose it is," he admitted. "But truly, lass, she'll be all right. I'll get to her even if I have to book passage to Scotland. You needn't worry."

"I can't *help* worrying." She pushed away enough to lift her tear-drenched face. "I'll drive myself mad unless you let me go. Promise me you will. Please . . ."

He rubbed away her tears with his thumb. "You'd be better off—"

"No, I wouldn't. *Promise* me. I'll pay for a coach or a gig, whatever you wish. I'll be quiet as a mouse, I swear, and you'll have nothing to worry about from me."

"All right, damn it," he murmured to stave off her litany. "We'll hire a coach and go on that way, but—"

Her face lit up at once. "Thank you, Daniel, thank you!"

"Let me finish. We'll go on as soon as I'm sure you haven't hurt your leg." He hated making even that concession.

"I'm sure I haven't."

"That's for me to determine, since I can't trust you to tell me the truth." He lifted her lame leg and set it across his lap before she could protest, then shoved up her skirts to examine it.

"It's fine . . . truly . . . you needn't . . ." She trailed off as he caught her leg and began gently kneading the calf, watching her face for any sign of pain that signaled a fracture.

He saw not even a wince, but she did blush prettily and avert her face. That's when it dawned on him that he had her leg in his hands again, just where he wanted it. What's more, her lovely, frail calf was not only uninjured, but as shapely as he remembered.

He told himself to release it. Instead he continued kneading, but more slowly, indulging in the luxury of her soft female flesh, savoring the delicacy of it, the way it moved so smoothly beneath her stockings.

Within seconds, the unquenchable thing inside his breeches stiffened, mad with the pleasure of touching her. He began to consider outrageous possibilities, like removing her stocking, peeling it down past her knees and right off.

"I think my leg is . . . all right," she whispered. "I'll be able to stand on it once I can rest it."

Still, he was loath to let go. "Are you certain?" he asked, drawing out the moment. He smoothed his thumbs over her knee, then up her trim thigh.

Her eyes widened, not with horror as he expected, but with anticipation, even excitement. His fingers no longer kneaded but caressed. She blushed again and shivered.

His blood pounded through his veins. So she felt it, too, did she? She mightn't know what to make of it, she mightn't approve of it, but she surely felt the powerful shock of awareness fracturing the scant air between them.

If he had an ounce of sense he'd flee the room and preserve his sanity. But when it came to her, his common sense always went on holiday. He leaned forward, unable to tear his gaze from her flushed cheeks and trembling chin. And her mouth—her fine, dainty mouth, opening on a breath.

"Bloody hell . . ." he whispered, and then his own mouth was covering hers.

Her lips were sweet and spiced with cloves, soft as a swan's breast. Though every instinct warned against kissing her, he ignored them. He took advantage of her willingness, measuring the heat of her mouth, the silky texture, all the things he'd wondered about when he'd been mad enough to imagine this.

He'd wanted to kiss her since he'd first spied her on the terrace at Swan Park last summer. Now he needed to do it too badly to stop, even if she slapped him afterward or froze up again.

Except she did neither. True, she remained utterly still at first. But then she softened into pure, lovely woman, giving him all the encouragement he needed. "That's it, Helena. Relax," he murmured against her mouth before taking it again.

Helena wanted to laugh at the command. Relax? Impossible! He was kissing her, for heaven's sake, like no man had ever kissed her before. It dazed her, intrigued her, excited her. It made her want to kiss him back. Somehow Daniel had undermined her defenses before she could even erect them, and now it was too late.

All she wanted was to go on like this forever, with his mouth on hers, stealing her breath, giving it back, heating her lips with the warmth of his own.

Until he ran his tongue along her lips, startling her. She jerked back to find his gaze wild and hungry on her. He brought his hand up to clasp her chin, sliding the pad of his thumb over her lower lip, pressing it down a trifle.

"Open your mouth for me this time, lass," he murmured.

She barely had a chance to prepare herself before he was kissing her once more, his hand holding her still for it, the palm firm against her throat.

Again his tongue swept her lips. *Open your mouth.* That sounded as fascinating as it did naughty, so she complied.

The moment her lips parted, he sank his tongue inside to touch hers, to tangle intimately with it. Dimly she wondered if there was any stricture in Mrs. N's guide about letting a man thrust his tongue into one's mouth—but then she stopped caring.

Because it was wonderful, absolutely wonderful. Hot and sensuous and delicious. He plunged slowly in and out, teasing all the sensitive parts of her mouth until she felt loose and fluid from head to toe.

Then he dragged her onto his lap. Although her leg had already lain there, it was a shock to find her bottom suddenly resting between his hard thighs. She tore her lips away in a panic. "You must stop this," she said shakily, pressing her hands against his chest.

"I'd rather not." Deprived of her lips, he scattered kisses along her cheekbone and down the slope of her neck. "Are you sure that's what you want?"

Pride demanded that she make *some* resistance as a proper lady. But the thundering excitement in her chest demanded that she not only let him do these scandalous things, but participate. She began to understand how Rosalind had let herself get into trouble with Griff.

When he nuzzled her neck and then her ear, his whiskers abraded her skin, yet that intensified the secret thrill of it. Her breathing grew erratic. "Please, Daniel . . . don't . . ." Yet her hands clutched his coat.

He chuckled, the sound guttural against her ear. "You'll have to do better than that, lass. I thought you wished to know what all the fuss is about?"

"I-I never said that—*you* did."

"Yes, but you thought it, didn't you?" He laved her ear with his tongue, making her gasp. How could something so odd feel so good? "I'll wager you've wondered about it more than once, too." His hands stroked her back now, up and down in long sweeps that made fiery shivers dance along her spine. What if he were to put his hand on her breast the way that man in the street—

She groaned. He was right—she did wonder. "Perhaps I *am* a trifle curious . . . but that doesn't mean I want you to . . . that you should . . ."

"If you don't like it, show me," he rasped. "Let go of my coat. Slap me. I'm a big man; I can take it."

Slapping him was the furthest thing from her mind, and the rascal knew it.

He pressed an openmouthed kiss to her ear. "It's a paltry thing to endure for the chance of kissing you." He nibbled on her earlobe. "Ah, lass, you rouse my appetite so sorely. I've been aching to make a meal of you for such a long time . . ."

A vague image of him nibbling and kissing her naked flesh—*all* her naked flesh—tantalized her, then angered her. Devouring naked women was his forte, was it not? "I suppose you say that to your fancy women, too."

"Trust me, you're the fanciest woman I've ever kissed, my beauty, and certainly the only one I'd try to win with words."

Disturbed by the sudden notion that he might consider her a kind of . . . elite conquest, she tried to wriggle from his lap, but he wouldn't let her. Instead, he caught her face in his hands and made her look at him. "Or p'raps I shouldn't try words with you a'tall, since you'll turn them wrong in your head." Kissing the tip of her nose, he whispered, "For once, let yourself feel. Just feel."

He feathered his lips down the curve of her nostril, brushed them over the corner of her mouth, then pressed them once more to hers. His tongue invaded her mouth again, taking what it wanted and making her insides jump and quiver. This she liked—the kissing. He did it so well, made it so . . . thrilling.

Especially when he kissed her slowly, leisurely, as if he had every right to feed on her mouth. He probably thought he did, since she was letting him handle her body so shamelessly. One of his hands splayed over the back of her head, crushing her upswept hair as his mouth grew bolder, harder, needier.

He stole her breath away, and all she could do was sway into him, intoxicated by the feel of his mouth taking hers like some marauding bandit. Or smuggler.

A knock at the door broke the spell. "Sir?" they heard

a male voice call through the door. "Is your wife all right?"

She jerked back from Daniel, her hands still clinging to his coat lapels.

"The innkeeper, damn it," Daniel grumbled under his breath. Then he called out, "She's fine." But his gaze bore into her with an intensity she'd never seen in him. "Full of surprises, aren't you, lass?" he whispered, one eyebrow cocked upward. "You may not ride, but you can bloody well kiss. And much better than I'd expect of so lofty a lady."

The hint of triumph in his voice brought her to instant mortification. She tried to scramble off his lap, but her legs wouldn't work, and she landed on her knees on the floor. With a curse, Daniel lifted her up under her arms as if she were a rag doll, then dragged her back onto the settee beside him.

"Stay there," he ordered.

The knock came again. "Can I do anything?" the man asked through the door.

"Yes. Come on in," Daniel responded.

By the time the innkeeper opened the door, Helena was sitting beside Daniel as demurely as possible under the circumstances, though she surely looked a fright. She'd excavated Daniel's handkerchief from her skirts, wanting to bury her entire face in it, but that would be just as suspicious as revealing her puffy eyes and red nose. Then she spotted her bonnet on the floor, which made her feel even more conspicuous.

Especially when the pockmarked innkeeper shot them both a knowing smile. "You can stay here the night, sir," he offered, much more genial than his wife had been. "We've got a nice room with—"

"As it happens, we can't." With a quick searching

glance at her, Daniel rose. "But we'll need some other way to travel. Have you a coach or a gig for hire?"

"I have a post chaise, and a fine well-matched pair to pull it. The postboy can be ready to leave at a moment's notice."

"That'll do nicely, thank you. Go have it readied, and I'll be there in a bit."

With a quick nod, the innkeeper left.

Daniel returned to the settee, where he loomed over her with an unreadable expression. "This is your last chance, Helena."

She gazed up at him, painfully conscious of the fact that she couldn't stand and look him in the eye. "For what?"

"To return to London. It's two hours by post chaise—you could be back at Griff's in time for dinner."

She crumpled the handkerchief in her hand. "I've already said I don't want to go back. Why would I change my mind now?"

His gaze drifted to her mouth and settled there as if marking his place. "Because if you go with me, I can't promise not to kiss you again."

She caught her breath. Oh, my. Nothing like honesty to shatter a woman's nerves. Or rouse her imagination.

Still, there was a certain presumption in his words. "I can promise not to allow it."

A half smile touched his mouth. "Can you?" He picked her bonnet up off the floor, then held it out to her. But when she reached for it, he caught her hand with his free one and bent his head to kiss it.

She couldn't help it—her hand trembled as he lingered over it, kissing first the back, then turning it over and pressing an openmouthed kiss to her wrist where it lay exposed above the edge of her glove. Her pulse did a wild dance beneath his parted lips.

When he released her hand and straightened, his gaze glittered with need and her entire body tingled with it as well. He flashed her an enigmatic look, triumph mingled with frustration. "If you think for one minute that your resolving against it can prevent it from happening again, then you don't know me very well, lass. Or yourself."

She couldn't think of a single retort that would sound convincing.

He scarcely waited for one before nodding. "All right then. As long as we understand each other." Looking suddenly grim and determined, he headed for the door. "Stay there. I'll be back to carry you to the coach once it's ready."

Oh, Lord, the coach. Now they'd be riding in a coach, alone together in a most intimate situation. Merciful heavens, what insanity had she agreed to?

Chapter 8

Her closed eyes, like weapons sheath'd,
Were seal'd in soft repose;
Her lips, still as she fragrant breath'd,
It richer dyed the rose.
Robert Burns,
"On a Bank of Flowers"

The coach rattled along the road to Tunbridge as Daniel watched Helena sleeping on the seat across from him. She'd fallen asleep almost from the moment they'd started off, probably exhausted from her stint on the horse. Except for a brief doze, he'd watched her the whole time, unable to look away. Helena asleep was fascinating, made even more lovely by the setting sun that caressed her slender body with gold-spangled fingers. The way he wanted to caress it himself.

What a fine piece of work she was—a long-limbed creature of such elegance he could scarce believe he'd kissed her. She even slept elegantly. No snoring or drooling for m'lady, oh, no. With her head propped against the squabs, she slept neatly in the corner of the seat. Her hands remained folded between her cheek and the carriage wall, and her feet stayed together on the floor.

He was something of a messy sleeper himself, thrashing about and snoring. It surprised him she could stay so nicely contained. It made him want to muss her, to take a seat beside her and buss her cheek. But that would be a mistake, no doubt about it.

It had been a mistake to kiss her the first time, to uncover the real woman beneath all that perfection, the one with yearnings and needs.

And the loveliest mouth this side of heaven, warm and tender and kissable. "Bloody hell," he swore under his breath as his St. Peter behaved less than saintly. The damned thing kept rearing up inside his breeches, thanks to her and her sweet lips. He could still taste them; he wanted to taste them again. More than that, he wanted to taste all of her from her wide brow down to her adorable toes, if only to test her vow not to allow him to kiss her again.

But he couldn't risk it. Kissing might lead to more—even a well-born virgin could be tempted to err under the right circumstances—and more would lead to nothing but trouble.

No man with sense seduced a woman like Helena, whose rigid ideas about morality made her dangerous. She was the sort to change her mind about what she wanted the minute the seduction was over, and then there would be hell to pay. She could blacken his character to his clients without ever revealing the truth, all it would take was a few well-placed insinuations that he'd insulted her person. If it came down to choosing her word or his, his wouldn't be worth a farthing.

No, he'd worked too hard finding himself a profitable niche in London trade to see his efforts destroyed by his unruly St. Peter.

She shifted in her sleep, and something tightened in his gut. Of course, if it was more than seduction . . . if she'd accept him as a suitor . . .

His throat tightened. Not bloody likely. She scarcely trusted men of her own rank; she'd never trust one of his. Especially a highwayman's bastard and erstwhile smuggler.

Besides, why would he marry a woman as distrustful as her simply to assuage his lust? He wasn't even looking for a wife, and her kind could only bring him grief.

No matter how lonely the prospect, he was better off with fun-loving lightskirts like Sall, who lacked the urge or the ability to harm him. He was better off not indulging any fanciful dreams of a future with the likes of Lady Helena.

The carriage hit a rut, jolting her awake. She stared at him in bewilderment. It took her a moment to awaken fully, and just watching the sleep fade from her fetching features made his blood quicken. How he'd survive the rest of this trip with her was beyond him.

With characteristic grace she straightened and let her hands float down into her lap. "I-I'm sorry, did I fall asleep? How very rude of me."

And how very like Helena to think in those terms. He smiled. "Not rude in the least. No doubt you needed the rest."

She smoothed out nonexistent wrinkles in her skirt, then fussed with her bonnet. "Did you sleep some, too?"

"A bit," he evaded. No sense in her knowing he'd spent almost the whole time watching her with rabid lust. She was already uncomfortable with him, careful to keep even her skirts separate from him, although that took some doing in the close confines of the post chaise.

"What time is it?" she asked.

He drew out his pocket watch. "Half past five."

She lifted a dainty hand to hide her yawn. "Will we travel all night, do you think?"

"No. I thought we'd spend the night in Tunbridge. We can't go farther until we know exactly where Pryce and Juliet are headed. They're likely to have stopped there, too, and from Tunbridge could've traveled either east to Dover or south to any number of coastal towns."

"Did the ostler at the Blue Boar tell you anything helpful?"

"He said Pryce did have a woman with him, and they were bound for Tunbridge. So for the moment we're on the right road. According to my friend Clancy, Tunbridge has an inn called the Rose and Crown where smugglers sometimes stop on their way to London. I figured we could take rooms; then I could visit the taproom later on and ask questions of any free traders I find. They might know where the pair was headed. They might even know if Pryce has his own cutter and where he keeps it. That'll help us when we reach the coast."

She nodded absently. Then she folded her hands in her lap and stared out the window, seemingly oblivious to the jerking of the coach over rutted roads. Her body was fluid, adjusting to the rocky carriage motion as easily as she'd done to the gelding's pace. It made him wonder if she weren't physically capable of far more than she thought. Perhaps if she could ease into riding more slowly—

"May I ask you something, Mr. Brennan?"

"I thought you were going to call me Daniel."

Her gaze shot to him, veiled and careful. "Of course. I was wondering . . . Daniel . . . will this trip cause you any trouble with your investment concern?"

Bloody hell, did the wench read minds? "What do you mean?"

"You seem to have several clients, and they'll surely be annoyed that you have left them without explanation."

Ah, so that's what she'd meant. "They'll survive."

"I'm not thinking of them, but of you and your new business. I would hate to be the cause of its ruin."

An ironic smile touched his lips. "You won't be." *As long as I can keep my John Thomas in my breeches.* "My short absence might reduce my profits for a time, but that's of no matter."

"No matter! I realize it's important, I assure you. If Griff refuses to compensate you adequately, I will do all in my power—"

"Let's have no more talk about that." Her worry over his finances amused him enormously. "Rest assured I can afford this trip, whether or not Griff compensates me."

"You need not keep up appearances with me, you know." She paused, as if gathering her courage. "I beg your pardon for being so rude as to mention it, and I do not mean it in anything but a friendly way, but I did notice how you live, Daniel. And where. I know that your funds are . . . probably limited."

Nobody had ever called him poor quite so politely before. She looked so very anxious over not shaming him that he had to laugh. "I live in St. Giles, so you've decided I can't afford better?"

"Why else would you live there?"

"Because I want to."

She shook her head. "No one would choose to live in such a slum."

"You're forgetting who I am, lass. I belong in St. Giles. What do you think—that I should buy a grand house in Mayfair and set myself up as gentry? Even if I wanted to spend my money so frivolously—which I don't—it would serve no purpose. A man is what he is, and no fancy lodgings or fine clothes will change that. It's only when he tries to hide his low beginnings and fool people about it that he gets himself into trouble."

She stared at him in complete bewilderment. "Then why have you taught yourself to speak properly and behave like a gentleman if not to be one?"

"So I could make the most of the chances for success that Griff gave me. But I don't need fancy lodgings to be a success at my business. My private life is my own, always has been. And in my private life I prefer not to pass myself off as what I'm not. I only did it once, for Griff, and it didn't suit me a'tall. Best to be honest. People don't accuse you of trying to deceive them if you're honest from the first. If anybody should understand that, it's you."

She looked skeptical. "So you tell all your clients—the duke, for example—that your father was a highwayman and you used to work for smugglers?"

"I don't tell them, but I don't hide it either. They generally find out, if they don't already know it. Most of my clients met me through Griff." He didn't explain that some had even been involved with smugglers themselves at one time. *Somebody* had to put up the capital for those boats and goods, after all. "They saw how I increased his investment income, and they wanted the same. So long as I make them pots of money, they don't much care who I am. My honesty on the subject makes them trust me even more."

She shook her head. Her ladyship probably couldn't understand a man choosing to be himself rather than put on a show. She put on a show every day, keeping her true self locked up so tight that scarcely a piece of the real woman peeked through.

But this afternoon, he'd glimpsed the woman trapped inside the brittle glass of her manner, like a lovely figurine imprisoned in a glass dome. Sheer perversity made him want to be the one to break the glass and set her free.

"Besides," he went on, "living in St. Giles works to my advantage in business. The fortunes of London aren't made only in the clubs, y'know. Where do you think the mine owners go to hire ruffians when they want to subdue their workers? Where do you think all those talkative sailors with juicy cargoes go when they're fresh in from sea? To the gin shops of St. Giles, that's where. And a clever man with an ear for business can use what he hears to figure out when the price of tea is about to soar or when the mines will prove troublesome."

She gaped at him as if seeing him through new eyes. "I never thought of it that way."

"Nobody ever does. That's why it gives me an advantage, lass."

"Yes, I see." She ventured a smile. "All the same, I want you to know that I appreciate your going to so much trouble for me and Juliet. After today I wouldn't have blamed you had you tossed out the whole idea and headed back to London."

"I said I'd find her, and I will. I don't renege on my promises."

Suspicion flickered in her hazel eyes. "Be that as it

may, you were not so eager to set off on this trip before. What made you change your mind in London? You're not keeping anything from me, are you? About Mr. Pryce, I mean."

Mr. Pryce. Now that was a subject that made him sore uneasy. "No. I've told you all I learnt. But I confess that it gnaws at me that he's a free trader. When you first told me of it, I thought for sure you were mistaken. I was wrong, and that's worrisome."

She lifted one delicate eyebrow. "You don't like to be wrong, do you?"

"No more'n you, I expect."

"True," she said gamely, and added a smile to boot.

What a smile she had. He saw it seldom, but when it made its appearance, it was like finding the ring in the wedding cake—an unexpected delight amidst what was already the pleasure of looking at her.

A pity it was so fleeting. She shot him an anxious look. "You don't think Mr. Pryce will hurt her, do you?"

"No. Smugglers are only interested in one thing—money. Even if he's marrying her for her fortune, it won't serve his purpose to hurt her other than to—" Bloody hell, he should've shut his trap sooner.

"Other than to ruin her," she finished.

He sighed. "Yes." Nor was little Juliet the only one in danger of being ruined. "Now let me ask you a question. Why are you so bent on this wild attempt to stop her? Why risk so much merely to save Juliet from marrying badly?"

"She's my sister," she said as if that were all the explanation he needed.

"And a grown woman old enough to know her own mind. But your reputation might also be ruined if anybody finds out you were traveling alone with me."

"No one will."

"You can't be sure. And if they do . . . well, I may not move in your 'refined circles,' but I know what happens to a woman of your position when she spurns the proprieties. She can be ruined without ever losing her virtue, and well you know it. Then no decent man will offer for her, let alone anybody of rank or wealth."

To his surprise, she laughed, though with some bitterness. "Don't worry—I long ago relinquished any expectation of marrying well."

"Oh? Why is that?"

Her eyes widened. Apparently, nobody had ever questioned her assumption. "It should be obvious."

"It's not." Not to him, anyway. Oh, he was fairly sure what *she* thought was the reason, but he couldn't believe that was the cause of her being a spinster.

"There are lots of reasons," she said evasively.

"What are they?" he pressed.

"For one thing, I'm the daughter of a man who's not really an earl, but merely the one who stole the rightful earl's title. Once Papa dies, everyone will know it."

"Griff will keep the details as quiet as he can."

"I know, but if he's to inherit, there's no way of avoiding revealing the truth, and it's to all our benefits for him to inherit."

"You said there were lots of reasons. Name another."

She tipped her chin up. "I am well past the age when women marry—"

He snorted. "You can't be more than twenty-five."

"I'm twenty-six, nearly twenty-seven. I'm on the shelf."

"Then the shelf is too low in my opinion, but go on. What else makes you so unmarriageable that you take no care for your reputation? Griff did give you a nice dowry."

She shot him a searching glance. "That merely means I have my pick of the fortune hunters."

"And we both know how you feel about fortune hunters," he teased.

She did not smile. "Exactly."

"What else?" *Say it,* he thought. *Say it, so I can tell you you're wrong.*

"I am not the wifely type."

He laughed outright. "And what is the 'wifely type,' pray tell?"

"Compliant and sweet-tempered. I'm neither."

"I'd have to agree with that." When she glared at him, he leaned forward to whisper, "Except when you're kissing a man. That's enough to make me suspect you have a bit more sweetness in you than you let on."

"Don't be so sure," she said archly.

"I'd lay odds on it. I'm a fair judge of character, y'know, especially in women."

"Because you spend so much time with so many of them."

"Probably." The jealous edge in her tone pleased him despite himself.

So did the way she reacted to his answer. She frowned very prettily. Then a tense stillness came over her as she turned to stare out the window. "Did you know I was engaged to be married a few years ago?"

That brought him up short. "No, I didn't. Who was the man?"

"A viscount named Farnsworth."

He thought a moment. "Heir to the Earl of Pomfret? Isn't Farnsworth the one who married a rich coal merchant's daughter last year?"

She rolled her eyes. "The very one."

"I take it you harbor bad memories of your courtship."

"You could say that."

When she refused to elaborate, he adopted a tone of nonchalance. "I actually met the viscount once, but what I most remember is his fine boots. I asked where he'd had them made, and he told me the name of a fancy cobbler in Oxford Street. That was the extent of our conversation." He studied her a moment. "I talked to his wife a bit longer, however. She was pretty, but a simpering fool without a brain in her head. She doesn't hold a candle to you."

"Is she lame?" she snapped as her gaze shot to him, hard as stone.

Ah, at last she'd said it. The bitter words made him want to haul her onto his lap and demonstrate how very little her lameness meant to a man of good sense.

He chose his answer carefully. "I don't see what that has to do with anything."

She sucked in a ragged breath. "It means she'll make him a better wife than I."

"Why? It's not as if you'd have to cook and clean for him, or do anything that required full use of your leg. You have servants to do everything, so it shouldn't make a difference one way or t'other."

"On the contrary, it makes even more of a difference. Well-bred young ladies should be perfect embodiments of womanhood." She recited it as if it came from a rule book like the one the groom had handed him out of her bag earlier.

"Ballocks," he retorted.

She gaped at him. "Wh-what?"

"You heard me. Ballocks, all of it. Maybe *you* think you have to be perfect, but nobody else does. I doubt even Farnsworth thought it."

Her eyes glittered in the dimming light of the carriage.

"Frankly, I have no idea what he thought. Unlike you, I'm no expert on the opposite sex. What I do know is that Lord Farnsworth courted me only as long as he believed I had a fortune. Once he discovered I did not, he ran as fast as his fine boots from Oxford Street could carry him."

"Then he was a fool, lass," he said earnestly, "and you deserve better."

She caught her breath, emotions flowing across her face in rapid succession—surprise, then hope, and finally disbelief. After a moment, she tore her gaze away.

"Actually, he was much cleverer than the ones who came after him. He had the good sense to pretend to care for me. He was always giving me elaborate compliments and treating me with cordial concern." Her tone grew brittle. "But I was on my guard for the others. Besides, since they knew from the outset that I had a lame leg and only my rank to recommend me, their attempts to woo me were rather halfhearted."

The way she lumped all the men together inexplicably irritated him. "Did you ever stop to think that it might not have been your leg that repulsed them? P'raps they got tired of your bitter tongue and frosty manner. P'raps Farnsworth did, too."

"I did not *have* a bitter tongue when Lord Farnsworth was courting me; that came later. You see, I was fool enough to believe his compliments. I fancied myself in love with him." Her soft sigh tore at him. "Indeed, I was always perfectly amiable to him. More than amiable."

The words hit him broadside. He suddenly found himself hating Farnsworth with great virulence, not only for hurting Helena, but for gaining her love before he dealt the final blow.

And what the devil did she mean, *more than amiable*? "Is that why you're so good at kissing?" he said without thinking. "Because you practiced so much with Farnsworth?"

She blinked at him. "Whatever are you talking about?"

"Your being 'more than amiable' to his bloody lordship, that's what."

She drew herself up in outrage. "I only meant that I was sociable, not that I . . . you couldn't possibly think that I . . ." Her voice hardened. "Oh, that is so much like a man—to boast of his own association with half the strumpets in London, then criticize a woman for even speaking to another man in a friendly way. You seduce me into kissing *you*, but chide me for possibly kissing *him!* How dare you?"

Struck speechless by her ire, he stared at her a long moment. Then he shook his head, shocked by the strength of the jealousy she'd roused. She had a good reason for her tirade, though he'd be damned if he let her know what had provoked his unguarded speech.

And must she speak of their kiss as if he'd forced it upon her? "I'm sorry, lass," he said, struggling to contain his emotions and sound sincere. "You're perfectly right. It was a foolish and unfair thing to say."

Apparently she sensed he wasn't saying everything, for she cast him a wary glance. "It certainly was."

"You can kiss whoever you want," he assured her. *Though I'd prefer it to be me.* He squelched that thought, and deliberately turned the conversation back into safer waters. "Certainly, you can be amiable to whoever you want."

"Thank you so much for giving me permission." She tipped up her nose, apparently still miffed. "But I know you think me incapable of amiability."

"Not a'tall. You were perfectly amiable during our luncheon today." *And even more so afterward . . .* Bloody hell, why couldn't he keep his randy thoughts off that kiss?

"You're not saying that just to flatter me, are you?" She dragged her pelisse about her as if the flimsy fabric would provide some protection from him.

A smile tugged at his lips. "I wouldn't dream of it."

"Because you do have a tendency to flatter women, you know."

"Do I?" Was she thinking of that bloody Farnsworth, the one who paid her insincere compliments?

"You do. Even Griff says you could talk your way into a queen's good graces."

He shrugged. "That isn't flattery. Flattery's when a man lies to a woman about what she is. I don't do that. I look for the hidden part of a woman, the virtues inside even the shyest or most arrogant, and I speak to that part, the best part. That's all."

"You mean, the way you ferreted out the one virtue of that nasty woman at the inn—her willingness to work hard?"

"That mightn't have been her only virtue, y'know. I realize she rubbed you wrong with her comment about the Irish, and I didn't much like it myself. But a woman like that has a hard life. It can turn even the best woman sour. You can't hold it against her if it comes out in foolish opinions. You never know—she might have been robbed by an Irishman once." He lowered his voice. "It's no different than you, seeing every man as untrustworthy because of Fickle Farnsworth."

"But I don't!"

"Oh, but you do. Or you wouldn't be so suspicious of my compliments."

"I have good reason for being suspicious, and well you know it. Last summer—"

"Let's settle one thing: I meant every compliment I paid you last summer, no matter what you think. I've never lied to you, not once, except to pretend to be Griff." He'd been evasive, but never out-and-out lied. "What's more, I promise never to do so."

He glanced down at her hands, curled up into defensive fists in her lap, then back to her wary face. "And surely you can't think I had any motive for kissing you this afternoon except honest desire."

Her eyes glittered. "The 'nice dowry' Griff gave me had nothing to do with it, I'm sure."

The words fell between them like a cannon shot, setting off a wild, hot fury in his breast. She might as well have slapped him. Indeed, he would've preferred it. Nor did it help that she'd confirmed his suspicions about her—that she'd turn on him in a heartbeat. "That's a low blow, Helena, and one I don't deserve."

Remorse instantly flooded her cheeks. "All right, perhaps it is. But I do have some reason for it. You were willing to take money from Griff to court us—or have you forgotten that?"

He glowered at her. "P'raps I should disabuse you of some foolish notions you have. I'm not so poor or lacking in prospects as you think. I left Griff's employ because I was already earning more on my own than as his man of affairs. But even before that, I'd started putting away substantial monies. At present, I have ten thousand pounds in a fund that I touch only when necessary. If I continue to live modestly, and my business continues to grow, I'll have twice that sum in a year."

He took a grim satisfaction from the look of shock on her face. She was so bloody conventional. She couldn't think outside the narrow lines drawn for her by her governesses and father and God knew who else.

"Yes," he continued, "I did accept Griff's offer of money to court you three. That's how I started my fund in the first place—by doing unusual tasks for Griff. But he didn't pay me to give you false compliments, nor would I have done it if he had. And in fact, I never took a penny of what he offered me. I'm not the least worried about my financial future, so I assure you that no dowry of three thousand pounds could tempt me to kiss a woman I didn't desire."

With that little speech, he knocked on the ceiling of the carriage to signal the driver to stop. He'd rather ride up there in the wind and the cold than spend one more minute in Helena's frosty presence.

"Daniel—" she began.

"Don't. I'm too bloody angry right now to hear any more. If you can't see that a man might desire you for something other than your damned money or station, if you insist on thinking so little of yourself, then I don't s'pose there's much I can do about it. But I don't have to put up with your thinking so little of me."

The coach shuddered to a halt, and he flung open the door. He'd been right to caution himself against her. Figures encased in glass domes weren't meant to be set free; they were meant to be kept on their little pedestals and admired from afar.

Because trying to free them gave a man nothing but glass shards in his fist.

Chapter 9

Here's to the man who drinks dark ale
And goes to bed quite mellow.
He lives as he ought to live . . .
For he's a jolly good fellow.
"Three Jolly Coachmen,"
anonymous ballad

Helena sat on a chair in the common room of the Rose and Crown, waiting for Daniel to return from speaking with the innkeeper about a room. Thankfully, she could walk with the help of her cane now, though not stand for any length of time.

Daniel probably would have balked at carrying her in, anyway. He hadn't spoken to her since their arrival. Not that she blamed him after her patently unfair accusations.

She knew he was not pursuing her for her dowry or anything ridiculous like that; he wasn't pursuing her at all—at least not as a wife. Plain desire had fueled his kiss, not courtship.

But when he'd implied that she'd shared intimacies with Lord Farnsworth, it had made her so angry! Especially when he wasn't the least ashamed of all *his* dalliances.

That was why she found his compliments suspect—because he gave them so indiscriminately. She'd never wanted to believe other men's compliments as badly as she wanted to believe Daniel's, which made him dangerous to her peace of mind.

Now there'd be no compliments at all. How she wanted him to greet her with his easy smile again, to fuss over her again.

To not be so very angry at her.

She sighed. She had sunk low indeed to be craving the attentions of such a rascal.

Daniel entered the room, his manner as stony as when he'd left her there. "The innkeeper says there's only one room available. We'd best go on to Tunbridge Wells."

"But you said this was the best place to—"

"I know what I said. We're *not* sharing a room, and that's the end of it."

"I don't mind sharing, if we have to."

His gaze pinned her in place. "*I* mind."

"It's only for one night." She lowered her voice as the innkeeper entered. "And if it will help us find them, we should do it." At least it would give her the chance to apologize. He could hardly avoid her in close quarters.

"Meaning to change your mind, sir?" the innkeeper asked as he approached. "Your missus looks right peaked, and the room I got is large enough for two."

And Daniel *had* said this was the ideal spot for gathering information. "Yes, my dear, I'm much too tired to go on. Can't we just stay here?"

Daniel glared at her, a muscle working in his jaw. She swallowed. Lord, it was going to be a very long night.

He swore under his breath and turned to the innkeeper. "Have you an extra mattress I can throw on the floor?"

"You won't want to sleep there, sir—"

"My wife's leg pains her at night, so we don't share a bed. We won't be staying here unless you provide us with a second mattress. I'm willing to pay for it."

The innkeeper shrugged. "I suppose that can be arranged."

"All right. Then give us the room."

Helena sagged with relief. Truth be told, she did not wish to spend one more minute in that wretched coach, with or without Daniel.

The innkeeper beamed. "I'm sure you'll find the accommodations more than sufficient, sir. Come right this way and I'll show you to your room. Then I'll see to having the mattress brought up."

As the man headed for the stairs, Daniel approached to help her stand, then put his arm around her waist so she could lean on him. "Don't think this changes anything between us," he muttered as they made their way behind the innkeeper.

"I don't." Though surely he could not stay angry at her forever. "I *am* sorry, you know. I should never have said what I did."

"It's too late to take it back. At least now I know what you really think of me."

"But Daniel—"

"Enough, Helena. I don't wish to discuss it."

Now who was being unfair? She felt his ire in the stiffness of his arm, in the way he touched her as little as possible. She missed his teasing and solicitude. She'd been foolish indeed to make him so cross.

They climbed the stairs in silence. She didn't need his help half so much as she pretended, but her enjoyment at having his arm about her waist prodded her to keep up the pretense.

As soon as they entered their room and he'd accompanied her to a chair, he left her side as if he couldn't escape her fast enough. The innkeeper swept his arm in an arc. "You see? Quite large, ain't it?"

Daniel gave it a cursory glance. "It'll do." He handed the innkeeper some silver. "Have our bags brought up, and bring a meal for my wife. She'll tell you what she wants."

"Whatever you have already cooked will be fine," Helena said softly. "And a flagon of wine, if you please."

"Very well, madam. And nothing for you, sir?" the innkeeper asked.

"No. I'll be eating in the taproom."

Ah, yes, the taproom. Where the smugglers gathered.

"All right then." The innkeeper looked as if he might comment on the odd arrangement, but when Daniel glowered at him like Samson in the barber's chair, the man seemed to think better of it and fled.

Daniel headed for the door as well, but she called out as he passed, "Will you be very late, do you think?"

He paused at the door. "As late as it takes to find out the information we seek." He swept her with a hard glance. "When I come upstairs, you'd better already be situated well out of my way, do you hear? Especially if you intend to sleep other than fully clothed, or so help me, God—" He broke off. "Just don't wait up, that's all."

Then he was gone, leaving her feeling all at sea. She dropped into a Windsor chair and surveyed her surroundings. It was a cheery wainscoted room, much nicer than any of the ones she'd had on the mad rush to London. It even boasted a comfortable-looking four-poster bed, though bedbugs probably lurked in the mattress. Mr. Brennan would have a devil of a time keeping vermin off him if he slept on the floor.

Perhaps *she* ought to sleep there. That would demonstrate her remorse. Although she didn't relish sharing the floor with the fleas and mice that inevitably inhabited coaching inns, she also didn't wish to spend the rest of the trip with Daniel so angry.

The mattress arrived a half hour later, brought by a footman. A maid entered behind him with a tray containing her dinner. The footman built a fire in the grate, then left, and the maid began laying out her meal on the deal table nearest the window.

Helena eyed the mattress suspiciously. "How long has it been since that mattress was used?"

"Lord have mercy, I've no idea," the maid answered. "Some months, I expect. Most people prefer a bed, y'know, even if two or three have to share it." The maid wrinkled her nose. "Sleeping on the floor ain't so pleasant, if you take my meaning."

Unfortunately, Helena took her meaning quite well.

The buxom girl shot her a curious glance when she went to make up the mattress. "My master says you prefer to sleep alone. Don't know as I could do that meself, not with a husband as fine as yours to share my bed."

The maid's tiny, knowing smile pricked Helena raw, and though Helena's frosty glare made it vanish, the chit's assumptions still irritated her. No doubt she was calculating how easy it would be to get Daniel into her own bed. After all, any man who refused to sleep with his wife . . .

Oh, Lord, now she was even thinking of herself as his wife. Next she'd be wondering what it would be like to share a bed with him, to have his large frame nestled against her, bared except for his drawers—

"Will there be anything else, ma'am?" the girl asked, having finished with the mattress.

Helena snapped her gaze away from the imposing bed and colored in spite of herself. "No, that will be all. Thank you."

As soon as the girl was gone, she sat down to her meal, but could do no more than pick at it. Food did not interest her just now. The Madeira, however, was another matter. She did not overimbibe as a general rule, but tonight she wanted to ease the ache in her heart.

Between sips of Madeira, she unpacked the meager contents of the saddlebag, hanging her other gown over the leather screen to air, examining what else she'd been allowed to keep. Her extra petticoat was there and her night rail, but little more beyond a few toiletries and her sketch pad. She sighed. Mrs. N's guide had been left behind.

Truth be told, however, she was finding its guidance vastly unhelpful. She began to suspect that Mrs. N had limited experience with men. Why else would she make rules so impossible to follow as *The Well-bred Young Lady never loses her temper?*

At least Helena had her sketch pad. Settling down with the remains of the flagon, she took out the pad and her pencil and sketched out the shapes of the furniture in their room. Then she set the whole mess aside.

She was in no mood to draw. She was in no mood to do anything but stare into space and replay her conversation with Daniel. The trouble was, every time she replayed it, she came out looking worse.

She'd been utterly wrong about him in more than one

respect. Considering his background, it was astonishing how much he'd taught himself, how he'd risen to a position of respect and responsibility. And to have amassed so much money, he must be very competent and far more intelligent than many privileged gentlemen. No wonder Griff placed such faith in him.

Contrary to Daniel's opinion of her, she did not believe birth was everything. After all, Mama had been a mere actress fortunate enough to marry a gentleman, yet she'd been the most refined woman Helena knew.

Helena *had* placed some store by breeding and education, but this afternoon Daniel had behaved in a more civilized way toward her than she had toward him. He'd proven kinder and more apt to look beyond appearances than any of the proper gentlemen she'd known, which made her feel quite ashamed of her unfair treatment of him.

She still did not approve of his dalliances, of course, and she still thought him annoyingly arrogant at times. But beyond that, he was a better man than she had guessed. That was what made him hard to resist, what tempted her into shameless behavior around him. It had been years since she'd met a man she truly believed was good at heart. And it was perhaps the only time she'd met one who roused such naughty thoughts and urges in her.

After a while, she glanced at the clock on the mantel, shocked to discover it well past eleven and the candles already guttering in their sconces. She ought to go to bed. After her exertions today, she needed rest, even if she didn't feel the least bit sleepy.

As she performed the necessary ablutions at the basin, she wondered if she dared change into her night rail. No, best not to. Daniel had been rather firm about her roaming the room in such a state, and she refused to give him anything else to complain about. Though she cringed to think how her dress would look in the morning, she kept it on, only taking down her hair. Trying not to dwell on the bugs lurking in the shadows, she lay down on the mattress on the floor and pulled the wool blanket up to her chin.

She was convinced she was too edgy to sleep, so it was with something of a shock when she awakened to discover from the clock that she'd been asleep nearly two hours. It must have been the Madeira she'd drunk on an empty stomach. Indeed, she still felt a trifle foggy-brained.

Sitting up, she glanced about to find the bed still empty. She grabbed her cane and got up, wincing as her aching leg protested. A quick examination of the clock revealed that it was indeed past one A.M. And Daniel was still downstairs.

For heaven's sake, how long did it take a man to question a lot of scoundrels? He'd been down there for hours.

An image of the buxom maid flashed into her mind, and her heart sank. What if he was doing more than asking questions? She'd certainly given him no reason not to practice his usual . . . indiscretions.

Well, she refused to wait about in the morning for him to rise after a night of drinking and . . . and other debaucheries. He could do his wild living on someone else's schedule—she wouldn't tolerate it on hers.

Hastily, she pinned up her hair. As she left the room to descend the narrow stairs, clinging to the banister for support, she told herself it was only her concern for their schedule that led her toward the taproom. Nothing more.

Finding the taproom was easy—loud and raucous snatches of drinking songs and laughter spilled from it. A faint apprehension seized her as she neared its entrance. She had every right to come fetch Daniel, she reminded herself. To all appearances she was his wife, and surely that was what wives did.

Still, she was unprepared for the sight that greeted her eyes. The walls of the low-ceilinged room were hung with sporting prints, and smoke clogged the air from freely lit pipes and cigars. The taps flowed in regular bursts, and the only women in the room—the taproom maids—were kept busy filling glasses and rushing them to tables where men clamored for "more ale." Though the girls were dressed a trifle . . . casually, and one or two flirted with the men, they seemed to have little time for more than that.

Which explained why the men were all in varying stages of inebriation. What a pitiful collection of drunken louts. One man stumbled over his companion trying to dance a jig beside his joint stool, another pinched a maid's bottom as she passed and only laughed when she swatted his hand away.

Oh, dear, this was no place for a woman of good reputation, to be sure.

"Helena?" rasped a disbelieving voice somewhere to the right of her. Swallowing hard, she turned to find herself the object of scrutiny by six men crowded around a lopsided oak table. Daniel was one of them, and his surprise rapidly altered to annoyance.

The others, however, looked pleased to see her. One even rose to bow and say, "Welcome, madam. Do come and join us. We'll buy you a pint of ale, won't we, lads?"

As the man's companions grinned and chorused the invitation, she hesitated. Lord, what had she got herself into?

"That's my wife you're talking to, you fool," Daniel ground out as he rose from the table, "and the only place she's going is back to our room."

That sparked her temper. Yes, she'd behaved badly this afternoon, but that was no reason to pack her off to bed like some child. These men did not look so awful as she might have expected. Why *not* join them?

She walked toward their table with a smile. "Don't be silly, Danny. I'm not going anywhere." His eyes narrowed ominously at her use of his nickname, but she ignored it. "I'm tired of waiting upstairs. I believe I *will* join you and your friends."

"Now see here, Helena—"

"Relax, Brennan, and sit down," the man who'd invited her said as he hurried to pull up a chair next to him. "Yer wife's perfectly safe with us, eh, lads?"

"Thank you," she said primly as she took the proffered seat. "Danny is far too overprotective sometimes. He thinks he's the only one who should have any fun."

Her overprotective "husband" did sit down, but he shot her a thunderous glare across the table. She sighed. If he insisted on being angry at her anyway, she could hardly make matters any worse.

"Well, now, Mrs. Brennan," one of the other men said, "mayhap your husband's got his reasons for bein' overprotective—with you such a fine woman and all."

"Pish-posh. A fine woman deserves entertainment as much as any other."

"She deserves ale, too," the first man said at her side.

"She don't need ale," Daniel put in. "She ain't staying."

She blinked, unused to such poor grammar from Daniel. But of course, he would want to play his part thoroughly, wouldn't he? Well, she would play a part of her own.

"Of course I'm staying." She bestowed a smile on the man beside her. "Ale would be nice, thank you." *The Well-bred Young Lady does not overimbibe*, niggled a voice in the back of her mind. Oh, a pox on that Well-bred Young Lady. She'd probably never had to chase after an unruly sister.

Daniel snorted and shook his head, but made no other move to keep her from staying. Not that she would have let him. She was tired of waiting on Daniel's leisure, taking only the crumbs of information he'd offered. She didn't see why she couldn't participate in their investigation.

The man next to her called for a maid, who hurried over to take his order. Then he laid his arm about Helena's shoulders and winked. "The name's John Wallace, ma'am, though it's John Thomas Wallace that the ladies like the best. And either one will suit for you."

At her bewildered expression, the other men burst into laughter. Daniel rose half out of his seat to growl, "Best be watching your coarse tongue around my wife, you sot!"

"It's all right," Helena put in, not sure what she'd missed, although Daniel's expression implied it was rather improper. Lord, were they all as flirtatious as Daniel? She picked up Mr. Wallace's arm and dropped it in his lap. "Actually, I think 'presumptuous' suits you best of all."

He chuckled. "'Pre-sump-tuous,' eh? By damn, you're a fancy female to be married to a rascal like Brennan there. Yer husband claims to be a dealer in smuggled goods—been tellin' us about it for the past hour." Suspicion glinted in his eyes. "But mayhap he's not such a rascal after all."

The tension at the table instantly heightened. She didn't dare look at Daniel. "Well, of course he is." She folded her hands in her lap to hide their trembling. "How else do you think we met?" Oh, dear, why had she said such a ninny thing?

"That sounds very interestin'," Mr. Wallace commented. "Met yer wife while free tradin', Mr. Brennan? Do tell us about this odd courtship."

"I'll let my wife do it," his deep voice answered. "She tells it much better than me."

Her gaze shot to him in a panic. Daniel was the one who could twist the truth—what was she to do now? But his cursed eyebrow just crooked upward in challenge.

She stiffened. He thought she'd ruin everything, didn't he? Well, how hard could it be to convince a lot of drunken men that her tale was true?

"It's very simple, really," she began, stalling for time. The taproom maid set a foaming glass of ale in front of her, and she stared at it, an idea forming. "My father is a London liquor merchant. Danny was the one to sell Papa French brandy and wine and such. That's how I first spotted him." She let a dreamy expression cross her face as she looked over at Daniel. "I lost my heart to him the minute I saw him at Papa's place of business."

A faint, mocking smile touched Daniel's lips.

"Oho!" one of the other men said. "And did your father approve?"

"Of course not. He had great aspirations for me, wanted me to marry a fine lord. How do you think I learned to speak like this? Papa sent me away to . . . Mrs. Nunley's School for Refined Ladies." She leaned forward and lowered her voice as she warmed to her tale. "My grandfather was a publican, and Papa improved his fortunes by marrying a merchant's daughter. But he wanted better for me, you see. And since he had the wealth to tempt a lord, he was determined to see me marry well."

"Yet you married *this* scoundrel," the man sitting next to Daniel said with a laugh, clapping him on the back. Daniel rolled his eyes.

She lifted her pint of ale and sipped, trying not to wrinkle her nose at the musty smell. It tasted far better than it smelled, though, sort of nutty.

She set the ale back down. "That's rather good."

"You *have* had ale before, haven't you?" Mr. Wallace asked. "I mean, with yer father bein' a liquor merchant and all."

Had her surprise been that obvious? "Now that I'm married to Danny, I drink what I want. But Papa always said that proper ladies do not drink ale, so he never let me have anything stronger than ratafia. And once in a while, champagne."

That sent the other men into gales of laughter. "Ratafia, eh?" Mr. Wallace remarked. "Well, you won't find any ratafia or champagne here, Mrs. Brennan."

"Thank heavens." She drank some more ale. "I prefer the stouter stuff."

They laughed again and Daniel snorted, but she was surprised to discover the taste was growing on her. As were its effects—a general warmth and feeling of grand well-being throughout her body.

"How did you get around your father's expectations so you could marry Brennan?" one of the men asked.

Best to stick as close to the truth as possible, Daniel had said. "Well, I realized Papa's hopes for me were far too lofty, even if he did not." She pointed to her leg. "It's hard to catch a fine lord if you can't even dance at balls."

"Have you always been lame then?" the youngest of the group asked from his seat on the other side of Mr. Wallace.

Mr. Wallace cuffed him. "That's a rude question, you chawbacons."

"I don't mind," she said quickly, unsettled by the casual violence against a lad who looked little older than

Juliet. But when they glanced to her expectantly, she froze. She rarely spoke of her illness to anyone, deflecting all questions with polite evasions. And to expose herself so wholly to these strange men . . .

Taking a fortifying sip of ale, she looked at Daniel. His encouraging smile oddly reassured her. "Well, you see, I contracted an illness, a very rare one, around the time of my coming out. I first had fever and headache, and then it attacked my muscles. When the fever passed, I discovered that my legs didn't work."

"Both legs?" Mr. Wallace glanced down at them. "But yer other one seems fine."

She nodded. "Papa consulted a surgeon familiar with the disease, and he said I might recover some facility in my limbs if I exercised them." She shrugged. "So I did, and I managed to recover all the strength in one leg and partial use of the other."

That was all she'd planned to say until Daniel spoke up. "Tell them how long it took you."

Her gaze shot to his to find a question in his eyes. Heavens, he wanted to know for himself, and his interest warmed her even more than the ale. "It was three or four years before I could manage with only a cane. My . . . er . . . maid Rosalind helped me enormously. She prodded and pushed me even when I didn't want to try. It's thanks to her that I can walk at all."

"Thanks to her and *yourself*," Daniel corrected. "It must've taken great strength of will. And I doubt your 'maid' would've succeeded if you hadn't wanted it so bad."

She stared at him, her heart in her throat. Approval shone in his face, and she drank it up more thirstily than any ale. "I suppose not," she admitted.

"So you didn't have your show in grand society after all," one of the men put in.

She tore her gaze from Daniel. "M-my show?"

"Your 'come out.' "

"Oh. No, I did not." She took a great swig of ale, drowning the memory of her first public appearance in Stratford when her cane had garnered her pitying glances from the squire's son. That pity was echoed later by men of higher rank. "By the time I regained use of my legs, I was too old and lame to suit any of those stuffy lords." The liquor spreading through her body made her reckless, made her want to confess things she told no one. "Besides, I didn't want them anyway. I think a man ought to appreciate a woman for more than just her appearance, don't you?"

The men quickly chimed their agreement, protesting that they wouldn't be so "mutton-headed," that she was fine enough for any man and all those "lords" were fools.

Their enthusiastic response surprised her, though she didn't quite believe them. They *were* smugglers, after all. "Thank you. But now you see why I was eager to marry Danny. He was so sweet to me. Those chaps Papa kept throwing at me only wanted my inheritance."

Mr. Wallace eyed Daniel with a hint of mischief. "And how did you know Mr. Brennan here did not want yer inheritance?"

Daniel bristled, but she hastened to say, "Oh, I knew I could trust him from the start." She caught his gaze and held it. "He's an honorable man. He'd never court a woman for her money."

She prayed that he'd accept her apology this time, and for a moment it seemed that he might, for his expression held a sort of bemused surprise.

Then it hardened. "My wife exaggerates. She wasn't always so trusting."

A keen disappointment sliced through her. She finished off her ale, taking solace from the heady brew. "Well, what did you expect? Your profession doesn't precisely inspire trust, my dear."

Too late, she realized she'd insulted the entire table.

But they didn't seem to take offense. Indeed, Mr. Wallace laughed broadly. "A clever woman, eh? So what did he do to change yer mind, Mrs. Brennan?" Leaning close, he whispered in her ear, "Did he dance the mattress jig with you *afore* the weddin'?"

"I told you, I can't dan—" She broke off, realizing what he must mean. A blush spread over her cheeks that she could only pray was hidden by the taproom's poor light. Daniel was looking as if he might dance a jig on Mr. Wallace's head at any moment, and he didn't even know what the man had said.

"Of course not," she whispered and edged away from the smuggler. Then she explained to the others, "I . . . he . . . asked for my hand from Papa, and when Papa threatened to disinherit me if I married him, Danny carried me off anyway. He didn't care one whit about my inheritance. That's how I knew I could trust him."

"I said she'd tell it better than me," Daniel remarked. "My wife's a born storyteller." The sarcasm in his voice wounded her, though no one else seemed to notice.

"Another pint of ale for the storyteller!" Mr. Wallace called to a maid passing by and tapped Helena's empty glass.

"No," Daniel ordered. "She's had enough ale for one night."

"Nonsense!" Helena protested, though she did feel substantially more foggy-brained than she had earlier. And her tongue seemed a trifle . . . unwieldy.

Still, if drinking ale was a requirement for the deception, she would drink ale. She turned to Mr. Wallace.

"You see what I mean about Danny? He's so careful of me. But I don't know why he bothered to bring me if he'd planned to be so cautious."

"I didn't want to bring you, remember?" Daniel downed the contents of a tumbler in front of him. As the taproom maid appeared with Helena's second pint, Daniel tapped his own glass. "More gin."

So *he* could drink and she couldn't? The taproom maid set down Helena's pint, and she drank from it with a defiant flourish, then wiped her mouth with the back of her hand as she'd seen the men do. "Well, I'm here now, so I intend to enjoy myself."

The smugglers cheered.

"I swear, Helena—" Daniel began.

Mr. Wallace cut him off. "Be a good sport, Brennan—it's just a touch of ale between friends. It'll liven up yer trip." He turned to Helena. "Where are you two goin' anyway, Mrs. Brennan?"

Helena shot Daniel a quick glance, wondering how much he'd told them. He looked thoroughly irritated, touched his hand to his coat pocket where lay the sketch, and gave a tiny shake of the head.

He hadn't yet asked about Pryce? For heaven's sake, he'd been down here all this time and *still* hadn't learned anything? Well, she'd take care of *that*. "Danny's going to the coast to buy things from free traders. And I came along to keep him company."

When Mr. Wallace's glance narrowed and Daniel went rigid, she knew she'd said something wrong. "Why not just go to Stockwell?" Mr. Wallace asked Daniel.

Stockwell was near London. Why would he go there?

"They cheat you in Stockwell," Daniel retorted. "I get a better price at the coast."

That answer seemed to satisfy Mr. Wallace, but only a

little. "But you never came to the coast before. I know all the dealers who come down to Kent and most of those who come to Sussex. I never seen you."

"This ain't my usual route." Daniel drank gin as casually as if he were speaking to old friends. "I generally go to Essex."

The suspicion in Mr. Wallace's gaze eased a little more. "Then you know Clancy in St. Giles."

"Clancy's a good friend of mine," Daniel said. "His son George works for me from time to time."

"I heard George was a clerk now," Mr. Wallace said conversationally.

"Aye, but ain't much money in clerking." Daniel winked. "Not as much as in free trading, to be sure."

The men laughed, and the tension around the table eased considerably. Talk began to center around smugglers in Essex. Helena found it an intriguing conversation. If anyone else had heard it, he would have thought these men fishermen or farmers. They spoke of their profession as if it were perfectly acceptable. They didn't boast of murder and mayhem; indeed, they didn't mention violence at all—which made her wonder if she'd been a trifle misinformed about smugglers.

And about Daniel's connection to them. He seemed awfully familiar with their world for someone who claimed not to have associated with them in years. He knew all about "tubmen" and "owlers" and "batsmen." She'd never seen this wicked side of him, and she found it shamefully appealing.

Had she misconstrued his involvement with smugglers? No, how could that be? He'd been so young. Yet the boy with them, who boasted of his last run to France, couldn't be more than eighteen. And Daniel did seem to know so much about their business.

Which meant he ought to be able to find out about Juliet and Pryce. From what she gathered, these men were returning from selling their goods in London. That was probably why they were so open in their speech. They had nothing incriminating in their possession at present, and Daniel had made it clear he was one of them.

Yet the rascal still didn't ask about Juliet. Well, she fully intended to correct that.

As soon as the conversation lagged, she jumped in. "Actually, we also came this way because Danny's looking for a friend he knew before. He heard that the man works in the south of England now."

A swift kick to her good leg under the table made her start. Her gaze snapped to Daniel; he scowled at her. She kicked him back, vastly satisfied when it caught him by surprise. If she left this matter to him, they'd be drinking with the smugglers clear into next week.

"I think the man's name is Morgan or something," she continued blithely. She gulped some ale. It tasted better the more she drank. "What's his name again, my dear?"

"Pryce," Daniel bit out. "Morgan Pryce."

"I know that fellow," one of the smugglers offered without any apparent suspicion. "Matter of fact, he stopped here a couple o' days ago when we was on our way to London. Had a lady with him."

Her heart began to pound. "Oh, he must be traveling with his wife, too. How odd. I didn't know Mr. Pryce was married."

"It weren't his wife," the young man on the other side of Mr. Wallace offered. "Mr. Wallace, didn't you say that—"

Mr. Wallace cut him off with a pop on the head. "Don't be talkin' about things you don't know nothin' about."

Helena's smile hid gritted teeth. "Well, that's neither

here nor there. It doesn't change the fact that Danny'd like to speak to Mr. Pryce. Wouldn't you, Danny?"

Daniel looked as nonchalant as ever, but his sharp gaze showed he was taking everything in. "I would indeed. He used to get me the best price on French brandy. Had a contact in Boulogne who gave it to him cheap. I was thinking he might tell me who the chap was."

Mr. Wallace leaned forward. "Trouble is, you can't deal with Mr. Pryce without talkin' to Crouch. Crouch don't take kindly to his men makin' private arrangements."

Crouch? Helena wondered. Her brain now felt truly soggy. What or who was a Crouch?

Daniel had gone pale. He knocked back another gin, then set the glass down hard on the table. "Pryce works for Jolly Roger?"

Mr. Wallace smiled, obviously pleased that Daniel knew of this Jolly Roger person. "Aye."

"For how long?"

"Not sure. Awhile now."

"You're sure he *works* for Crouch and ain't just using Jolly Roger's contacts on occasion?" Daniel probed. "Or p'raps sharing one of his cutters?"

"*Who* is Crouch?" Helena couldn't help asking, though she followed the question with a mortifying hiccup.

The men laughed. "Jolly Roger Crouch, the King of the Smugglers," Mr. Wallace explained. "He's got a large gang on the coast. They control all the free tradin' in Sussex. That's where Pryce and the lady were headed—toward Hastings or thereabouts."

And Daniel looked miffed about it. She couldn't imagine why. They already knew Mr. Pryce was a free trader, and Daniel had said he might be headed for the coast. What did it matter whom he worked for?

"Why does the King of Smugglers have such a

shhtrange name?" she asked. My, that sounded rather slurred. How odd. She tried again. "Jolly Roger." There, that was better. "It shounds . . . sounds like a pirate."

Mr. Wallace chuckled. "I think the ale is goin' to yer head, Mrs. Brennan."

"It is not!" she protested, then hiccupped again. Was hiccupping covered in Mrs. N's guide? She couldn't remember.

She drank the rest of her ale to silence her hiccups, but when she set the glass down, it fell over. Now how had *that* happened?

All the men laughed now. Then one of them added, "His Christian name is Roger and he likes to jest with his men, so they call him Jolly Roger."

"He's also got a pirate's greed," Daniel grumbled. "Not to mention lack of scruples."

"You seem to know the man well enough," Mr. Wallace commented, eyes narrowing.

"I've heard of him," Daniel said. "Who hasn't?"

Mr. Wallace leaned across the table and stared at Daniel. "Wait a minute. Yer name's Brennan, ain't it? Like Wild Danny Brennan, the highwayman? Didn't Jolly Roger used to have—"

"Aye, he did," Daniel interrupted. "And now, if you'll excuse me, I'd best take my wife upstairs. She's had all the 'fun' she can stand for one night."

Chapter 10

I took this fair maid by the lily white hand
And on the green mossy bank set her down
And I planted a kiss on her red ruby lips
And the small birds a-singing all around.
"Queen of the May,"
anonymous ballad

Daniel had to get them both out of here before they said or did something to give themselves away. So far matters had gone well, but now that he realized Crouch was involved, not to mention that Helena was drunk to the gills . . .

Christ, on two pints of ale and naught else. He'd never seen her drunk, never even imagined the possibility. This was pure disaster.

He called the taproom maid over. "How much do I owe for the drinks?"

She glanced over to Wallace, then back to Daniel. "You've got to settle up at the bar, sir. The proprietor keeps accounts up there. He don't let me take money at the table."

"Be right back," he told Helena as he rose and headed for the bar.

The proprietor took his time about settling the bill, and when Daniel headed back to the table he discovered why. Apparently Wallace had signaled the taproom maid to delay Daniel, for he now had Helena on his lap and was trying to kiss her while she protested. Rage seared Daniel, even after he saw Helena draw back and slap the man.

"What was that for?" Wallace asked, rubbing his cheek. "All I wanted was a little kiss, and you said you wanted fun—"

"Not that kind. And not with you." Helena attempted to climb off the man's lap, but instead fell heavily onto the chair next to him.

At her cry of pain, Daniel nearly hurdled the table in his eagerness to get his hands on Wallace. Daniel lifted him bodily from his chair and held the smaller man dangling in the air so they were nose to nose. "In future, you keep your bloody hands off my wife or I'll break them both. D'you understand?"

Wallace glared at him, and Daniel shook him until the smuggler nodded. Then Daniel set him down.

Straightening his clothes, Wallace said with a sneer, "Don't worry. Nobody wants yer crippled wife anyhow."

Daniel heard Helena's pained gasp and saw red. Before he could even think, he'd planted a facer on Wallace, laying him out flat. As he stood staring down at the man who lay moaning on the floor, he growled, "That'll teach you to insult a lady, you bloody arse."

The others half-rose from their chairs, and he brandished his fists at them. "The rest of you want a bunch of fives? Do you?"

But they weren't as stupid as their leader. He glowered at them all, and they took their seats again, mumbling into their ale. They might outnumber him, but anybody could see he wasn't nearly as drunk as them. Besides, he was in the right, and they knew it. Nobody touched a man's wife, even smugglers.

He turned to Helena. "Are you all right?"

"Yes," she whispered, her eyes riveted on Wallace.

"Let's go." He picked her up and strode for the door. Between the ale and her weak leg, she probably couldn't manage to walk.

As they headed for the stairs, he grumbled, "You do know how to shake up a room, lass."

"So do you."

He glared down at her, only to find her laughing—laughing, the little witch! "What do you find so funny?"

She twined her arms about his neck and smiled with the breezy manner of a woman well into her cups. "You warn'd me not to insult people. Then *you* go and knock 'em in the head. P'raps you ought to take your own advice, Danny."

"If you hadn't been so bloody friendly with that arse Wallace and got yourself drunk, I wouldn't have had to knock him in the head."

"I do appreciate your rescuin' me, y'know. I didn't like Mr. Wallace at all." Her eyes shone up at him. "I like *you* so much better."

Despite being a mite slurred, her words turned all his annoyance into pure need. Combined with the soft weight of her in his arms, they sent a sudden surge to his wayward pego that was downright criminal. Christ, he wished *he* were drunk. At least drunkenness would blunt the edge of his lust.

He climbed the stairs as fast as he could manage, trying not to think of her breasts a few inches from his hand, her legs draped over his arm, her sweet little arse bumping against his belly every step he took.

She stared up at him with an unsteady gaze. "Danny?"

"Yes?" Strange how it didn't bother him so much when *she* called him Danny. She meant it for an endearment, not a reminder of his highwayman da, and that made all the difference.

"You're still cross at me, aren't you?"

He glanced down at her and raised an eyebrow. "Do I look like I'm cross at you?"

She bobbed her head. "You look ex-tre-e-emely vexed."

He bit back a smile. She was going to have a devil of a headache tomorrow. "I'm not vexed, although God knows I ought to be. I told you to stay in our room, and you didn't. Our agreement was that you were to do as you were told, and you've already broken it repeatedly."

Her brow wrinkled up in a frown. "Our 'greement was that *you* were s'posed to find out what happen'd to Juliet. If not for me, who knows how long it would've taken?"

"I was coming to it, Helena. I didn't want to rouse their suspicions." *Which I probably have now.*

"Pish-posh." Her lips curved into a pout, and it only made him want to kiss them. "Thanks to me, we know where Pryce took Juliet. Yet you're vexed."

"I'm not bloody vexed!" he growled, then lowered his voice as he reached the floor where their room was. "Not at you, anyway." No, he was far more vexed at himself.

For not seeing what should have been obvious—that Crouch was involved in this. For letting her come along.

For wanting her so badly he ached with it.

"Then who're you vexed at?"

"Never mind who. We'll talk about it in the morning." Not that he wanted to discuss the implications of Crouch's involvement, but he must. She should know all his suspicions. "You're in no condition to discuss anything now."

"I'm perfectly well, y'know," she said with a lofty air so typical he laughed at her.

"I can see that."

"Even if I did drink a bit too much, everything turn'd out wonderfully."

"You nearly got mauled by an arse—I don't call that 'wonderfully,'" he muttered as he strode down the candlelit hall toward their room.

She stabbed a finger at his chest. "You're only annoyed 'cause a lot of men were nice to me. You think it's fine for women to drape themselves naked over *you*, but let *me* have a teeny bit of fun and you turn into a bully ruffian."

"A bully ruffian?" he said, amused. "Wherever did you hear that term?"

"That awful Mr. Wallace said it."

He scowled. "D'you know what it means?"

"It means you're a bully and a ruffian. And you are, sometimes."

"No. It means I'm a highwayman who's rude to his victims. You should be sure of your cant before you start throwing it around."

"Oh." She frowned, apparently trying to assimilate the new information. Then her brow cleared. "Well, you were rude to those men, y'know."

He rolled his eyes. "They'll get over it."

She looked pensive all of a sudden. "They weren't at all like what I'd expect of smugglers. Except for Mr. Wallace, they were terribly nice."

So nice they'd steal her blind as soon as look at her. He chuckled as he reached their room. "And you, sweetheart, are drunk."

"I am not!"

Setting her down, he reached for the door, but he'd scarcely shoved it open when she lost her balance and swayed into him. He picked her up again, laughing. "You're right—you're not drunk, you're *very* drunk."

She peered up at him as he strode into the room and kicked the door shut. "Are you sure?"

"Absolutely." He scanned the room, noting the extra gown hanging over the screen. "D'you have something to sleep in?" But then he'd have to put her in it, and he'd never survive that. "Never mind, you can sleep in your gown."

"Nonsense. It'll get all wrinkled, and I only have two. I'll sleep in my chemise." With typical Helena loftiness, she added, "But you have to play lady's maid, since you wouldn't let me bring one."

He supposed he deserved that, though the thought of helping her undress made his pulse pound madly. "Very well."

After setting her down on the edge of the bed, he knelt to pull off her half boots. The sight of her fragile leg reminded him of her astonishing tale about regaining its use. No wonder she was so bitter about the men who condemned her for her lameness. He would've felt the same if he'd accomplished a minor miracle through sheer will, only to have it taken for nothing by a lot of arses who saw her leg as a weakness instead of the strength that it was.

She was more amazing than he'd realized. And if she

weren't so drunk, he'd be tempted to show her exactly what he thought of her. Which would not be wise a'tall.

Swiftly he quelled the urge to strip off her stockings and kiss his way up from her trim ankle. Instead, he rose to sit on the bed next to her, then turned her so he could work loose her gown's tiny buttons.

But the more he uncovered the transparent linen beneath, the more his John Thomas stiffened. Christ, any more of this and he'd explode. Quickly, he shoved the top of her gown off her shoulders.

Her delicate shoulders were barely veiled by her linen chemise. In a trance, he lifted his hand to cup one, then caught himself. Swearing under his breath, he jerked to his feet. "You can manage the rest yourself. Throw me the gown when you're done, and I'll hang it over the screen."

It took all his will to cross the room. She'd made it clear that she thought him a conscienceless whoremonger; he wasn't about to prove her right by taking advantage of her while she was drunk, no matter how tempting the notion.

Careful to keep his back to her, he dragged off his boots and untied his cravat. But when he shrugged off his coat, the slim volume he'd confiscated from Helena's bag earlier bumped his hand.

He extricated it, remembering the peculiar title. *Mrs. Nunley's Guide to Etiquette for Young Ladies*. Probably the source of all her notions of propriety. Later he'd have to read it, if only to find out why it took ale to loosen her up.

For now he shoved it under his discarded coat and took off his waistcoat. Once he was sure she was asleep, he'd remove his breeches. That was as much as he planned to disrobe. Being in the same room with her would be difficult enough without being half-dressed as well.

Her gown and petticoat came flying at him and he

hung them over the screen, then turned, expecting to find her in the bed with the covers dragged up to her chin.

Instead, she sat on the edge, clad only in her chemise. Sweet Jesus. The flimsy bit of nothing clung greedily to her darling breasts and lithe thighs, firing his own greed to new intensity. His fingers itched to touch every inch of feminine flesh. What in God's name had he done to deserve this torture?

To make matters worse, she'd taken her hair down, too. Just as he'd imagined, it was long and thick and bloody gorgeous. Like the rich dark ale she'd drunk all evening, it frothed over her shoulders and down her arms past her waist, where the last bit curled sweetly about her hips.

It made him almost imagine he could see its echo between her legs beneath the linen. At least she still wore her stockings. Knowing Helena, she probably wore drawers as well. Not that it helped much. Helena with her hair down, in chemise and stockings, looked so damned erotic he wanted to vault across the room and take her like a savage beast.

She seemed oblivious to his arousal, however. She wore the smile of an innocent as she swung her good leg back and forth, her calf thumping rhythmically against the oak bedstead. "I'm not sleeping in the bed, y'know. You're to have the bed. I'm sleeping on that." She pointed to the mattress with her big toe. "See? I've already used it."

He glanced down at the mattress, startled to find a blanket crumpled on top and a pillow that still held the indentation where her head had been. "Why did you do that?"

"Because you were cross at me. I hate it when you're cross. You get all grumbly and . . . and arrogant. You make stern pronouncements and order me about. I don't like being ordered about."

"I'd never guess," he said dryly.

"I thought you'd be in a better mood if you had a good night's sleep. That's why I'm sleeping on the mattress."

He shook his head. The woman never ceased to amaze him. "It would be better if you took the bed."

"No!" Her voice retained some of its usual imperious tone. "I told you—you're to have the bed, and I'm to sleep on the floor. It's all settled."

She rose as if to move in that direction. Only his quick action prevented her from collapsing without her cane for support.

Unfortunately, that put her in his arms again, every lovely, half-clad inch of her. When he tried to set her aside, she looped her arms about his neck and gazed up at him with a secretive smile that made his head spin.

"Helena," he ground out, "let's not quarrel over who sleeps where. You take the bed."

She was already shaking her head. "The bugs will plague you all night."

"I daresay they'll plague us both, no matter which one we take." Annoyance crept into his voice. "Now for God's sake, stop all this and let me put you to bed. We both need our sleep." *Not that I'm likely to get any tonight.*

She pouted. "You're cross at me again."

"I am not," he gritted out.

"Yes, you are."

"Helena—"

"If you're not cross, then prove it."

That flummoxed him. "Prove it? How?"

"Kiss me, Danny."

Hot need slammed into him, and he groaned. *Steady*

now, lad. She doesn't know what she's saying and won't feel the same about it in the morning.

He pretended he hadn't heard her. "Time for bed, lass," he muttered as he started backing her toward it.

"Kiss me. I know you want to."

She'd kill him before the night was done. "As I recall, you vowed not to let me."

"I changed my mind."

His John Thomas—his infernal John Thomas with a mind of its own—was raring up in his breeches. He practically shoved her toward the bed in his haste to get her out of his arms, but he misjudged her strength. And her determination. As she fell onto the mattress she dragged him down, too, and in seconds, he found himself lying atop her.

"Oops," she said with a shaky little laugh. "I fell."

He was falling fast himself. It felt so bloody good to have her beneath him, soft and eager. His gaze swept her hungrily. The chemise left little to the imagination, and his weight pressed the linen so tightly to her skin that he could easily make out the rosy tips of her breasts and the sweet valley where he wanted to bury his face. Her hair, silky and sensuous against the pillow, begged for his touch.

She twined her arms even more tightly about his neck. "Kiss me." Her eyes shone up at him. "Or I'll never believe you've forgiven me for the mean things I said."

He looked at her luscious lips. Her waiting lips. What could it hurt to give her a little kiss? Just a peck to reassure her that all was well between them.

He quickly brushed her mouth with his. Even that brief contact made his head reel, but it worsened considerably when he felt her tongue dart out to sweep his closed lips. He jerked back, his blood thundering through his veins.

With the enticing smile of a woman just beginning to guess the depths of her feminine power, she touched her thumb to his lower lip. "This time when you kiss me, open your mouth," she said, teasing him with his own damned words.

It was too much. His flimsy restraint broke, and he seized her mouth with near savagery, blindly seeking the pleasures she didn't even realize she was offering.

Or did she? She met his kiss with enthusiasm, not only letting him drive his tongue deep inside, but toying with it, drawing it in. She was passion and inexperience combined, need and innocence mingling, a heady brew indeed. She gave far more than he'd hoped to have, and far less than he wanted.

Time vanished when he kissed her—long, slow kisses that heated his blood until he felt drunk with it, with the ale taste and honey water scent of her. He came up for breath, struggling to regain his control, to find some way to untangle himself from the insanity, but that only made him more aware of her lissome body lying beneath him, willing and supple and tempting.

"I like it when you kiss me," she admitted with a kittenish smile, and every muscle in his body responded.

"I like it myself, lass." The heavy weight between his thighs said he liked it far too much. Yet he couldn't bring himself to move off her.

Her eyes glowed as she gazed up at him. "Danny, will you do something for me?"

"What?" he growled, though he could imagine what it was. She was banishing him now that she'd got her "proof." Even if it was for the best, he found himself loath to go.

"I want you to . . ." She paused, and a giggle escaped her lips.

He'd never heard her giggle before. She really was

drunk. All the more reason to get off her now, before he did anything he regretted. He started to lift himself away, but she clung more tightly to his neck.

"Not yet!" Her face lit up with excitement. "First you have to . . . oh, it's too naughty of me . . ."

Now she'd got him curious. "What is it you want?"

She seemed to be screwing up her courage. "I want you to . . . put your hand in my clothes and touch me."

"Christ Almighty in heaven," he swore as images of doing that very thing swirled through his randy mind.

Releasing his neck, she dropped one hand to her breast. "Here. Touch me here. But inside my chemise."

He nearly came off in his drawers at just the sight of her delicate hand touching herself with such innocence. "Have you lost your mind? Is this a joke? Or are you only trying to drive me insane?"

Her excitement dimmed a bit, but she tipped her chin up stubbornly. "I wager you do it to that Sall woman. Don't see why you won't do it to me."

"Sall is a lightskirt. You are a respectable lady and a virgin. Not to mention that you're drunk. I'm damned well *not* going to touch your breast."

"I'm not that drunk," she protested. "And why are lightskirts the only ones who get to have men touch them? It's not fair." Before he could stop her, she yanked the ties of her chemise loose and tugged the neckline down.

One luscious breast sprang free, and he groaned. It was as tempting as he'd have guessed, pert and taut, the way a virgin's breast ought to be.

She scowled down at it. "Isn't it pretty enough? I know it's not as big as hers, but—"

"It's beautiful, sweetheart—the perfect size." *To fit a man's hand. To fit my hand, damn it.*

"Beautiful enough to touch?"

Beautiful enough to eat. And that's what he wanted to do: taste it and lick it and suck the pretty nipple until she cried out. The woman was a bloody seductress when she was drunk. It was a miracle she hadn't lost her innocence years ago.

She grabbed one of his hands and pressed it to her breast. "Here. I want to know what it feels like, Danny. Please?"

Her nipple puckered up into a sweet kernel beneath his palm, and he swore. It felt so natural to have her breast in his hand. A man could take only so much.

Cursing himself for a fool, he bent his head to kiss her thoroughly again. He rubbed her breast, kneading and teasing, plumping it up, then smoothing it out. Her hands crept under his shirt to feel their way along his ribs and stroke tentatively over his chest. He shuddered, wanting more. Ah, such gentle fingers, such virginal touches.

Virginal. It took all his will to tear his mouth from hers, though his fingers continued to play with her breast, ignoring his command to stop.

The look of delight on her face didn't help. "That feels so good, Danny. Do it to the other one now."

He would've laughed if he hadn't been so bloody aroused. "Lass, you don't know what you're asking."

Her gaze as it met his was surprisingly clear-eyed. "Yes, I do." She flattened her hands on his chest inside his shirt, and he groaned as they covered his own nipples. "You said I was curious. Well, you're right. I am. I want to know what all the fuss is about."

All hell broke loose in his breeches. He damned well wanted to show her what all the fuss was about. And why was he fighting it? He needn't take her innocence to show her a bit of pleasure, and he might never have another chance to touch Helena intimately, to know her sweetness.

Yes, she was drunk, but not as drunk as he'd first thought. Her slur was less pronounced and she *had* managed to remove her gown, not to mention get him onto thc bed.

Besides, when sober, she followed a lot of creaky rules that made her feel safe but kept her from having any fun. Who was he to tell her she shouldn't enjoy herself while her conscience was nodding off? Not to mention all her fool notions about her undesirability. He wouldn't mind showing her that was nonsense.

His own conscience protested that these were wild rationalizations, but he silenced it ruthlessly. He could taste her and touch her and give her pleasure without ruining her, for God's sake. Surely he possessed enough strength of will for that.

"All right, lass," he murmured. "Just be sure to tell me when you've had enough." He only prayed he could stop when she did.

This time when he lowered his head, he indulged his urge to taste her. As he obliged her request to fondle her other breast, his mouth seized on the one he'd just been caressing.

Ah, such lovely breasts—he'd never seen a pair of dearer ones. He fed on them, devoured them, teased them both until he heard Helena moan and felt her hands clutch his shirt, urging him nearer.

"Oh, yes," she whispered, "like that. Yes, Danny, yes."

He'd bedded more women than he could count, yet her innocent "yes" made his heart thunder with pride more than any lavish words of praise. It made him ache to please her, give her something to think on in her bed at night.

He wanted her thinking of *him*, damn it, desiring *him* as badly as he desired her. Once sober she might tell herself he was too low for her, but he'd damned well ensure that she remembered *he'd* been the one to pleasure her.

Thankful that he still wore his breeches, he ground his erection into her softness, making her gasp. He stared down at her, one of his hands thumbing her breast. Deliberately, he rubbed his hard ridge against her sweet cunny again, watching as her eyes widened and her face flushed. He waited for her to shove him away in shock.

Instead she asked, "Is that . . . is that your man's thing?" Her eyes were alight with curiosity.

He laughed. "'Man's thing'? Is that what refined ladies call it?"

"That's what Rosalind called it. And some other naughty words Griff taught her."

"Like what?" He bent to nuzzle her breast.

She shook her head, her blushes setting her skin aflame. "I could never use them."

"You won't talk about a man's pego, eh? We'll see if you're so missish after you've felt the pleasure it can give a woman. Like this." Smiling, he pressed into her most sensitive spot again. She sucked in a breath and arched into him instinctively. He chuckled. "You see, lass, you don't have to speak of it to enjoy it."

"I shouldn't speak of it *or* enjoy it . . . I mean—" She broke off when he rocked against her rhythmically. "Oh, Lord . . . that's . . . amazing. I never thought it would feel . . . so good. Rosalind said it did, but I never believed . . . yes . . . do that . . . yes . . ."

"Anything to please m'lady," he teased as he returned to sucking her delicious breasts. She was melting and shimmying beneath him, hot and beautiful, her face flushing pink with her enjoyment. Thank God she still had her chemise on and he still wore his breeches and drawers. Otherwise he didn't know if he could bear it.

He ached to be inside her, but he knew better. Once sober, she'd regret all this and hate him for taking advantage of her. If he ruined her, she'd never forgive him.

Still, he *could* give her pleasure without ruining her. He wanted to see her face rapt from the "little death," see her reach release in his arms. If it killed him, he'd do that. He'd have her dreaming of him for weeks to come.

Through a delightful haze, Helena saw Daniel slide down the bed between her legs. He lifted her chemise, and shock rocketed through her. What in heaven's name was he doing? She wasn't so tipsy that she didn't realize how terribly wicked this was. Thanks to the slit in her drawers, her most intimate parts were fully exposed to his eager gaze. How mortifying!

She tried to draw her legs together, but he wouldn't let her. Instead his large hands held her thighs open, pressed them even wider apart. "Let me look at you, sweetheart. You're so bloody beautiful."

"Th-there?" she stammered.

He shot her his most devilish grin. "Yes, there. Everywhere. I want to taste you now. Let me taste you, lass."

"T-taste me?" She'd barely spoken the words when his mouth covered her *there*, between her legs, in an intimate kiss. She went utterly still. She'd had no idea . . . Could a man really . . . Did men really . . .

Clearly, they did. Merciful heavens, how delicious! He was doing to her *there* what he'd done to her mouth, using his tongue, darting it inside her . . . *inside her,* for heaven's sake!

Worst of all, she lacked any urge whatsoever to stop him. It was surely the effects of that cursed ale, yet she squirmed beneath him, shamelessly wanting more, and his mouth supplied it with relentless perseverance. His tongue gave no quarter, lapping at the soft folds of skin, then driving deep inside her with quickening strokes until she began to forget where she was, who she was, why she was here.

Before she knew it, she was clutching his head, crushing his thick, dark blond locks beneath her fingers, straining against his teasing tongue. She felt as if he pushed her ever closer to a secret abyss that might swallow her up if she stepped any nearer.

"That's it," he lifted his head to growl, though the sensations between her legs continued as he used his fingers to pluck at her, rub her, drive into her. "Enjoy it. Just forget everything and enjoy it."

So she did precisely that. As he returned to his intimate kisses, she closed her eyes and let her head fall back, let herself think only of the shivering pulse of his tongue inside her, the way it made her feel, the thrill that swept further with each heady stroke. Suddenly she fell off into the beckoning darkness, and it roared through her like a dangerous drug, more potent than ale, more glorious than anything she'd ever known. She cried out and surged against his mouth, her body afire, her senses exploding.

Afterward, she lay there gasping, stunned by the power of what had just possessed her. Several moments of mindless drifting followed before she thought to open her eyes and look at him.

Daniel's head lay cradled against one of her thighs, and his gaze was riveted to her face in pure triumph. "Now you know what all the fuss is about."

Oh, yes. Dear Lord in heaven, she knew.

She ought to feel embarrassed or something equally virtuous. She oughtn't feel this delirious happiness, this . . . this urge to wheel about the room in drunken delight.

How awful of her not to feel ashamed at having a man between her legs, nuzzling her bare thigh inside her drawers, planting openmouthed kisses on the sensitive inner skin. He was stroking places only a husband should be allowed to touch.

A husband. Her eyes went wide as her curiosity got the better of her. "Danny?"

"Hmm?" he murmured.

"Is this what happens between men and women when they . . . make love?"

He went still, then rose up on one elbow and drew her chemise down over her legs. "Sometimes." He avoided her gaze. "Depends on what you mean by 'make love.' "

"Rosalind said when a man makes love to a woman he puts his thing—"

"Yes. Generally he does." He slid back up her. Briefly he hovered over her, pressing himself against her again, letting her feel the bulge in his breeches. "That's why it's firm like this." He stared down at her, his features as rigid as what lay between his legs. "It's meant to be put inside a woman, the way I put my tongue inside you."

Her face flamed. "I-it's hard like that all the time?" She tried futilely to imagine men walking around with a pole in their breeches. Why had she never noticed it before?

He smiled faintly, but behind the smile shone a rapacious hunger that made her breath catch in her throat. "Not all the time. Only when a man is in a state of unrelieved arousal." He rubbed against her, eyes darkening. "Like this."

Unrelieved? Did that mean what she thought it did? "So we didn't actually . . . I'm still . . . a virgin."

A muscle tightened in his jaw. Lifting himself off her, he rolled away to lie on his back and stare up at the ceiling. "Yes. I haven't ruined you, if that's what you're asking."

But he'd wanted to.

Or had he? Abruptly he rose and left the bed, as if he couldn't escape her quickly enough. Even in her inebriated state, she had to wonder at that. She watched, relieved, hurt, as he strode to the mattress on the floor with seeming nonchalance and dragged his shirt over his head, then slipped out of everything but his drawers.

Had he wanted to make love to her? And if so, was it only because she was a woman near to hand? Because she'd behaved so wantonly that he couldn't help himself?

She *had* behaved wantonly, to be sure. If he'd pressed her, she might even have done the unthinkable.

A sob rose in her throat at the realization. She'd wanted him to ruin her, hadn't she? Until now she'd refused to acknowledge how truly joyless her life was, how devoid of passion. Tonight—with her brain not nearly fogged enough by liquor—she admitted it freely. Ruination suddenly seemed infinitely preferable to her old life of lonely pride.

She was so far gone she nearly asked him why he'd stopped. The bulge in his unmentionables made it perfectly clear that she'd roused his desires. But not enough to prod him into making love to her. Why not?

He caught her staring at him and scowled. "Go to sleep. You've only got a few hours. We have a long day ahead of us tomorrow and much to discuss in the morning."

She swallowed back her question. No, she wouldn't show herself to be so foolishly besotted with the man that she'd beg him to bed her. He'd indulged her dangerous requests for kisses and touches and . . . things she should never have asked for. If he could get aroused by it yet still not be tempted to "ruin" her, then he must find her a dull companion indeed.

Not that she could expect otherwise when he had

women as obviously well-versed in seduction as that Sall begging to leap into his bed. A tear leaked out, and she swiped it away viciously.

Turning over, she drew the blanket up to her ears and squeezed her eyes shut. She should be glad that he'd spared her, that he'd left her a virgin. But all she could think of was the low tingling in her nipples, the heat simmering between her thighs, the incredible excitement she'd felt when his mouth devoured her breasts and his tongue drove inside her most private place.

A pox on you, Danny Brennan, she thought as she lay there quivering with need. *Why am I not woman enough for you?*

Chapter 11

There came a knight from over the sea
And stole my sister away
O shame on him and his company
In the land where e'er they stay.

"Fair Annie,"
anonymous English ballad

Juliet shivered and rubbed her arms beneath her cloak. In the dead of night, the sea air bore the chill of early autumn, making the flimsy velvet useless. Dampness crept under and around her, as insidious as her unease.

She peeked around the edge of the massive Pipewell Gate, a structure left from the days when Winchelsea had been a walled town, to where Will stood waiting near the road to Rye. He was more warmly dressed than she, but then she'd had little time to dress when she'd awakened to hear him leaving the cottage. All she'd known was that he was sneaking out, and she'd decided then and there to find out where he was going.

Two days they'd stayed in the tiny stone cottage, two days awaiting the arrival in nearby Rye Harbour of his friends who owned the ship. The time had passed pleasantly enough, she supposed, though he'd kept her in the cottage, saying he didn't want to risk her being seen by anybody looking for them.

Still, they'd played chess and he'd brought her several books. He bought her anything she asked for. Indeed, except for in the bedchamber—which she inhabited alone while he slept on a bedroll in the other room—they carried on almost like husband and wife. It ought to have overjoyed her to be settled for a short while, to be living with him in every way but one.

So why was she lurking out here in the middle of the night, spying on him?

Because something was wrong. She didn't know what, but something. He'd been different these past two days, as courteous as ever, but tense and edgy, too. Sometimes she caught him deep in thought, as if contemplating serious matters. Could he be regretting their elopement? Was that why he wouldn't even kiss her?

The possibility of his refusing to marry her would be too awful to endure. Still not married after nearly a week away from home, she'd finally begun to realize the enormity of what she'd done. If he *did* change his mind, she'd be ruined for life, even though he'd never touched her in anything less than a gentlemanly manner.

Suddenly she heard hoofbeats up the cobblestone street, though they came not from Rye but through town. Watching from behind Pipewell Gate, she saw a shadowy figure on horseback emerge from the darkness and halt beside Will. Could this be his friend who owned the ship and the cottage? But if so, why meet in the middle of the night in such stealth and secrecy? And why here?

"Hello, Jack," Will said.

The man dismounted and glanced furtively around. "Hello, Pryce."

Juliet froze. Who was Pryce? Did he mean Will? She wrapped her cloak more tightly around her with growing unease.

"So you've got the girl, do you?" Jack asked.

"I've got her."

"Did you have any trouble getting her away? It's the eldest, ain't it?"

"No. I tried for her, but she'd have none of me. I had to take the youngest."

The cold practicality of Will's words struck panic in her. The eldest? Did he mean Helena? Helena had claimed that Will was a fortune hunter. Good heavens, could she have been right?

"But she still thinks it's an elopement?" Jack asked.

"Yes."

Fear exploded through her. No, no, she couldn't have been that wrong about Will, could she? She circled the gate's brick tower, trying to get close enough to hear better, hoping she'd misheard or misunderstood.

"Good, it'll be easier if she keeps on that way," his friend Jack replied. "Better for her and better for us. How long do you think you can keep up the pretense?"

"As long as it takes. She's a sweet girl, very innocent. She believes what I tell her." Will's low voice was remote, emotionless. It struck a chill to her heart. "Just make sure that Crouch holds to his end of the bargain, or I'll bring her back to her family before he's got what he wants, do you hear?"

What did he mean? And who was Crouch?

"He'll hold to his part, never fear," Jack answered. "Keep the girl quiet and occupied until the ransom money comes, and you'll have what you asked for."

Ransom! She sucked in a breath. This wasn't an elopement at all, but a kidnapping! And like a fool, she'd walked right into it. Tears started in her eyes, but she forced them back.

This had to be a nightmare. She would wake in her own bed at Swan Park and laugh at her foolish dream.

No, a cold voice inside her said, *the other was the dream.*

Indeed it was. She'd known it shortly after they'd left Stratford-upon-Avon, when Will had continued to treat her with his curious courtesy, lacking any outward show of love. *I tried for the eldest.* Helena had warned her, but she'd been too much in love to listen.

With this . . . *this* scoundrel! A man who not only didn't love her, but didn't even care about her. Pain tore savagely through her as she realized he planned to hand her over to this Crouch person without a qualm. And for what? Money?

In her distress, she must have made a noise, for the men suddenly fell quiet. Heart pounding, she plastered herself against the brick tower and prayed they hadn't heard her. As soon as they left, she'd flee in the opposite direction. She must get away. Away!

"Did you hear that?" Jack asked, and she held her breath.

"It was the wind," Will said easily, and she sagged against the brick in relief. "You might as well go on back to Hastings. I'll contact you if I need to."

His friend's only answer was the creak of saddle leather as he mounted, then the slow clopping of hooves on cobblestone as the horse walked off. Juliet held her breath, her eyes fixed on the corner of the brick tower beyond where Will stood. She'd wait until she was sure he'd gone, too, and then—

"You heard everything, I suppose."

She nearly leaped out of her skin. Whipping her head around, she discovered that Will had circled the tower on the opposite side and stood a scant foot away. She bolted, but had scarcely gone two feet before he caught her around the waist, yanking her hard against him.

"Let go!" she cried, realizing too late she would have been better off pretending not to have heard the men's conversation.

Now all she could do was fight, striking out blindly, kicking at his legs. Her boot heel hit his shin, and he swore. Then before she knew it, he'd thrust her against the gate tower and covered her body with his to hold her still.

"Calm down, you little fool," he hissed. "Do you want Jack to hear you and come back?"

"What does it matter if you hand me over to him now or later?" she cried.

He shoved his hand over her mouth. "It matters a great deal, I promise you. As long as he thinks you haven't seen him, you're safe, do you hear me?"

Safe! In a pig's eye! She struggled against him, but he was hard as steel and twice as relentless.

Yet regret showed in his moonlit face as he thrust it within a breath of hers. "Listen to me, Juliet—you may have made a mistake in running away with me, but you can emerge from this unharmed if you'll only continue to trust me."

She raised both eyebrows in mute disbelief, letting her thorough contempt show in her gaze.

His voice softened. "I won't hurt you or let anyone else hurt you, either. In a few days, a week at most, you'll rejoin your family—and I promise that when you do, you'll be whole and healthy and no different from when you left. Perhaps a little wiser, but that's all. So fighting me will merely distress you for the short time we're forced to be together. It won't gain you your freedom any sooner, I assure you."

With a warning look, he loosened his hold on her mouth. "Now I'm going to let go. You can scream and fight if you like, but if you do, you'll merely force me to bind and gag you for our return to the cottage. And since the town is asleep, I don't think it will be too hard to sneak you back in, even bound and gagged."

She swallowed hard, remembering how deserted the streets had been when she'd moved through them.

"Do you understand?" he murmured.

She hesitated, then nodded.

He released her mouth and shoved away from the wall. "Now we're going to walk back to the cottage, and you're going to be a good girl until we're inside. Then you may fight me all you wish, but if you try anything in the street, I swear I'll tie you up."

"May I ask you . . . one question?"

His midnight gaze bore into her. "What?"

"Why are you doing this? For money? Because I'm sure Papa or my brother-in-law would pay you more than this Crouch person if you'll just return me now."

"It's not money, and I can't bring you back until I have what I need. I can only swear on my father's grave that you will not be hurt."

She sniffed. "That's not much consolation, since you seemed to have been spawned by the devil."

His soft chuckle took her by surprise, made her heart wrench in her breast. "Will it help if I swear on my mother's grave instead?"

"Nothing will help," she whispered as a tear spilled down her cheek. "I wouldn't believe you now if you swore on a stack of Bibles as high as this tower."

He reached up to wipe the tear away with his thumb, and she shoved his hand back. A muscle worked in his jaw. "Nonetheless, you have no choice but to trust me. Until this moment, have I mistreated you? Have I hurt you in any way?"

Yes, he'd hurt her—but not physically. And now that she knew what he was, she could hardly complain about his lack of affection and how it had made her feel.

There were other complaints, however. "My reputation will be ruined after this."

"No, it won't," he retorted, though a hint of remorse showed in his eyes. "Your family thinks you've eloped, and you said yourself that Helena couldn't—or wouldn't—leave the house to come after you. So they'll keep it quiet until you come home married. And though you won't go home married, you *will* go home eventually as long as you behave yourself. I promise you that, Juliet."

His indulgent tone rubbed her raw. "It's *Lady* Juliet to you, sir," she said, falling back on the rules of propriety her older sister had drummed into her, which she'd so foolishly neglected. Well, she'd learned her lesson. She would *never* be so stupid again. "You will address me as Lady Juliet or not at all, Mr. Morgan or Pryce or whatever your name is."

"It's Morgan. Morgan Pryce." A faint smile played across his lips as he held his hand out to her. "Pleased to meet you, *Lady* Juliet."

* * *

Helena now understood why Mrs. N cautioned the Well-bred Young Lady not to overimbibe. Because the aftermath was not well-bred in the least.

Crouching over the basin on the bedside table, Helena prayed she was done throwing up. Morning had dawned gray and dreary, wracked by thunder and lightning and the clatter of rain on the tiled roof, an appropriate accompaniment to her current hell. Clearly ale was a devil that plagued a person most when leaving. She swore never to renew its acquaintance.

At least she'd had privacy for her torment. Daniel's overcoat still lay over one chair so she knew he hadn't gone far, but thankfully he'd left the room. The last thing she wanted was for him to see her like this, her chemise damp with sweat and her body trembling like a babe's.

She wiped her mouth with a washcloth, then dragged her apron off a nearby chair and fumbled in the pocket for her packet of cloves. As soon as she bit into the spice and its familiar fragrance and taste filled her senses, she felt better. Perhaps she would live through this after all. And if she did, she would never flout that particular stricture of Mrs. N's again.

A pity that wasn't the only stricture she'd ignored last night. It was all a bit of a fog, but she *did* know she'd behaved as indecently as any of Daniel's tarts. And she very much feared that if Daniel had wanted her last night, she would have behaved worse still. Lord, but she was a mess.

A knock at the door made her groan. Curse it, he was back. Why couldn't he have stayed away longer?

The door opened a crack. "Helena, I'm coming in. Cover yourself."

Hastily, she spit her clove into the basin, then wrapped a sheet around herself.

"What's wrong?" Daniel said from the open door.

Glancing over to find him eyeing her with alarm, she cast him a weak smile. "Just the aftereffects of too much to drink."

The alarm faded from his face, replaced by a look of masculine superiority. "Ah, yes. I thought that might prove a problem." He carried in a tray. After setting it down on the table, he brought her cane to her, and added, "P'raps next time you'll think twice about ignoring me when I say you've had enough ale."

Arrogant wretch, she thought as she took it. "It wasn't only the ale, you know. I had some wine before I went downstairs. And I didn't eat all that much last night. It's not as if I can't hold any liquor at all."

"Could've fooled me. Never seen anybody get so drunk on two pints."

"I was not *that* drunk."

"That's what you said every time you asked me to—" He broke off abruptly and scowled. "Anyway, for a woman who wasn't 'that drunk,' you were quite . . . friendly."

"Thank you for reminding me," she bit out. She certainly didn't need any reminders. Every minute was burned into her memory—the kisses, the caresses, the wild, scandalous excitement he'd made her feel. Oh, no, she remembered it all with astonishing clarity.

She merely felt a trifle embarrassed about it this morning. And he seemed to feel the same, for after he hovered there a moment looking awkward, he pointed to the basin and mumbled, "Are you done being sick from *not* being drunk?"

She nodded.

"Then I'll get rid of that before it spoils our appetites."

"Mine is beyond spoiling," she grumbled, "but I'd hate to ruin *your* breakfast."

That seemed to restore his good humor, if not hers. Chuckling, he picked up the basin and headed for the door. "Somebody's a mite testy this morning."

She scowled at his back. *He* was obviously fine. No doubt he could outdrink a hundred smugglers and still feel splendid the next day. Why, he even looked splendid. His buff trousers and sage-green coat were hardly wrinkled, his hair was nicely combed, and he'd even managed to shave.

While she sat here, grimy and frumpy and perspiring. How utterly mortifying!

He set the basin outside for the servant to take away, then closed the door and gestured to her cane. "Shall I help you stand?"

"I can do it." She snatched up her cane. Why must she always appear so weak in front of him? For once, she'd like to see him laid low by something—a cold, a sore throat . . . a stubbed toe. She snorted. That would never happen. Apparently the great ox possessed not only a bottom of iron, but a hard head and an unassailable constitution.

She waited until he'd returned to laying out their breakfast before she grasped her cane with both hands, then shoved to her feet. She teetered there for a moment, but noted with grim satisfaction that her few hours of sleep seemed to have restored her former mobility, such as it was.

"Why don't you come try to eat something?" he coaxed. "We've important matters to discuss."

The very thought of food made her belly churn. "Must I eat? Or talk? My head aches, and there's a war going on in my stomach."

"What a surprise," he teased, but when he caught her frowning at him, he added gently, "You'll feel worse if you don't at least drink some tea. And since we can't get on the road yet—it's storming like the devil out there—we might as well talk."

"Oh, very well, if you insist." Wrapping the sheet more securely about her body, she limped to the table. For a moment, she thought she'd be sick again. It held enough food for a regiment—rashers of bacon, a mound of toast, pots of jam and butter, four boiled eggs at least, not to mention the sausages and scones and Lord knew what else.

"Do you eat like this at every meal?" she asked peevishly as she dropped into a chair.

"You ought to be grateful that I do. How else can I keep up my strength for lugging you about?" He glanced up with a grin, but it died as his gaze met hers.

She could see he was thinking of what had happened the last time he'd lugged her about. Her stomach did flip-flops, only this time it had nothing to do with last night's ale. "I'll try not to make it a necessity again." Her hand trembled as she reached for the cup of tea he'd poured.

"I don't mind it so much."

With just those words he revived all her yearnings from last night. Oh, how were she and he to go on? Every time she looked at him, she remembered his head buried between . . . Lord, she shouldn't even *think* of that.

Yet she couldn't help it. No matter how much she chided herself for last night's shameless behavior, she kept replaying every glorious minute. Which was ludicrous. Though she might never have a chance to marry, she certainly didn't want to become Daniel's latest light-o'-love.

Not that it was all that likely to happen. He did not desire her as he desired other women. Or at least not enough to act on it.

The realization still rankled so much that she spoke before thinking. "Daniel, about last night and what we did . . ."

"What about it?"

She could tell from his suddenly wary expression that she should not have brought it up, yet she couldn't help but press on. "Why did you . . . well . . ."

"Touch you?" With stiff, controlled movements, he began ladling food onto a plate. "Take advantage of you? Behave like a randy—"

"No. Why did you stop?"

His gaze shot to hers, as astonished as if someone had just crowned him with an anvil. "Why did I *what*?"

"Stop." She ducked her head, embarrassed by her own bluntness. Lord, she was becoming as brazen as Rosalind, and that was *not* a good thing. "You . . . you could have . . . well . . . you know . . ."

Carefully setting down the platter, he leaned back against his chair to eye her intently. "I'm afraid you'll have to be more specific, lass. Because I can't believe you're saying what I think you are."

She swallowed and forced herself to meet his gaze. "Why didn't you . . . um . . . 'dance the mattress jig' with me?"

He blinked. "The mattress jig? Where the devil did you get that bit of cant?" His eyes clouded. "No, don't tell me. I can guess. Our friendly Mr. Wallace. I s'pose the bloody arse suggested that you dance it with *him*."

"Actually he thought that you and I might have . . . that the reason we married . . . I mean, supposedly married . . . Well, why didn't you? You could have." Her tone grew self-mocking. "I clearly wouldn't have minded it in the least last night."

"Yes, but you would've minded it this morning, I expect." With a snort of disgust, he snatched up a platter of sausages, then began forking them onto his plate. "Well, I'm not such a blackguard as to seduce a drunk virgin, no matter what you think of me."

His answer quickened her pulse. Was he saying he'd been trying *not* to take advantage of her? That it had nothing to do with her . . . inadequacies?

She pretended not to understand him, wanting to know the truth but too proud to ask. "No, I don't suppose a drunk virgin would be adept enough at seduction to please a man of your . . . experience."

A harsh laugh boiled out of him as he dropped the platter onto the table. "Drunk or no, you were plenty adept at seduction, trust me. It took all my will to leave that bed last night without deflowering you. If you'd been any more adept, you'd have driven me stark raving mad."

Such a frank admission shattered her composure. She stared at him, unable to speak, unsure what to say.

His eyes blazed at her, hot as fired steel. "So now you know. You can make me lust after you with hardly any effort. That should please you: another way to torture me for my arrogance."

"I wasn't trying to torture you," she whispered. Despite the chilly room and her inadequate attire, her skin heated beneath his gaze.

"If that's what you're capable of when you're not trying, then God help me if you ever make an effort." He searched her face, eyes narrowing. "Why d'you want to know why I stopped? Isn't it enough for you that I did?"

"I merely wondered . . . it seemed surprising that you . . . well . . ."

"You're not trying to tell me you're *disappointed* that I didn't make love to you, are you?"

"Certainly not!"

Frustration flared briefly in his face before he masked it. "I didn't think so, even if you did seem to find the idea appealing last night. In the cold light of the sober morn, I expect it doesn't seem so appealing." He swept her with a gaze so intimate, she felt it whisper over her skin. "I'm right, aren't I?"

"I . . . yes, of course." What else could she say? *I'm so shameless I want to join the legions of strumpets clamoring for your attention?*

She feared it might actually be true. Sober or not, when he looked at her with those smoldering gray eyes, all she wanted was to feel his hands and his mouth on her again. He wasn't the only one going stark raving mad.

Thankfully he was wise enough not to act on her madness or his, and she would make good use of her reprieve. "I do want you to know that I appreciate your not taking advantage of me when I was . . . inebriated."

"You're welcome," he said tightly. He settled back in his chair, but his gaze continued to drift over her with that dark hunger that made her ache. "Still, I suggest you be more careful in the future. Last night stretched the bounds of my control. Next time I won't let you go so easy." His gaze rested briefly on her parted lips, then lifted to lock with hers. "But I promise you this—when I make love to you, you'll be stone-cold sober and willing, or I'll have none of you. D'you understand?"

She sucked in a ragged breath. He had not said "if," but "when." *When I make love to you.* A slip of the tongue? She didn't think so. He was warning her that if she wanted to behavc like a tart, he wouldn't hesitate to oblige her. And to her shame, the idea made her blood run hot with anticipation.

"Yes," she breathed. "I understand." She only hoped she had the good sense to heed his warning.

"Good." He stared a moment longer, making her all too conscious of how awful she looked, what a sight she must be with her hair unkempt and her face pale as death.

Self-consciously, she dropped her gaze and busied herself with buttering a piece of toast. "You said we had . . . other matters to discuss?"

Silence. Then he picked up his fork. "Yes. We need to talk about your sister and Pryce."

That caught her off guard. "What do you mean? We know where they're going now, so all we do is follow them to Hastings, then convince her to leave him before they sail off to Scotland."

"It's not so simple anymore." He served himself some bacon, but just sat staring at it. "Do you remember Wallace speaking of Jolly Roger Crouch last night?"

"Yes." She sipped some tea.

"Crouch and his men are situated in Hastings."

After last night, she wasn't entirely surprised to discover he knew so much about this man Crouch. Clearly, he'd dealt with hundreds of free traders in his youth. "What does that have to do with Juliet and Mr. Pryce?"

He scowled. "I told you—they're going to Hastings."

"Yes. Because he has friends there—this Crouch person he works for—who will help him take a ship to Scotland."

"No, damn it, not because of any ship." He picked up a piece of bacon, then tossed it down. "When I thought Pryce was an independent free trader, it made sense for him to be a fortune hunter, too. Often as not, free traders have regular professions and only do the smuggling on the side. They're as liable to marry for money as anybody. But he's with Crouch. And that changes things."

"Why?"

"Because Crouch's men are smugglers by profession rather than necessity. And notwithstanding your pretty tale about how *we* met last night, smuggling and marriage to gentry don't mix."

"What are you saying?"

His gaze met hers, cold, fearless. "I think this is a kidnapping, Helena."

She caught her breath. As she set her cup back down, it rattled in the saucer. "K-kidnapping? Juliet?" Her nausea returned full force, and she had to fight to keep her gorge from rising. "That can't be! Pryce . . . *courted* her. He—"

"He probably thought it would make it easier to get her to Hastings. I doubt he told Juliet he was kidnapping her."

Her heart beat unsteadily in her chest. "But I never received a request for ransom. Papa would have notified me in London if a letter had come to Swan Park."

"It's not you or your father they want the money from—I'm sure Pryce learned that your family isn't rich. No, they want money from Griff. He's her brother-in-law and he's wealthy—who better to pay a ransom? So any ransom note would have gone to him." With a sigh, he raked his fingers through his hair. "I think it might already have."

"What do you mean?"

He glanced away, his jaw rigid. "Two days before you arrived in London, Griff's clerk mentioned that a man had come to Knighton Trading and insisted on having a letter sent personally to Griff on the Continent. The clerk tried to convince the man to broach his business with me, but the man refused. I didn't think much of it at the time—some men would rather deal with Griff than me. Then you came to London and all this happened, and I forgot about it." His gaze swung back to her. "But with this new information, I have to wonder. The timing was right. It could easily have been Pryce."

"So you think Mr. Pryce kidnapped her, then sent a ransom note off to Griff on the Continent before carrying her the rest of the way to Hastings?"

"I don't know." He sighed. "For all his wicked reputation, Crouch isn't the sort to engineer a kidnapping. He's limited himself to smuggling to date, which is a fairly innocuous criminal profession."

"Innocuous? The Hawkhurst Gang tortured and murdered people!"

"True, but that was years ago, and they were a very bad lot. Your average smuggler is only trying to make a living in a part of the country where times have been hard. But kidnapping . . ." He shook his head. "I wouldn't have thought it, that's all. Still, it's the only thing that makes sense. Otherwise, why would Pryce take a false name? And you said yourself he could've sailed to Scotland quicker from Warwickshire. You said he'd been seen with other free traders before he went to Stratford, too. They must've been Crouch's men."

"Merciful heavens." Everything fit. It fit far too well. "There's also the fact that he tried to court me first. If he'd merely been looking for a fortune, he would have seized on *her* first because she's younger and prettier."

"Younger maybe, but not prettier," he corrected with a faint smile.

She waved off his compliment. "Yes, but he chose me first. And why? Because I'm lame. He probably thought I would fall in with his plans more easily."

"Thank God for your suspicious mind that made you see right through him." His voice was fierce, protective.

"I wish I hadn't. I could have held my own with the scoundrel, but Juliet—" She broke off, pressing her hand to her mouth as she thought of the horrors her little sister must be suffering.

He reached across the table to clasp her hand. "He won't hurt her."

"How do you know?" she cried.

"If Jolly Roger's behind this, you've naught to fear. It's not in his interests to hurt her. He's too canny for that."

"So you know him personally?"

He blinked, then glanced away. "No . . . that's just what I've heard about him, is all. And I'm thinking like a smuggler." His gaze shot back to hers. "That's why you wanted me to help you, isn't it?"

She nodded warily, not entirely satisfied with his answer.

"Any smuggler would realize that Griff would gladly pay a ransom to get Juliet back. They'd also assume he wouldn't involve the authorities after she's restored to him. They'd figure that Griff wouldn't want people looking into his old connections to free trading." He fingered her bare hand absently. "But they'd know that if she's harmed, Griff would no longer have a reason to be circumspect. If they hurt her, he'll see them hanged, no matter what it does to Knighton Trading. So she'll be safe with them. I'm sure of it."

His explanation made sense, but left her uneasy all the same. Daniel seemed very adept at "thinking like a smuggler." And no matter how much he sat there stroking her fingers to soothe her, she could feel the tension in him.

He was hiding something. She was sure of it. "Is that why they chose her? Because of our family's connection to Griff? Because Griff has a shady past they can use to their advantage that will keep them from being pursued?"

Abruptly, he dropped her hand, a shadow passing over his face. "Yes, I expect so." He busied himself with cutting his sausages, making sharp, downward stabs at them. "And because Griff is rich."

Aha! He *was* hiding something. "But that's so much trouble to go to. Why not just choose some rich man's daughter from Hastings?"

"Well, for one thing, their friendly townsfolk wouldn't be so friendly anymore if the smugglers preyed on their own." His gaze met hers, so remorseful and concerned that she forgot her suspicions. "I'm sorry, sweetheart, that it came to this. I hate that it had to happen, especially to her. But I do believe she'll be all right. So far, everything I've learnt since we left has confirmed that Pryce is treating her carefully. He's taken separate rooms for her at the few inns where they've stayed, and she's appeared to be content. The innkeeper here says the man behaved like a perfect gentleman. He and Crouch both know just how far to push Griff. They'll treat her like a queen, I expect."

She wished she felt as confident as he did. "But the longer she stays among those men, the more chance—"

"Yes."

His curt answer sent fear curling about her heart.

"And that's why," he went on, "she needs to be spirited out of there as soon as possible. It might be weeks before Griff can pay them off. I don't like to think of her with them for that long."

"You have a plan to get her out?"

He sighed. "I wish we could just alert the revenue officers, but if I know free traders, they've bribed the excisemen to look the other way. And we don't know where he's got her. Besides, if Crouch feels cornered, there's no telling what he'll do. What if he flees to France and takes her with him? He can still demand a ransom from Griff, but then he mightn't be so eager to keep her safe."

He shook his head. "No, the best approach is a furtive one. I wish we hadn't revealed our interest in her and Pryce last night, but that can't be helped now. We can only hope Wallace won't speak of it to Crouch's men. They *are* rival gangs, from what I understand."

She leaned forward. "So what is your 'furtive' approach?"

Lifting an eyebrow at her, he ate a slice of sausage. "If I had my druthers, it wouldn't concern you, lass. I'd be sending you back to London this very morning." When she started to protest, he held his hand up. "But I don't have my druthers. That bloody Wallace is still hanging about, asking questions of the innkeeper about you and me. If I send you off to London alone, he'll be after you like a fly after treacle. I can't take that chance. I can look after you better if you're with me."

"Yes," she agreed. If he'd even attempted to send her back, she would have fought him.

"Hastings isn't but half a day's journey away, if this storm will ever quit. I'll take you with me as far as Sedlescombe—and we'll try to shake off Wallace on the way if he follows us. Then I'll leave you in Sedlescombe while I go to Hastings and nose about for Juliet. It might take a day or two to figure out where Crouch and Pryce are holding her, but once I learn it, I can steal her right out from under their noses."

"Won't that be dangerous?"

Her concern must have shown in her voice, for he smiled warmly. "Not if I do it right. They're not expecting anybody to come after her—Pryce took great care to cover his tracks in London and travel under a different name. They're probably figuring on a long wait until Griff receives their ransom request. Even then, I'm sure they kept Crouch's involvement quiet so Griff wouldn't know to come after them. And they took great pains to keep me from knowing of it, so they won't be expecting me. I can be in and out with her in a trice as long as—" He broke off. "Well, in any case, it shouldn't be any trouble."

"As long as what?" she prodded.

His face grew shuttered. "Nothing to worry you. I'm just thinking aloud is all."

"Daniel, *tell* me."

He stared her straight in the eye. "There's naught to tell. Now eat your breakfast. Looks as if it might be clearing outside, and the muddy roads will slow us down as it is. If we eat hearty, we might make it to Sedlescombe without having to stop for another meal."

While he returned to eating, she sat there seething. The man could be so infuriating! She *knew* he was hiding something from her.

But what? She thought back through the past two days, their many conversations, their discussion with the smugglers, and this morning's revelations.

A horrible suspicion crept over her. Could it have been *Crouch* that Daniel had worked for in his smuggling days? Could that be what he was hiding?

It made sense. If Daniel had worked for Crouch, then he knew precisely how the man would behave. Her stomach sank. That would also mean Griff knew the man well, too. So this entire elopement/kidnapping had been planned with Griff and Daniel in mind. A gang of smugglers had come after her poor sister because she was connected to their old compatriots . . .

Wait a minute, she chided herself sternly, *there you go*

again, jumping to conclusions about him. Remember what heartache that caused you yesterday?

She simply must stop this. If Daniel had worked for Crouch, he would have said so. She'd asked him if he'd known the man, and he'd answered quite plainly that he hadn't. What's more, he'd sworn never to lie to her again.

Besides, he'd revealed his suspicions about Crouch and the kidnapping when he hadn't needed to do so. Why tell her all that if he wanted to hide some connection to Crouch?

Though he'd sometimes tried to keep her from being involved in his plans—probably wisely so, last night—he'd been forthright about the situation from the beginning. So why should he start lying now?

No, this time she would not allow her overdeveloped sense of caution about men to rule her thinking. If ever there'd been a man she could trust, it was Daniel. For heaven's sake, the man didn't even hide his past from his clients! Why bother to hide it from her?

So if he said there was nothing to worry about, then there was nothing to worry about. Because she refused to believe that after all they'd shared, all he'd promised, he would look her in the eye and lie to her.

Chapter 12

So gaily sings the lark and the sky is awake,
With the promise of a new day
for the road we gladly take.
Tramping song from the Outer Hebrides
off the coast of Scotland

Damn it, he'd lied to her, Daniel thought for the fiftieth time in the three hours since they'd left Tunbridge. He was driving them in the only equipage for hire at the Rose and Crown: an ancient gig with two dips worn into the seat and tarnished harness buckles. The post chaise had been rented for a return trip to Bromley and nothing else had been available.

What had possessed him to lie after swearing never to do it? He'd never hidden his connection to Crouch from anybody else. He'd never hidden any of his past. That was why he lived in St. Giles, to make sure people understood who he was, what he was. They knew who they were getting when they consulted Daniel Brennan.

The trouble was, he didn't care about those other people. It was Helena he cared about. He cared too bloody much. This afternoon she'd turned to him for help with her problems, her eyes full of trust and respect, and he'd balked at telling her the truth. It was as simple as that.

He'd had no choice—it was either lie and have her keep trusting him, or tell all and risk shattering that trust. He couldn't do it. Her faith in him intoxicated him, made him want to leap mountains on her behalf. When she looked at him, she didn't see a highwayman's son or Danny Boy, the smuggler. She saw only Daniel Brennan, the man she trusted to rescue her sister.

So he bloody well would never tell her the one thing sure to make her despise him. If she ever learned that he hadn't been some errand boy for free traders, that he'd worked for the very man who'd kidnapped her sister . . .

His fingers tightened into fists on the reins. It didn't bear thinking on. Besides, she needn't ever know. He could snatch Juliet out of the jaws of her captors without their even realizing who'd done it.

"Watch it!" Helena cried as a hare darted in front of the horse's hooves, barely missing being struck. "You nearly hit that poor creature! And look how you're hugging the side of the road—we're liable to end up in the ditch. Lord, who taught you how to drive?"

"Clearly somebody you wouldn't approve of," he said dryly.

"I should say not," she grumbled, but he could tell he'd squelched her complaint for the moment.

It wouldn't last long, judging from how she'd been

since they'd departed from Tunbridge. Though the day had turned fine after the storm passed, it had left the road so pockmarked with puddles and ruts that it might as well have been Romney Marsh. He'd tried his damnedest to keep the great wheels from bogging down in the mud and avoid slinging too much water and filth on them both, but still Helena had complained about every maneuver he made.

Under other circumstances it might have sparked his temper, but he knew she was feeling poorly in both body and mind after her night's drinking and the revelations about her sister's situation. Her complaints about his driving masked a great and understandable worry, so he didn't protest them too much. Especially since he'd lied to her, was still lying to her.

She grabbed at his arm. "Be careful of that curve . . . oh, heavens, you're taking it too fast!"

"Do you always go on like this when somebody else has the reins?"

"Only when they don't know what they're doing," she snapped. Then, as if realizing she was being unreasonable, she added, "I'm sorry, Daniel. I'm being a trifle annoying, I suppose."

"A trifle," he said mildly.

"I promise to hold my tongue from now on."

He bit back a smile. She'd said that three times in the past hour. "I have a better solution."

She eyed him nervously. "What?"

"Why don't you drive? I could use a rest." Besides, the best way to keep a woman's mind off her troubles was to put her in charge of something.

"Me? Drive the gig?"

"You do know how, don't you, lass?"

She blinked at him. "Why, yes."

"Good. Then have at it." He held the reins out to her expectantly.

She hesitated only a moment before taking them. "Very well. Since you need a rest."

Settling back against the seat, he watched as she began tooling the gig with a deft hand. He shot her a surprised glance. "I take it you've done this before."

She kept her eyes fixed on the road. "At home, my only choice was to take the coach or our gig, since I couldn't ride or walk into town. The coach was far too much bother, so the gig and I became well-acquainted."

"Then you should have little trouble driving this one."

And taming the bad road would keep her from thinking too much about Crouch.

Damn that Will Morgan or Morgan Pryce, or whoever the bastard was. To seduce Juliet into Crouch's power was unconscionable. He couldn't wait to get his hands on the blackguard. He'd teach him a thing or two about not taking advantage of young women.

The way you took advantage of Helena last night.

He swore under his breath. What a bloody stupid thing to do. He was lucky she'd reacted as she had this morning. Any fool knew you didn't seduce a woman while she was drunk, no matter how willing she appeared. Because when she sobered up, she gave you hell for it.

Though Helena had done something worse—she'd looked at him with those soft hazel eyes and made him wonder if perhaps she *had* been willing. He shook his head sadly. He was merely imagining things. She'd told him only too clearly that she hadn't wanted him to make love to her.

Yet she'd also seemed awfully eager to know why he hadn't. It was enough to give a man hope . . .

He snorted. Hope that a woman like her would come

willingly to his bed? He'd lost his bloody mind. Last night had happened only because she'd been upset about their quarrel and drunk enough to want to make amends. Probably she'd also needed reassurance about her desirability after Wallace's insulting remark. All that, combined with a virgin's natural curiosity, was sure to make even the most virtuous woman slip.

And if she ever slips again? When she's sober?

He'd have her in his bed so fast her head would spin.

His gaze drifted over her elegant form. It was a bloody shame that refined women had to wear so many clothes. Still, now that he knew what lay beneath all that fabric, memory quickly supplied the details. The creamy thighs, no less attractive to him for being marked by her illness. The trim waist with its dainty navel. And those lovely breasts puckering up beneath his kisses last night.

Ah, yes, it had almost been worth going to bed iron-hard just to see her in all her glory. And then to watch her reach her peak of enjoyment . . . that was something he'd never forget.

Thankfully, she'd been too drunk to notice him finding his own release later in his bed. Not that he would've minded too much if she had. He'd had only two choices—toss off or climb back into bed with her and make love to her until morning.

"Daniel?" she asked, yanking him from his pleasant ruminations.

"Yes?"

"About this Crouch person . . ."

He stiffened, preparing himself for the worst.

"Was he smuggling while you worked for smugglers? Is that why you know so much about him?"

His gaze shot to her, but he saw no evidence of distrust. She looked curious, that was all. "Yes, that's why."

He had to get her mind off this bloody subject. The gig lurched, throwing him to one side, and as he straightened, a hard object in his coat pocket bumped against his thigh. Perplexed, he reached in and pulled out a slim volume.

Mrs. Nunley's Guide. Ah, yes, just the thing. "Why don't I read to you while you drive? It'll make the hours pass more quickly."

"You brought something to read?" She glanced over at it, then groaned. "Where did you get that?"

He rifled through the book. "It was in your bag—the groom gave it to me before we left. I thought to leave it behind, but now I'm glad I didn't. It might prove interesting."

"For *you*?" she said skeptically.

"Why not?"

"Because as far as I know, you're not planning a coming out. Or didn't you notice that the title says it's for young ladies?"

"You're a young lady. I'll read it to *you*."

"There's no point. I have it memorized."

He gaped at her. "All of it?"

"Of course. I've been reading and following it for twenty years."

"You're shamming me! Twenty years?"

"Mama gave it to me when I was only six. She died when Juliet was born, so Juliet doesn't have one, but she gave Rosalind and me copies as soon as we could read."

"Hard to believe Rosalind even looked at it."

Helena smiled for the first time since they'd left Tunbridge. "She conveniently 'lost' hers some years ago."

"Now, that I can believe." He eyed her soberly. "But you kept yours and memorized it." Was it any wonder the woman had such rigid notions?

"Yes, Mama may have been an actress, but once she married, she knew her duty to Papa as his countess. She tried to instill a lady's behavior, manners, and speech in both Rosalind and me."

"It didn't work with Rosalind. Why did it work with you?"

She shrugged. "Because I'm the oldest, I suppose. And the closest to Mama in temperament. I admired her very much." A faraway look passed over her features as she maneuvered the reins. "She was so lovely, so elegant and graceful. Even after she died, when I was ten, I wanted to grow up to be just like her." She cleared her throat. "That's why I learned the rules so well—because it seemed the best way to follow in her footsteps."

His throat tightened. Poor motherless lass, clinging to the likes of Mrs. Nunley for advice because her own mother was gone. Daniel glanced down at the book. "Now you've made me all the more eager to read the thing."

"Why?"

"Because it'll help me understand you better."

Her gaze shot to his, perplexed and a bit alarmed. "What's there to understand?"

"Everything. But mostly, why you keep your real self locked up tight inside where nobody can see it." Bending close, he whispered, "Except when you're drunk, of course."

Against the dark green of her bonnet, her cheeks glowed as pink as peaches. "You'll find Mrs. N's guide to be very dull reading."

"I doubt that." Settling back against the seat, he opened the book to a random page. It was a mite hard to read with all the jouncing and the wind ruffling the pages, but he managed it. "Let's see. 'The Well-bred Young Lady refrains from arguing.' Hmm. You must've skipped this part."

She cast him an arch glance. "You make it rather difficult to follow the rules."

"Thank God. I like you better when you break them." When that coaxed a small smile from her, he grinned and thumbed forward a few pages. "Here's an interesting bit. 'The Well-bred Young Lady does not show her stockings in public. She must arrange her skirts to protect her modesty at all times.' Fancy that." He reached down and lifted her skirt to peruse her lovely leg, and she swatted his hand away. "Very good. Seems you've mastered that one."

She laughed, though a fresh blush bloomed on her cheeks. "I swear, Daniel, sometimes you are such a rascal."

"Is that the best insult you can manage? Tell me, where's the part about what the well-bred lass is s'posed to say when a man misbehaves?"

"Page fifty-five."

"Bloody hell, you *do* have it memorized, don't you? Though I s'pose it's fitting that you marked *that* page in your mind." He found it, read the rule, and then chuckled. "So this is the grand insult of fine ladies: 'You are no gentleman, sir.' A milk-and-water remark if I ever heard one."

"It's generally effective," she said primly.

"Then how come you never use it on me?"

"Because you'd probably consider it a compliment."

He smote his chest in a mockery of injured pride. "You wound me to the heart, lass!"

She snorted. "If you have such a thing."

"That's more like it—a fine insult, to be sure," he teased. "I see you're not deterred by Mrs. N's lack of set reproaches for a highwayman's bastard. You improvise your own insults bloody well."

"If you don't behave, Daniel Brennan, I shall improvise a way to leave you standing by the side of the road," she warned, eyes gleaming with suppressed amusement.

"You wouldn't do that, and you know it." He chuckled. "You need me."

"True, though I wish it were otherwise."

"Liar."

He could see her fighting the urge to smile, but she lost, and he laughed. Feeling decidedly cheerier than before, he flipped to another page in the book. " 'The Well-bred Young Lady keeps a respectable six inches between herself and her gentleman companion at all times.' " He glanced down to where her thigh lay flush against his. "Move over, Helena. Your improprieties are embarrassing me."

She rolled her eyes. "You'd have to be capable of embarrassment, which you clearly are not. You illustrated that amply the day I came to your lodgings."

"Because I answered the door wearing only my drawers?"

"Because you considered drawers to be adequate attire for home."

"You caught me at a bad time, y'know. You ought to be glad I bothered to dress a'tall." He bent close and murmured, "As I recall, you didn't mind the sight of me in my drawers so much."

"Don't be absurd!" she protested, but she blushed a lovely shade that made his blood run fast and hot. He did enjoy making her blush. Sometimes it seemed the only way to melt the haunting sadness in her eyes.

"D'you know what seems to be missing from this fascinating little book?" he went on as he flipped through it, scanning here and there.

"Sketches of naked women?"

He laughed at her snippy tone. "That, too. But what I

was about to say before m'lady so rudely mocked me is that this book lacks any rules about not getting drunk in a tavern with a lot of free traders. Is that why you figured it was all right to do it?"

That got her dander up. "I was playing a part," she said defensively. "I was trying to help you. And for your information, the book does mention getting drunk. Page twenty-two states that 'The Well-bred Young Lady does not overimbibe.' Believe me, I'm fully aware of my folly in ignoring that rule last night."

He grinned at her. "Ah, but you're great fun when you overimbibe."

She glared at him. "Precisely why there's an admonition against it."

"Seems to me, lass, that there've been entirely too many admonitions in your life, or else you wouldn't have been tempted to break them all at once. Sometimes even a Well-bred Young Lady should have fun and enjoy herself."

"Mrs. N would not approve," she said dryly.

"Then to hell with her." He flashed the book in front of her face. "This is ballocks, all of it. Pure drivel. Telling a woman how to live her life—or rather, how *not* to live it. Nobody's got the right to do that to you, and you don't have to take it, either."

"That's easy for you to say." Her back was straight and her shoulders firmly set, though her face showed every nuance of her agitation and confusion. "No one expects you to follow the rules."

He bristled. "You mean, because I'm a scoundrel and my da was a thief?"

"No! Because you're a *man*." Her eyes were fixed on the cantering horse, but the bitter glint in them had nothing to do with the road's perils. "You're rewarded for taking risks. You're not punished for your . . . enjoyments. A woman's life is different. She must follow the rules or be cut off from her family and good society, from any possibility of a future."

"I thought you already said you had no possibility of a future."

She blinked. "Well . . . yes, but—"

"And even if you became the toast of London tomorrow, you'd still be imprisoned by all these petty proprieties. You'd be even more imprisoned than you are now. So what have Mrs. N's rules gained you? Have they made you happy? Do you wake up each day glad that you're alive, that you're safe and warm and healthy? That the day holds boundless opportunities? It's one thing to follow rules if they lead to happiness, but when they hold you back—"

"What about you, Daniel? Does *not* following rules make *you* happy? Are you happy living in St. Giles among people who couldn't possibly understand you? Or working for gentlemen who probably despise you for your upbringing when you know you're cleverer than any of them?" Her voice shook. "Are you happy having your romps with fancy women who don't care about anything but the money you give them?"

"Bloody hell, you know nothing of it," he growled, and threw himself back against the seat.

But he was lying. She knew a great deal more than he'd expected from a woman who'd barely been out in the world. Damn her for seeing things no one else ever saw.

The gig raced past hedgerows and heath, with Brent geese honking overhead on their way south for the winter and white-wooled sheep bleating from surrounding pastures, but he scarcely noticed. Her perceptive words thundered in his brain.

All right, perhaps he wasn't all that happy these days.

Perhaps loneliness did plague him at times. It wasn't like he could do anything about it. He didn't belong with Clancy and his lot, and he certainly didn't belong in Griff's world. He felt comfortable enough with Griff, but Griff was married now and he'd be spending his time with Rosalind and eventually their children.

Besides, Griff's companionship had never assuaged his loneliness. Not even the lightskirts could manage that. The only person who'd driven out his loneliness for a time, who'd crawled inside him enough to really warm him was—

Helena. He felt a kinship with her that bridged the chasm of blood and breeding. Like him, she knew what it was to struggle fiercely for her place in the world. She knew what it was to not truly belong. People looked at her and saw her game leg and her coldly protective manner. People looked at him and saw his da or his past as a smuggler.

Yet they were both so much more than that. For the first time in his life, he felt as if somebody really saw him for what he was.

It shocked him that it should be Helena. Amazing, surprising Helena, who was game enough to brave a taproom for her sister, and bold enough to coax a table full of rough free traders into spilling their secrets. Helena, who'd defended him when he least expected it, warming him with her veiled apology made before all those men.

"There's something I've wondered about since last night," he said.

She eyed him warily. "What?"

"Why did you come downstairs after me? I thought for sure you'd be asleep almost as soon as I left the room."

"I did sleep awhile." She fidgeted with the reins. "Then I woke up and you weren't there and I was worried."

"About me?"

"Of course. You were downstairs with a lot of shady characters."

"So you thought if you came down, you could protect me?"

"Something like that."

"What did you plan to do—rap all the free traders on the head with your cane?"

A small smile touched her lips. "Don't be silly. It just seemed that you were taking an awfully long time. I thought perhaps I could help." Her smile faded. "Besides, how was I to know that you weren't . . . well . . . that you didn't linger downstairs because . . . because . . ."

When she fell silent, he prodded her. "Because what?"

"Because you were enjoying one of your dalliances."

That was an explanation he could believe. "You were expecting to find me bouncing a taproom maid on my knee?"

She colored. "I-I wasn't sure."

"Either you think I have an insatiable appetite, or you're jealous."

"Jealous! Don't be absurd. I don't care a whit about your . . . fancy women."

She said "fancy women" with such vitriol that he knew she cared a great deal, and her jealousy made his blood quicken. "Don't you?" He let his fingers tangle in the gauzy fichu that hid her lovely swan's neck from his view. "I would've thought otherwise from the number of times you mention them." He lowered his voice. "But I don't mind if you're jealous. I rather like it."

He tugged her fichu away from her gown just enough to bare the silky nape of her slender neck. When he ran his finger along the soft skin, she trembled.

"Daniel," she said on a breath. "You should not . . . I should not . . ."

"What? Want each other? Need each other? Too late for that, lass." It was too late for him, anyway. No matter how much he told himself she would never let them have a future together, he wanted to believe that they could. He wanted very badly to believe it.

He stroked along her neck, beneath the perimeter of her bonnet, then followed the ribbon around to her chin. A light touch against it had her sucking in a breath and turning to lift her face to his.

That's when all hell broke loose.

At first he thought he'd distracted her so much that she'd dropped the reins, but when the horse sprang right out of the traces and galloped off furiously down the road, it dawned on him that something far more serious had occurred.

Then the front shafts of the gig dropped and dug deep into the road, halting the gig at once and sending them both sailing forward off the seat.

"Jesus Christ!" Daniel swore as he landed on his arse in the mud, Helena's book flying out of his hand into the ditch. He sat stunned, his teeth jarred half out of his head, and watched as their horse disappeared around the curve in the road. In a trice, he turned toward Helena, only to find her sitting straight up in a puddle with a look of utter bewilderment on her face.

"What happened?" She stared down at the dirty water soaking into her skirts. "What in heaven's name happened?"

"Goddamned shoddy old gig—the traces broke," he grumbled as he pushed himself to a kneeling position. "I'll strangle that innkeeper the next time I see him. Are you all right? Does anything feel broken? Are your legs hurt?"

She wiggled, then groaned. "My posterior is bruised, but I think that's it. What about you?"

"My arse is more than bruised, I tell you, but I don't think it's broken. My legs feel fine." He rose, the mud sucking at his knees as he pulled free of it. He glanced down the road. "And it appears that our fearless mount decided he was better off without us. He's running for Sedlescombe, damn his hide."

Leaving them not only without transportation, but in no condition to walk any distance. Every bone in his body ached from the impact with earth. Ignoring his protesting muscles, he bent to pick up Helena, then set her on her feet.

She stood there swaying, her weight mostly balanced on her good leg. Lifting her sodden skirts with dainty hands, she stared down at them morosely, then dropped them with a loud sigh. "Ruined, utterly ruined."

"At least it wasn't one of your fancy gowns," he said, trying to find some humor in the situation. "Aren't you glad I cautioned you to dress simple?"

She glowered at him. "I would be, if this weren't all your fault."

"*My* fault? How the devil do you figure that?" He looked around for his hat, which had flown off. "*You* were driving. And don't try to tell me that it was because I distracted you. The traces broke, and that's neither of our faults."

"All the same, we could have been riding comfortably in my coach if you hadn't insisted on taking horses instead." She wiped her muddy hands on her ruined skirt. "Admit it, Daniel—the only reason you wanted to go by horseback was to make me balk at going with you. If you hadn't been trying to scare me off, we would have been in a decent carriage today, and none of this would have happened."

Leave it to Helena to find a way to blame him for it—though in this case, she was mostly right. He spotted his hat in a clump of flowering gorse and snatched it up to clap it on his head. "You're too shrewd for your own good, lass," he said gamely. "I do admit it—I underestimated your determination. But I've paid for my mistake time and again, don't you think?"

She looked at his hat, then burst into laughter. "Yes, I believe so." She pointed to his head. "Don't look now, but there's a rather large spider patrolling your hat brim."

"Bloody hell," he grumbled, jerking off his hat and knocking it against his thigh. The spider dropped to the ground with peculiar grace, then ambled away as if lacking a care in the world. If only he and Helena could do the same.

Walking stiffly to where the gig had dug in its heels, Daniel surveyed the damage. It didn't look good. When he glanced over and saw Helena standing motionless, he retrieved her cane and threw it to her. Then he squatted to examine the broken traces.

He fingered the leather ends, his frown deepening. "As it happens, lass, this particular accident wasn't even an accident."

She leaned heavily on her cane as she limped toward him. "What do you mean?"

"Someone cut the traces partway through before we left Tunbridge."

A low gasp came from her. "Are you sure?"

"Yes." He held up one end. "See how smooth this cut is? It goes halfway, just enough so it would take some time for the strain to make the leather tear all the way."

She looked closely at it and paled, her hands clutching the silver head of her cane. "B-but why? Who?"

"I have a suspicion who. It's the why I'm not so sure of." He straightened. "In any case, we won't be traveling by gig any longer." He gazed along the road in the direction the horse had disappeared and sighed. "Looks as if we'll be walking to the next town, unless some good soul is kind enough to stop and give us a ride."

As if summoned by his wishful thinking, the clop-clop of horse's hooves sounded down the road. Daniel glanced back to see a lone rider approaching on horseback. Uneasily, he watched until the face of the rider came into view. Then his gut clenched into a knot. "Well, well, here's our savior now, come to our rescue in the nick of time. What a coincidence."

"Hullo!" called the rider, shading his eyes from the sun with one hand. "Had a bit of trouble, have you?"

"Mr. Wallace?" Helena said, then shot Daniel a questioning glance.

He nodded. None other than John Wallace had arranged this little accident. Now all that remained was to find out why.

Chapter 13

Then here is a health to the lass,
That the risk of her life she has run;
She tricked the highwayman completely
Out of his horse, money and gun.
"The Highwayman Outwitted,"
from a broadside by Harkness

A sickening premonition settled in Helena's belly as she watched Mr. Wallace come abreast of them. He reined in his dappled mare but did not dismount. Instead he sat staring down at them with a superior gaze, his hands resting on the pommel of his saddle. So Daniel suspected him of cutting the traces? Or had she misunderstood?

Mr. Wallace did seem inordinately satisfied by the damage to the gig. "Looks like the traces broke—a pity, that. But it was half in the grave anyway. I s'pose it was only a matter of time afore it fell in."

"Or was pushed in," Daniel said evenly.

Mr. Wallace ignored Daniel's comment. "I tell you what. I shouldn't want yer missus to have to walk. I can't carry you both, but I can carry her, at least. So why don't I take Mrs. Brennan into the next town and send somebody back for you and the gig while you wait here?"

"Not bloody likely," Daniel ground out, coming to her side with instant protectiveness.

"I may be 'crippled,' Mr. Wallace," she put in, "but I can walk sufficiently to reach town, I assure you." It was a blatant falsehood, but the very thought of going anywhere with the villain made her cringe. She slid her hand into the crook of Daniel's elbow. "Besides, I prefer to stay with my husband. But we would be obliged if *you* would send someone to our aid once you reach town."

Her hand shook, and Daniel slid his over hers to give it a reassuring squeeze.

"Come now, Mrs. Brennan," Mr. Wallace said in a placating tone, "you wouldn't want to be sittin' out here till evenin' waitin' for help, would you? After dark it can be dangerous."

"She isn't going anyplace with you," Daniel said, "so you'd best be on your way. If you truly want to help, you can send someone back for us both. But we'll manage all right if you don't."

Shaking his head, Mr. Wallace reached into his pocket and pulled out a cruel-looking flintlock. "I didn't want to have to do this, Brennan, but you force me to it. Yer wife is comin' with me, one way or t'other."

Helena dug her fingers into Daniel's arm. Merciful heavens, anyone who'd go so far as to draw a pistol was surely not to be trifled with!

"You might as well put that away," Daniel warned. "You only have one shot, and you'll have to kill me with it before I'll let you take her."

Mr. Wallace leveled the pistol on Daniel. "Now that's a tempting thought—"

"No!" Releasing Daniel's arm, Helena stepped between him and Mr. Wallace. This was partly her fault for blundering in last night where she hadn't belonged, and she wouldn't allow Daniel to die for it. Besides, she had a plan. "I'll go with you as long as you don't harm Daniel."

"Get out of the way!" Daniel hissed behind her and grabbed at her arm, but she twisted free to hobble forward a few steps.

When Daniel started after her, Mr. Wallace aimed the pistol at her. "Stand back, Danny Boy, or I'll give yer wife grief."

"Damn you, Helena!" Daniel roared, though he halted in his tracks. "Have you gone mad, woman?"

She was beginning to wonder about the possibility herself. She'd never stared down the barrel of a pistol before, and certainly never purposely drawn its aim.

"Let her do as she pleases," Mr. Wallace said, cocking the pistol. "You don't want to see yer pretty wife hurt, do you?"

"Why are you doing this?" Daniel demanded of Wallace.

"You'll know soon enough." He nodded toward Helena. "Now come here, Mrs. Brennan. But move slow and careful if you don't want to lose the use of yer other leg."

Ignoring Daniel's low growl of rage, she did as he commanded, but all the while her mind was working on her plan. She wasn't about to simply ride off with Mr. Wallace. She wasn't insane, for heaven's sake.

Her fingers tightened on the silver head of her cane. It was weighty, hard. It wasn't much, but perhaps . . .

Mr. Wallace shifted the pistol to his left hand so he could reach down to her with his right. Although his aim on her wavered for no more than a second, his gaze was fixed on Daniel.

Which meant it was not on her.

He removed his foot from the stirrup, but never even glanced in her direction. Clearly it was Daniel he worried about. "Give me yer hand and put yer right foot in the stirrup," he ordered her. "I'll pull you up behind me."

She took his hand in her left, shifting her grip lower on her cane. Then with a sudden motion, she brought her cane up and knocked his pistol hand high into the air. The pistol went off, sending a ball whistling over their heads.

After that, everything happened at once. Daniel lunged forward. She grabbed Mr. Wallace's arm, trying to pull him off the horse. The sound of the men's swearing filled the air as the mare danced between them like a wild thing. It was all Helena could do to stay clear of its hooves.

The next thing she knew, Daniel had yanked Mr. Wallace off the mare onto the ground. The two men rolled over and over together as the horse shied away. Daniel was stronger and bigger, so he quickly had Mr. Wallace pinned beneath him. Then Mr. Wallace used his empty pistol to give Daniel a stunning blow to the head that sent him reeling back.

When Mr. Wallace shoved Daniel off, then lifted the pistol to strike him again Helena saw red. Coming up behind Mr. Wallace, she hit him squarely on his skull with the silver top of her cane, using such force that the cane broke and the silver head spun off into the bushes.

Mr. Wallace slumped to the ground.

She stood there staring at him and trembling, hardly

able to believe that she'd just crowned a man. "Oh, dear, have I killed him?" she asked, a note of frantic concern in her voice. She could see it now: the trial, the ride to the gibbet . . . the scandal!

Daniel rose to his knees beside Mr. Wallace, then felt for a pulse. "No, he's still living, more's the pity." He shot her an admiring glance. "You've got an arm on you, lass. Wallace didn't know what hit him." Then he leaped to his feet, his face darkening into a scowl. "Though that was a bloody stupid thing to do."

"Yes, he should have known better than to accost us, with you so large and—"

"I'm not talking about *him*." Daniel grabbed her by the shoulders. "You could've got yourself killed with that little trick! Attacking an armed man with a walking stick—are you mad? You're lucky he didn't shoot you!"

The broken half of her maligned cane slipped from her fingers. "What else was I to do?" she protested, though her trembling had turned to an uncontrollable shaking at the thought of her rash action. "You were practically *daring* him to kill you!"

"He wouldn't have shot me in cold blood."

"How do you know? It's not as if he likes you. And if he'd shot you, I couldn't have borne it!"

He stared down at her, his leaden gaze slowly warming, melting. "I was in a bloody terror myself, the whole time he was aiming at you. If he'd hurt you, I swear I would've killed him with my bare hands." He cupped her cheek. "So don't ever do anything like that again, all right? You damned near took ten years off my life, you did."

A sweet warmth stole through her, banishing all her trembling. A shaky smile touched her lips. "It was partly *your* fault I did it, you know. If you hadn't mentioned knocking the free traders over the head with my cane this afternoon, I wouldn't even have thought of it."

"I s'pose that's what I get for giving you ideas."

Mr. Wallace groaned. Daniel abruptly released her, went to Mr. Wallace's side, and knocked him on the head again with the butt of the pistol lying close at hand. Removing the man's stock from around his neck, Daniel then tied his hands with it.

Then he hurried to the gig with Mr. Wallace's pistol and shoved it into a bag, swearing as he rooted around for something else. Once he found it, he returned to her side to press it into her hand. "If you're itching to murder somebody, at least use a proper weapon. Aim this at him while I finish tying him up." He started working loose his cravat. "Next time you can be sure I'll keep it a lot closer to hand."

She glanced down at what he'd given her and nearly dropped it. Another pistol, this one bigger and more intimidating than Mr. Wallace's. And probably loaded, too. Lord, she'd never used a pistol in her life. "Next time?" she echoed. "Surely you don't think we'll need to defend ourselves again."

Daniel slid his cravat from around his neck. "Wallace had other men with him, remember? I don't know why they're not here now, but I don't intend to wait around for them to show up."

Mr. Wallace stirred, and she jerked the pistol up toward him as a hysterical giggle bubbled up in her throat. What was the proper etiquette for holding a pistol on a man? Yet another area Mrs. N had not addressed. Did one inform the man that he might die at any moment? Wave it in his face? Oh, what was a Well-bred Young Lady to do?

Thankfully, she did not have to ponder the possibilities long. Within seconds, Daniel had bound the man's ankles. Mr. Wallace began struggling as he grew conscious, but his struggles were fruitless. Daniel had tied him exceedingly well.

Rising from the ground, Daniel rolled Mr. Wallace onto his back, then planted his boot in the middle of the man's chest. "Where are your men?"

Mr. Wallace glared up at him. "Go to hell!"

"Odds are good that I will, but in the meantime—" Daniel leaned forward, placing weight on the man's chest. *"Where are your men?"*

"They'll be along any minute," Mr. Wallace spat.

"Then I won't waste time talking." Daniel held his hand out to her, though he kept his gaze fixed on Mr. Wallace. "Give me my pistol, lass. We might as well finish off the scoundrel now, before he can cause us any more trouble."

"Daniel!" she protested, both fascinated and horrified by his savagery.

But one black look from him made her hand him the pistol. He aimed it at Mr. Wallace's head and cocked it.

"Wait!" Mr. Wallace croaked out. "They're . . . they're up ahead, in Sedlescombe."

"That's better." Daniel uncocked the pistol, eliciting sighs of relief from both her and Mr. Wallace.

"They'll be watching for me," Mr. Wallace warned, "and if I don't show up they'll come back here. See if they don't."

"Why didn't they come with you in the first place?" Helena asked, genuinely curious.

He said nothing, avoiding her gaze.

"Answer the lady!" Daniel dug his boot into Mr. Wallace's chest, and the man coughed.

"That's enough, Daniel," she interjected. "I'm sure Mr. Wallace is more than willing to explain, and we are not barbarians, after all."

"Speak for yourself," Daniel grumbled, but he eased the pressure on Mr. Wallace's chest. "Well, Wallace, it appears my wife is too softhearted to see me crush you like I ought, but you've got ten seconds to answer our questions before I lodge a ball in your idiot skull. Tell us why your friends didn't join you in this escapade."

Mr. Wallace eyed the pistol warily. "They didn't want to."

"Why? Did they disapprove of your nasty plans for her?"

There was so much venom in Daniel's words that Mr. Wallace looked alarmed. "Now see here, don't you go jumpin' to conclusions. Pretty as yer wife is, I meant her no harm."

"You were going to carry her off!"

"Not because I wanted to hurt her or nothin'."

Daniel stared down at him in clear confusion. "Then why?"

Mr. Wallace struggled against his bonds once more, then, recognizing that it was futile, slumped back on the ground. "Because of Crouch, of course."

"Crouch? What have you to do with Crouch?" He waved the pistol at him. "If you think claiming some connection to him will frighten me into letting you go, you're a bigger fool than you look."

"That ain't what I mean!" Mr. Wallace swallowed hard. "I just figured it weren't no coincidence you were lookin' for his man Pryce. And I figured that he'd like to hear of it, considerin' who you are an' all. I thought he might even pay me for it, 'specially if I was to lure you to him meself, using yer wife."

Helena's heart thumped madly. Had Mr. Wallace somehow figured out the connection between her and

Juliet, between Daniel and Griff? "What do you mean, 'who we are and all'?" she asked in a panic.

Mr. Wallace looked over at her. "Not who *you* are, Mrs. Brennan. Who yer husband is. Y'know what I mean—one of Jolly Roger's lot from years back."

The words tore through her, shredding her heart, making her stomach roil. So Daniel *had* lied, after all? After all the promises he'd made, he'd lied to her again?

"That's enough from you," Daniel spat, pressing down against Mr. Wallace's chest, confirming the truth of his words.

Fighting back tears, she stepped forward. "Stop it! I want to hear."

"Helena—" Daniel began, his eyes suddenly a stormy gray.

"I have a right to know, since Crouch has abduct—" She broke off, all too aware of how Mr. Wallace listened to every word. She met his gaze with determination. "Tell me about my husband and Jolly Roger Crouch. Danny has been rather reticent on the subject." Perhaps she'd misunderstood. Oh, please, let her have misunderstood!

Mr. Wallace glanced warily from her to Daniel. "Make him take his foot off my chest, and I'll tell you whatever you want."

"Daniel?" she said softly. "The man is tied up, with a pistol aimed at his head. I hardly think he'll be escaping."

Daniel stared at her a long moment, a muscle working in his jaw. Finally, he cursed and jerked his foot back. Mr. Wallace sat up awkwardly, forced by his bonds to hunch his shoulders and keep his legs bent. Daniel continued to aim the pistol at him, but the man ignored it.

"All right, tell me," she whispered.

He lifted sullen eyes to her. "Not much to tell. Back

when the war was on and Customs an' Excise in London couldn't spare the men to catch us, smugglin' was a mite easier. And Jolly Roger was the best, with two hundred men at his command."

"But what did Danny have to do with it? How long did he work for Jolly Roger?"

He shot Daniel a hostile look. "More'n eight years, from what I heard. They said he joined the gang when he was nine. That's why they called him Danny Boy, 'cause he was so young."

Oh, Lord, it made perfect sense. Danny Boy. That was why he hated the nickname so much and why that tart in St. Giles had called him by it. He'd *said* he was raised in Sussex, which was where Crouch's gang was located. She'd forgotten about that.

"Even as a young one," Mr. Wallace went on, "Danny Boy was more clever than most. Knew plenty about figures an' all. By the time he was seventeen, he was payin' his way an' then some. That's why Jolly Roger made him his lieutenant. Jolly Roger tripled his profits when Danny worked for him."

His *lieutenant?* A knot tightened in her stomach. It was even worse than she'd thought. Not only had he blatantly lied about knowing Crouch, he'd deliberately deceived her about what he'd done for the man. A lieutenant did not hold the horses. "It's true, isn't it, Daniel?" she accused him, her hurt rapidly flaring into anger.

At least he had the decency to look guilty. "Yes." Then his gaze locked with hers and grew belligerent. "I never claimed I was aught but a smuggler all those years ago, y'know. You're the one who assumed I was something less."

Yes, because he'd twisted the truth to suit her impressions of him, the way he'd done with the innkeeper's wife. What a smooth liar he was, the wretch! "But you knew what I thought. And you let me go on thinking it."

He merely jerked his gaze back to Mr. Wallace, who seemed to be enjoying the little contretemps.

"Didn't you tell yer wife about yer adventures with Crouch?" Mr. Wallace grinned maliciously. "No, I don't s'pose you did, her bein' gentry an' all. I'll bet she wouldn't have been so eager to marry you if she'd known it, and her father would've had the hounds after you."

"Stubble it!" Daniel snapped, glaring down at the man.

How terribly ironic that Mr. Wallace had hit accidentally on the truth. Papa probably *would* be unhappy to hear the full extent of Daniel's past. Or did he know it all, as well? It would be just like him not to reveal what he knew about Daniel's and Griff's pasts.

After all, he believed in keeping women ignorant, not telling them what they needed to know. Unshed tears clogged her throat. Just like Daniel, whom she'd thought was a better man than Papa.

But they were two sides of the same coin. God forbid that a woman should be secretive, but men could be as closemouthed as they liked, and they were praised for it. A pox on them all!

Another awful thought occurred to her. How long had Daniel known that it was his former compatriot who had Juliet? Since London? Was that why he'd agreed to go after her? Had he intended *never* to reveal any of this?

Through a dim haze she heard Daniel tell Mr. Wallace, "So you thought to lure me to Crouch by taking Helena, did you? And you thought Crouch would pay you for it?" Daniel laughed mirthlessly. "Then you don't know him very well. He wouldn't pay you—he'd just send his own men out for me and wish you to the devil." Daniel wouldn't look at her. His features seemed carved in stone as he glowered down at Mr. Wallace. "You still haven't explained why your men didn't join you in this grand plan."

Mr. Wallace shot him an insolent look. "They didn't like the idea, is all." He twisted against his knots, then lapsed back into stillness. "Aside from the lot of them bein' cowards an' afraid to cross you *or* deal with Crouch, they—" He glanced at Helena. "Well, they liked yer missus. They said I should leave well enough alone an' let the two of you go on about yer business."

"Good advice. You should've heeded it." Turning to Helena, Daniel handed her the pistol. "Don't let him out of your sight. And shoot him if you must."

"Where are you going?" she demanded, feeling the awful weight of the pistol settle in her hand once more as he strode back to the gig.

"He's probably telling the truth about his men—they'll head back this way looking for him when he doesn't show up in Sedlescombe." Daniel unloaded their meager belongings from the gig and set them beside the road. Then he pried the gig shafts out of the mud. "I don't want to make it too easy for them."

He pulled the carriage off the road and behind the copse, where it was scarcely noticeable unless someone looked closely. Then he returned to Mr. Wallace and hefted the bound man over his shoulder.

"Now see here," Mr. Wallace protested, "you're not going to leave me out here, are you? It'll be hours before they find me!"

"I'm counting on it."

Still heartsick from Mr. Wallace's revelations, Helena followed Daniel to watch as he tossed Mr. Wallace roughly onto the seat of the gig. While Wallace was still wriggling, Daniel leaned close to clasp him about the throat. "Listen to me, you bloody arse, and listen well. Your men had the right idea. If you'd taken Helena, I would've hunted you down like the dog that you are and cut your heart out."

His protective vehemence thrilled her, before she reminded herself that she wouldn't have needed protection if he hadn't been so secretive. She certainly wouldn't have taken any chances last night by telling those men about Mr. Pryce if she'd known that Daniel was such a notorious smuggler.

But Daniel wasn't through with Mr. Wallace. "I suggest that when your men show up here, you return to Kent where you belong. Forget about Crouch and forget you ever saw me or my wife. This isn't your concern. And if you make it your concern, you'll regret it. I'd slit your throat as soon as look at you. Understand?"

Mr. Wallace said nothing, clearly mute with fear. Daniel was beyond anger, acting like the dangerous character he must once have been.

She wanted to despise him for it, but some small, clearly uncivilized part of her admired his fierceness.

"Do you understand, you bloody sot?" Daniel asked again, tightening his hold on Mr. Wallace's throat.

Mr. Wallace's head bobbed up and down, and Daniel thrust him back against the seat. Removing a handkerchief from his pocket, Daniel started tying it around the man's mouth. Mr. Wallace protested, but his words came out as muffled gibberish.

As Daniel strode back to her side, Helena felt she ought to protest. "You're not really going to leave him here like that, are you? What if no one finds him?"

"For God's sake, the man wanted to kidnap you." Daniel took the pistol from her and shoved it inside his frock coat pocket. With a glance at Mr. Wallace, he lowered his voice. "If I let him go and he alerts Crouch to our presence in Sussex, we'll never sneak Juliet away. We can't take that chance. At least this'll keep him quiet a bit longer."

"Oh." She swallowed. "I hadn't thought of it like that."

"Well, you'd best start thinking of such things. These men are not to be trifled with."

"You'd know that better than anyone," she snapped.

Anger sharpened his features. "I would indeed." Glancing away from her, he added gruffly, "I know you have questions you're itching to ask, Helena, but now isn't the time. We'd best leave here right away, before his men come looking for him and find us instead."

"Leave? How do you intend to do that?"

"We'll use Wallace's horse." He gestured to where the mare stood grazing peacefully by the roadside. Then he glanced down at her leg, and his voice softened. "I'm sorry, lass, there's nothing else for it. You'll have to ride, and astride, too."

She tipped up her chin. "I'll do whatever I must. Besides, I wouldn't get far on foot now without my cane."

"Damn, I forgot about that." He headed back to the trees and returned a moment later with a fallen branch. Snapping off twigs and leaves, he fashioned it into a crude walking stick. "Here. This'll do for now."

She took it, her heart lurching as she watched him walk off to fetch the mare. What kind of man was he? One minute he was threatening to slit a man's throat and the next he was crafting her a cane.

Slowly she made her way back to their bags. Daniel's deception provoked other disturbing thoughts. Why had he kept the truth from her? Were matters worse than he'd implied? Did he know even more horrible secrets about this Crouch than he let on?

He led the horse to her, looking grim. "You'll have to ride behind me, because my weight would injure the horse. I'd walk and let you ride, but we need to move quickly."

"It's all right. I'll manage."

Daniel replaced the contents of Mr. Wallace's large saddlebags with their belongings, but he hesitated over the sketch pad. She held her breath. Large as it was, it did take up some room. Then with a glance at her that hinted of remorse, he added it.

Remorse? No, she must have imagined it. The man who'd once ordered her to follow his commands and not ask questions was unlikely to feel remorse merely because she'd found out all his secrets.

And she wasn't even sure of *that*. He might be lying about other matters concerning the abduction, too. Was his assertion that Juliet would be safe with Crouch's men even true? Her heart began to pound. She'd thought she and Daniel were partners, sharing the same information, working with the same risks. But they were not partners at all, were they?

It took some effort for them both to mount the horse. They had to walk until they found a stile, since Daniel had to mount first and couldn't lift her into the saddle. He set her on the stile, climbed onto the horse, then pulled her up behind him. Moments later they were back on the road.

Riding astride was sheer agony after yesterday, but she choked down her moans. For safety's sake, she ought to wrap her arms about Daniel's waist instead of hanging on to his frock coat, but touching him so intimately was impossible when she felt like strangling him. Nor did she want to be reminded of all they'd shared the night before, when she'd foolishly thought she'd begun to understand him.

She didn't even know him.

Her brother-in-law's man of affairs figured investments and advised dukes. Danny Boy Brennan, Crouch's lieutenant, threatened to slit men's throats. Danny Brennan lied whenever it suited him.

Oh, why must she have the instincts of a ninnyhammer when it came to men? How could she have been so foolish as to be taken in by him yet again?

They'd ridden only a few miles before Daniel suddenly turned the horse off the road onto a smaller one nearly hidden by overhanging willows. "Daniel? Where are we going?" she demanded above the thundering of the hooves. Daniel had kept the horse at a steady gallop, which, along with their positions, made conversation difficult.

"We need to find somewhere to lie low," he called back. "I'll explain when we stop."

You certainly will. She would not let him shut her out any longer. She'd make him tell her everything, if she had to beat him over the head with her makeshift cane to do it.

Soon they emerged from a grove of autumn-red sycamores to gallop past a wide expanse of marsh humming with grasshoppers and blue dragonflies. The narrow road ended abruptly before a small farmhouse and barn. Daniel stopped the horse in front of the wattle-and-daub house and dismounted, then turned and lifted her down. Her legs were sore, but thankfully the ride had been short enough not to tax them beyond her strength.

But even after her demi-boots were firmly on the ground, he stood there with his hands on her waist, his gaze trailing over her with a dark need that sent her blood racing in anticipation of more.

Lord, what was wrong with her? All he had to do was touch her and everything she'd learned today was blotted out by the memory of him lying atop her last night, kissing her and caressing her and . . .

With a groan, she twisted out of his arms and reached for her makeshift cane. She moved a few feet away to face the tiny farmhouse. "Why are we stopping here?"

He came to stand beside her. "Wallace's men are sure to come upon us if we continue on the main road. If they see us riding his mare, they'll guess what happened and then there'll be hell to pay. At least this way they may assume he was successful and that he went on without them."

"So they might not look for him at all?" she said hopefully.

"Or they might be headed here now. Either way, we can't go on so openly with him and his men around. We need to hide for a bit and find better transport."

"But if they do find Wallace while we're hiding, he might convince them to go to Crouch."

"P'raps. P'raps not. They don't seem as foolish as him, and God knows I tried to put the fear of God into him." He sighed. "It's not as if we have a choice, lass. At least if we lie low for the night, we might continue in the morning without trouble. But if we go anywhere near Sedlescombe tonight, we're sure to be seen by some of them—and the only road to Hastings from here goes right through Sedlescombe."

She glanced around. The timber-framed house was small. The barn looked ancient and scarcely capable of housing more than a few horses. In a nearby enclosure four pigs lolled about in the mud, and some Jersey cows grazed on marsh grass beyond. All in all, a struggling farm.

"So this is where you plan to 'lie low'? Do you know the owner?"

"No, I took a turn at random." He started toward the house. "But farmers hereabouts are friendly, especially if you cross their hands with silver. They probably won't see anything wrong with letting us sleep in the barn, and that's all we need—a night off the road."

She followed him to the door, watching as he knocked on it loudly. There was no answer. He knocked again and they waited, but no one came. Finally, he tried the door. Just as the knob turned and the door opened, a youthful voice sounded behind them.

"Best get away from that door, mister, unless you wish to die."

Chapter 14

Instead of his stomach he feasted his eyes
On the charms of her beauty, which did him suffice.

"Love in the Tub,"
anonymous ballad

So much for friendly farmers, Daniel thought as he turned around.

Then he caught sight of their challenger, and relief curled through him. It was a lad of no more than fifteen, clad in a dirty laborer's smock and nankeen breeches. A lock of ginger-brown hair drooped into the wary blue eyes that darted from him to Helena. The stripling brandished a pitchfork at them, but the sweat dripping down his freckled cheeks made it clear he wasn't as brave as he pretended.

"Here now, boy, we mean you no harm." Daniel took a step toward him. "Why don't you just put that thing down and—"

"Stay back!" The stripling swung his pitchfork out toward Daniel. "And I ain't no 'boy'! I'm man enough to put this through your heart if I have to!"

Daniel stifled a laugh. What would the boy say if he knew of the pistol in Daniel's pocket? "No doubt you can, but I'm not sure why you'd want to. We've done nothing to warrant it."

"You were breaking into my house!"

"My husband merely wanted to see if anyone was home," Helena put in. "When no one answered his knock, we thought perhaps it had not been heard."

Helena's cultured tones seemed to give the boy pause. He shifted his attention to her, his eyes flicking over her muddy gown and the makeshift cane she leaned upon. He lowered the pitchfork a fraction. "What happened to you? Y'look as if you've been rollin' about with the pigs."

She winced. "I certainly feel like it. I'm afraid we had an accident while on our way to the seaside. It quite destroyed our gig and tossed us both in the mud. As you can see, it ruined my best frock. It broke my cane, too, which is why I'm having to use this pathetic tree branch to walk." She held out a hand with a cordial smile. "My name is Helena Brennan, and this is my husband Daniel. We're very sorry to intrude, but we thought perhaps you could help us."

The lad hesitated, glancing from her to Daniel with wary eyes. At last he set the pitchfork on end and took her hand. "I'm Seth Atkins. I live here."

When the lad held Helena's hand longer than necessary, Daniel said gruffly, "P'raps if we could speak to your father . . ."

Seth dropped Helena's hand and shot Daniel a sullen look. "Father ain't here just now." The boy thrust out his chest. "So you'd best be talkin' to me about what it is you want."

"Of course." Helena cast a warning glance at Daniel as if to say, *Let me handle this.* Then she gave Seth a bright smile. "Your father will undoubtedly be pleased to hear how well you are protecting the farm. But I assure you, we are not beggars or thieves. We merely need a place to stay this evening. We were hoping you might oblige us by letting us stay in your barn."

Seth shifted from one foot to the other. "Why d'you want to stay in a cold barn? Sedlescombe's only a few miles south, and you c'n get a nice room at the inn there."

"With my poor leg, a few miles might as well be a few hundred. I can't ride more than a short distance, and since the accident with our gig forced us to rely on only the one horse . . ." She trailed off with a pitiful look of supplication. "Please, you won't make me get back on it, will you? We'll be no trouble, I assure you."

Christ, Daniel thought, and she said *he* was smooth-tongued.

Seth relaxed his stance and scratched his chest. "Well, I don't know . . ." he began, but it was clear he was softening.

Daniel shook his head. The poor lad hadn't had a chance once Helena turned her powers of persuasion on him. She'd done the same thing to Daniel in London, convincing him to bring her along against his better judgment. And now he was suffering for it.

"We can pay you very well," she said.

"Yes," Daniel put in, figuring that was his cue. He withdrew his purse and opened it. "We don't mind paying. And once your parents return, they can decide whether we stay or no."

Seth glanced from Helena's leg to the horse and then back to the purse in Daniel's hand. "They ain't comin' back till tomorrow evening. They left me in charge. But I suppose it won't hurt none. Long as you pay."

"Thank you," Helena said softly. "That's most generous."

The lad gave her a crooked grin. "You're welcome. I'd let you stay in the house, but Father would tan my hide for it."

"The barn will be fine, I'm sure," Helena said. "It's very kind of you to take pity on us."

Helena flashed Seth a smile and the fool thrust out his chest, a bantam rooster crowing to a hen.

Daniel rolled his eyes. And to think that the lass believed she couldn't attract a man. Was she bloody blind? Already the boy looked as if he'd pitchfork his way through hell to save her.

Daniel cleared his throat. "We'd like something to eat, too, if it's all right." Daniel drew out a handful of silver and waited until Seth's gaze shifted to it. "It needn't be anything fancy, you understand. Just bread and whatever else you can spare."

"Mum left me some supper I'll be happy to share." Seth jerked his thumb toward the barn. "You can stable your horse in there. My parents took our only two, so there be plenty of room. I'll bring the food to you in a bit, soon's I dress." He paused to scan the two of them. "If you want to wash the mud off, you c'n use that." He indicated a pump with a jerk of his head. "There's soap in the pail next to it if you like."

"We're much obliged," Daniel said, handing the coins to Seth, who took them, then stood staring down at the silver as if waiting for it to evaporate in his hand. Poor lad had probably never seen that much money in his whole life, judging from the appearance of his family's farm. Indeed, Daniel wondered what the boy had thought he was protecting.

At last Seth shoved the coins into his trouser pocket. "Be right back," he mumbled, then strode toward the farmhouse.

As the lad set his pitchfork by the door, then disappeared inside, Daniel strode back to Wallace's horse. Out of the corner of his eye, he saw Helena limp toward the pump and felt his gut twist into a knot. He hated this, forcing her to wash in the icy water of a pump and bed down in hay when she deserved hot baths and fine linen on feather beds. He hated dragging her from pillar to post, not knowing what trouble they might find in the next town.

But most of all, he hated the look of hurt betrayal in her eyes. He wished he'd shot that scoundrel Wallace before the man had told her about him and Crouch.

Daniel drew himself up with a scowl. She had him acting as if he ought to be ashamed of it. It wasn't *his* fault that she'd leapt to certain conclusions about his past. Nor did it change anything between them, not as far as he was concerned.

Yet the memory of how disappointed she'd looked when Wallace was gleefully exposing Daniel's old connection . . .

Damn the man! Now she knew for certain what a scoundrel Daniel had been. She'd already thought him a whoremonger, but now she thought him a villain, too. He could tell from her frosty manner, her angry glances. His only consolation was that she still seemed willing to let him guide their actions—though she probably felt she had little choice.

He led Wallace's horse into the barn and set about unsaddling it. When Helena entered a while later, she had her bonnet in one hand and a now-dirty handkerchief in the other. She hung both on nails in a nearby post. She'd scrubbed her face clean and had rinsed out her hair, for the chestnut weight of it clung damply to her shoulders, crisscrossing the back of her bodice with dark, wet swaths as translucent as paper.

His blood quickened at the sight. Jerking his gaze away, he concentrated on rubbing down the horse. He was nearly finished when Helena spoke.

"Daniel?"

"What?" he growled.

"When you said this morning that you could rescue Juliet from Crouch unless something went wrong, were you talking about Crouch's men finding out that you were coming? And them knowing who you are?"

He flinched. "Yes."

"And I suppose with Wallace around that's still a possibility."

"Damn it, yes." He couldn't stand the way she danced around the issue. "But that's not what's bothering you, is it?"

"What do you mean?" Her voice held a hauteur he hadn't heard in it since London.

"I mean the reason you stiffen when I touch you, the reason you can hardly bear to look at me. You've gone back to thinking you can't trust me."

"Now why should I do that, I wonder?" she said sarcastically.

He turned from the horse to throw down the curry brush. "Goddamn it, Helena, I couldn't tell you about me and Crouch."

Her gaze burned steadily into his. "Oh? Why not? Because it was 'nothing to worry' me?"

Her blatant echo of his lie sliced right through him. "That's it exactly. I didn't figure your knowing would make any difference, seeing as how I'd already promised to help your sister escape her captors."

"If it made no difference, then why not tell me?"

"Because I knew you'd react like you are now—assuming the worst, deciding I'm as bad as the ones that took her."

She gaped at him. "I'm not doing that!"

"I saw how you looked at me after Wallace spewed out his poison: like I was a bloody insect you wanted to squash. Like I'd betrayed you. Here you'd been thinking I was some poor lad forced to live among smugglers and do a bit of their dirty work, and apparently that was all right by you. You didn't mind so much having me touch you, then."

"You don't understa—"

"But it's not quite the same to learn I was Crouch's right-hand man in my youth, is it? That I was as much a criminal back then as Wallace and his gang, if not more. Well, you listen to me, lass. I'm the same man who kissed you last night, the same man you claimed to trust while you sat before all those free traders. And if you think I—"

He broke off as he heard the door to the farmhouse slam. The boy was coming.

Daniel dropped his voice. "We'll finish this later, d'you hear? In the meantime, you'd best decide what you want from me. Because like it or not, we'll be enduring each other's company for the next few days, and I don't plan to spend it as your whipping boy."

He regretted his harsh words the instant she recoiled

from him, shock and pain in her features. Filled with self-loathing, he wheeled away to lead the horse into a stall. He shouldn't have said that last bit, but Christ, she made him insane when she looked at him like he was the worst devil hell had ever spawned. It made him want to roar and stamp about the barn.

She hadn't looked at him like that last night, oh, no. Last night, she'd been all soft and eager to have him in her bed. And it hadn't just been the liquor talking, either. After this afternoon in the gig, he was sure of it. But now she thought to blot all that out of her head, just because of a few matters in his past. How dare she?

He wanted to go back and drag her into his arms, remind her of what had passed between them, the heat and the need and the sweetness. He wanted to make her see it made no difference what he'd been in his youth.

But their young host's footsteps could be heard rounding the barn. The stripling had chosen a devil of a time to bring them supper. Schooling his features into some semblance of calm, Daniel left the horse, closed and latched the stall door, and returned to where Helena was still standing, mute and stricken. He couldn't look at her. He couldn't bear to see the sure contempt in her eyes.

"There was more food than I thought," Seth announced cheerily as he walked into the barn carrying a tray heaped high. Dressed in the simple garb of a farmer, he seemed oblivious to the tension that clouded the air in the barn.

Helena seemed to shake herself. "Oh . . . thank you. We much appreciate it."

"Mum even left a cake," he went on. "I'll get it after you're done with all this."

"We wouldn't want to take your cake," she said softly. "You keep that for yourself."

Though the smile she then offered looked wooden, it further enraged Daniel. How easily she could turn pleasant when some unlicked cub cozied up to her. "*I* wouldn't mind a bit of cake," Daniel grumbled. "God knows I paid for it." He strode up to the boy and surveyed the tray, then grudgingly conceded, "Although it does look as if you gave us our money's worth, lad."

"Mum makes right fine bread and butter," Seth boasted. "And there's pickles and ham and even some cold boiled potatoes if you like."

"It sounds delicious," Helena whispered, "though I confess I'm . . . not as hungry as I thought."

When Daniel's gaze shot to her, he saw naught but bleak pain, so palpable it was like a blow to his groin. He knew why she'd lost her appetite—who'd made her lose it. And with a savage twist of guilt, he remembered that she'd barely eaten any breakfast.

"Why don't the two of you set up a place for us to eat while I go wash up?" he muttered. Maybe if he left her alone for a bit, she could find her appetite. Besides, it was too bloody hard to be near her at the moment.

He strode outside to the pump. He shed his clothes to the waist, being careful to remove his pistol and hide it beneath the pile. Then he gave himself as good a scrubbing as he could manage in the rapidly fading light. He didn't mind the icy water or the chill autumn air; at least it helped to cool his anger. After he'd finished and put his shirt and waistcoat on, he gathered up his muddy coat and the pistol and returned to the barn.

Seth and Helena awaited him, seated on milking stools at a jury-rigged table of planks set across a cart. They'd lit a couple of lamps, sending cheery light around the dusty barn and over the plentiful meal. As Daniel tossed his clothes in a corner and hid the pistol in them once more, he realized he'd lost his appetite, too. Though the food looked mighty enticing and Seth had brought them fresh milk to wash it all down with, what he desperately wanted was some ale. For himself *and* Helena, since that seemed to be the only thing that took the starch out of her spine.

Why could she only be easy with him when she was half-drunk? Why must her expectations for him be so bloody rigid?

Then again, it served him right for hiding his true self from her. He'd learned long ago not to do that, because it always ended with people discovering he was something other than what they thought. He'd known she'd get her back up if she found out that she'd allowed one of those "nasty, evil men" to kiss her and touch her intimately. Yet the reality of it was twice as agonizing as he'd expected.

Because a tiny part of him had hoped she might be different.

She wasn't. That was clear enough throughout their meal, which she only picked at. She ignored him pointedly, bestowing all her queenly kindness on Seth. Never had Daniel felt so much like wringing a boy's neck just for being young and friendly. Why couldn't the stripling have slunk off into the house without bothering them?

Instead, Seth had eagerly accepted Helena's invitation to join them for their meal. At first, he stuck to questions about where they were headed. But when he heard they'd come from the city, it sent him into a fever of excitement.

He exclaimed that he'd dearly love to see London. Question tumbled after question, and Daniel soon realized that the lad wanted to hear about every bloody piece of the entire wretched town. Even worse, Helena seemed more than eager to oblige, though she probably knew as little about London as Seth. No doubt she wanted to postpone the moment when she and Daniel were alone. God knew he dreaded it himself.

Not to mention that he wasn't sure how to handle the sleeping arrangements. Letting Seth prattle on to Helena, he left the table to survey the barn. Helena couldn't climb a ladder, so the loft wouldn't do. They'd have to use a stall. Thankfully, there was one that looked as if it had been empty for years. No doubt the family had been forced to sell some of their horseflesh when the farm fell on hard times.

Lending only half an ear to the boy's chatter, Daniel climbed into the loft and tossed down some hay. Then he brought a lamp into the unoccupied stall and swept the dust and cobwebs out. Laying down plenty of fresh hay made him all too aware of how small the stall was. Christ, for all intents they'd be sharing a bed if they both stayed here, yet he didn't like the idea of sleeping in the loft and leaving her down here alone. What if by some chance Wallace's men showed up?

No, he and Helena would have to share the space. It wasn't much, but it would do once he threw a horse blanket and his greatcoat over it. And surely he could keep his hands off her for one night—especially since she'd probably shoot him before she'd let him touch her again.

She and the lad were still jawing when he finished, but Daniel had had as much as he could stand. Though it took repeated hints about their tiredness before he could get rid of the boy, he did at last succeed. Even then the lad insisted on coming back to bring them linens to throw over the horse blanket that Daniel had tossed down.

"Won't your mother be angry to find her linens filthy?" Helena asked as Seth held out a pile of sheets and a blanket.

He shrugged. "I'll wash 'em out in the morning. Besides, a fine lady like yourself shouldn't have to bed down on a horse blanket."

"I agree," Daniel snapped, whisking the linens from the boy's hands. "Now if you'll excuse us, Seth, we need our privacy. My wife and I would sorely like to shed these mud-caked clothes and go to bed."

Seth colored, then mumbled about how he understood and scurried out the barn door. Daniel shut it with a rush of relief.

"You didn't have to be so rude to the poor boy." Helena stalked to where their saddlebags were hung over a stall door and began to rummage about in them. "He was only trying to help."

Snorting, Daniel added his coat and pistol to the pile of linens and strode past her into the stall. "Trying to get into your good graces, is what he was doing. I should've warned the boy it was pointless." Daniel spread the sheet and blanket over the horse blanket, then placed the pistol in the corner of the stall.

"And what is that supposed to mean, pray tell?"

He strode back to where she was tossing out the contents of the saddlebag with jerky movements. "What that means," he snapped as he halted a few feet from her, "is that you are bloody unforgiving. Let a man make one mistake and—"

"One mistake? Is that what it was? A mere *mistake?*"

Noting her haughty posture, he gritted his teeth. "All right, so it was more than that. Yes, I was Crouch's lieutenant." The carefully banked anger that had smoldered in his breast all evening flared to blazing heights. "But it was a long time ago, damn it! I haven't dabbled in free trading in years, yet you act as if I'm still doing it!"

She dropped the flap of the saddlebag and whirled on him. "I don't care about the free trading! You were young and you did what you had to. I can't pretend to understand what it's like to have to scrabble for every penny, so I couldn't possibly judge you for doing whatever you did."

"Now who's the one telling lies?" he growled.

"You arrogant wretch! I'd already begun to figure out you were not some child apprentice to smugglers. Last night you were quite expert on the subject of free trading. I wasn't so drunk that I couldn't tell you knew a great deal more than I'd expected."

That took him off guard. Then his eyes narrowed. "But you didn't know I was *Crouch's* smuggler, did you? You didn't know of my connection to the man who had your sister abducted. And now that you do, you think me even more of a scoundrel than before!"

"Yes, you're right!" she snapped, her eyes clouding with hurt. "But not because of your connection to *him*. Because you *lied* about it, damn you! You promised never to do so, then turned around and did precisely that!"

He stood there stunned, his own anger ebbing as he tried to grasp the source of hers.

"I trusted you," she went on, warming to her subject, "I told you things I'd never told any man. I asked you to do things that I would never—" She broke off, averting her wounded gaze from him. Her breath came in harsh gasps, and every one stamped an echo in his conscience.

She went on in a whisper. "All the while, you weren't showing me the least bit of trust. You were keeping the truth from me, pretending not to know Crouch when you really did, pretending the situation wasn't that dangerous, lying to me about why Crouch kidnapped Juliet—"

"I didn't lie to you about that. I told you exactly why I think he did it."

"But you assured me you'd told me everything, and that was all a lie."

His gut twisted into a painful knot as he saw the look of betrayal on her face. Christ, he'd mistook everything. It wasn't his past that bothered her, but the fact that he'd kept it from her.

What had he been thinking? Farnsworth had lied to her, her father had lied to her, and he and Griff had lied to her and her sisters last summer. Just when she'd started thinking that perhaps not all men lied to get what they wanted, just when she'd forgiven him for his part in Griff's scheme, he'd gone and lied to her again.

What an idiot he was.

He reached out to grip her shoulders, and she flinched. She tried to wriggle free of his hands, but he wouldn't let her go. "Listen to me, sweetheart, just listen," he murmured. "I should've told you about Crouch—I see that now. I'm so sorry I didn't."

"Y-you sat there this morning pretending that Crouch had chosen Juliet simply because Griff is rich. Yet you must have known he'd chosen her because of his connection to both of you."

"It's probable, but—"

"How long have you known about his involvement?" she persisted. "Since we left London? Have you known from the beginning that your . . . former friend had my sister?"

"No! Bloody hell, is that what you've been thinking? That I kept it from you all this time?"

Her lower lip quivered. "I wasn't sure. The day I went to your lodgings, you seemed determined not to help me. Then you changed your mind the next day, and I've always wondered why."

"Only because I'd learned that Pryce really was a free

trader. I would never have taken you with me if I'd thought Crouch was mixed up in it. Never! I wouldn't have risked it." He softened his tone. "I found out about his involvement the same time you did, sweetheart—last night at the inn. You have to believe me."

She glanced away, blinking back tears. "How? Every time I start to believe you, I find out how foolish I was. I thought you were being honest with me. I thought you were different from the others—"

"Please, lass, please understand—I couldn't tell you." He cupped her cheek, brushing tears away with his thumb. "I couldn't bear to have you look at me with contempt in your eyes."

The minute her gaze swung to his, fiery and furious, he knew he'd said the wrong thing. "*That* was why you lied to me? Because you thought knowing about you and Crouch would make me despise you?"

Her anger gave him pause. "The possibility did occur to me, yes."

"Why, you . . . you . . . big . . . stubborn . . . ox!" She punctuated each word by poking a finger at his chest, tears coursing down her cheeks. "After last night, did you really think that could possibly make me stop wanting you?"

The words thundered in his ears, tilting his world on its axis. She wanted him. She was stone-cold sober, yet she wanted him—despite everything she'd learned about his past, and all her rules of propriety.

"Yes, I did," he said in a husky whisper. "But now I know better."

As if realizing how much she'd revealed, she paled. Wrenching free of him, she backed away. "I-I didn't mean that the way it sounded—"

"Too late to take it back now, lass," he said as he

stalked her. "You want me. You said it, and we both know bloody well you meant it. So I'll be damned before I'll let a few of my stupid lies stand in the way of you and me being together."

She continued her retreat. "You shouldn't have lied to me, Danny."

"I know." He caught her and hauled her into his arms.

Her chin quivered as she stared mutinously up at him. "You . . . you should have told me everything about Crouch this morning."

"I know." He bent his head toward hers. "And I'm sorry for it. Let me show you how sorry I am for it."

"No!" Panic flared in her eyes, the panic of a woman who was afraid to trust her own instincts. "I'm not going to let you . . . get away with lying to me, blast it!"

"That's your pride talking, not your heart." He caught her chin, held it still. "Well, lass, I think it's time you tell your pride to stubble it."

He didn't give her time to think, to argue, to protest. He just kissed her the way he'd been wanting to all day, seeking solace from her soft, sweet lips. And though she balked at first, she didn't balk long. With a little moan of acquiescence, she threw her arms about his neck and opened her mouth to him.

Yes, he thought, *yes, sweetheart.*

Suddenly she tore her lips from his to whisper, "A pox on you, Danny! You're such a devious rascal."

He scattered kisses over her cheeks. "If I am, it's only because I want you so badly I'd do anything to have you."

"You mean, lie and deceive me," she grumbled even as she arched her body against him. "You ought to be ashamed of yourself."

"I am thoroughly, heartily ashamed." His voice

thrummed low. "Let me show you the full extent of my remorse."

"Now see here—"

Silencing her with his mouth, he kissed her more boldly this time, thrusting his tongue deeply, intimately into her mouth, giving her full warning of what he wanted from her. He kissed her like a man kissed the woman he intended to seduce.

Because that was exactly what he intended. If he didn't make Helena his this very moment, he feared he'd never have a chance with her again. And he very badly wanted a chance with her—any chance.

If he waited to make love to her until he was sure of her, she'd spend every minute hardening her heart against him. She'd invent a thousand nonsensical rules for why she shouldn't allow him in.

Well, he wouldn't let her. It was time to shatter her rules once and for all. Time to make room for him in her heart. And if that meant making love to her in a goddamned barn on a bed of hay, then that's what he'd do. Because he refused to lose her.

Chapter 15

And when we arose from the green mossy bank
Through the meadow we wandered away
I had plowed my true love on the green mossy bank
And I plucked her a handful of may.
"Queen of the May,"
anonymous ballad

It's not fair, Helena thought as Daniel's mouth plundered hers, intense and needy. *Why must he be the one who does this to me? Why can't I push him away?*

Because she wanted him, wanted this. She hated that she did, but it changed nothing. From the minute he'd explained why he'd lied, she'd begun weakening. How could any woman resist a man who'd lied to keep her from despising him?

Yet he'd promised not to. He'd promised! She wrenched her mouth from his. "You cannot simply kiss me into submission, Daniel. It will not work." Actually, it was already working, but she didn't *want* it to work.

"It's not submission I want from you, sweetheart. It's your fire and your need that I want." He looked as starved for her as she felt for him. His hot gaze drifted over her, hinting at all the delights he had to offer.

"You had my 'fire' and my 'need' last night, and you didn't appreciate it."

She whirled away from him, but not swiftly enough. He caught her from behind, wrapping his brawny arm about her waist. When he tugged her against his massive body, remembered pleasure swamped her, draining her will to resist.

"That's not true, y'know," he rasped. Nuzzling her damp hair aside, he brushed her ear with his lips. "I appreciated it far too much or I wouldn't have lied to you today trying to hold on to it. It was stupid—I admit it. And it didn't even work. It only made you despise me." He kissed her ear sweetly. Too sweetly.

She stifled a groan. "I-I don't despise you."

"Don't you? At the very least, you're extremely vexed."

Vexed? That sounded vaguely familiar. Then he tugged on her earlobe with his teeth, sending a wanton shiver dancing along her spine and driving all rational thought clear out of her head. "I am not."

"Not what?" He ran the tip of his tongue around the outside of her ear, and delicious feeling flooded her, mocking her feeble resistance.

"Extremely vexed."

His free hand slid around her to cup her breast, and his voice rumbled seductively. "If you're not vexed, then prove it."

Now she remembered why this exchange seemed so familiar, yet the words were out of her mouth before she could stop them. "Prove it? How?"

"Let me make love to you."

It was the merest whisper, yet it thundered along every nerve like a siren's lyric, shattering her defenses, stealing around her heart. She fought to block its seductive song. "You can't make me forget that you lied to me merely by . . . making love to me."

"P'raps not. But I can show you how sorry I am for it." He brushed her nipple with a light caress that she felt even through the layers of muslin and linen. "Let me make amends by giving you pleasure." His hand was hot where it stroked her breast, deftly, cleverly.

Tempting her to all manner of wickedness. "You are . . . very naughty, Danny," she said, trying for sternness and disapproval and instead speaking his nickname in a throaty whisper.

"Compliments upon compliments." Both hands were kneading her breasts now with sweet, silken caresses that made her ache and yearn. "Though I've come to learn you can be naughty yourself when you wish. Show me your naughtiness, lass. I know you want to."

As he played with her breasts and branded her neck with kisses, her very bones melted. Lord, he was right—she wanted to be every bit as naughty as that woman under the lamp in London being fondled by her companion. She loved how he rubbed her breasts until they tingled and hardened.

"Daniel . . ." she whispered, grabbing for one of his hands. But she merely succeeded in pressing it more firmly to her breast.

He groaned. "That's good, lass. Show me what you

want from me, what you need. Show me how to make amends."

Horrified that she was *helping* him touch her, she dropped her hand, but he did not drop his. His hands were like waves lapping rock, wearing her down, smoothing her out, softening her rough edges. Already the place between her thighs grew as damp and warm as it had last night, craving more of his touch, his scandalous touch. His arousal thickened against her bottom, and his breath came hard and fast against her ear.

One hand left her breast to unbutton her gown. In seconds, he had it open and was sliding it off her shoulders. Her head fell back against his shoulder as he divested her of gown and petticoats, then resumed fondling her breasts. With only her chemise separating his flesh from hers, she felt every caress of his large, warm hands with an acute intensity near pain.

She'd thought that her memories of last night's pleasures had been heightened by the drink, but now she knew better. If anything, tonight it was more vivid, more pleasurable. More irresistible.

"Ah, sweetheart," he murmured, "I could hold you like this for hours. I love to touch you. You have a body made for touching."

A thrill shot through her that she fought to temper. "You're such a flatterer. And as Mrs. N says, 'The Well-bred Young Lady must ignore flatterers.' "

"It's not flattery, it's the truth." He nipped her ear. "Isn't it time you replaced the old harridan's rules with ones better suited to your new status?"

"My new status?" she echoed, then gasped as one of his hands slipped down to stroke her belly, then lower to the juncture between her legs.

"Yes." He cupped her there through the thin linen of her chemise. "As a Naughty Lady. And the first rule is that a Naughty Lady enjoys a man's compliments."

"Does she?" She could hardly think while he touched her so intimately, one hand rubbing between her legs and the other thumbing her nipple deliciously. "She sounds very . . . naive."

"Second rule," he said thickly, "is that a Naughty Lady doesn't question the rules."

She arched an eyebrow. "That sounds like Mrs. N."

"Ah, but the rules of pleasure are very different." He dragged up her chemise just enough so he could slide his fingers into the slit between her drawers.

Merciful heavens, it was sweet feeling him flesh to flesh—his callused and hard, hers soft, wet, and yielding. He rubbed a sensitive nub, and she nearly jumped. Instinctively, she undulated against that magical finger, only half conscious of what she was doing.

"You like that, do you, lass?" When she said nothing, hardly capable of speech, he added, "Rule three: A Naughty Lady tells her lover how to pleasure her."

Her lover. Yes, he was going to be her lover. And she wanted to let him.

"So tell me, sweetheart," he murmured devilishly, "is this what you want? Does this make you feel more kindly toward me?" His finger delved inside her, centering all her rampant urges at that one aching spot. "Does it please you to have me touch you here? Shall I go on?"

He paused his motion as if waiting for her answer, and she cried, "Yes, go on!" Only when his finger plunged deep did she realize she was gripping his forearm to urge him on. But heavens, it felt so very good!

"I'll have more than my finger there in a bit, y'know," he vowed. "You won't escape me tonight, lass. I plan to lay you down and fill you with my flesh. I plan to make you mine."

A shiver of excitement rippled over her, the fierceness of her sudden yearning for him overwhelming. "And will you be . . . mine, too?" she couldn't resist asking. "Only mine?"

Abruptly, his caresses stopped. He turned her to face him, his gaze locking with hers. "Rule four: The Naughty Lady trusts her lover not to hurt her. As her lover trusts her to do the same." His voice softened. "I swear to be only yours." He unknotted the ties of her chemise. "Do you believe me? Do you trust me, love?"

"I don't know." She wanted to. How badly she wanted to. But what did "only yours" mean to a man like him? Did it mean marriage?

Even if it didn't, she still wanted him. She'd become that shameless, that eager to know what other women knew—the lovemaking of a man who found them desirable. And if she brought up the subject of marriage and found out that Daniel's idea of marriage was one where he kept his tarts and she waited for him to show her a drop of affection, it would ruin everything.

She didn't want to know. For once in her life, she wanted to do something reckless, without thought for the future. Something enjoyable and yes, naughty.

"At least trust me with this," he urged, dragging her chemise off her shoulders. "I'll never hurt you, love. I swear it."

The chilly air hit her bare skin as he dispensed with her chemise and then her drawers, but it barely cooled the furnace building inside her. His eyes were like silvery flames licking over her, scorching and needy.

"Christ, you're the loveliest thing I've ever seen." His hands whispered over her body as if marking her breasts and belly and hips for future caresses. "Your skin's as sleek and fine as Chinese silk. I knew it would be." He caught a lock of her hair and twined it about his fingers. "And this hair . . . do you know how many times I wanted to take it down? How many times I imagined it flowing over your naked breasts?"

The adoration in his voice made her tremble with need. "I wish you had."

His gaze shot to her, intent, earnest. "Helena, I said I'd have none of you unless you were sober and willing. The sober part I'm sure of, but the willing part you must confirm while I can still bear to let you go. I want to make love to you. Will you let me?"

The uncertainty in his eyes reassured her. It was not the look of a man jaded with women and lovemaking. It was the look of an anxious lover. And that she understood. She was feeling rather anxious herself.

She swallowed, her gaze dropping shyly to his waistcoat as she reached for the buttons. "A Naughty Man never leaves his lover standing naked while he's dressed. It is rude, you know."

He made some choked sound, and her gaze shot up to find stark need flaring in his face. "God forbid I should ever be rude to you," he rasped, brushing her fumbling hands aside to undo his waistcoat hastily.

Anticipation swirled through her, pooling in the hot, eager place between her legs, curling around her heart. This was probably sheer madness, but she didn't care. She wanted him for her own, if only for tonight.

Her mouth went dry as she watched him unveil his flagrantly male body. The last time she'd seen him nearly naked she'd been too embarrassed to look her fill, but since this might be her only chance at it, she intended to memorize every inch. The well-wrought chest with its sprinkling of dark blond hair, the taut waist, the thickly muscled thighs, and between them . . .

Oh, dear Lord in heaven. So *that* was a man's "thing." It was not at all what she'd expected. Even the sketches of Greek sculpture in the art books she pored over in secret had not prepared her for such a magnificently impudent appendage.

Curiosity momentarily overcame maidenly shyness. "Danny?"

"Yes, love," he said tensely.

"You said that your . . . that it got firm. You didn't say it stuck out." The ones in the books were tame and lay nicely between a man's thighs. *This* was anything but tame. It sprang wildly from a bed of golden, springy hair that made him seem more earthy than any hairless Greek statue.

She looked up to find him struggling vainly against laughter. With a wicked gleam in his eye, he stepped closer and caught her hand. "Haven't you ever noticed how a hound's nose lifts and sniffs the air whenever his ladylove prances by? This randy beast of mine sniffs the air whenever you're near. It's aching for you, sweetheart." Taking her by surprise, he laid her hand on his "beast," closing her fingers around his hard flesh. "But first, it needs a bit of petting."

When her gaze shot to his in alarm, he lifted his other hand to stroke her breast. "You pet me. I pet you. That's how we learn what pleases each other."

Daniel could tell he'd shocked her. Her eyes were round as saucers, and when he released her hand, she held him like he was made of glass. Though it felt bloody good having her hand on him, she was too gentle, too timid. It was like tossing a dram of water onto a blistering stone—all you got for your efforts was steam.

And Christ, was he steaming.

Hesitantly, she swept her fingers along him, and he thought he'd erupt right there. His pego moved in her hand, and she dropped it like it was a brand. "It's rather . . . large, isn't it?" she said uncertainly.

"Not too large to fit inside you, love, if that's what worries you," he growled, torn between amusement at her maidenly hesitation and the urge to force her fingers back around his John Thomas and make her wring him with her hot little hand. But that would send him off for sure. As it was, even her gaze on it was rousing him to a stiffness sure to frighten her.

It seemed to him that someone as sheltered as Helena would enjoy lovemaking more if she knew what to expect. So he strove to stand motionless while she looked him over, curiosity warring with virginal fear in her face.

When he could endure the wait no more, he caught her to him and kissed her hard. Then he lifted her in his arms and carried her back to the stall. "We've got hours for you to learn me. Now it's my turn to learn you."

The straw crunched beneath the layers of coat and linens as he laid her down on the makeshift bed. He removed his boots and hose in record haste without taking his ravenous gaze from her. Even the scent of hay and horses and leather couldn't dampen his pleasure at seeing her long-limbed body stretched out on the sheet, wearing only stockings and demi-boots, and swathed in golden lamplight.

When he knelt beside her, a shaky smile quivered on her lips. "Aren't you going to snuff the lantern?"

He stripped off her boots. "Not yet. A man would be daft to make love to you the first time in the dark, my beauty."

He reached for her garter, but she caught his hand, a look of sudden panic on her face. "No, leave them on."

"Come now, lass." He tucked one finger inside the bow of her lacy garter. "No lace allowed, remember?" he teased. When she didn't respond to his little joke, he added, "I want to see all of you."

She ducked her head. "I . . . I . . . my leg is not . . . pretty."

Tipping up her chin, he forced her to look at him. "It'll be pretty to me. Every bit of you is pretty to me."

"But—"

"Shhh," he said, laying his finger over her mouth. "I know what I want. And that's you—all of you—lying naked and open beneath me. If I can have that, naught else matters."

Keeping his gaze locked on her face, he untied her lacy garters and whisked them away. But when it came to removing her stockings, he couldn't stand not to look at her legs. First he bared her good one, sucking in a harsh breath at the sight of her lovely thigh and lovelier calf. She was a work of art, too good for the likes of him, though that wouldn't stop him from relishing every inch.

When he dragged the stocking down her left leg, he felt her stiffen. To be sure, this leg wasn't as plump as the right, and the muscles lay withered beneath the skin, but it wasn't so awful as she seemed to think, either.

"I'm sure it's the ugliest thing you've ever seen," she whispered.

He glanced up to find her wearing an expression of pitiful vulnerability, as if she half-expected, half-feared he would share her opinion. It nearly broke his heart. "No." He pointed to his John Thomas. "*This,* sweetheart, is the ugliest thing I've ever seen. Yet I wouldn't trade it for a prettier one, if such a thing was to be had."

She fixed her gaze on his pego and a hesitant smile touched her lips. "I suppose it *is* rather . . . unusual-looking."

"So is your leg—unusual but pretty in its own way, just as a man's pego can be attractive to the right person." He bent to kiss her poor maligned limb, feeling her flesh tremble beneath his lips. "Besides, both your leg and my pego have their uses, don't you think?"

She buried her fingers in his hair. "I don't know about your 'pego,'" she whispered wistfully, "but my leg is good for nothing except making me limp."

"I like your limp," he said as he kissed his way up her thigh.

"Don't be silly." Hurt glimmered in her eyes. "Now you're lying again."

"Not at all." He grinned up at her. "I like it because it makes it easier to catch you. And because it made you refuse all your suitors, leaving you to me." He positioned himself over her, nudging her legs apart, planting his hands on either side of her shoulders. "Best of all, I like it because it'll keep you from dancing with all those fine lords at balls and making me mad with jealousy." He bent his head to suck her breast, tonguing her nipple until she gasped and arched up into his mouth.

"B-but it keeps me from dancing with you as well," she stammered.

"I've never been much for dancing. This is the dance I prefer." He rubbed his John Thomas against her cleft, watching her expression grow heated and her lips part in surprise. "So tell me, love, would you like to dance the mattress jig with me?"

A shy smile spread over her delicate features. "Yes."

She dug her fingernails into his muscles. "Oh, yes, Danny. I'm yours tonight."

Not just tonight, not if he had anything to say about it.

So he set about making her need him as much as he needed her. He found all her tender spots, kissing the hollow of her throat, the sweet little dip in her collarbone, her nipples . . . all the parts of her that deserved kissing and had never got it. Every murmur she made fired his need, every gasp of discovery heightened his pleasure. Only when he had her trembling and begging and pressing her darling cunny instinctively against him did he enter her.

He tried to do it gently, but Jesus Christ, she felt good—warm and tight and so wet. And his, all his. The fierce possessiveness he felt when he gazed down at her astonished him. And when he came to the barrier of her innocence, it humbled him to think that she would give herself to him, the highwayman's bastard, when she could have other, better men if she wanted.

That thought gave him pause. If he took her now, he'd ruin her for any of them.

"Helena," he whispered, "listen to me."

She gazed up at him, her face flushed, angelic and wanton all in one. "What is it, Danny?"

"Are you sure this is what you want?"

"Yes," she breathed, without a moment's hesitation. Sliding her fingers down his chest to his waist, she latched on to him, trying to pull him into her, even though her inner muscles tensed with her fear. "I want to be a Naughty Lady. I want to be *your* Naughty Lady."

He swelled uncontrollably within her. To hell with those other, better men. None of them could possibly want her in their lives as badly as he did. "Then you damned well will be."

He could make her happy—he was sure of it. Once this nightmare with her sister was over, he *would* make her happy, no matter what it required. He'd make this a foretaste of what they could have together. He'd take precautions this first time, but he'd have her all the same.

Seizing her mouth, he kissed her hot and long, until he could feel her muscles relax around his St. Peter. Then he plunged in deep, shattering her innocence with one controlled thrust. She cried out against his mouth, and he swallowed her cries, soothed her with kisses as he tried to ease his guilt at having hurt her, however necessary it might have been.

"That's the worst of it," he murmured, trying to hold still, clenching his muscles against the urge to drive into her again. "It'll be better now, love, I promise. Just let me show you. Relax."

"It's not so bad," she whispered. When he drew back to stare at her, she managed a tremulous smile. "I've had much worse pain, you know. So go on, Danny, I can take it."

His heart lurched in his chest. His darling lass had indeed had a great deal of pain in her lifetime, physical and otherwise. From her expression, she clearly expected the rest of this to be at best uncomfortable.

"There'll be no more pain for you," he vowed. "Not ever. I won't ever let you hurt again."

Then he began to move, clamping down on his ravening lust so he could keep his strokes slow and shallow. But she threw herself wildly into every kiss, her lips seeking his, her fingers digging into his arms. And before he knew it, he was driving into her lush heat with deeper, harder thrusts, trying to immerse himself in her secrets, in the soft mystery that was Helena. She was wet and warm and giving . . . He lost himself in her so completely it frightened him. He'd never lost himself in a woman before, never been so overwhelmed by need that he feared reaching his release before he could pull out. His craving for Helena had grown from the day he'd met her, and now it was so wild and urgent he'd perish if he couldn't satisfy at least some of it.

First, however, he'd satisfy hers.

He reached down between their straining bodies, searching out the place they were joined, finding her pleasure spot and fondling it. Tearing her mouth from his, she moaned, "Oh . . . Danny . . . yes, dear Lord, yes . . . like that . . . yes . . ."

Her litany poured over him, flooded him with power. They were one force, straining together, moving toward a fulfillment he sensed he'd never known. And when she convulsed around him, it drove him over the edge into the insanity that was the "little death." With a hoarse cry that echoed her own, he jerked out and spent himself, his own need exploding.

As he drifted back to consciousness, the purest contentment he'd ever known stole over him. This was where he belonged, with her, beside her, around her. Right now she might only want him when he coaxed her like this, when he tempted her with pleasures beyond her ken. But he'd make her want him for more. He'd make her want to keep him.

Because this was a woman he fully intended to keep.

Chapter 16

'Tis of a brave young highwayman this story I will tell
His name was Willie Brennan and in Ireland
he did dwell
It was on the Kilwood Mountain he commenced
his wild career
And many a wealthy nobleman before him
shook with fear.

"Brennan on the Moor,"
anonymous Irish ballad about a real-life Irish highwayman

Helena lay in Daniel's arms spoon fashion, filled with a sweet lassitude. His breath riffled her hair, and his hand gently stroked her belly. She couldn't remember when she'd felt so safe, so protected . . . so wanted.

Glancing idly down at his hand, she caught sight of the scarlet smear on her thighs. Her virgin blood, a stark reminder of the enormity of what she'd just done.

She waited for shame to assault her, but there was nothing but the warm aftermath of pleasure and the exultation of having known him intimately. Apparently Rosalind wasn't the only one in the family with a wicked streak.

"Daniel?" she whispered.

"Yes, love."

"Have you ever . . . that is . . . am I your first virgin?"

He chuckled and pressed a kiss to her shoulder. "Most assuredly my first virgin. My first lady of rank, in fact." He paused. "And my last, too, if I have anything to say about it."

Her pulse quickened. "Wh-what do you mean?"

"I intend to marry you, lass."

A treacherous thrill swept through her before she could tamp it down. She turned onto her back to stare up into his face. The lamplight left half of it in shadow, reminding her that only half of him was honest gentleman. The other half was wicked rascal, through and through.

But his eyes looked perfectly sincere as they fixed on her face. "I want to marry you, Helena, if you'll have me."

Hope and desire and some emotion she'd always carefully squelched blossomed in her heart. Then it wilted as her sense of fairness overtook it. "You don't have to marry me just because you ruined me. I knew what I was doing. I made a conscious choice to become your . . . your lover."

He bent his head to brush his lips across her cheek. "And I'm making a conscious choice to marry you." A teasing light flickered in his eyes. "Besides, you weren't the only one ruined, y'know. What about me? Now that you've taken advantage of me, aren't you going to do the right thing?"

She snorted. "If *men* were ruined the first time they made love, you'd have been married back when you were . . . what, nineteen or twenty?"

He winced. "I'm not sure you want to know."

"Oh, but I do. If you mean to marry me, I should hear what I'm getting into. So how old were you?"

A sigh whiffled out of him. "Fourteen."

"Fourteen! Lord, you started your oat sowing early, didn't you?"

"I had a bit of help," he grumbled. "Crouch and the others decided it was time I bedded my first woman, so they took me to a Hastings inn and paid for a tart for me. That started me on the road to perdition."

"A road you've been paving with bad intentions ever since, I expect." She knew she sounded jealous, but that was because she was. She couldn't help it.

He cupped her cheek, his expression suddenly earnest. "I'll not lie to you, Helena. I've had a wild life—and yes, quite a few women in my bed. But I'm not a reckless young fool anymore, and I've been thinking I'd like to settle down with a wife."

"Is that what you were doing at your lodgings when I went there?" she asked archly. "Auditioning women for the role?"

"Christ," he growled, "you'll never let me forget that, will you?"

"It was rather unforgettable."

"For you, p'raps, but I'd have forgotten it instantly if not for you bringing it up all the time." He fixed his gaze on her lips and lowered his voice. "Whereas I know I'll never forget one minute of our lovemaking tonight.

You're dancing around the subject, love, but I won't let you avoid it. I want to know—will you marry me?"

She bit back her instinctive "yes." Part of her would like nothing more. Daniel was the first man who'd taken her for what she was, who'd noticed her advantages but accepted her flaws, too. He was the first to think it worth his while to coax her from behind her aloof shield.

But charming women was his peculiar talent—and that gave her pause. Could she handle marriage to a man who'd spent half of his life bedding women ten times more experienced in the sensual arts than she? What if he grew bored with her and wanted to return to his "wild life"? She'd never live through that. She just knew she wouldn't.

Her silence made him scowl. "I know I'm beneath you," he said, "and that you could probably do better, but all the same—"

"You're not beneath me," she protested, "not in any sense that counts. And it's not as if my bloodlines are substantially superior to yours. Papa used treachery to get his title, and Mama was an actress." She laid her hand over his. "As for doing better, you're all I could want in a man."

He let out a long breath. "I can support you, too, y'know. P'raps not as richly as you're used to, but certainly not so poorly as to make life difficult. In time, when my business is more secure, we might live quite nicely indeed." The corner of his mouth quirked up. "I'll even move out of St. Giles for you."

"I'm afraid I'd make that a condition of marriage," she quipped. Her humor faded. "But that's not what concerns me."

"Then what is it, lass?" He swept his hand over her

shoulder, then down her arm to her hip, where he rested it possessively.

She couldn't meet his eyes. Instead, she stared at his chest, at the whorl of hair around one flat nipple. "*Why* do you want to marry me, Danny?"

His hand jerked on her hip. "It's not for that dowry Griff gave you, if that's what you're thinking."

At his defensive tone, she glanced up. For once, he looked vulnerable, wary. She brushed his stubbled jaw with her fingers. "I know that."

"I don't need Griff's money. Or yours." His face was stiff with pride. "In fact, I'll tell him to keep it."

"You will not!" she protested. When he lifted an eyebrow, she added, "We can use it, for heaven's sake. And Griff owes it to both of us, after the way he made you deceive me last summer."

He relaxed, a smile tugging at his lips. "True enough." He traced a circle on her hip with his thumb. "Are you saying you'll marry me?"

"I-I don't know. You haven't answered my question. About why you want me to."

He looked guarded. "Why does anybody marry? For companionship, for affection . . ." Desire flickered in his gaze as he caressed her hip. "For lovemaking."

For love? she thought, but didn't say it. She didn't want him just speaking the words to secure her, the way her former fiancé had done. Besides, it ought to be enough that he offered marriage, which she certainly hadn't expected.

But it wasn't.

She managed a shaky laugh. "You don't need marriage to sanction your lovemaking, from what you've told me."

"Ah, but I'd need marriage to sanction lovemaking with *you*, wouldn't I? I think I know you well enough to know that." He added softly, "I've never asked a woman to marry me before, Helena. That should tell you how badly I want you in my life. I've never wanted a woman as much as I want you. Tonight and beyond. For good."

She turned away to hide her face, shifting onto her side and tucking her hands up under her head. "It's understandable that you might . . . feel that way just now . . . when we've been forced to be in such close company . . . and . . ." *And when I'm such a novelty—your first conquest of a gentlewoman.*

"I know my own mind, Helena."

"Or that you might feel obliged to marry me because—"

"I don't feel 'obliged' to marry you, damn it." He turned her back to face him, his eyes flashing fury. "Is it really so hard for you to believe a man might simply want you?"

"Yes!" The word tore from her before she could stop it. As she lay there fighting back tears, she realized it was what she truly felt. "Yes, it *is* hard to believe. No other man has done so. No other man has looked at me and seen anything but a tart-tongued spinster with a distasteful deformity. And you are a man who routinely beds beautiful women, who's used to—"

"That's what troubles you, isn't it? All those other women." His anger had faded as she spoke, and now he lifted his hand to brush away her tears. "You're more beautiful to me than any of them ever were. Not a single one of them held my interest for more than a night."

He flashed her a wry smile. "To be honest, I never held theirs for more than that, either. They liked me for the money or the moment's pleasure, and one or two liked the idea of a dalliance with the famous Wild Danny Brennan's bastard. They were a fun lot, but none of them cared about *me*. Because I knew that, bedding them was naught but an entertainment. And a lonely business, too, when all was said and done."

He tipped her chin up, forcing her to look at him. "But with you it's different, because you look at me and see Daniel Brennan, not my da or my purse or even my pego. That's why our lovemaking is so much more. It's what passion should be, what I've never had from it before—two bodies as one, two hearts entwined, a great glorious joining of two people who care for each other. When I can have that, why should I want any other woman?"

Her heart beat triple-time as she stared up into his dear face. He did have such a talent for sweet words, and she wanted so badly to believe him. If not for his vast experience with women, she might not be balking.

"You needn't give me an answer now, love," he whispered. "Just give me time to prove that I mean what I say, that I intend to be faithful to you. Let me court you properly. All I need is the hope of a future with you and your promise that you'll consider my offer."

"All right," she whispered back, feeling her heart lift as she said the words. "All right, Danny." *My love.*

She caught her breath. Could she have been so reckless as to fall in love with the rascal?

Any woman would. He was brave and strong, yet so tender. She couldn't forget how he'd hovered protectively over her this afternoon, yet readily asked for her help, assuming she was perfectly capable of holding Wallace at bay with a pistol.

Then there were his wicked ways—his teasing and his seductions and his daring. They enticed her beyond endurance. He dared to say what she'd always thought, to do what she'd always wanted to do, to be shocking in ways she'd only imagined in the dead of night.

That was precisely why allowing herself to fall in love

with him would be utter madness. She'd given her heart to Farnsworth and had lived to regret it dearly when he'd betrayed her.

Though she didn't believe Daniel would betray her, she wasn't ready to let down her guard, either. Still, she didn't resist when Daniel kissed her long and deep, as if to promise that if she'd just trust him, he'd make it worth her while.

Then he lay back and pulled her into his arms. "Come, lass, we'd best get some sleep."

"I can't sleep yet," she said, extricating herself from his arms. "I wish to wash off . . . well . . . the blood. You know."

He groaned. "What an oaf I am. I didn't even think of it. But then, I'm not used to virgins." Dragging the blanket up to his waist, he added, "Go on, but don't be long. Morning'll come all too soon."

She bent to give him a swift kiss, then gathered up her chemise and pulled it over her head. Taking the lamp with her, she left the stall. She did wish to wash herself, but that was not her only reason for leaving the bed. Excitement thrummed through her like the aftermath of some delightful drug, and she knew she would never be able to lie still, much less sleep. After all they'd said, she had a great deal to think on. And she always did her best thinking with a pencil or paintbrush in hand.

Outside by the pump, she shivered in the frigid air. The water was dreadfully cold, so she finished her ablutions quickly, praying that their young host did not take this inopportune moment to come out. Then she reentered the barn and pulled on her pelisse for warmth. Finding their saddlebags, she removed her sketch pad and pencil, then returned to the stall.

Daniel was already asleep. She was not terribly surprised. It had been a taxing day for both of them, more so for him because of driving the gig and fighting with Mr. Wallace. Settling herself on the straw at his feet, she hooked the lamp where the light would fall partly on her sketch pad and partly on him. Then she carefully stretched her legs out beside him and began to sketch.

The blanket covered his muscled thighs and the naughty appendage between them, but his chest and arms were plainly visible as he lay on his back with his hands tucked under his head. She sketched his body first, the sculpted chest and the shoulders roped with muscle. Later she would add the tufts of hair under his arms and the thick sprinkling of it on his chest that narrowed down to the shadowy navel.

But first, she'd do his face. He truly had an artist's dream of a face. Not the classic sort of handsome, of course, but the sort that would make any viewer stop and remark upon the hints of character and struggle in it.

She laid down her pencil. He did possess a great deal of character. She was probably being foolish, balking at accepting his proposal. Even if he did go to a tart once in a while after they were married, would it matter so much?

Pain constricted her throat. Yes, it would. It would break her heart. And she had spent so many years protecting that bruised organ that she found it hard to simply hand it over to someone now.

He said he would be faithful, and she wanted to believe him. Perhaps she would feel better in a more conventional situation, where they could come to know each other at a leisurely pace. Where she could determine that their unusual circumstances weren't all that prompted him to marry her. Once they'd rescued Juliet they could spend time together, and that would make her more easy about marriage.

Juliet. She groaned. She'd completely forgotten about Juliet. Tonight Daniel had created a cocoon for them where time halted, and she'd been perfectly happy to lie wrapped up with him in it. But in the morning, all of that would end, and they'd be back to dealing with Crouch and his cronies.

Poor Danny, to be raised by a man like Crouch. How had that come to be? Had he even known his parents at all, the ones who were hanged? She had a thousand questions for him, a thousand things she wanted to know before she gave her life and future into his keeping. But for now, it was enough just to be here with him in their cozy nest.

She turned back to sketching. She'd sketched out his entire upper body and was just beginning to put in shadow and refine shapes when she looked up from her sketch to find him staring at her. "Oh," she said, startled, "I didn't mean to wake you." He dropped his hands from behind his head, and she said, "Don't do that! Don't move!"

"Why? What are you sketching?"

"You asleep." At his grin, she added, "Though now that you're awake, I'll have to change it to you looking very pleased with yourself."

He laid his hand on her calf beneath the pelisse, then slid it slowly, sensually up to her knee. "I *am* pleased with myself."

"Are you?" She returned to sketching him, wanting to get further along before he altered his pose any more.

"What man wouldn't be pleased to find himself being sketched by a beautiful, half-naked woman?" He opened her pelisse, exposing her thinly clad form to his ravenous gaze. The dark glitter in his eyes made her suddenly conscious of the nearly transparent chemise and the lamplight falling on her barely concealed breasts.

She wished she could capture that look of his—the one that said, *I want you.* The one that always shot her through with hunger and need. She concentrated on her sketch, feeling the inevitable blush rise beneath her skin. "I thought you wanted to sleep."

"I did. I take it you didn't."

"I couldn't."

"Dare I hope it's because you're considering my proposal?"

"Yes." She angled a shy glance up at him. "Although I was also . . . well, wondering about some things, too."

He turned his face just enough to put it fully in shadow. "Like what?"

"You spoke of Crouch taking you to your first . . . fancy woman at fourteen. You went to live with him when you were nine, is that right?"

"That's right." His voice was decidedly wary.

"And how old were you when you went to the workhouse?"

"Why?"

"I just want to know. I want to know all about you. Should that surprise you?"

"I s'pose not." He sighed. "I was six, I think. I don't remember much about that first day, just that it was bitter cold and I was hungry. But then, I was always hungry after my parents were hanged. I was shuffled from relative to relative—nobody wanted me. They all feared my bad blood."

"Oh, Daniel," she whispered, dropping her pencil. "That's awful."

He shrugged. "The last one fobbed me off on the parish, and I was sent to the workhouse in Maldon. That's in Essex, where I was born."

"So you lived there three years until Crouch found you?"

"Yes. He happened to be in Maldon buying a cutter, and he needed an extra body to sail it back to Sussex. So he came to the workhouse and picked me out, paid them good money for me. I was large for my age, large enough anyway for what he wanted—someone to scurry up and down rigging—and I expect that Crouch found it amusing to have Wild Danny Brennan's son join his gang."

"The owners of the workhouse knew who your parents were? They told him?"

"Yes," he said tersely.

"I suppose they thought nothing of sending you off with a smuggler," she said, trying to imagine being sold like so much chattel. "Even though you were only a child."

"They did me a favor, to be honest. Crouch treated me ten times better than the workhouse. Before I met Griff, I thought Jolly Roger the finest man I knew, because of how he took me in." He shifted to lay on his side. "That's why it's so hard to think of him doing something like this—kidnapping Juliet. He's a rascal, to be sure, but except for that fight between him and Griff, I never thought him a villain. This isn't like him a'tall."

"I suppose he must have *some* goodness in him to take an orphan of nine into his care." She played idly with her pencil. "What about your parents? Do you remember anything about them?"

A wild, bleak yearning touched his rough features. "A bit. I have one snatch of memory that never leaves me. Mother used to always kiss the tip of my nose when she put me to bed. 'There's a brave boy,' she'd say. 'Brave as your da.' " His face hardened. "Yes, he was the bravest man alive, wasn't he? Tangling my mother in his reckless adventures, taking her to the gallows with him, not caring what might happen to his own son—that was right brave of him. Shows a great nobility of character, don't you think?"

His voice blew like a frigid wind, as if the pain were so great that he could only speak of it in that cold, dead tone. It made her heart ache to realize how much he had suffered. "It was his fault that your mother was hanged?"

"Partly. She rode with him the night they were captured, y'see. But it wasn't his fault she was caught. I had an uncle with a part in that."

"An uncle?"

"My mother's brother. He's the one who betrayed my parents to the soldiers. I didn't even know about it until a few years ago, when I went searching for information about my family. After I heard what my uncle did, I wanted to track him down and kill him with my bare hands." Hot fury flashed in his face, reminding her for a moment of the murderous rage he'd shown toward Mr. Wallace.

Suddenly it faded, and he sighed. "But he'd drowned himself shortly after my parents were hanged. I s'pose he couldn't live with what he'd done."

"Oh, Danny," she whispered, unable to keep the pity from her voice.

He glanced up and stiffened. "That's my family in a nutshell. Quite a band of rogues, wouldn't you say?"

She fumbled for an answer that would soothe his injured pride. "Well, you've beaten me, but not by much."

"What d'you mean?" he asked warily.

"I have a scoundrel father, too, remember? I don't have any scoundrel uncles, however, so your scoundrel relatives outnumber mine, two to one."

He stared at her a long moment. Then a faint smile touched his lips. "If you count my mother, it's three to one. But mine are all dead, and yours is still alive making trouble. I'd think one live relative beats out any number of dead ones."

"Probably." She shook her head and smiled sadly. "Oh, Danny, think of our poor children. We might as well hand them pistols and teach them deceit from birth, since their bloodlines will surely send them in that direction."

He leaned forward, his eyes warming. "You give me hope, love, by speaking of children. Though I do want a better life for any child of mine. Let's pray they take after you and your mother."

"I wouldn't mind so much if they took after you," she said shyly. "At least a little."

He chuckled. "So you don't think I'm such a devil after all, do you?"

"I didn't say that," she teased. "But every child should have a bit of the devil in him."

Catching her by surprise, he rose up on his knees to snatch her sketch pad, then toss it aside. "This particular devil is thinking he ought to live up to his image. Especially with a lass like you tempting him to devilment." The blanket fell to reveal his "pego," which seemed to thicken before her very eyes.

Her mouth went dry and desire pooled between her legs, despite the faint soreness there. "I have not yet accepted your proposal of marriage, remember?" she said, a warning both for herself and him.

It did not deter him in the least from sliding her pelisse off her shoulders. "Ah, but you will, love. You will."

Young Seth glanced out the window of his house. At last: the light was out in the barn. He slipped out and crossed to the barn door. Opening it soundlessly, he paused to listen, but could hear nothing except snoring. Although it was pitch dark inside, he figured he could find the horse by the sounds of its nickering and shifting in the stall.

For a moment, he reconsidered his plan. Mr. Brennan was a giant, he was, and could beat him senseless if he chose. Still, Mrs. Brennan was a nice lady, and he felt sure she wouldn't let the giant beat him. Besides, he was only borrowing their horse, not stealing it, and he'd have it back long before morn. They'd never even know he took it.

And when would he have a chance like this again—silver in his pocket and his parents gone? A horse standing at the ready? It was perfect! Once Meg saw him swagger like a man into her parents' taproom, order his own ale, and pay for it with his own blunt, she'd see at once that he wasn't the mere boy she took him for. She wouldn't be so quick to laugh at him the next time he tried to kiss her behind the inn.

He moved with utter stealth, grabbing the saddle and leading the mare from the barn, then closing the door an inch at a time behind them. As soon as he'd saddled the horse and was on the road to Sedlescombe, his mind filled with thoughts of lovely Meg's red mouth. The moon was bright enough to see by, so he scarcely had to guide the horse along the tiny road from the farm.

He felt a twinge of guilt when he reached the main road to Sedlescombe and thought of his parents. His mother, who'd recently joined the Wesleyans, would certainly disapprove of him spending good silver to drink at the taproom when it could be better spent on the farm. Still, he hadn't taken all the money—just enough to impress Meg and have a drink or two. The rest was for his parents, who'd never know how much Mr. Brennan had given him anyway. He forgot his guilt as dreams of kissing sweet Meg resurfaced.

He was nearing the bridge over the Brede River into Sedlescombe when two hulking shapes appeared as if from nowhere, and a voice called out, "Stand to!"

Terror splintered his soft thoughts. Highwaymen? And so close to Sedlescombe? He'd heard tales of highwaymen from Father, but none from recent years and certainly none brave enough to attack within shouting distance of town. He jerked the horse around, meaning to flee, but a loud whistle pierced the night, freezing the horse so that it refused to budge no matter how much he urged it.

Rough hands pulled him off and pinned his arms behind his back. One of the black shapes in front of him lit a lantern, then shoved it up to his face. Beyond the lantern, he could make out only glittering eyes and a sullen mouth.

"Who are you, boy?" the sullen mouth demanded. "And where'd you get this horse?"

"I . . . I . . ."

"Speak up!" the man growled, and gestured beyond him to Seth's captor, who twisted his arm hard behind his back and made him cry out. "This is *my* horse you've stolen—"

"I didn't steal it! It was them what stole it!" he burst out, then cursed his quick tongue when a calculating smile twisted the man's lips.

"Them? A big man and a crippled woman? Is that who you took it from?"

"I-I didn't take it from them. I just . . . borrowed it. I swear!"

"And where are they now?" the man asked.

He swallowed. The last thing he wanted was to lead this mean bastard to his house, but he didn't want to be beaten for borrowing a horse, neither. Or worse yet, taken to the gallows. Though he'd never have guessed the Brennans were thieves, he did remember how Mr. Brennan had been opening the door to the house when Seth had happened upon them. He wasn't about to pay for *their* crimes.

"I didn't know they stole it, or I would never have let them stay in our barn."

"Are they still in your barn?" the man demanded.

He hesitated, then nodded. "They're sleepin'."

"Do they know you're out with the horse?"

"No. I . . . I didn't mean to stay out long." He prayed that the man and his companions didn't find the silver in his pockets. That was probably stolen as well, but no matter who the blunt had belonged to before, it was his now.

"Tell me where they are, where your barn is."

Seth explained how to find the road to the farm.

The lantern was suddenly snuffed, and the man holding it spoke to someone lurking in the shadows to Seth's right. "You heard that. Now go tell Crouch's man Seward we've found them, and bring him back here. He says he won't pay unless he sees Danny Brennan in the flesh. Go on, and be quick about it."

Shame engulfed Seth. He'd heard the name Crouch before; this was not about stealing a horse, to be sure. This was some other dark work, having to do with the smugglers. And damnation if he hadn't just turned over his hapless guests to them.

Chapter 17

When I was awakened between six and seven
The guards were all around me in numbers
odd and even.
"Whiskey in the Jar,"
anonymous Irish ballad

In his dream, Daniel was in the workhouse again, scrabbling with the others for a spoonful of extra porridge. One of the older boys kicked him down, then stood on his chest, poking him in the neck with a fork. "Go 'way," Daniel mumbled and pushed against the fork. His hand met a blade of cold steel. That brought him abruptly awake to find a sword pressed to his neck.

Fighting off the fog of sleep, he blinked his eyes and lifted them to the man holding the sword. Wallace, with his foot planted firmly on Daniel's chest. Bloody hell. So much for putting the fear of God into the son of a bitch. And how had he found them so quickly? Judging from the dim light in the stall, it was barely dawn.

Wallace looked damned pleased with himself as he dug his heel into Daniel's chest. "How does it feel to have the boot on the other foot, Danny Boy? Or shall we say, on the other chest?"

Daniel felt a stirring next to him and remembered with horror that Helena was with him. Though he couldn't turn his head to look at her, he could see out of the corner of his eye that her naked body still lay covered by the blanket. Thank God.

"Take me if you want, Wallace, but leave my wife be. She's got naught to do with this."

"Danny?" Helena shot up next to him, clutching the blanket to her chest. "Mr. Wallace! Take that sword away! Don't you dare hurt him!"

"That's enough, Wallace," came a vaguely familiar voice from beyond the stall. "You've had your fun. Now take your money and be off with you—you and your scurvy lot."

Wallace hesitated before apparently deciding that money was far more useful than a petty revenge. But before he took his foot off Daniel's chest, he dragged the blade along Daniel's neck just hard enough to score it. Daniel ignored the bite of steel, the blood trickling down his throat, and as soon as Wallace backed out of the stall, he lunged for his pistol.

His hand froze on it as the unmistakable sound of another pistol being cocked echoed in the barn.

"I wouldn't do that, Danny, if I were you," came that familiar voice again, much nearer this time. "Move your hand away from the pistol. I shouldn't like to shoot you."

With a heavy sigh, Daniel turned his head to stare up into the face of Jack Seward. Crouch's oldest friend and cohort.

Though Jack kept his pistol cocked and ready, he grinned down at Daniel without an ounce of hostility. "It's been a long time, Danny Boy. You're looking well."

"I'd be looking a lot better if you weren't aiming that thing at me."

"Pass yours over, and I won't have to shoot you, will I?"

Anger mingled with a softer emotion in Daniel's breast. Jack might be an aging rogue still in service to a scoundrel, but he'd also been a good friend once. Indeed, he'd been the person who'd most looked after Daniel all those years ago.

"Listen, Jack," Daniel said. "I don't know what you're about or why you're in league with a whoreson like Wallace, but I know you'd never kill me."

"'Tis true, old friend." Jack waved the pistol toward Daniel's hand and smiled, though it was a sad sort of mirth. "And you wouldn't use that on me, neither, would you?" When Daniel didn't answer, he added, "Shove it over here, Danny Boy. I mightn't have the heart to kill you, but I wouldn't hesitate to shoot your hand off."

That much Daniel suspected was true. Nor did he need Helena's anxious voice saying, "Daniel, please do as he says," to convince him to comply.

As soon as Jack had picked up the pistol, he uncocked his own and slid it into his overcoat pocket. "Sorry to frighten you, ma'am," he told Helena. "The name's Jack Seward. Me and Danny go back a long ways."

"My association with him is more recent," she said evenly, "but I do appreciate your not shooting my husband."

Daniel noted with approval that she'd neglected to give her name. He might be able to negotiate her freedom if Crouch and his men didn't know who she was. He wasn't sure how much they knew about Griff's new family. He wasn't even sure if they realized why he and Helena were in Sussex in the first place.

Sitting up, he slid his arm about her waist and played dumb. "What's all this about, Jack? My wife and I come down here to do a bit of trading, minding our own business. Suddenly you chaps show up with pistols and swords. What d'you want with us? We've done naught to warrant it."

"Naught, eh? Then why was this in your pocket?" Jack pulled two objects from inside his coat and waved them at Daniel: the miniature of Juliet and the sketch of Pryce.

Daniel groaned.

"I may be getting gray, m'boy, but I ain't stupid. It's plain why you're here. I'm just not sure how you learned of it. It was s'posed to be taken for an elopement by the girl's family. And Crouch told Pryce to take great care you didn't hear of it. Pryce was s'posed to send that ransom note direct to Knighton."

With a squeeze, Daniel cautioned Helena to silence. "All the same, I found out."

"So you planned to play the hero and get her back without paying, eh?" When Daniel said nothing, he chuckled. "Well, it's too late for that. Get up, Danny Boy—you're coming with us, both of you."

Daniel's arm tightened about Helena's waist. "There's no need to drag my wife into this. You can leave her here."

"You know damned well I'm not leaving nobody to go running to Knighton telling him that Crouch is behind this. And if you hadn't wanted her to be part of it, you shouldn't have brought her."

Daniel groaned. Unfortunately, Jack was right. He should never have brought her, no matter how much she'd complained. But he'd thought it was an elopement, damn it!

"You know we won't hurt her," Jack added. "We don't hurt women."

"No, you only kidnap them," Daniel snapped.

Jack shrugged. "When there's a great deal of money in it, yes. But I swear on my honor none of us will hurt you or your wife, m'boy. Not if you behave yourselves." Jack gestured behind him. "Now come on, I ain't got all day."

Helena clutched the blanket closer to her chest. "Please, would you be so good as to give us some privacy so we can dress?"

Jack hesitated, glancing from her to Daniel, then scouring the stall as if looking for weapons. "I s'pose I can manage that," he surprised Daniel by conceding. "But five minutes and no more, d'you hear?"

"Thank you," Helena said. "And if you'd kindly give us our clothes—"

"Polite little thing, ain't she?" Jack grumbled to Daniel. "All right, ma'am." He motioned to someone behind him and the clothes were brought to him. He threw them inside. "Five minutes, remember." Then he swung the stall door shut.

The second it was closed, Daniel searched his trouser pockets for his penknife. Unsurprisingly, it had been removed. Scowling, he stood and jerked on his drawers and trousers.

Helena stood up as well. "Danny?" When he glanced at her, she spotted the scratch on his neck. "Why, you're bleeding!" She stepped up to him and used one corner of the sheet to dab at his neck. "That wretched Wallace. I wish I'd shot him while I had the chance."

Her vehemence amused him. "Or hit him hard enough to kill him. I'll have to buy you a bigger cane."

"That's not funny." Her hand stilled on his neck, and she lowered her voice. "What do you think they'll do with us?"

"I don't know," he said truthfully. "Crouch won't like it that I'm involved, though if he learns who *you* are . . . That'll only make things worse, give him two Knighton relations to ransom. Let's keep your identity secret, all right?"

"But Pryce will recognize me," she pointed out.

He sighed. "I forgot about that. Still, there's no point in tipping our hand any sooner than necessary, so let's hide it as long as we can."

She nodded, but she couldn't quite hide her fright, and something caught in his chest at the sight of it. Cupping her face in his hands, he planted a swift kiss on her lips. "Don't worry yourself, love. It'll be all right, I swear. Somehow we'll get out of this. We may just have to sit tight until Griff sends the ransom, though it plagues me to think of Crouch profiting from this treachery. Still, I don't believe he or his men will hurt us as long as Griff pays what they ask." Not if he had anything to say about it.

"I believe you, Danny. I do trust you, you know."

The faith shining in her eyes made his chest hurt. He only wished he could be sure he warranted it.

"Hurry up in there," Jack called out.

"Stubble it, Jack," Daniel replied. "You damned near scared my wife to death, and I'm reassuring her that you won't hurt her none."

"I already told you I wouldn't," Jack grumbled, though he made no move to come back in the stall.

They dressed quickly. Picking up her sketch pad and pencil, Helena glanced at Daniel. "I don't suppose they'll let me take this."

"I imagine not."

With grim determination, she opened the pad and tore out the sketch of him, then folded it up and stuffed it into her pelisse pocket along with her pencil. When he chuckled, she stalked past him. "Don't you be getting a swelled head. I merely hate to see some of my finest work lost."

"And here I was thinking you were starting to feel a certain affection for me, lass," he teased.

She paused at the stall door to cast him an earnest glance. "Oh, Danny, I am. Promise me you won't do anything to get yourself killed."

Her concern warmed him, taking the edge off the chill of their capture. "You needn't worry about me," he said as he caught her to him. "I've got no inclination to be feeding the worms just yet."

He kissed her, not sure if he'd get the chance again anytime soon and needing to reassure her, to reassure himself, that all would be well. For a moment he forgot where they were, lost in Helena's sweet mouth clinging to his with desperate urgency.

"Time's up," Jack's voice rang out over the stall door, and they broke apart.

"Ready, love?" Daniel whispered and offered her his arm.

She took it, smiling faintly. "I'm ready for anything as long as you're with me."

Christ, he hoped her faith in him was not misplaced. If he failed her and Juliet, he'd never forgive himself.

When they moved into the barn, Jack's men were milling about. A couple he recognized, but the other five were strangers. They eyed him with blatant curiosity, making him wonder what Crouch had been telling them all these years about his former lieutenant who'd run off to London to make his fortune with Griff Knighton.

Young Seth was also there, sitting on a bale of hay, looking sullen and wary and guilty as the devil. As soon as he saw them enter, he jumped to his feet and came toward them carrying a walking stick.

"Oh, Mrs. Brennan, they haven't hurt you, have they? If I'd known the horse didn't belong to you, I would never have borrowed it and taken it to town. I didn't mean to bring them here. I swear I didn't!"

Daniel scowled. So that's how Wallace had found them. If he ever got out of this, he'd take that damned fool lad over his knee.

"It's all right, Seth," Helena answered. "You didn't know."

Seth held the walking stick out to Helena. "I . . . um . . . thought you could use this. It was my grandfather's. I dug it out of an old chest."

"Are you sure your parents would approve?" Helena responded gently.

"Please take it," Seth said. "It's the least I can do after I've . . . caused you so much trouble."

Helena hesitated, then accepted the cane. "Thank you."

"Are we carrying the boy with us, too?" one of Jack's men asked, jerking his thumb toward Seth.

Seth's eyes widened in clear fright.

"Don't be absurd," Helena snapped before Jack could answer. "He has nothing to do with any of it. He merely let us sleep in his barn. Besides, his parents are returning today, and they'll call in the constable if they find him gone. He doesn't know what this is all about, so what can he possibly do?"

Jack considered that a moment, then turned to Seth with a grim expression. "Now you listen to me, boy. You've heard of Jolly Roger Crouch, haven't you?"

Seth bobbed his head.

"Then you know he eats boys like you for breakfast. So you'd best keep your tongue in your head if you don't want it sliced off."

Daniel snorted. Jack had never sliced off anybody's tongue in his life.

"And if you're not worried for yourself, then you'd best be worried for your parents," Jack added. "We know where you live, remember."

"Oh, you can't be hurting my parents!" Seth cried. "They're good people, and they've naught to do with this."

"You just make sure it stays that way, d'you hear?" Jack took one look at the boy's now sickly pallor and rolled his eyes. Removing his purse from his coat, he counted out some silver. "Now then, you helped us find Danny Boy, and we do remember our friends. So take this. For your help and your silence."

"Th-thank you," Seth whispered and took the silver, though he shot Helena an apologetic glance as he did so.

Daniel felt Helena's hand on his arm relax, and he gritted his teeth. It would've served the lad right if Jack *had* taken him. Then again, Daniel didn't need to be worrying about the boy as well. Bad enough that Helena was mixed up in it.

When Jack herded them out of the barn, Daniel was surprised to see a coach-and-six awaiting them. "Traveling in style these days, are you?" he told Jack.

"Better than putting you on a mount alone," Jack answered. "Though I don't suppose you'd run off and leave your wife behind."

"No." And that was the worst part. Even if he could escape Jack's guard of seven men, he couldn't manage it with Helena at his side. Which meant there wasn't much he could do to get them out of this just now.

"I couldn't believe it when Wallace said you'd married," Jack went on as he accompanied Daniel and Helena to the coach. He eyed Helena askance. "Given your habits with women, I figured he was wrong. Before I heard her talk, I thought for sure she was just one of your . . . well, you know—"

"Strumpets?" Helena said in outrage. "You thought I was a strumpet?"

Jack blinked at her forthright manner. "I didn't mean nothing by it, ma'am. But you have to admit that you weren't even wearing nightclothes . . . and Danny here . . ." He shot Daniel a helpless glance.

"Don't look at me," Daniel said. "You were the one stupid enough to insult her."

"I only meant that I didn't expect any woman in *Danny's* bed to be respectable. That is—"

"It's perfectly clear what you meant," Helena snapped. "You, sir, are no gentleman."

Daniel couldn't help laughing. "I doubt that'll work any better on him, lass, than it does on me."

"Perhaps not, but it had to be said." Chin held high, she hurried ahead to the coach.

"I ain't no gentleman, that's true," Jack called after her, "and I'm proud of it!" Then he lowered his voice. "Fractious woman, your wife. Is she always so plainspoke?"

"Yes, especially when she's rousted out of bed by a lot of scoundrels brandishing swords and pistols."

Jack frowned. "I told you before, you've got naught to fear from us as long as you cooperate. And nobody will lay a hand on your wife, neither."

"Good. Because the first person who does will draw back a stump." Daniel stalked off to help Helena into the carriage, leaving Jack mumbling to himself about people who got above themselves and turned into gentry.

Once they were in the coach, Daniel tried to sit next to her, but Jack would have none of it. He put her beside him, then took out his pistol, which he kept none too casually resting on his knee, pointed at Helena.

It was uncocked, and it was possible Daniel could wrestle it away, but he wasn't taking any chances with Helena's life. Besides, he might be better off playing along for a while and trying to find out where Crouch had Juliet.

Despite the pistol, Jack seemed determined to treat this like a bloody social call. As the coach rumbled off, he turned to Helena with his smoothest smile. "So how long have you been married to our Danny?"

In typical Helena fashion, she straightened her spine and shot back, "I believe he is no longer *your* Danny, nor has he been for some time."

Take that, you old fool, Daniel thought smugly. Helena mightn't have consented to marry him yet, but she was loyal to him all the same.

"Ah, but we did have good times when he was," Jack replied, not to be put off. "Didn't we, Danny?"

Daniel lifted an eyebrow. "D'you mean all those cold nights playing spotsman and dodging the preventive officers? Or the predawn mornings running up the beach with two loaded tubs while the icy rain pelted us?"

"You're leaving out the good stuff—the thrill of slipping past an exciseman in the dark, and those evenings when the sky was so scattered with stars, it was like a thousand spilt shillings."

Daniel snorted. Only Jack could wax poetic about free trading. Jack's eyes twinkled with mischief now, which put Daniel on his guard.

"As I recall, Danny Boy, there were certain tasks you didn't mind a'tall. Like the letting down."

"Letting down?" Helena asked.

Although Daniel glared at him, Jack was in the mood for devilment. "Ain't Danny told you about that?" At her shake of the head, Jack explained, "When we transport the liquor into England, it's over-proof, y'see. That's so more of it can be brought in. Once it's here, we got to dilute it for sale. Water's added a bit at a time, and we put numbered glass beads in it that float to the top when it's at the right mix. When he was only a wee bit, Danny was in charge of watching the beads until the right one floated."

"Danny always was good with numbers," Helena said, straightfaced.

Daniel's gaze shot to her, but she actually seemed amused.

"Aye," Jack retorted. "But that wasn't the part he liked best. He fancied the reward for getting it right: a dram of the brandy. You can be sure that Danny learned right quick how to get the dilution perfect."

"Damn it, Jack, you make me sound like a tippler at the wee age of ten."

"As I understand it, my dear," Helena interjected, "tippling wasn't the only vice you began at an uncommonly early age."

Impudent wench.

Jack went on gleefully. "Danny enjoyed the letting down so much that he even got testy when another boy took it over from him." Jack nudged Helena. "Can you believe it? Danny tried to sabotage the lad by rubbing the paint off the beads and painting new numbers."

He'd forgotten all about that, and despite his annoyance, he smiled. "I got into trouble for it, too. Had to spend the week mending sails, and I loathed mending sails."

"You got off easy, in my opinion," Jack commented. "I wanted to tan your hide, but Jolly Roger wouldn't let me. Always did coddle you too much, m'boy."

"Do you call sending his men out to carry me and my wife off 'coddling'?" Daniel retorted.

"Oh, he don't know about this. He's off on a run, won't be back until early morn. But when Wallace told me you were nosing about, I figured I'd best take care of it. I know Jolly Roger will want you where he can keep an eye on you once he returns."

Yes, so Daniel couldn't sneak Juliet away. He sobered at the thought. "So you've stooped to kidnapping now. I wonder what Bessie thinks of that?"

That seemed to suck the wind out of Jack's sails. He glanced away quickly. "Bessie's dead, Danny. She died of the consumption two years ago."

When Daniel's face undoubtedly reflected his shock, Helena glanced in bewilderment to Jack. "Who's Bessie?"

"Jack's wife," Daniel answered. The closest thing he'd had to a mother during his years smuggling.

He glanced out the coach window, barely registering the town of Sedlescombe they now passed through. Bessie was dead. It was hard to fathom. Though he'd lived in a house with Jolly Roger and some bachelor free traders during his youth, it was Bessie who'd kept an eye out for him, making sure he was well-fed and well-treated. She was probably the real reason he'd escaped having his hide tanned by Jack.

His gaze swung back to Jack. "I'm sorry, I didn't know."

"You might have if you'd ever bothered to come back and see us," Jack grumbled. Then, as if embarrassed by that show of sentiment, he shrugged. "Anyway, it was her time, is all."

Daniel was used to the stoicism of free traders, for whom the dance between the sea and the exciseman occasionally ended in death, but it suddenly seemed too cruel for the likes of Bessie. "She was a good woman. She didn't deserve to die so young."

Jack flinched. "No, she didn't. And you're right about what she would've thought of this—she wouldn't have liked it a bit. I know that." His chin jutted out. "But times are harder now than when Bessie was alive, and liable to grow harder still. There's rumors of a new coast guard being formed. It's been plaguing Crouch to distraction. He's thinking of giving up the free trading now that he's getting old."

"Not too old for kidnapping, clearly," Daniel said sarcastically.

Jack looked affronted. "Wouldn't none of this have happened if Knighton had considered Jolly Roger's proposal in the first place."

A sudden chill wrapped about Daniel's gut. "Proposal? What the devil are you talking about?" He glanced at Helena, who looked as bewildered as he.

"You know what I mean," Jack said. "The one Jolly Roger offered last spring. When he went to London and told Knighton that he'd expose your connection to us if Knighton didn't start doing business with us again."

"He did *what*?" Daniel leaned forward, his hands clenching into fists on his knees.

Jack shifted nervously on his seat. "Knighton must've told you about it. Jolly Roger threatened to go to the papers with the story of how you used to be a notorious smuggler and how you were the son of Wild Danny Brennan. He figured Knighton wouldn't want to see you tarred and feathered in the press, possibly even arrested. It mightn't set well with his lofty friends if they knew you'd been a criminal."

"Those 'lofty friends' already know most of it." Still, Daniel reeled from Jack's revelation. Crouch had tried to force Griff by using Daniel's past? And Griff hadn't told him?

"That's what Knighton said. He told Jolly Roger to go to the devil, said he didn't care who knew and he didn't figure you cared, neither."

"Bloody right!" Why hadn't Griff told him all this? He'd probably thought to protect him, knowing that Daniel would cut off his right hand before letting his connections harm Griff or Knighton Trading.

Jack went on. "Knighton said he'd make damned sure Jolly Roger was hanged for it if he went to the papers about you."

"Good for Griff," Daniel snarled. "That's what Crouch gets for assuming that Griff would be an easy mark. He should've known better. Griff would sooner lance a vein than give him hush money."

"It wasn't money he wanted," Jack reminded Daniel as the coach clattered over a bridge, jarring them all. "He just wanted Knighton to go back to buying our goods. Nobody wants to fund the runs anymore—and Jolly Roger thought that p'raps with a bit of pressure, Knighton would consider it." His tone turned acid. "He never dreamed you and Knighton had got so respectable you considered yourselves too good for shady profits."

Daniel shook his head. "Even if Griff wanted to finance the runs again, he sure as the devil wouldn't choose Crouch. The man nearly had him killed, for God's sake!"

Jack made a dismissive gesture. "That was ten years ago, Danny. Tempers were high, and hasty words were spoke. I don't think Jolly Roger had any idea Knighton still held that against him."

"Then he's more of an idiot than I took him for."

"Anyway, Knighton didn't take kindly to any of it. Said it was blackmail. He had Jolly Roger thrown into the street on his arse."

"I'm not surprised." But if Griff had told him, Daniel could've warned him that Crouch wouldn't stop at blackmail. Griff had badly underestimated Crouch, something Daniel never would've done.

"To be honest," Jack went on, "the way Griff humiliated him is what fired Jolly Roger's temper. If not for Knighton's threats to set the excisemen on him, he would have marched down to the *Times* there and then. But when he heard about Knighton's wedding a few months later, he saw his chance for a better revenge."

Helena made a little whimpering sound, and Daniel's gaze shot to her. He'd forgotten what she must be thinking of this, of him. Bloody hell, what if she thought he *had* known of it? Bad enough that Griff had unwittingly brought this on Juliet, but if Helena thought Daniel had kept it from her . . .

He groaned. He couldn't even reassure her without revealing her identity to Jack.

Especially when Jack was already eyeing them both curiously. "Jolly Roger half-expected you to come later and offer him hush money yourself. He was surprised you let Griff speak for you."

"Griff never told me about any of it." Daniel's gaze shot to Helena, who looked stricken. "Griff kept it from me," he repeated, more for her sake than Jack's.

Though her eyes were alive with emotion, she seemed to have mastered her agitation. But that only made it worse, because now he didn't know what she thought. Did she believe him? Surely she wouldn't blame him for this, too.

His heart sank as he tore his gaze from her. What did it matter if she did? She had every right to. Griff may've brought this on her family initially, but it couldn't have happened without Daniel's past. The weapon had always been there—Crouch had just taken his sweet time about using it.

"So Jolly Roger kidnapped Juliet for money because he was angry at Griff," he said. "Didn't he realize that

Griff would send the excisemen after the lot of you once this was over?"

"He wasn't supposed to find out it was Crouch." Jack's arch look made it clear that he blamed Danny for that change in affairs.

"Come now, surely you realized he would figure it out in the end."

"Pryce covered his tracks, took a false name and everything."

"*I* found Pryce, so why couldn't Griff?"

Jack rubbed his chin. "You're better at looking for our sort than Knighton. Not to mention that fool Wallace opening his mouth. If not for him, you wouldn't have known what we were about, would you have?"

Probably not, though he'd be damned if he told Jack that.

"Besides," Jack went on, "the ransom note wasn't signed—it just gave instructions for switching off the money and the girl, which ain't happening in Sussex."

Daniel stored that bit of information. "Surely you realized that once Juliet was freed, she'd tell Griff . . ." He trailed off, icy apprehension stealing his breath. "Unless Crouch never intended to free her. Unless he'd decided he wasn't above killing."

"No!" Jack protested. "No, killing was never part of it. That's why we didn't let the girl see nobody but Pryce. We figured Knighton would think it was Captain Will Morgan running the show, and he'd not be able to track him down, since there's no such man."

"But that's all changed now," Daniel reminded him grimly. "You've got me and my wife to contend with, don't you? Crouch isn't going to let us go now that *we* know, you can be sure of that."

"Danny! Don't talk like that." Jack looked annoyed. "You know him better than that. He ain't gonna lift a hand to you." He paused, then fixed Danny with an earnest gaze. "You'll understand better when you see him, Danny Boy, but he's faring poorly. Right ill, he is. He's giving up the free trading to go live somewhere comfortable. This was his last chance at making money to keep him the rest of his days. Once Griff pays him the ransom, he'll take off for parts unknown. Then it don't matter if you know."

Daniel had to bite his tongue to keep from pointing out that Griff would pursue Crouch to the ends of the earth for kidnapping his wife's sister, and Rosalind would be right behind her husband, wielding a sword. No point in giving Crouch any more reason to consider killing them all. "How much is he asking for, anyway? It'd have to be a lot to stretch to all of you."

"Not so much. Nobody else's getting any of it, because nobody else had a part in it but Pryce and me and Jolly Roger. Pryce don't want money for his part, and I don't, either. I'm taking over for Crouch when he's gone. That's enough for me." His voice softened. "Besides, I ain't the least worried about your turning me in, m'boy. You wouldn't hand me over to be hanged, and we both know it. Just like I'd never harm you or your missus or the girl. Crouch will get his money from that arse Knighton and be gone. Then it'll be over. Simple as that."

Daniel persisted, unconvinced. "So he'll hold us until the money comes, and then let us go? I find that hard to believe."

"I can't be certain exactly what he'll do, that's true. But I can be certain he'd never hurt *you*, of all people."

Daniel laughed bitterly. "And why not?"

"Because he ain't gonna hurt his own blood."

Seth Atkins stared down the road long after the coach had trundled off. They were gone, thank God. He was safe again. So why did he have this sickening feeling in his chest?

He stared down at his hand, dawn's light gilding the shillings that lay there. Blood money. For his silence, Mr. Crouch's man had said.

But what did Jolly Roger Crouch want with the Brennans? And why did he want them bad enough to send men with pistols to take them away? He'd never heard tell of the smugglers doing such a thing. Father's friend Robert Jennings had done a run with Mr. Crouch's gang, before he got into trouble with his wife for it. He was always saying as how it paid good money and they treated their men well. And most of Mr. Crouch's men only did the free trading when there was no work to be had at the failing ironworks.

Could Mr. Brennan be an exciseman? The smugglers didn't take kindly to customs officers from London, and he *had* come from London . . . Yet he didn't seem the sort. Besides, excisemen didn't bring their wives along with them.

Well, it was none of his concern *what* Mr. Crouch wanted with the Brennans, was it? Seth hefted the silver in his clammy hands. Surely he'd done more than enough by letting them stay in the barn. They'd stolen that other fellow's horse, after all. And they'd been sneaking about when Seth had come across them, too.

Still . . . they didn't seem like thieves, and they'd been awful nice to him. He counted the shillings. Thirty. Thirty pieces of silver, like what Judas was given to betray Our Lord. With a little cry, Seth dropped the money.

It was a sign, it was. He'd done wrong, after all. He shouldn't have taken their horse, even for a minute. Mum would call it stealing, especially since he'd took it to do something wicked like go off drinking in town.

He stared down the road. There was something mighty wrong here. But he daren't go to the constable, not after what Mr. Crouch's man had threatened to do to him. His tongue itched, already feeling the touch of a blade against it.

All the same, it didn't sit right with him to let it pass, neither. He had to do something to help the two escape their captors. Perhaps he could sneak a weapon to them. If he got it past Jolly Roger's men without them knowing who done it, they'd never know to come here after him.

And he was fairly certain where the Brennans had been taken—everybody knew that Jolly Roger's gang came from Hastings. Perhaps if he went to Hastings and asked around a bit . . .

He gazed down at the thirty shillings. He'd walk the few miles into Sedlescombe and use the blood money to hire a horse to carry him to Hastings. It wasn't that far. With the rest of it, perhaps he could pay somebody to tell him what was going on and where the Brennans were.

Because he couldn't bear being the cause of any harm done to them.

Chapter 18

His gown was large, made of good serge;
his petticoat was yellow
And such a bouncing girl was Dick,
in Belfast had no fellow.
"Dick the Joiner,"
anonymous ballad

His own blood.

Mr. Seward's words had shocked Helena, but she could tell from Daniel's slack jaw that they'd shocked him even more.

"His own blood?" Daniel growled. "What the devil are you talking about?"

Mr. Seward fidgeted, his fingers steadily drumming his knee. "I swore to Jolly Roger I never would tell you this.

But I can't stand to see you thinking so ill of him, after all he done for you."

"All he— If you call trying to use me to blackmail Griff—"

"He took you out of the workhouse, and at great risk to himself, damn it!" Mr. Seward cried.

Daniel went very still. "How in God's name do you figure he risked anything?"

"He's your uncle, m'boy. Your mother's brother."

Helena's heart caught in her throat at the look that passed over Daniel's face—shock, anger, and finally a dangerous calm that would give a wise man pause. "My uncle is dead," he enunciated, the words echoing stark and cold above the clattering carriage wheels.

"No, he ain't." Mr. Seward's voice quivered, then steadied. "Come on, Danny, you ain't thinking! He went to Essex for *you*, not to buy a damned cutter. You ain't never seen Crouch in Essex before nor since, and there's a reason for that. If anybody in Essex ever recognized him as Tom Blake—the man who rode with Wild Danny Brennan—he'd be caught and hanged!"

"My uncle never rode with my da," Daniel bit out. "I don't know why you've got this fool idea in your head, but my uncle drowned himself—"

"No, Jolly Roger only did that to escape capture. Your parents got caught, but he didn't. He confessed it all to me when he was drunk a few months back, shortly after Knighton refused him. He blubbered about being ashamed of hisself for using his own nephew to get money. He said next time he wouldn't involve you a'tall. That's why he was hoping to keep you out of it. *And* why he's going to be damned angry to find you here." He softened his voice. "He don't like

Knighton much, but he'd slit his own throat afore he'd hurt you."

"Is that so?" Daniel's eyes were steel in ice. "In the midst of all his 'confessing,' did Jolly Roger happen to mention why he never told *me* that he was my uncle?"

Mr. Seward shrugged. "Because he was a wanted man. He didn't tell you when you were a boy because he was afraid you'd let it slip, and then later . . . there just never seemed a right time. And once you worked for Knighton, he wasn't going to put a weapon into the man's hands, was he?"

"*Now* who's not thinking?" Daniel snapped. "He spun you a pretty tale, man, and you swallowed it whole." When Mr. Seward drew himself up stiffly, Daniel added, "The reason he never told me was he knew I'd find out the truth about my parents' capture one day, and then I'd be after him, bent on making him pay."

"For what? Not getting caught?"

"For betraying my parents to the soldiers!"

Mr. Seward paled. "What're you talking about?"

"I'm talking about Crouch—or Tom or whatever his bloody name is! He never rode with my da, you arse. He was the one who turned them in. That's why he didn't want me to learn who he really was, because he knew what I'd do to him if I found out." Daniel snorted in disgust. "When he moved to Sussex, he changed his identity not because he feared capture, but because he realized that no free trader with an ounce of sense would work for the man who'd betrayed Wild Danny Brennan!"

Mr. Seward was shaking his head over and over. "Jolly Roger wouldn't have done that. For God's sake, your mother was his sister."

"Yes. But that didn't stop him from telling them where

to find her and Da the night they were taken. I went back to Essex a few years ago and talked to one of the soldiers. My uncle did it for the reward. He turned his own sister in for a bag of gold. And *that's* the man you're defending, the man you claim would never kill anybody!"

Fear wrapped itself around Helena's heart. Daniel did have a point.

Apparently Mr. Seward recognized it, too, for he slumped against the squabs to stare bleakly out the carriage window. "I can't believe it. Crouch betray his own sister? It don't . . . seem like him."

"All the same, he did it." Daniel dragged in a harsh breath. "That's why I distrust him and his motives now. And if you help him do this, Jack, then you're as bad as he is."

A mutinous expression crossed Mr. Seward's face. "You're making this all up, aren't you? You want to twist me against him so I'll let you go. Well, it won't work, Danny Boy, so you may as well give up. I can't believe it of him. I won't."

Daniel's features seemed carved from stone. "Do as you please. Or better yet, ask *him* and see what he says."

"I will, don't you worry," Mr. Seward said stoutly.

An awful silence fell on the carriage, punctuated only by the wind whistling through the windows. What else was there to say? Mr. Seward was fretting, and Daniel looked ravaged. Helena wished she could take him in her arms and just hold him to ease his pain, but she doubted Mr. Seward would allow it.

She kept hoping he would look at her, that she could show him her sympathy with her eyes. But he held himself remote, as if too shattered to allow any connection with another human being.

Thankfully they soon arrived in Hastings, and the

coach shuddered to a halt before a half-timbered cottage at the top of a hill in the center of town. Mr. Seward's companions dismounted and called for help with the horses. They were joined by more men, which made Helena decidedly nervous. She glanced at Daniel, but he was staring morosely out the window, as he had for the last few miles.

"Here we are," Mr. Seward said grimly as he descended from the coach. "This is where you'll stay for the moment."

"At your house?" Daniel said in surprise. He disembarked, then turned to help her out.

"Why not? Nobody in Hastings will think aught of it. Besides, with Bessie . . . gone, the lads who aren't working spend their time here while waiting for darkmans."

"Darkmans?" she whispered to Daniel.

"Night." He laid his hand protectively in the small of her back. "That's what smugglers call it."

Lord, these free traders were as elaborate as spies with all their code words and odd practices. No wonder the excisemen couldn't keep them under control. Without Daniel playing Virgil and leading her through the Inferno, she would have been quite lost. She only hoped they made it at least into Purgatory. Paradise seemed unreachable at the moment.

Mr. Seward led them toward the entrance. "You and your missus can have a bit of breakfast if you like, m'boy."

A faint smile touched Helena's lips. She'd never get used to Mr. Seward's calling Danny "m'boy," as if the man who now towered over him were still in leading strings.

A chorus of "Danny Boy! It's Danny Boy!" erupted from the occupants of the cottage as soon as she and

Daniel crossed the threshold. Daniel's hand on her back tensed at the greeting, and her heart broke for him. Poor Daniel. No doubt he found this as difficult as she did.

She surveyed the oak table crowded with men, in the center of what had once apparently been a parlor. Framed needlework samplers still graced the walls and a set of pewter plates were displayed on the stone mantel, but now they were nearly obliterated by soiled crockery, gunpowder bags, and even a sword or two. It was clearly a male preserve now, with free traders playing cards, drinking, and laughing raucously. Instinctively, she drew nearer to Daniel.

"Sit down, and I'll fetch you something to eat," Mr. Seward said as he hurried off into another room.

By the time Daniel found them seats at the table, Mr. Seward had returned with their food. As she ate breakfast, Helena surveyed the faces of the men at the table. That broke at least one of Mrs. N's rules—a Well-Bred Lady wasn't supposed to stare—but until Mrs. N wrote a book on etiquette for kidnappings, Helena would have to improvise. Besides, the men ignored her staring, too intent on questioning Daniel about what he'd been up to since they'd last seen him.

That left her free to sort them out in her head. The tall red-haired man with the scar at his temple. The man with crooked teeth and clear blue eyes. The boastful, flirtatious youth they called Ned. If she and Daniel ever got out of this alive, she wanted to be able to recognize them all. Perhaps Griff wouldn't want them brought to justice, but if he did, she wanted to help.

If only she could sketch them. She still had the sketch of Daniel and her pencil—it wouldn't be hard. And if she could pass the sketches to someone who'd carry them to Griff in London, Griff could take *some* sort of action . . .

Well, there was no chance of that at the moment. It appeared that she and Daniel were to stay in the company of these men for some time.

The one man she didn't see among them was Mr. Pryce. Was he off alone with Juliet even now? The thought was most unsettling. When she finished eating, she drew a clove from the packet in her apron and chewed on it, then leaned over to whisper to Daniel, "Pryce isn't here. That probably means Juliet isn't here, either."

He nodded and whispered back, "I'll find out what I can, but you're to keep quiet about it. I don't want them guessing who you are."

"What are you two muttering about?" Mr. Seward asked with a frown.

Daniel squeezed her hand, warning her to silence. "My wife's a bit tired, since we were so rudely awakened this morning. D'you have a room where she can go rest?"

Taken by surprise, she shot him a sharp glance. She didn't want to leave without him, for heaven's sake.

"Aye, there's one upstairs for you both." Mr. Seward rose from the table, gesturing toward the staircase. "I'll take her up there."

"Thanks, Jack." Daniel's gaze met hers, imploring her to go.

Perhaps it was for the best. The men would talk more freely about Juliet and Mr. Pryce if she was gone, and it *would* give her a chance to sketch their faces.

Removing her clove, she dropped it onto her plate and stood. Then she took the arm that the old smuggler offered and let him lead her up the stairs. She tried to memorize everything she saw, for her sketches. When they reached the top, she noted three doors, all closed.

Mr. Seward caught the direction of her gaze. "The girl

ain't here, if that's what you're wondering. Like I told you, she's been kept separate."

"I see," she said, swallowing her disappointment.

The room he showed her into was large and neatly furnished, though not terribly clean or tidy. Mr. Seward hurried about, picking up a discarded shirt here, a sock there. "Beggin' your pardon, ma'am, but I didn't have time to make it presentable before we rode out early this morn. And I'm not much of a housekeeper myself."

"This is *your* room?"

"No. My son's. I got three of 'em, and they're all as slovenly as their father."

A jolt of sympathy hit her. It had been easy to dismiss Mr. Wallace as a plain villain, but Mr. Seward, with his dead wife and untidy sons, didn't seem the least villainous.

He didn't even look villainous. She examined him with an artist's eye, trying to figure out why. She supposed it was his age, the graying hair and the fine wrinkles about the eyes and mouth. She'd guess him to be about fifty, which seemed a trifle old for a smuggler, considering what she'd learned of the rigors of the profession. There was also his obvious affection for Daniel.

An affection that stopped at helping them escape Crouch, she reminded herself. None of these free traders could be trusted, even the ones with families. Daniel's own wary expression around them told her that he knew very well how far their amiability extended, and the distance was short indeed.

Mr. Seward faced her with a smile. "I'll leave you to rest now, Mrs. Brennan. You make yourself comfortable. It'll be a few hours before we send round to the Stag Inn for dinner, so you've plenty of time to sleep."

"Thank you."

As soon as he left, she flew to the one window, but it

had been nailed shut. She might succeed in breaking out the panes without being heard by the rowdy men downstairs, but even if her leg *could* handle a descent from a second-floor window, the flagstone walk below was being patrolled by an armed man.

Discouraged, she sat down at the table and drew out her pencil and the sketch paper. When she unfolded it, Daniel's face stared up at her.

At least one thing had come of this nightmarish capture. She now knew what she wanted. *Whom* she wanted. The morning's events had made her realize that life was too short to worry about her foolish pride. Daniel was right—she had to grab on to life, take a risk. He'd certainly managed it. Despite his parents, despite being raised by a scoundrel, he'd carved a respectable place in the world. He'd made himself into an honorable man.

If they escaped this, she'd be a fool not to marry him.

For she did love him—she knew that now. She loved the strength beneath the rascally exterior, the integrity beneath the rough manners, the tenderness beneath the bluster.

And he wanted her for his wife, after all. If he didn't love her yet, she could wait until he did. Besides, he'd promised to be faithful, and oddly enough, she believed that he would. So she would marry him.

If she ever got the chance. Turning the sketch over, she began to draw on the back. She'd do what she could to recount these events, complete with names and places.

And pictures. Yes, lots of pictures.

Daniel sat at the table of smugglers, trying not to think of Helena alone upstairs, anxious and distraught. It had taken all his will to watch her leave, and her scent still lingered, fragrant with cloves and honey water. If anything happened to her . . .

He clenched his fists, then clenched them tighter, remembering all that Jack had revealed in the carriage. Crouch was his uncle. Christ, how had he not figured it out before? Jack was right—he should have realized that Crouch wouldn't have taken a boy from the workhouse to raise in a den of smugglers several counties away.

The bitter realization that he was linked to Crouch by blood hammered in another fact he'd tried to ignore all morning: he would never escape any of this. He might manage to take Helena and Juliet out of here safely, but that wasn't the same as escaping, not for him. Why had he thought he could struggle free of his free-trading past? Why had he fought to wrest a future from it? This was his destiny, like it or not—to be dragged down into the mire with the likes of Crouch and Wallace and all the rest. His investment concern . . . a marriage to Helena . . . they were castles in the clouds.

Well, he wouldn't play in the clouds any longer. This was reality, *his* reality, and it was time he accepted that it would follow him all his life.

But that didn't mean it had to be Helena's reality, too. Once he got her out of here, he'd make damned sure it never touched her again.

"So," he asked his companions, "which one of you rascals is Morgan Pryce?"

"Pryce ain't here," the young man called Ned answered. He and three others were playing cards to pass the time.

Daniel settled back against his chair, trying to appear nonchalant. "Will he be around later? I'd like to meet the man."

"Oh, he ain't been here in weeks." Ned laid down a card. "He's tied up with some private project of Crouch's. Don't know what it is. Jack's keeping all mum about it."

A surge of relief hit Daniel to realize that Jack hadn't lied about that. "So you don't know where Pryce is now?"

Jack answered from the doorway. "No, he don't. None of them do."

That didn't stop Daniel from probing further. "How long has he been with Crouch?"

Shrugging, Jack took a seat at the table. "Awhile."

"I hear he's a gentlemanly sort, so why did he take up with you rough lads?"

"Boredom, I s'pose," Jack answered. "A need for money. Who knows why a man of breeding dabbles in free trading? If you want an answer to that, you ought to ask your friend Knighton. He did it long before Pryce ever did." Taking up a bottle, he poured some brandy into a cup and shoved it at Daniel. "But we don't want to talk about all that. Have a drink and relax, Danny. Enjoy yourself."

Gritting his teeth, Daniel had a drink. And another and another and another as the day dragged on. By late afternoon, he'd been handed more drinks than he could count. Thankfully, they drank smuggler's brandy—the colorless liquor that hadn't yet been doctored with burnt sugar to make it brown—so it was easy to water it down without anybody noticing, or pour it into the nearby chamber pot.

He had to keep his wits about him, try to find out where Juliet was. If he and Helena could escape, he wanted to reach the girl quickly. Unfortunately, Jack seemed to be the only one who knew, and he seemed determined not to let the information slip.

Late in the afternoon, a timid knock sounded on the cottage door. Ned jumped up to answer, since he wasn't playing cards just then. "That'll be the food from the Stag Inn. It's about damned time. I told them to bring it for three, and it's long past that."

"I'll fetch us some plates," Jack said, disappearing through the door into what Daniel remembered was the kitchen. That's where he'd eaten many a meal. He smiled a bit sadly. What would Bessie think to see her house so invaded?

Ned entered with a huge tray, accompanied by a spindly maidservant who kept her head down as she brought in a second tray. Since she wore the biggest poke bonnet Daniel had ever seen, he could hardly make out her features.

"They sent over a new girl," Ned announced as he set his tray down, and the maid ducked her head even more. "Bashful thing, ain't she?" Ned swatted her arse, and she nearly dropped her tray. Ned laughed. "You needn't be shy of us, missy. We're an amiable lot, aren't we, boys?"

Her whispered response, "I'm sure you are, sir," sounded oddly familiar, but Daniel doubted he knew any Hastings girl of her age.

She moved up next to him to set her tray on the table, and as her hand came back, something dropped into Daniel's lap. Bloody hell, a hunting knife! He reacted instantly, sliding it hilt-first inside his coat sleeve. Then he glanced up to find the maid regarding him with a steady blue gaze.

He didn't know whether to laugh or shake "her" senseless. Seth Atkins—Christ, was the lad insane?

Jack reappeared, and Seth turned quickly away. Jack addressed "her" offhandedly as he set down the plates. "Empty that tray there, girl." As soon as Seth did, Jack filled a plate and put it on the tray. "Richard, you take this upstairs to Danny's wife."

"Aw, Jack, let Ned go. I'm about to win this hand."

"Aye," Ned said with a leer, "I'll be happy to take it up to the lady."

Daniel bristled, but Jack cast him a cautioning glance and said, "I'm not letting you anywhere near Mrs. Brennan, Ned."

"I'll go," Seth whispered, playing the part of shy maiden with astonishing believability. As long as they didn't get a good look at his face, that is. Christ, but he made an ugly girl. "I'll take it for you, sir."

Jack hesitated, then shrugged. "All right. The man at the top has the key to the door. He'll let you in. Tell him I sent you up."

Seth bobbed his head, then picked up the tray and left.

Daniel waited until he heard Seth's steps upstairs, then stood and stretched nonchalantly. "I think I'll take my food up and join my wife, if you fellows don't mind. I've had enough of drinking rotgut for the time being."

"Then wait until the girl comes back down," Jack said, eyeing him with suspicion.

"Come on, Jack, my food will be cold by then." Daniel picked up his plate and headed for the door. Ned rose to bar his way.

"P'raps I should remind you, Danny," Jack said, "that the servants from the Stag Inn are all completely loyal to the free traders, since it relies on us for its brandy. And you wouldn't involve some poor innocent in an attempt to escape, would you?"

"Escape?" Daniel laughed harshly. "I've no weapon, and my wife is lame. You've got ten armed men down here, not counting your guard upstairs. Do you think I'd be so foolish as to take you all on? I just want to dine with my wife is all." He forced a wicked smile to his face. "You and your cronies rousted me out of the hay too early for me to have my morning's entertainment, so I thought I'd hurry the maid along and . . . take advantage of the wait for Crouch."

Jack studied him a moment, but apparently remembered Daniel's appetites well enough. He jerked his thumb toward the door. "All right, go on then. Ned, let him by, but watch him go up."

Daniel could feel Ned's eyes on him as he climbed the stairs. At the top was a burly man standing guard—the one they'd called Big Antony, an Italian as big as Daniel and probably twice as mean. The door next to him was open.

Daniel spoke to Big Antony as he reached it, but received only a grunt in response. Good, perhaps he didn't speak much English. It was common enough for foreigners to work in smuggling gangs, and Crouch's was no exception.

As Daniel entered, he found Helena seated at a table where Seth seemed to be dawdling. She glanced up, showing by a jerk of her head that she'd already determined the "maid's" identity. Daniel nodded. He wasn't sure what use he could make of the lad, especially with Big Antony watching them, but he wanted at least a word with him, if only to send the bloody fool home unharmed.

Helena was drumming her fingers on the table as he set his plate down. At first, he was too intent on transferring the knife in his sleeve to his coat pocket while his back was to the guard to pay much attention. But when her drumming grew loud and he frowned at her, she slid something ever so slightly out from under the empty tray.

He saw a fragment of sketch paper and moved around the table beside her. "How are you feeling, my dear?" he asked as he bent to kiss her cheek. Seth shifted into position across the table from them, blocking the guard's view of what was there.

Daniel scanned the writing and images she'd apparently produced on the back of the sketch she'd done of him. Then he straightened, a slow smile spreading over his face. This was good, very good indeed. Perhaps he and Helena would make it home unscathed after all. Helena pressed the pencil into his hand, and he began commenting on the food as he wrote furiously across the paper, sure that Seth's body blocked Big Antony's view of his hands. Then he glanced up to find the Italian watching him with narrowed eyes.

"Go distract that bloody guard," he bent low to whisper to Helena. "I need to speak to Seth."

She nodded and left the table. As soon as he heard her ask the guard if she could obtain cleaner linens, he folded the sketch paper, slid it across to Seth, then sidled around to stand beside him, both of them with their backs to the door. The guard was trying to make sense of Helena's words, and she was speaking in loud English the way idiots do when faced with a foreigner who doesn't understand.

"Will they figure out that it's you who came here?" he murmured to Seth. He wasn't about to risk the lives of Seth or his family.

"No, I was wearing Mum's clothes when I showed up in Hastings." He grinned sheepishly. "I thought they might let a girl inside if I gave 'em a clever enough tale. Then I saw the maid from the inn bringing the food. I told her that her master had sent me after her with news of her family, and that she had to go home right away. It'll take her a while to find out nothing's wrong."

"Good." Daniel only hoped it would buy them enough

time. He tapped the sketch paper with his finger as he whispered, "Take this to London—I've written the direction on it. Give it to Mr. Griffith Knighton if he's there, and if he's not, wait at Knighton House until he arrives. There's plenty of money in it for you, I promise. I told him to pay you a hundred pounds for your service, but I'm sure he'll be happy to give you more if you succeed."

Seth's low gasp at the amount was followed by a hissed protest. "I want to help you *here,* now. I couldn't get a pistol, but I've got another knife and—"

"Certainly not," Daniel bit out. When Seth drew himself up stubbornly, he added, "There's too many of them, lad, and you might be recognized." Not to mention that he still didn't know where Juliet was being held, and any escape with Helena would prove difficult. "We'll be all right, I swear, but only if you get out of here with that piece of paper. Now do as I say."

"What you talk about?" thundered Big Antony's voice from the doorway, and it took a second for Daniel to realize he was speaking to them and not Helena.

"Danny," Helena said in her loftiest tone, "you had best not be flirting with the maid, or I swear you'll sleep alone tonight."

Following her lead, he laid his arm around Seth's shoulders. "I'm just being friendly is all."

"Hey!" Seth protested, then amended it to a more feminine-sounding protest, though he shot Daniel a foul look.

Daniel laughed for real and called back to Helena, "Oh, come now, love, it doesn't mean anything. The lass here knows that. Don't you, sweetheart?"

Daniel smacked Seth on the arse with one hand while shoving the paper into his apron pocket with the other, and Seth muttered something in a high voice that sounded oddly like, "Bugger it all." Thankfully, Seth's decidedly unladylike response escaped the Italian's notice.

Especially when Helena began bellowing her protests over Daniel's "flirting."

"Best go on," Daniel said loudly to Seth and handed him the tray. "My wife'll have your hide if you stay around here any longer."

Seth fled past the guard, who seemed more interested in the brewing argument between Helena and Daniel than in some homely servant. Determined to draw attention from Seth long enough for the boy to make his escape, Daniel began shouting at Helena about how she was the most jealous wench this side of the Thames. She cried that he was a lecher and a rogue.

She threw herself into it with such enthusiasm that they soon heard footsteps pound up the stairs. Jack appeared in the doorway. "Here now, what's all this ruckus?"

Helena would've made Mrs. Nunley proud, for she drew herself up like the bloody queen and said primly, "He was flirting with the maid."

Jack chuckled . . . until Helena glared at him. Then he smothered his amusement. "I'm sure he didn't mean naught by it, did you, Danny?"

"Nothing a'tall, but you can't tell *her* that," Daniel retorted in apparent disgust. "Any time she sees me with another woman, her eyes turn green."

"What do you expect when you flirt with everything in skirts?" Helena snapped. "What I ought to do is—"

"See here," Jack put in with a glance down the stairs, "the maid has gone anyhow, so there's no need for this fuss."

Relief surged through Daniel so powerfully it took all his will to disguise it.

"I'm sorry, lass," he told Helena. "You know how I am when I'm drinking—"

"Drinking!" She snorted. "Well, don't think that'll excuse it. And why were you drinking, anyway? Here we are, probably about to be murdered in our beds, and you're downstairs having the time of your—"

"I'll leave you to discuss this in private," Jack muttered as he backed out. Then he halted with a frown. "I almost forgot. There's something I got to do before I lock you in."

Jack disappeared. Helena looked at Daniel questioningly, and he shook his head, not sure what Jack was up to. They didn't have long to wonder, however, for when Jack returned moments later and Daniel saw what he was carrying, he groaned.

A leg shackle. Bloody hell.

Chapter 19

Among the pleasant cocks of hay,
There with my bonny lad I lay
What lass, so young and soft as I
Could such a handsome lad deny?

"Spinning Wheel,"
anonymous ballad

"You're not putting that thing on me, Jack, so just forget that idea."

Daniel's protest was the first thing that alerted Helena to what Mr. Seward carried. She turned to see him holding a long length of chain attached to two wicked-looking iron cuffs.

"I got to do it, Danny Boy." Mr. Seward stalked toward Daniel. "I can't leave more'n three or four men here tonight, because Jolly Roger needs us for the landing when he comes in. And I don't trust you to stay put."

"You're already lockin' us up, so why the devil do you need to shackle me?"

"Because I don't want nobody havin' to deal with your shenanigans, m'boy."

Mr. Seward stepped closer. Daniel lifted his hand to the pocket where she'd seen him slide a knife earlier. Oh, dear, surely he wouldn't fight Mr. Seward over the shackle—that would be terribly unwise with an armed man standing in the doorway. He must have realized it, too, for he dropped his hand abruptly.

Mr. Seward bent to fasten one cuff around Daniel's leg. "There's ten feet of chain here so you can move about easily," he pointed out, "and it's only till the morrow. But I ain't gonna leave you in here without something. And don't be getting any ideas about coaxing Big Antony into letting you out of 'em, because I'm keepin' the key meself."

He straightened, a sudden grin flashing over his face. "It's not so bad, y'know." He turned and clamped the other cuff to the iron bedstead. "With it locked to the bed, you oughta have an easier time of mending your quarrel with the missus. You want I should shackle her, too?"

Fire leaped in Daniel's face, though she couldn't tell whether it was anger or something more . . . interesting. "Don't you dare," he said quickly. "She has enough trouble with her leg as it is."

A pox on my leg, she thought wickedly. Shackled to a bed with Daniel sounded quite intriguing. She shushed the little murmur of anticipation in her breast. Merciful heavens, she was turning into such a naughty creature. "Can't say I didn't offer." Mr. Seward winked at her. "Now it'll be up to you to mend the quarrel, Mrs. Brennan."

"I think I can manage." They *were* trapped here until

tomorrow, and they'd done their best to prepare for the coming confrontation with Mr. Crouch. It was enough to tempt even the most inflexible woman to err, and she was feeling more flexible by the moment. Especially with Danny shackled to a bed . . .

Mr. Seward paused on his way out the door. "I'll tell Big Antony that nobody's to bother you, including him. So enjoy yourselves."

As soon as Mr. Seward shut the door, Daniel brandished his fist at it. "Damn that Jack! Even if I could trick the guard into coming close enough for me to overpower him, I couldn't shake this bloody shackle."

She chided herself for thinking about lovemaking at a time when she ought to be helping him plot their escape. "Can't you pick the lock?"

"I was a smuggler, not a thief. I don't know any more about picking locks than you do." He muttered an oath. "I'd hoped for a chance to slip us both out, stash you away, then hunt for Juliet, but that's impossible now."

"You still don't know where she is?"

He shook his head. "One thing is certain. None of them know of her but Pryce, and he has the care of her."

"That blackguard," she hissed. "If he dares to hurt her—"

"Don't worry—I'll be the first to wring his neck." He paced the floor like a bear at a baiting, heedless of the chain that clanked behind him. "Well, at least we've got a chance for survival now that Seth is on his way to London."

"What did you tell him?"

"To take that sheet of paper to Griff." He shot her an approving glance. "You did well, lass. Your sketches and what I wrote will send Griff down here quick as can be. Not to mention that he can use them if we—" He broke off with a curse.

"Are murdered? I thought of that. It's why I drew them up in the first place."

"Jack said Crouch wouldn't kill us."

"But you don't trust him, do you? Even if he *is* your uncle."

Pain slashed over Daniel's face. "Exactly. But if he proves villainous, we'll threaten him with all that information you gathered. It just might keep us alive."

"Do you think Seth can get it to London?"

A smile ghosted over his lips. "He sneaked in and out of here successfully, didn't he? The boy's half-mad, I swear. And he makes a damned ugly girl. Good thing, too, or that randy arse Ned would've tried to buss the poor lad and probably got his teeth kicked in for the effort."

She laughed at the outrageous image. "It was rather clever of Seth to come dressed as a girl, wasn't it?"

"Reckless, more like."

"I suppose." She sidled up to him. "Though I have no doubt you were just like him at that age."

Inexplicably, he stiffened and whirled away from her. "I was *nothing* like him." With quick, angry strides, he walked toward the window, but the chain didn't go that far and forced him to halt short of it. His back was to her, but she could see the tension in his broad shoulders and rigid arms. "I only wish I had been."

Bewildered by his stormy reaction, she folded her arms over her chest. "I wasn't trying to insult you. I only meant that he's bold and brave. And clever. I'm sure you were clever at his age."

"Oh, yes, very clever," he said sarcastically. "Clever enough to start my wenching and drinking early on. Clever enough to keep the books for my own uncle's smuggling gang without even knowing who he was." He spun back to her, his gaze bleak. "Clever enough to get your sister tangled up in *my* dirty linen."

"You had nothing to do with it! You didn't know Crouch tried to blackmail Griff, or I'm sure you would have done what you could to prevent Juliet's abduction."

Surprise flickered in his features. "Well, at least you trust me enough to believe that."

Ah, so he'd thought she might not? It hurt to hear it, but she couldn't blame him. She'd certainly been stingy with her trust until now. "Of course I trust you. Completely, utterly." She cast him a shy smile. "Why wouldn't I trust the man I plan to marry?"

For a second, hope flared in his face, fierce and feverishly bright. And then it was as if the fire burned out, leaving nothing but cold gray ash. "No."

Confusion clamored in her mind. "No? No what?"

"We are not marrying, Helena."

"What?" she whispered. "Why not?"

He turned back to the window. "I should never have asked you. I see that now. It was bloody stupid, and I'm sorry, but I cannot, will not marry you."

The words hammered her, beat at her self-respect, and nearly undid her. Her first impulse was to accuse him of being exactly what she'd feared from the beginning—a more wily rendition of her worst suitors.

But he wasn't, and she knew it. Perhaps she'd always known it. Why else had she let him close to her when she'd never done so with the others? Why else had she exposed herself so wholly to him? Because she'd sensed that he, of all men, was exactly what he seemed, that he would never strive to hurt her.

Until now. Somehow this morning's revelations had brought on this sudden reversal. Perhaps she could find the root of it if she ignored her wounded feelings and dug deeper into his.

She spoke as steadily as she could manage. "As it happens, I don't think it was 'bloody stupid' at all." She tipped up her chin and prayed she was not misjudging the situation. "In fact, I accept your offer of marriage."

"Too late for that. I've withdrawn it, m'lady."

"Don't call me that!" How dare he try to negate these past few days! With furious strides, she rounded him, forcing him to look at her. "I have no such rank, and you know it. Even if I did, it wouldn't stop me from wanting to marry you." She paused, gathered her heart in her hands, then added, "It wouldn't stop me from loving you."

He flinched as if struck. Looking hunted, almost wild, he rasped out a curse that seemed to contain all his frustration. Then he glanced away from her. The light of the setting sun limned his taut features. "That . . . doesn't matter. It has naught to do with it."

She swallowed down her hurt. "Well, it happens to matter to me, and I'd say it has everything to do with it." She pressed him, determined to push past this sudden change in him. "Last night you said you wanted me for your wife, and as far as I'm concerned that's the only thing that counts."

A muscle ticked in his jaw. "A man will say anything to a woman when he's bent on seduction."

"Perhaps," she retorted acidly, "but if that's what you were about, then you did it very badly. You said it after you'd already seduced me, when it could gain you nothing." She tried to provoke him. "Are you claiming that you lied when you said you wanted me? That you are merely one more Fickle Farnsworth after all?"

He refused to answer. He just stood there, remote, his hands clenching into fists at his sides.

A pox on him! She would make him talk to her if it killed her. Walking up close, she said with deliberate coldness, "Or have you merely reconsidered the wisdom of settling down and decided that you would miss not being able to bed all your strumpets? Is that it?"

"At least strumpets know better than to ask a man for what he can't give," he ground out.

At last she was getting somewhere. "Like what? Trust? Honesty?"

"A future, damn it!" His belligerent gaze shot to her as he jerked his leg to rattle the chain. "I can't marry you when I'm leg shackled for life to . . . to Crouch and his bloody gang!"

Her breath hitched in her throat. "Don't be silly. Once we're out of here—"

"Once you and Juliet are out of here, you mean. I'll *never* be out of here. Weren't you listening in the coach this morning? No matter what happens, it'll never stop. My past with Crouch follows me around like . . . like this damned shackle!"

So that was the source of all this: Mr. Seward's unsettling revelations. "What if it does? You've never let it stop you before, and that was clearly wise. As long as you're open and honest about your past—"

"For all the good that's done me." His pain was starkly evident in the drawn cheeks and rigid jaw. "I thought to rid myself of the monster under the bed by shining a light on it, by acknowledging it openly. But that only works for a child, not an adult. Shining a light on it just made it come after me. It didn't banish it a'tall."

His gaze was heartrending in its remorse. "And this time it came after more than me. It came after Juliet and Griff and now you. Even if we escape it this time, it'll always come back in some fashion. He's my blood, damn it, which means it's not an association I can escape!" He released a ragged breath. "So we won't be marrying, lass. I might have to live with shackles, but I won't put you in them. And that's the end of it. I'll not change my mind on this."

Helena's heart twisted in her chest. Her poor, sweet love, so foolishly determined to protect her. And she doubted that saying she didn't care about the "shackles" of his past would convince Daniel once he'd set his mind to something.

Nonetheless, she wasn't about to lose the stubborn lout merely because he'd decided to be noble. She knew exactly how to bring him to his senses: use his nobility against him. "You mean you're abandoning me now that you've ruined me?"

The barb hit its mark. He glanced away, flustered, guilty. "It's better than dragging you down with me. I'm very sorry for taking advantage of you last night. It was a great mistake. But that doesn't mean we should compound it by making a worse one."

She pressed her point. "I can see how marriage would be a mistake for you, but I'm still confused on how it would be a mistake for me. *I* am the one who'll suffer the consequences of being ruined, you know."

He gritted his teeth. "You're not ruined. I daresay many men would marry you, no matter what you think. When Griff and Rosalind return, they'll launch you properly into society. They'll see that the right men court you, men of your rank and breeding, who'll see you for the treasure you are, who won't care about your leg or your . . ."

"Lack of innocence?" she finished for him.

He nodded curtly.

She gave a mirthless laugh. "I was unaware there *were* any men of my rank and breeding who would ignore a maid's 'lack of innocence.'"

To her satisfaction, he looked decidedly uncomfortable. "There are . . . ways for a woman to . . . disguise—"

"What a grand idea," she snapped, infuriated that he'd even suggest such a beastly thing. "With Griff's money and Rosalind's help, I can sell myself to some paragon of virtue who would take me despite my lameness. Then I can deceive this paragon about my chastity to ensure marital bliss." Her voice dripped sarcasm. "And if I should happen to find myself with child by you, I can always fob the baby off on him."

His shocked gaze swung to her. "Good Christ, Helena—"

"That is, as long as Griff and Rosalind find me a husband quickly enough." She planted one hand on her hip, the other gripping her cane so tightly it was a miracle she didn't crush it. "Or have you forgotten talking about the possibility of children after you made your 'mistake' last night? Made it *twice*, I might add."

"I took precautions," he protested. "You won't find yourself with child."

That hit her like a physical blow. True, he had not spilled his seed inside her. Had he been thinking even then that they had no future?

No—he wouldn't have proposed marriage if he hadn't wanted to marry her. "Are you sure your 'precautions' are foolproof?"

He blanched, his eyes flitting over her belly as if considering it. "No. But if by some rare chance you should . . . become pregnant, that would change matters, of course."

"You mean that forcing a child into 'shackles' is all right, but forcing me is not?"

A dark flush spread up his neck. "Damn it, you don't underst—"

"You're saying that if you haven't sired a child on me, it won't bother you in the least for me to marry some other man. Even though I gave myself to you, and you claimed to want me."

She went on relentlessly. "Or perhaps you're assuming that a marriage to another man needn't stop me from taking you for my paramour. I understand that such things are acceptable as long as one is discreet. Then your 'past' wouldn't cause us so much trouble." She swallowed, wondering if she was just torturing herself with this little speech. "Is that what you were hoping for all along? To be my paramour while some other man keeps me?"

"You know I wasn't!" he gritted out.

She did know it, but she was determined to force him into considering the possibilities. "For you, it would be no different than going to one of your tarts, except that you'd not have to pay me, since I'd rely on my husband for my allowance—"

"Stop it!" Catching her by the shoulders, he shook her. "You know I don't want you to be my 'tart'!"

"I'm not good enough for that?" she said, deliberately pretending to misunderstand him, determined to goad him past his irrational nobility. "No, I don't suppose there are many men who'd want a crippled strumpet."

"Don't talk about yourself like that, d'you hear?" he shouted. "You could be blind, deaf, and dumb, and I'd still love you, damn it!"

The words rang very clearly in the room, the most poignant declaration she could ever have wanted. Hope leaped in her chest. "You . . . you love me?"

Raw emotion flashed over his features. "I shouldn't have said it, but yes, of course I love you. Why else do you think I don't want you to marry me?"

She caught his face in her hands and whispered, "I won't let you get out of it, my darling."

He shut his eyes as if to block her out. "Oh, Christ, Helena . . . you know I'd marry you this instant if . . . if . . ."

"If what? You were a different man? You'd had a better

upbringing, a nicer set of parents, a less complicated past? Then you wouldn't be who you are, and I wouldn't want you."

His eyes shot open. Powerful hands gripped her shoulders, and a powerful need shone in his face. "I want to protect you, is all."

"From what? Happiness and a future with the man I love? Thank you very much, but I can do without that kind of protection."

"You are so bloody stubborn," he growled, but he did not thrust her away.

She wound her arms about his neck so he couldn't. "I certainly am. How do you think I managed to live when the surgeon said I would die, to regain the use of legs he swore would never work again? And I shall be *very* stubborn about marrying you. Because the possibility of having your shady past occasionally overshadow our lives is not nearly as fearsome to me as the possibility of losing you."

"Then you're as daft as you are stubborn." He was weakening—she could see it in his face, in the hint of hope that he kept trying to banish with a scowl.

"If I am, it's all your fault. You made me see that being the soul of caution and propriety has merely brought me a lonely bed and a cold future. So if you think I shall let *you* turn into the soul of caution and propriety all of a sudden, you're more daft than I."

"Propriety?" he said, arching one eyebrow. "Me?"

"In one respect, yes. Like a proper gentleman, you're trying to protect me from things I don't wish to be protected from." She tugged his head down until his mouth was a mere inch from hers. "I really wish you'd stop. I like you much better as a wicked rascal." She brushed her lips over his.

With a groan, he grabbed her head to hold it still. His

hands cupped her jaw, and he shook her head just a little, as if to shake her wild ideas from her brain. "So you think to marry a wicked rascal, do you?"

"Yes," she whispered fiercely. "I'm very set on it."

"Last night you weren't." He dragged his thumbs roughly down her throat. "Last night you barely dipped your toe in my wicked past, and it sent you running. But if you marry me, you'll be swimming in it. You won't be able to banish it with your tart tongue. I can't change what I am and what I've been. So you either swim with me or you drown. And I don't know if I could bear to see you drown, love."

"Ah, but I'm a very good swimmer." She tightened her arms about his neck. "You might as well give up this ridiculous resistance, you know. I'll become as wicked as you if that's what it takes."

Untempered need flared in his face. "You couldn't be wicked if you tried. A little naughty, p'raps, but not wicked."

"What about that night at the inn, when I practically threw myself at you?"

"You were drunk, that's all. People are different when they're in their cups."

"Are you sure that's all it was?" She dropped her hands to his waistcoat and began undoing the buttons. "Shall I tell you what I was thinking just now, while Mr. Seward was shackling you? It wasn't about your criminal past or your free-trading uncle or anything like that, I assure you."

"What, then?" he said hoarsely.

Opening his waistcoat, she slid her hands inside. "I was thinking how I wished he would shackle me to the bed with you. I was anticipating you and me, naked and trapped together, unable to do anything but make love all night long—"

With a groan, he brought his mouth crashing down on hers. He tasted of brandy and desperation—wild, hot, urgent—and oh, how she reveled in it. She had him now, whether he knew it or not.

His kiss teetered between anger and desire as he drove his tongue deep, taking what he wanted with a single-minded purpose that made her give her heart to him with complete abandon. He loved her. He might not want to, but she would change that. Tonight, now. And once this nightmare with Juliet was over, she would make him marry her if she had to hold a pistol on him to do it.

Suddenly he jerked back to stare at her with glittering eyes. "All right, prove it to me."

Dazed by need, she murmured, "What?"

"Prove you're wicked enough to be married to a man like me. Last night I had to seduce you. You wanted none of it at first—admit it. You came to my bed because you were coaxed, and afterward you regretted it—"

"I did not!"

"You acted like you did." His eyes searched her face. "But if you marry me, I want you to be damned sure you chose it freely. So prove that it's your choice." Abruptly, he dropped his hands from her and stepped back. "Seduce me. Coax me into *your* bed. Show me you want me badly enough to throw out all the rules of your fine upbringing, and act like the wicked woman you claim to be. Do that, and I might be convinced that you mean what you say."

She gaped at him, taken utterly by surprise. Seducing him would indeed mean throwing out all the rules. She was sure a Well-bred Young Lady *never* seduced a man, probably not even her husband. And certainly not a man to whom she wasn't married.

Well, here stood the man she loved, and if the only way to show him that they belonged together was by seduction, then by God, she would seduce him.

If only she had any idea how to go about it without looking like an utter ninny. It had been one thing to allow his attentions, to follow his guidance in lovemaking, to never take the initiative except when drunk.

But seduce him? What did she know about seducing a man who was clearly determined to resist her?

His lips curled up in a grim smile, as if he knew how his suggestion had flustered her. "Not feeling so wicked after all?"

The taunt firmed her resolve. "How little you know me," she shot back. She dragged her hair loose of its pins, letting them tinkle on the floor like so many raindrops. Striving to hide her self-consciousness, she shook it out to tumble about her shoulders.

"Taking down your hair hardly counts as being wicked," Daniel rasped even as desire blazed in his face.

That was true. If she wanted to seduce him, she'd have to be bolder. "No, but this does." Trying not to blush, she unfastened her gown, which thankfully buttoned and laced in the front. She hesitated a moment, feeling open and exposed to him in a way she'd never felt before.

Then she caught him watching her skeptically, and that was all it took. Swallowing hard, she shimmied out of her gown, then her petticoat. As they drifted to the floor, leaving her in her chemise and stockings, she glanced up to find pure hunger sharpening his rough-hewn features.

It gave her confidence, as if by shedding her gown, she'd shed some of her usual reserve. Perhaps she *could* seduce him. Certainly it didn't seem so difficult when his fiery gaze ardently raked her scantily clad body.

Her blood thundered in her veins, and a decidedly wicked smile crept over her face. "Do you wish to see more?" Without waiting for his answer, she undid the ties of her chemise, then pushed one sleeve off her shoulder.

"That's not seduction, that's teasing," he choked out, though she noticed that he clenched and unclenched his hands as if trying to keep from tearing her chemise off.

It encouraged her even more. "Isn't it seduction when I make you want me?" She slid the chemise off both shoulders and let it whisper down her body to the floor, baring her breasts to him shamelessly. Feeling bolder, she dropped her gaze to his trousers. "Because judging from that bulge in your breeches, I'd say you do want me, Danny."

"Wanting you and acting on it are two different things, remember?" he ground out. "You have to make me act on it."

"You'll act on it, never fear," she replied, buoyed by a sense of feminine power beyond anything she'd ever known. "But first I need you naked." She stepped closer and tugged at his coat lapels. "Come on, darling, take this off."

He arched one blond eyebrow in challenge. "A wicked woman would do it for me."

He did have a point. A wicked woman like that Sall creature would brazenly take what she wanted, not wait until it was offered. And to Helena's surprise, she found the idea of taking what she wanted more intriguing by the moment.

"Very well." Shoving the coat off his shoulders, she tossed it to the floor, then removed his waistcoat and shirt. An admiring smile curved up her lips at the sight of his bare chest, so broad and firm and deliciously male. "You were right, you know, when you said I liked seeing you half-naked at your lodgings that day. I did. I liked it a great deal."

He groaned. "You said you didn't."

"I lied." She smoothed her hands over the hair-roughened skin, relishing the way his muscles bunched and flexed beneath her curious fingers. Teasing the flat male nipples with her thumbs, she whispered, "I wondered even then what it would be like to touch you." She slid her hands up to his shoulders and leaned forward to rub her bare nipples against his chest. "To have you touch me."

At his sharp intake of breath, she smiled. He stared down at her, stiff-jawed, tight-lipped, remote, but his ravenous gaze belied his control. She locked her gaze with his as she let one hand drift down to the fall of his trousers. Profound feminine satisfaction swept her to find him hard as stone beneath the fabric. She fondled him shamelessly, glorying in his ragged breathing.

Quickly she bent to remove his boots. It took her longer to divest him of his trousers, drawers, and stockings, since she couldn't entirely remove them off the shackled leg, but had to shove them down past his ankle onto the chain. Nor did it help that he stood as rigid as a stone Zeus, letting her do it all, making no move to touch her.

So he was determined to make this difficult, was he? She would make him pay for that. Now that she had him quite naked, she stepped back to look him over the way he'd looked her over in the horse stall yesterday. She took her time about it, prolonging his agony purposely. Trailing her gaze down his well-formed chest, muscled ribs, and lean, hard belly, she let it skitter to a halt at his jutting shaft and ballocks.

"My, my, but aren't you the perfect figure of a man," she said. When his pego bobbed in response to her words, she laughed and stepped forward to catch it in her hand. He muttered something under his breath, half oath, half groan.

"Hmm," she went on, "what would be the most wicked thing I could do with this, I wonder?"

"If you have to wonder, then you're not very wicked, are you?" he choked out.

"It was a rhetorical question, Danny. I know precisely what to do with it."

Remembering how he'd put her hand on him that day, she swept her fingers up the length. "It needs a bit of petting, doesn't it?" She caressed him lightly until his hand shot out to catch hers.

"Bloody hell, lass, I said seduce me, not tease me into insanity." He forced her hand around his erection. "Hold it tighter."

Sheer triumph roared through her. He was not so aloof anymore, was he? "Like this?" she said, gripping him hard.

He growled his assent and moved her hand on him, showing her what to do, not even pretending to resist anymore. She had him now. Oh, yes, she had him in every sense of the word.

When he released her hand, she continued the motion he'd initiated, marveling at the satin smoothness of his rigid flesh, exulting in his groaned response. Grabbing her upper arms as if to anchor her to him, he slid his eyes closed and threw his head back.

It was irresistible, having him at her mercy like this, watching the play of emotion over his face. He was hers to "pet," hers to touch, and she couldn't get enough of him.

Emboldened by his crumbling control, she stroked him more quickly. "Do you like that, my love?"

"Oh, yes, sweet Jesus, yes!"

She stopped abruptly, still clasping the heavy weight of him. "Then touch me, too."

That was all it took to finally have his hands on her, fondling her breasts avidly, brazenly. With a smile, she resumed stroking his pego, and when she lifted her parted lips to kiss him, he responded with savage fervor, feasting on her, devouring her.

Then she felt his fingers delve inside her drawers—inside *her*—and it was her turn to groan. He stood kissing and caressing her for endless moments, until her leg began to ache from being forced to bear so much of her weight for so long.

Abruptly, she released him and pushed away. "Do you want more?" She slipped out of her drawers, watching in delight as he surged toward her. Backing toward the bed, she smiled a taunt. "Do you want to see how truly wicked I can be?"

He stalked her, eyes glittering. "On the bed, lass. Now!"

A thrill of delight shot through her at the command. "I thought *I* was supposed to be seducing *you*," she teased as she climbed onto the bed, still edging back from him.

"You're taking too bloody long." He lunged after her, the chain clattering against the iron bedstead as he hit the mattress close by.

With a laugh of triumph, she whirled to escape, but he had her before she could leave the bed on the other side. Throwing himself back onto the bed, he dragged her on top of him so that she lay along his length, with his pego a stiff rod between their bellies. He moved his leg and suddenly she felt cold iron against her good ankle. He'd wound it loosely in the long chain.

"You wanted to be shackled to a bed with me, did you?" he whispered. "You wanted to make love to me?"

She grinned down at him. "That was the general idea." She planted a hot, moist kiss against his collarbone, and he groaned.

"Then up on your knees, lass." His eyes blazed with his need. "Time for you to proceed with the seduction."

Up on her knees? It took her only a second to figure

out what he wanted, and another to drag the chain up so she could straddle him.

But before she went on, she wanted something from him. "Does this mean you've decided I'm wicked enough to satisfy you?" His erection now thrust up between her spread thighs, and she rubbed her damp, aching cleft against it.

He grabbed her hips. "Wicked enough to satisfy ten of me, I'm beginning to suspect. Now make love to me, Helena. Take me inside you before I go mad."

She wanted to elicit a more lasting promise from him, a promise of marriage, but she suspected he would not make it until all of this was over and done with. For now, this was enough.

As soon as she rose up and came down on him, he let out a feral growl. "Christ Almighty . . . ah, yes, love . . . yes, like that . . ."

My, this was amazing, being on top of him, filled by him, joined to him so completely. She had him entirely at her mercy, didn't she? The very thought flooded her loins with hot pleasure. She could be as wicked with him as she pleased, and he would let her, even encourage her.

That's when it dawned on her that this was why she loved him. Because he let her be herself, even when she wanted to forget she was a lady. He accepted her with all her flaws—her tart tongue, her distrustful nature, her lameness. He did not ask her to hide her leg or her physical weakness—he simply found a way to accommodate them.

Staring down into his dear face, she whispered, "I love you, Danny. I will always love you."

His thorough satisfaction made him look almost angelic. "You remember that you said that when you're back in London at one of your fancy balls, d'you hear?"

he said softly. Then he tugged her head down for a warm, intimate kiss so sweet she could have cried.

After that, she was utterly lost. She took him deep inside her, welcoming his thrusts, undulating with every plunge. Yet it was not just her body she laid open, but her heart.

All her life, she'd kept a small portion of herself hidden from everyone—her parents, her sisters, and even Lord Farnsworth. And then Daniel had come, refusing to let her hide from him. Now she wanted him to have it all, to know her completely. If she'd kept anything from him before, it was now all his: her secrets, her needs, her lifelong yearnings. With every precious thrust of his, she gave him more, dragged him further inside her, sucked him into herself as she'd never done with anyone.

As if he sensed it, he swept his hands and his mouth over all of her, everywhere he could reach, seeking, caressing, branding her with his touch. He kissed her hair and her breasts, he nuzzled the soft inner skin of her arms, he fondled her cleft until she felt herself shattering, a thousand shards of herself that were all his, would be his forever.

"I love you, too," he whispered fiercely as she convulsed around him. "And I'll ne'er let you forget it."

Then with a guttural cry of his own, he drove deep and spilled himself inside her.

Chapter 20

It was Brennan on the moor, Brennan on the moor
Bold, brave and undaunted was young Brennan
on the moor.

"Brennan on the Moor,"
anonymous nineteenth-century ballad
about a real-life Irish highwayman

It was dawn, the light growing too quickly. Soon the room would be as bright as polished brass. Propped up against the iron bedstead, Daniel watched the morning come, one hand stroking Helena's hair as she slept and the other rubbing his whiskered jaw.

He wished he could shave. He wished he wasn't shackled. He wished he was back in London. Most of all, he wished he wasn't a randy bastard who couldn't keep his hands off Helena for more than a moment.

Now I've gone and done it. I've gone from building castles in the clouds to moving into them.

With Helena, of all people. It was enough to make his heart leap. Or weep, he wasn't sure which.

He gazed down at her sleeping form and sighed. The lass had such faith in him, such trust in their future. Just the sight of her leg tangled in his shackle chain made his gut clench. He'd tried to keep from ensnaring her in his life, but the woman persisted in infecting him with all her mad hopes.

And to think she loved him! He'd never dared hope for that, hadn't allowed himself to love her, because he'd feared she could never love him back. Now it felt so good to love her, to have her say she loved him, as if she believed it with her whole heart and body and soul. No one had ever loved him like that. He hadn't realized till now how badly he'd wanted it.

One fear still hounded him—that this was a moment's aberration. She said it was not, yet he knew all too well the sort of promises one made when in danger. But would those promises hold once this was over and she returned to her proper place, once she saw what she'd recklessly thrown herself into? Back in London, she might very well realize she'd made a dreadful mistake.

He could only pray that she didn't. Because if he lost her love now—after having its sweetness dangled before him—it might very well kill him.

There were sounds of activity in the hall, and he shook her gently. "Come on, love, wake up. Looks like something's happening, and we want to be dressed for it."

She shot out of sleep like a startled swan, all rustling feathers and blinking eyes and flailing wings. "What?

Where am I? What's happening?" Then her gaze flew to his, and she blushed. "Oh, I'm here." A slow, seductive smile spread over her lips. "So it wasn't all just a lovely dream."

"No, or I'm sure you would've had us locked up under far better circumstances."

"True." She snuggled up next to him to press a kiss to his mouth. "Good morning, Danny."

"Morning, love."

"Are you feeling as grand as I am this morning?" She stretched her arms, letting the sheet drop enough to reveal her darling breasts.

His unruly John Thomas woke up and stretched as well. "Lass," he said in a strained voice, "any minute, our captors will be opening that door to take us to meet Crouch. So unless you want to be doing the mattress jig when they do, I suggest you not go tempting me."

With a look of horror, she grabbed the sheet and plastered it to her chest. "They're coming for us? Now? Why didn't you say so?"

"I just did," he retorted.

Whipping the sheet around her sweet curves, she left the bed and went in search of her clothes. "Why would they come for us so early?"

He, too, got up and began to dress. "Crouch was on a run last night. If he acts true to form, he'll be wanting to settle all his business before he finds some lightskirt and drops into bed. They're probably stowing the goods as we speak, which means they'll be here for us soon."

"What do you plan to do?" She dressed quickly.

"I don't know. First I'll have to see what he intends." He finished putting on all but his coat and strode to where she knelt on the floor, hunting for her hairpins. Plucking two from her hand, he returned to where his coat lay. He removed the knife from the pocket, used it to make a hole in the lining of his coat sleeve very near the wrist end, slid the knife inside, and closed up the hole with the hairpins.

"Do you think you'll need it?"

He glanced over to find her watching him with a mixture of horror and worry. "I hope not. I'm hoping Jolly Roger will listen to reason. I'd just as soon avoid bloodshed if I can."

The rattle of the doorknob cut into their conversation. The door swung open and Jack stepped inside, Big Antony looming up behind him. "So, did you two lovebirds sleep well?" Jack's eyes twinkled. "I hear the chain was clanking something fierce half the night."

"I had trouble sleeping with an iron bracelet on my ankle is all," Daniel snapped, annoyed by the idea of Big Antony—or any of them, for that matter—listening in on his and Helena's lovemaking. Strange, he'd never cared about something like that before. But then he'd never been in love with the woman he was bedding.

"Well, I'm glad you're both ready," Jack went on. "It's time to go."

"Did you ask Crouch about what I told you?"

Jack's amusement vanished. "Not yet. I haven't even told him you're here, and I ordered the boys not to mention it. I want to watch how he reacts when he sees you."

Jack spoke to Big Antony in fractured Italian. Within moments the foreigner was binding Daniel's wrists while Daniel did his best to keep the coat sleeve containing the knife from bumping the Italian. Only when Big Antony had him well-tied did Jack remove the shackle.

"You find me quite the dangerous fellow, d'you, Jack?" Daniel said sarcastically.

"Just a precaution, Danny. The last time I got into a fight with you, there were five of us against you and

Knighton, and you won. I learned then not to underestimate you."

Daniel glanced over at Helena, whom they'd left unbound. Judging from how Helena clutched her cane, he wasn't the only one Jack ought not to underestimate: Helena was liable to break it over Jack's fool head. He only hoped she chose to do it at a more opportune time. So he breathed easier when they hustled him past her and she acquiesced to Jack's order for her to follow right behind Daniel.

They moved down the stairs, with Big Antony in front of Daniel and Jack taking up the rear. Between Helena's difficulties navigating the narrow passageway with her cane and Daniel's being bound, it was impossible to move quickly.

That made it easier for him to work the knife from his sleeve into his hand. Helena hot on his heels blocked his arms from Jack's gaze, and the poor light helped. As soon as he had the knife hilt in his grip, he slid it up between his wrists and went to work on his ropes.

When they reached the bottom floor and headed to the staircase leading into the basement, Helena said, "Where are we going?"

"To the caves," Daniel answered for Jack. He should've known that was why they'd been brought to Jack's, but he'd forgotten about the caves. "There's a tunnel in the basement that leads to the St. Clements Caves inside West Hill. That's where Jolly Roger stashes his contraband."

"Very good, Danny Boy," Jack called down behind him. "I see you haven't forgot us entirely. If you ever decide you want to come back to work—"

"Thank you, but I prefer not to spend my days avoiding excisemen," he retorted. "Not to mention that I'm doing a damned sight better making my money the honest way."

Jack chuckled. "Then perhaps Jolly Roger should've come to *you* about the financing."

"Aye. Because I would've done more than toss him out on his ear. I would've sent him to Newgate. Especially if I'd known he was my uncle."

That shut Jack up, thank God.

When Big Antony reached the basement, he tossed aside the rug that hid the tunnel door. Soon they were descending an angled sandstone passageway illuminated by torchlight.

As Daniel sawed more quickly at the rope binding his hands, a weight of memory settled on him, oppressive and bittersweet. Jack had been right about one thing—there'd been both good times and bad in these damp dominions. He'd spent so much of the past few years suppressing it that he'd forgotten the simple pleasures of playing hide-and-seek with the other boys, exploring hidden passages, playing jokes on Jack and Jolly Roger when they were in their cups.

The rope binding his hands suddenly broke. He dropped it, praying Jack would tramp over it without noticing. Then he kept his hands clasped together around the knife hilt, hiding the blade inside his sleeve. He must continue to appear bound until he could assess the situation.

The tunnel was already opening into the largest of the sandstone caverns. They entered to find a blond stick of a man barking orders to a half-dozen others who scurried to and fro, repackaging tobacco for transport to Stockwell and stowing anker tubs in hidden nooks. The well-remembered sight swamped him in a wave of nostalgia. This was what he'd come from, like it or not.

"Crouch," Jack called out as they entered, "I've got a surprise for you!"

The blond man turned, and Daniel halted, slack-jawed to see the familiar features. Bloody hell.

Ten years had roughed Crouch up almost beyond recognition. The gray threading his blond hair was to be expected, since he must be past fifty now, but it was more than aging that had changed him. There was a stoop to his shoulders, and his skin seemed dried to his bones. The once-burly man looked as if any stiff wind might carry him off. Jack hadn't lied about the man's health, to be sure.

Crouch—his *uncle*, for God's sake—looked as if he danced just this side of the grave. The thought staggered him. Despite all Crouch had done and was attempting to do, Daniel hated seeing him so ill.

The man had his good side, after all. He could've left Daniel in the workhouse to rot, but he hadn't.

Crouch squinted through the murky darkness as he made his slow way to where they stood in the tunnel entrance. When he got close enough to see Daniel, he froze. "What in the divil— Is that Danny Boy?"

"Aye, it's him, all right," Jack said, laying his hand on Daniel's shoulder. "He's come to pay us a visit, he has."

"Hello, Jolly Roger," Daniel said blandly. "Been a long time, hasn't it?"

For a second, Crouch looked pleased to see him. Then anger clouded his features, directed at Jack. "Have you lost yer mind? You brought him *here*?"

"He didn't give me much choice," Jack retorted. "He was snooping around Sussex for the girl. Wallace's gang stumbled across him and sent me word. You were at sea, so I did what I thought best. I sort of . . . took him prisoner."

"You bloody arse—don't you know that Knighton can't be far behind? They wasn't supposed to know we was tied up in this!"

"Danny already knew," Jack protested. "He found out on his own."

"Your man Pryce wasn't careful enough covering his tracks," Daniel said smoothly.

Crouch swore under his breath. Then he seemed to notice Helena. "And who's this, pray tell?"

"His missus," Jack answered.

A dry laugh rattled from Crouch. "So you've got a missus now, have you, Danny? Let me see her."

Daniel tensed as Jack prodded her forward, but dared do no more than grit his teeth as Crouch ran his gaze over Helena. To his surprise, Crouch gave her a sketchy bow. "You're Danny's wife, eh?"

"Yes," she lied with a proud tilt of her chin.

"Then you got your hands full. He's a rascal, that one is."

Daniel snorted. The pot calling the kettle black. "What do you intend to do with us?" he demanded.

"Don't have much choice, I s'pose," Crouch said. "I'll have to take you with me."

That startled Daniel. "Where are you going?"

"The Isle of Wight. As soon as Knighton returns to England, he'll receive instructions from my man in London to go directly there. We're leaving for it shortly. When Knighton arrives on the island, he'll meet my man as we watch to make sure he's alone. He'll be able to see the girl from my ship, and this'll keep him from sneaking men in to try and take me. As soon as the money is there, we'll give him the girl."

Crouch sighed. "Of course, now that you're in it, he might think to come this direction first. But we won't be here, and when he don't find us, he'll go where he belongs. I'll make sure he knows that the girl's life is forfeit if he don't."

Daniel's gut clenched and he saw Helena stiffen at his side. "So you'd stoop to murder."

"Danny!" Crouch protested. "Damnation, boy, I thought you knew me better than that. I won't lay a finger on her. But Knighton don't know that. He thinks I'm the divil. It don't matter what he thinks, long as he leaves that ransom the way he's s'posed to. Because once I've got my money, I'm off for France."

"What about me and my wife?"

Crouch averted his gaze. "Do as you're told, and all will be well."

A far too evasive answer for Daniel's satisfaction. Go out to sea, where anybody could be thrown overboard without an ounce of suspicion? Hope that his uncle wouldn't turn on him, the way he'd turned on Daniel's parents?

Daniel wasn't taking that chance. He didn't trust Crouch that much, and certainly not with Helena's and Juliet's lives. Crouch could just as easily take the money, dispense with them, and be off to France as not. Then he'd never be taken, and he was bound to know it.

No, Daniel would have to make his move before they boarded ship. Now if only there weren't so many bloody free traders milling about . . .

Crouch suddenly glanced across the cavern and smiled. "And here is Pryce with the girl, right on time for departure."

Daniel looked up to see a young man coming out of a nearby tunnel, one of the others leading into the main cavern. Better dressed than the other men and carrying himself like a bloody lord, Pryce halted suddenly to scan the cavern. He kept Juliet behind him, but Daniel glimpsed enough to see that she was well.

Pryce's eyes narrowed on Daniel and Helena. Then he turned to whisper to Juliet, who'd just caught sight of them, too. To Daniel's surprise, Juliet didn't cry out to her sister, which was what he'd feared. Instead, she drew nearer to Pryce, her gaze darting anxiously from Crouch to Jack.

Pryce thrust her farther behind him, but approached no nearer. "I see you have visitors, Jolly Roger."

Crouch scowled at Pryce. "It's Knighton's man of affairs, Danny Brennan. He and his wife tracked you down, you fool. You were careless."

"Apparently so," Pryce said mildly, his gaze flicking to Helena. "His wife, is it?"

"Aye," Crouch answered. "It seems Danny made the mistake of bringing her along."

Daniel held his breath, waiting for Pryce to set Crouch straight, to explain that he had not one but two Knighton relations in his power.

But Pryce merely shifted his gaze to Daniel. "That was a mistake indeed, Mr. Brennan. You ought to know better than to carry your . . . er . . . wife with you into a den of smugglers."

Helena's sharp intake of breath said she was as surprised as Daniel to find Pryce concealing her identity.

"I thought it was an elopement," Daniel retorted, "or you can be sure I would have left her behind." What was Pryce up to? And why did he continue to stand back, keeping Juliet thrust behind him with one hand while the other remained shoved inside the pocket of his greatcoat?

"Does this mean that Knighton knows you're involved?" Pryce asked Crouch.

"Probably," Crouch retorted. "That's why I'll have to change the plan a bit, take Danny Boy and his wife with me, too. And you'll have to stay here."

Pryce stiffened. "Why? To serve as target practice for Knighton once he descends on Hastings with the soldiers?"

"I don't think he'd be that stupid with the girl's safety at stake, but I can't be sure. So I need you to make it clear that he won't get the girl unless he pays the ransom."

"No," Pryce said calmly.

Crouch drew his emaciated frame up taut like a bow string. "What d'you mean, 'no'?"

"I mean, she isn't going anywhere without me."

"You'll do as you're told," Crouch growled.

Pryce's black eyes snapped. "I've kept my part of the bargain, Crouch. I brought her here without attracting attention. You, however, haven't kept yours. So I'm not letting her out of my sight until you do. I'll be happy to stay here to greet Knighton, but not until after you've given me what you promised."

Good, a little dissension in the ranks can't hurt, Daniel thought. "Knighton will pay you better than Crouch ever could," he called out to Pryce, hoping to stir it up further. "If you'll get the girl out of here safely, there'll be a hefty reward in it for you."

From beside him, Crouch croaked out a laugh. "Nice try, Danny, but Pryce don't want money. What he wants, only I can give him."

Crouch nodded to Jack, who moved toward Pryce.

Pryce whipped out a pistol and aimed it at Jack, and the blood drained from the older man's face.

Pryce had chosen his position wisely. In the mouth to the tunnel, he had an escape route, for the complicated tunnels would delay pursuit. He could be outside with Juliet before they even got near him.

"Now, Morgan," Crouch wheedled, "why do you want to go and do something foolish like this?"

"Give me what I want, Crouch," Pryce merely repeated.

Though Daniel found this discussion more fascinating by the moment, he wasn't about to let this chance go by. He could already see the other free traders coming in their direction, having finally noticed the little drama taking place on the other end of the cavern. So while everybody was preoccupied with Pryce, he sidled closer to Crouch, the knife firmly in his grip.

Crouch's ravaged features were mottled with rage. "You blasted fool! You didn't do your part! You were found out, and now I've got to deal with Danny Boy and change all my plans!"

"Nonetheless," Pryce said calmly, still keeping Juliet behind him and his pistol steadily aimed at Jack, "you have Mr. Brennan and his wife—that gives you something with which to blackmail Knighton. And you'll have the girl, too, if you do as you promised." He stepped back into the tunnel. "If you don't, I'm taking her out of here and you'll never have her. I'll make my own negotiations with Knighton."

Daniel chose that moment to strike, darting behind Crouch to grab him about the waist and thrust the knife against his throat. "Helena, come on!" he barked as he dragged a cursing Crouch back toward the nearest tunnel. Big Antony lunged for Helena, but she brought her cane up into his jaw so hard Daniel heard both the jaw and the cane crack.

As she hastened to Daniel's side, he muttered, "I've got to buy you a bigger cane, love."

"I'd prefer a pistol," she retorted as she swept behind him.

"Good idea. Come see what you can find in Crouch's pockets. He usually carries a pistol when he's in the caves."

She quickly did as he bade, finding not one, but two. "An embarrassment of riches, it appears."

"Very good, lass. You'll make a fine smuggler's wife yet."

"I do my best." She held them up. "Whom do I shoot?"

Bloody hell, the woman would probably do it, too. "No shooting yet, love. But aim one of them at Pryce." Daniel met Pryce's gaze with grim purpose, then called out, "Let Juliet come with me or I'll have my wife shoot you."

Pryce laughed. "You wouldn't do that, and you know it. I feel fairly certain that your 'wife' has never shot anything in her life, and the likelihood that she'd risk hitting my captive is very small, I should imagine."

Damn, but the man was clever. "How about this then? I'll just slit Crouch's throat and you'll never get whatever it is you want from him."

"Danny, you wouldn't slit your own—" Jack began.

"Stubble it, Jack. I'll do as I damned well please." Now was not the time to let Pryce know that Crouch was Daniel's uncle.

Yet Pryce still kept hold of Juliet. "If you kill Crouch," Pryce countered, "you'll force me to shoot Jack. Then neither you nor I will have anything left to bargain with, and we'll both have a devil of a time escaping with the women."

Escaping with the women? Was that his purpose? Or was this just his ploy to get Juliet away so he could "negotiate with Knighton," as he'd put it?

Crouch's men inched closer, and Daniel steadied the blade against Crouch's neck. "Tell them to stay back, Crouch, or I swear I'll cut you. You know I will, too. I fought you once before, and I'll do it again."

Crouch cursed him roundly, but ordered his men back.

"Now give Pryce what he wants," Daniel barked, "so he'll let the girl go!"

For a moment, everything froze in the cavern, each man judging the other's determination, Crouch shaking as Daniel pressed the blade as firmly into the man's flesh as he dared.

At last Crouch slumped against him. "Damn you, Pryce, you're a bloody arse. Do with the information what you will. It's the *Oceana*. July seventeenth."

Daniel nearly throttled him for that enigmatic remark, but Pryce seemed to be well satisfied. "Are you sure? Because if you're lying, you know I'll find you and cut your heart out for it."

"I'm sure. You got what you wanted; let Danny have the girl."

Pryce's lips curved up in a smile as his gaze met Daniel's. "Not just yet. It seems to me, Mr. Brennan, that you have your hands full at the moment. So if you don't mind, I'll hold on to Lady Juliet a bit longer until I'm sure you will prevail. We'll meet you outside." He whispered to Juliet, and though she seemed to protest, he thrust her back into the tunnel.

"Pryce, come back here, damn you!" Daniel shouted, but Pryce shot his pistol into the roof of the tunnel mouth, raining sandstone down that quickly hid him and Juliet from view.

"Get him!" Crouch yelled to Big Antony, who started for the clouded mouth of the tunnel.

In that moment, Daniel made a split-second decision. Keeping the knife to Crouch's throat with one hand, Daniel grabbed one of Helena's pistols with the other and shouted, "Stop, or I shoot!"

At least the Italian understood *that* much English, for

he halted in his tracks. Jack did the same. Daniel returned the pistol to Helena. "Aim that at Big Antony, love. And keep the other on Jack."

"But Daniel, what about Juliet?"

"God help me if I'm wrong, but I think she's safer with Pryce than with Crouch."

Pryce had been right—Daniel was hardly sure he could get Helena out safely, much less Juliet.

"I wouldn't have hurt the girl," Crouch muttered. "I swear it."

"If you think I'd take your word for it, Uncle," Daniel shot back, "then you're a bloody fool."

Crouch stiffened in his arms. "U-Uncle?"

"Jack told me all about you being my Uncle Thomas. Made for a fascinating tale."

"Damn you, Jack—" Crouch began.

"I had to tell him." Jack pivoted to stare at Crouch. "He was so sure you'd murder him and his lady that I had to convince him you meant no harm. But he says . . ." He hesitated, glanced to Daniel, then went on haltingly, "He says you were the one what handed his parents over to the soldiers. I told him he was mad, but he'd have none of it. He's wrong, ain't he? He's wrong?"

Crouch slumped against Daniel. "Oh, lad," he whispered, "so you heard of it, did you? And I can see what you thought."

Jack paled. "Then it's true? You . . . you . . ."

"All these years," Crouch blathered on, ignoring Jack's reaction, "I was afraid you might learn of it, Danny Boy . . . Sweet Jesus, how did you find out?"

"I went back to Essex," Daniel growled. "I asked around."

Crouch was shaking his head, heedless of the knife at his throat. "It's not what you think—"

"No?" His hand on the hilt quavered against Crouch's neck. Right now he could easily kill the man. "Then what is it? Pray explain why you turned your own sister over to the soldiers, if you can."

Crouch's men were listening in rapt amazement, and everybody else—even Big Antony, who probably didn't understand a word—stood frozen, awaiting Jolly Roger's answer.

"I turned your father in, damn it, but not her!" Crouch shook in Daniel's arms. "Molly wasn't s'posed to ride with him. I didn't know she was with him, I tell you! The bastard was short a man when he headed out, so he took her at the last minute."

He jerked in Danny's arms, rocked by the violence of his emotion. "I always hated that blasted Irishman, y'know. He wouldn't marry her—treated her like a whore. She deserved better. I thought if I got rid of him, she could find a good husband. I knew where he roamed the road, so I did it, yes, I told the soldiers."

"And took their gold for it," Daniel snapped.

"Aye. But it was for her, to use in raising you. And when they told me she was with him, that she would hang with him . . ." His voice cracked. "Oh, God, Danny, I wanted to die. I tried to die. I threw myself in the river, but I was too much of a coward even to drown myself. Poor Molly . . . my poor, sweet sister . . ."

Crouch's words thundered in his brain, battering against Daniel's long hatred of his uncle.

All the same . . . "That gold came in handy, though, when you ran off to Sussex, didn't it? You used it to start up the free trading."

"It was all I knew," Crouch retorted. "How do you think your mother met Wild Danny in the first place? He and I used to do a bit of smuggling in Essex."

A heavy silence weighted the musty air of the cavern, smothering him. Daniel wondered if he'd ever be able to breathe again. His hand dropped away from Jolly Roger's neck, and he stumbled back a pace. The past was choking him, welling up from wherever he'd banished it, and the pain was so intense he was drowning in it, trying to claw his way back into the light and the air.

All this because of his bastard of a father. He'd never hated Wild Danny Brennan as much as he did now.

The other men seemed unsure what to do. With bewilderment and betrayal etched in his aging features, Jack stared accusingly at Crouch.

But Crouch didn't notice, for he'd already faced Daniel. Tears glinted in his eyes—an old man's tears, filled with regret. Daniel had never seen the man come close to crying. Never.

"Don't it mean nothing to you that I came after you?" Crouch whispered. "That I took you out of the workhouse?"

"Yes," Helena put in stoutly, "you hurried right back for him, didn't you? You left him in that workhouse for three years! He was only a boy!"

Helena's fierce protests on his behalf soothed some of the ache in Daniel's heart.

But they made Crouch blanch. "When I left Essex, I thought my family would look after him." He cast Daniel an imploring glance. "Believe me, Danny, I was in no condition to take a boy with me. It was only later that I heard roundabout how they'd abandoned you to the workhouse. Bloody arses." He sucked in a tortured breath. "But I'm sorry I didn't come for you sooner. I thought you were being taken care of, or I would've never left Molly's boy to . . ." He trailed off, unable to go on.

"When you finally did get around to coming for me,

why the devil didn't you tell me I was your nephew, you bloody sot?" Daniel choked out, years of suppressed hurt and anger oozing to the surface. "All those years, pretending, lying to me—"

"You would've hated me, and you know it. You were always yearning so for your parents. I was sure you'd go prying one day into what happened, and when you found out you'd never forgive me. I couldn't tell you, Danny Boy. And to speak true, although I was angry when you first chose Knighton over me, I didn't do naught about it because I knew he'd give you a future, make something of you. You deserved a better life than what I could offer."

Daniel stiffened. "Oh? Then why did you come back and try to ruin it, using me to pry money out of him? Why kidnap an innocent girl?"

A peevish look crossed his face. "I never claimed to be no saint." Resentment flared in his eyes. "Besides, it made me angry that you never returned. Ten years, and you forgot all about us. I thought it was time I reminded you—and him—that *I* was the one who had you first, who gave you a chance long before he came along." He hunched one shoulder. "Then he treated me no better than a villain and had me tossed into the street."

"That's what happens when you act like a villain," Daniel retorted, fists clenching.

"All the same, it wouldn't have hurt that arse to give me a bit of blunt, to throw me a bone now and then. He has all the money *he* needs and then some, made for him by you and your clever mind."

There was a wealth of bitterness in his tone, and Daniel suddenly realized why. Crouch envied Griff for more than his money; he envied him for garnering Daniel's loyalty and respect. No doubt it had frustrated Crouch not to be able to admit his blood ties to Daniel.

Not to mention that he'd lost the benefit of having Daniel's "clever mind" at his disposal, which must have grated on him.

"Trust me," Daniel responded, "I may have done my part for Griff, but he earned every penny of his money." *And my respect and loyalty, something you never sought until you lost it.* "He had a right to do what he wished with his fortune. What's more, he didn't earn it by kidnapping young women or attempting blackmail. He did it by hard work, by facing up to his responsibilities."

Daniel's implication was lost on Crouch, unfortunately. The old man scowled at him. "I only wanted enough money to go away, that's all. Jack can tell you that."

"Yes, he already did." Daniel glanced at Helena, whose lovely features were marked with worry, for her sister, for him. "But you involved innocent people in it, Uncle, and that's crossing the line."

Crouch stiffened, his face as implacable as Daniel remembered from his boyhood. "So you're passing judgment on me, are you, boy? Your own flesh and blood, who done his best to see that you had a good life? You think to hand me over to the excisemen and watch me hang?"

"No." Daniel took a shuddering breath. "Unlike you, I have some respect for blood ties. But that doesn't mean I'll let you go on wreaking havoc in my life. You've had a good run of it, Uncle. Now accept that it's all come to an end. Time for you to retire to France as you planned. As long as you stay there, you can end your days in peace."

"Danny, if you won't let me have the ransom and you won't let me free trade—" Crouch began.

"Knowing you, there's a nest egg somewhere you can use to set yourself up. It's probably not as plump as you'd like, but it'll have to do. And I'm damned well not going to have you staying in England, plotting new ways to bedevil me and mine."

"My boys won't let you do this to me," Crouch grumbled.

Daniel glanced up to see Crouch's men standing hesitant, some of them clearly still shocked by the revelations of Crouch's betrayal of Daniel's parents. "Oh, I think they'll do whatever I say. Especially when they hear that a package is on its way to London with sketches of Jack's house, Jack's face, the faces of some of your men, a few little tidbits about your free-trading operation, and a full account of the kidnapping and who was responsible for it. Griff should be receiving it about now."

The men started grumbling.

"You're bluffing," Crouch spat.

"Not at all. Jack, do you remember the sketch of Pryce you found in my coat pocket when you took me?" Daniel called over to him.

"Yes, Danny," Jack said in a curiously muted voice.

"My wife drew that. She's quite talented. She drew the other sketches, too, and I assure you they're good enough likenesses to send all of you to Newgate. That maid from the Stag Inn was obliging enough to agree to carry them to London for a price."

Jack's sigh made it clear that he remembered only too well all the ruckus they'd made over "her," and had figured out why.

"Griff's instructions are to use that information however he can if Juliet and Helena and I don't return within the week." Daniel let his gaze play over the men. "But as long as all of you leave me and mine alone, I swear I'll never let him use it. You can go on free trading until you rot." He lowered his voice to a threatening growl. "But if you ever again perpetrate any scheme like this against me and my family, or Griff and his family, you can be sure I'll have you all turned over to the excisemen in a heartbeat. And I've got plenty of evidence to do it, believe me."

"It's all right, m'boy, you've convinced us," Jack put in. "The rest of them had naught to do with the planning anyway. And none of us is gonna stop you."

Daniel took a pistol from Helena. "As for you, Uncle, I'm personally putting you on a packet boat to France. And if I ever see you in England again or hear that you've returned, it'll be your neck, do you understand?"

Crouch turned and shot his men a look of mute appeal, but they were no fools. Grumbling about "Crouch and his mad schemes," they wandered back to their tasks. Even Big Antony lumbered off to join them.

"All right, Danny," Crouch complained, "looks like you've won. I hope you're pleased with yourself."

"That isn't exactly how I'd term it," Daniel muttered as he took Crouch's arm and led him back toward the tunnel to the house.

As they passed Jack, the older man stepped up to Daniel. "P'raps you'd come visit once in a while, Danny? Just for old time's sake."

Daniel smiled sadly at Jack. "P'raps."

Jack jerked his thumb toward Crouch. "Don't be too hard on him, m'boy. He was only trying to look out for his kin."

Daniel glanced at Helena, who had endured insults, threats, kidnapping, and bullying to save *her* kin.

"That might be true. But some people risk their lives and future to do it. They accept their mistakes and don't try to avoid the consequences of their cowardice."

Jack could make no answer to that, because there was none.

And as Daniel ushered Helena and Crouch up out of

the caverns toward the light and air, he realized that having a murky past wasn't what shackled a man. It was how the man chose to deal with it. As long as Daniel didn't choose Crouch's way of dealing with it, he ought to remain free of shackles for the rest of his life.

Chapter 21

Tumultuous tides his pulses roll,
A faltering, ardent kiss he stole . . .
"On a Bank of Flowers,"
ballad by Robert Burns

Juliet and Morgan stood hidden in an alley where they could watch Jack Seward's house without being seen. Juliet trained her gaze anxiously on the door, and if Morgan hadn't prevented it, she would have rushed over and inside, down to the tunnel he said was in the basement.

"Oh, Morgan, they're taking too long. Are you sure it will be all right? I would never have let you drag me out of there if I'd thought—"

"Don't worry, your friend Brennan seemed an enterprising sort. He was well on his way to extricating himself from the situation. We'll give them a bit more time, and if they don't come out, I'll go in after them. One thing I'm fairly certain of—Crouch won't hurt them."

He sounded as worried as she, which surprised her. But then, everything he'd done had surprised her.

She gazed up at him, lower lip trembling. "If Crouch hadn't given you what you wanted, would you have . . . I mean, you *said* you'd try to get a ransom from Griff—"

"Haven't you ever heard of bluffing, my dear?" Morgan's gaze snapped to hers. "I had to threaten to take away something he really wanted—the ransom—to get what *I* wanted."

"And if he hadn't fallen for it?" she whispered.

He smiled down at her. "I'd be mad as hell. But we'd still be standing here, waiting for your friends."

Despite everything, his words made her heart leap. Oh, how could she be so foolish? "Why?"

"Why what?"

"Why did you kidnap me, then refuse to give me over to them?"

"Crouch has had his mind set on kidnapping you for weeks. I thought that if *I* were the one to do it, I could—" He broke off, a cynical smile touching his lips. "And it did seem the perfect way to make Crouch tell me what I'd been trying to get out of him."

"Yes, but what did it mean, all that about July seventeenth and the ship?"

His expression grew shuttered as he swung his gaze back to the door. "Nothing that concerns you."

"I have a right to know!" she protested. "You . . . you enticed me away from my family, you *kidnapped* me for some secret purpose, and now you won't even tell me what it is? I could be ruined forever. Everyone in London might know of my elopement, and when I come back unmarried . . ." She swallowed. "The least you can do is tell me why."

A muscle jumped in his taut cheek, but he merely said, "By thunder, Brennan, what's taking you so long? You had two Manton flintlocks and a knife at your disposal—you should have been out by now."

He was evading her questions as he always did, the wretch.

"Morgan—" she began.

"Look!" he interrupted, gesturing to the house.

She turned to see the door to Jack's house open and Helena limp out, blinking in the bright sun. Daniel quickly followed, shoving Crouch out ahead of him.

Relief brightened Morgan's features. "I told you he'd manage it." He gazed down at Juliet. "I told you."

"Yes, you did," she said quietly, wondering what would happen to Morgan now. Not that she wanted any more to do with him after what he'd done. And yet . . .

"It's time for you to go, sweeting." For a moment, his gaze trailed almost greedily over her face, as if he were trying to fix it in his mind.

"I suppose I ought to thank you," she whispered.

"For what?"

"For keeping your promise. You said you'd protect me, and you did."

His eyes darkened. "You once asked me to kiss you. Since this is good-bye . . ."

Without warning, he clasped her close and kissed her hard, as no man ever had, as if he wanted to make sure she never forgot it. There was no likelihood of that. His kiss scrambled all her insides, confusing her feelings toward him even more.

When he drew back, raw hunger flickered in his gaze. "Have a good life, Lady Juliet."

She stared at him, not sure what to say, how to react.

Then Helena's voice penetrated her haze. "Juliet! Where are you? Juliet!"

"Go on," Morgan said, almost harshly, giving her a little push. "They're waiting."

That was all it took. Juliet whirled and ran from the alley toward her sister. "Helena!" she cried. "I'm here, I'm here!"

The two of them met in a fierce hug, crying and laughing like little girls. As Daniel stood beaming at them, Helena clasped her so close that Juliet could hardly breathe.

"I'm all right," Juliet whispered. "Truly I am."

Helena held her at arm's length. "He didn't hurt you?"

"No, not a bit." He'd bruised her pride perhaps, but that was all. "Morgan watched out for me the whole time. I'm fine, I swear it!"

"And he didn't . . . you aren't . . ."

It took a second to figure out what Helena was trying to discover. "No! No, nothing like that! He didn't even kiss—" She broke off. "That is, he treated me with all respect, almost as if I were his sister." *Almost.* That final, searing kiss still lingered on her lips.

Helena scanned the road behind her. "Where is the villain, anyway?"

Juliet turned. "He was right—" A keen disappointment settled in her chest to find the alley empty. "Right there. But he's gone now."

A short time later, Helena sat with Juliet in a private room at the Hastings Arms, waiting while Daniel made travel arrangements downstairs. To her surprise, Mr. Seward had followed them outside the cavern to give them the belongings he'd confiscated at their capture, including Daniel's purse, still intact. He'd also offered Daniel the use of his horses for the return to London. Daniel had declined, but she could tell he'd been warmed by the offer.

For herself, she suspected that Crouch's revelations had badly shaken Mr. Seward. They'd certainly shaken her. Although Crouch's tale had gained him a tiny bit of her sympathy, it hadn't negated his abominable actions in ordering the kidnapping of her sister.

She searched Juliet's features, but could see nothing to indicate that Mr. Pryce had harmed her. That didn't mean, however, that he hadn't, and the thought made her heart twist in her chest.

"Are you sure you're all right?" she asked for what she knew was the tenth time at least.

"I'm quite well, I promise." Juliet patted her hand.

"I only wish that scoundrel hadn't run off," Helena grumbled. "I could happily wring his neck for what he did to you."

When Juliet remained silent, Helena frowned. The girl had been adamant that no one was to pursue Mr. Pryce. She'd insisted that his behavior at the end redeemed his other actions.

In Helena's mind, it didn't in the least. But that would be a matter for discussion with Griff. Right now, the most important thing was getting home safely.

Juliet shifted in her chair and eyed Helena curiously. "By the way, what was all that nonsense in the cavern about you being Daniel's wife?"

Lord, she'd forgotten about that. "Daniel . . . er . . . that is . . . he told people we were married while we were on the road. He did it to protect my reputation."

"That was very clever of him."

"Yes, very," she said wryly. She hesitated to reveal that she might actually become Mrs. Brennan. First she wanted to be sure that Daniel still meant to marry her. Despite their lovemaking last night, he hadn't exactly renewed his proposal.

The parlor door opened just then, sparing her any more of Juliet's embarrassing questions. Daniel entered with Crouch in tow. "The mail coach to London comes through in a few minutes, and I've booked passage for the two of you."

"Aren't we going to Dover with you?" Helena said apprehensively.

Daniel laid his hand on her shoulder. "I don't think that's wise. If Griff has reached London, he and Rosalind will be frantic, and I'd feel safer with you both there anyway. You can be at Knighton House by this evening on the mail coach."

"So quickly?" Helena said.

He smiled wryly. "You'd be surprised how quickly you can travel when you're not tracking leads and having gigs collapse under you and hiding from treacherous free traders."

And getting drunk in taverns and making love in barns, she thought, her cheeks warming. "How long will you be gone?"

"No more than a couple of days, I hope. I may have to help him tie up some loose ends, if only to get him out of here for good."

There was a noise in the hall, a porter calling the arrival of the mail coach. "Go on now," Daniel urged. "I won't feel easy until you're bound for London."

He hurried them out, and as he handed Helena into the crowded coach, she turned to stare anxiously into his face. "You will come back to me, Danny, won't you?"

"Yes, love." He brushed a kiss across her hand. "I promise."

Nonetheless, she fretted all the way to London. Since

she and Juliet could not talk freely in front of the other passengers, all she could do was think and worry. Last night with Daniel had been the most incredible, earth-shattering night of her life, but they had not spoken of marriage again. And today Daniel had heard more wretched things about his family. She would just die if he reacted as he had yesterday, pushing her away again.

Well, if he tried it, he would have a fight on his hands. Because Daniel Brennan was not going to escape marriage to her, no matter what fool notions he had.

When they arrived in London at Knighton House, all was chaos. Griff and Rosalind had returned, and Griff had already summoned runners and soldiers. They filled the halls and spilled out of Griff's study, looking as scruffy and ill-mannered as Crouch's men, or worse. Helena and Juliet swept past them into the room to find poor Seth Atkins under siege. Griff sat behind his desk with Helena's sketches, going over them with a fine-tooth comb as Rosalind fretted and demanded answers.

"We're back!" Juliet announced brightly, effectively halting any other conversation.

The shock on Rosalind's face was rapidly replaced by joy. "Juliet! Helena!" she cried as she bounded across the room.

More chaos ensued, punctuated by tears, hugs, and innumerable questions, each following so hard and fast on the other that sorting them out took forever. It was even longer before the household returned to normalcy, the runners and soldiers banished, Seth sent off to a guest room, and a modicum of sanity restored.

Now Helena and Juliet sat on the settee in Griff's study with Rosalind between them. She gripped both their hands as if afraid they might vanish into thin air.

Helena had begun by recounting the final confrontation with Crouch, so now they were working their way backward through the tale, trying to relate everything that had happened.

"What I don't understand is all this nonsense about Helena being Daniel's wife," Griff said. "That lad Seth insisted that he helped a Mr. and Mrs. Brennan."

"Oh," Juliet explained cheerily, "Daniel and Helena had to pretend to be married while they traveled so they could protect her reputation."

Griff raised an eyebrow. "Did they indeed? Seth seemed to think there was more to it than that."

Leave it to her rapscallion brother-in-law to divine the truth. Helena cast Griff her chilliest look. "Seth was wrong." One thing she wouldn't tolerate was meddling questions about her and Daniel and what they'd done. Not until he could be present, too. Much as she wanted to proclaim him as her fiancé, she would not do it until he'd returned and confirmed that he still wanted to marry her.

Unfortunately, Griff would not let it end there. "All the same, there is the rather intriguing matter of the sketches you sent home. Not those of the smugglers. The other one on the back."

Of Daniel half-naked, lying in the horse stall. Helena's face flamed. "That is private, and none of your concern."

"You're my sister-in-law now, so you've become my concern."

"Now see here, Griff Knighton, if you think that just because you married my sister, I will tolerate your trying to—" Helena began.

"You say that Daniel won't be back for a few days?" Rosalind jumped in quickly.

Helena glared at Griff a moment before meeting her sister's gaze. "Yes."

"Then there's not much point in discussing this until then, is there?"

Though Helena wondered why her sister had unexpectedly turned into her ally in this, she was not about to protest it.

For her part, Rosalind had already decided something would have to be done about Helena and Daniel when the blasted rogue returned. She'd seen that sketch, too—Daniel bare-chested and asleep, lying beneath what looked like a blanket. Helena could only have sketched it if she'd been sharing a room with the rascal, and probably his bed, too. It was hard to imagine Helena—who lived by the most stringent rules of propriety—succumbing to any man, yet *something* had certainly happened. And if it was what Rosalind thought, then she intended to make sure Daniel offered her sister a more respectable position than bed warmer.

She felt fairly certain that he would. She'd always suspected Daniel of having feelings for Helena. If Helena refused to speak of it, however, it might mean she still clung to her distrust of men. Then again, she might simply be uncertain of Daniel's intentions herself.

Either way, Rosalind would make sure her dear sister found happiness—if not with Daniel, then with *some* worthy gentleman.

But to ensure it, she had to address certain other matters. She rose to pace the room. "With you and Juliet back, we need to set about repairing any possible damage to your reputations."

Helena raised an eyebrow. "Since when do you care about reputation?"

"She may not always care about her own," Griff put in dryly, "but she's very particular about her sisters'."

Rosalind glared at her husband. "Especially when

your wild friends make matters difficult by dragging them about the countryside unchaperoned." Her brow furrowed as she faced her sisters. Juliet sat blushing, her head bowed, but Helena was even more intractable than usual and stared her down. "The sooner you're both seen publicly, the easier it will be to squelch any rumors. We can pretend you just came up from the country to visit me now that Griff and I have returned from our honeymoon."

"I don't see why we need to cover anything up," Helena said loftily. "No one knows us in London. Who could possibly know what we did or whom we did it with?"

"One thing I've learned since coming here is that servants talk," Rosalind retorted. "How do you think I found out that you went off with Daniel alone? Griff's servants told me."

Helena sighed.

Rosalind went on. "Fortunately, few people are in town now, but still I know neither of you is probably in the mood for society affairs, but you'll have to marshal your strength, I'm afraid. Tomorrow morning we begin paying calls and doing whatever we can to pretend that you haven't been gallivanting around the country alone with young men. Because I refuse to see my sisters' futures ruined because of some blasted free-trading friends of Griff's and Daniel's."

Chapter 22

He swore he'd adore her,
And to her ever constant prove;
He'd wed her, he'd bed her,
And none on earth but her he'd love.
"Una's Lock,"
anonymous nineteenth-century Irish ballad

Nothing in fashionable London had changed in eight years, Helena thought as she entered yet another ballroom with Rosalind, this time for a ball at Lord and Lady Rushton's Mayfair mansion.

For a week, Rosalind had dragged her and Juliet from one event to another—breakfasts and routs and appearances at the opera. Helena had acquiesced for her sisters' sakes. It wasn't as if she had anything else to do, as long as Daniel remained absent.

She did wish, however, that he'd send word of where he was or when he would return. She swallowed down the lump in her throat. He would come. He had promised.

But what if he didn't? What if he stayed away because he'd changed his mind? Because their time together had all faded into an amusing adventure that was now over and done? What if the wonderful night of mutual vows she remembered had been very one-sided?

No, she wouldn't think of that. He loved her. She knew he did. He would come.

In the meantime, she had no choice but to resume her role as Well-bred Young Lady. Strange, how ill-fitting it seemed these days. For the first time in her life, she chafed at the restrictions of her rank. She'd discovered that one minute with Daniel held more excitement than a week in "good society."

Tonight was no exception. She wished Juliet were here to bolster her spirits—but Juliet had not come out yet, and so hadn't been allowed to attend the ball. Instead, Helena listened to Rosalind engage yet another gossiping matron in conversation.

She smiled at her sister's deft lies. Rosalind chattered on, discussing what they'd been doing, how tedious the country was, anything to make it seem as if Juliet and Helena had not left Warwickshire until their appearance in London a week ago. It was easy to see how Rosalind had succeeded as an actress for her brief stint on the stage.

"And did you hear about the new Baron Templemore?" the gossiping matron commented. "He's just come into the title, and you should see how shamelessly Lady Feathering has been shoving her daughters at him. He's quite the handsome mystery man. Have you met him?"

Rosalind and Helena exchanged glances. At the moment handsome mystery men were not high on their lists. "We haven't had that pleasure," Rosalind replied. "I've heard quite a lot about him in the past week, but he never seems to be at the same functions we are."

The matron's gaze flicked briefly to Helena. "Well, I'll be sure to introduce you and your lovely sisters if I have the chance. Though I don't suppose they need any help from *me*, what with the hordes of men scrambling after them this week."

As soon as the matron walked away, Rosalind chuckled and murmured, "Shall we go sample the ratafia before the hordes of men descend on you?"

Helena raised an eyebrow. "That woman is certainly prone to exaggeration."

"Not entirely. You must admit there's been a steady procession of gentlemen wishing to be introduced to you. They fall all over themselves trying to fetch you punch and engage you in conversation. You've been the belle of thc ball *everywhere*, you and Juliet."

"Juliet perhaps, but not me and not here. One can hardly be the belle of the ball when one cannot dance."

"It hasn't stopped anyone from seeking you out."

That was true actually, and she found it surprising. "I suppose now that Griff has provided us with portions—"

"Nobody knows about that yet. I've been too busy trying to repair your reputations to bother mentioning your eligibility."

"What?" Helena spotted a couple of gentlemen she'd already met headed their way, and groaned. She wasn't ready to end this intriguing conversation. Swiftly, she tugged Rosalind into a nearby alcove. "If that's true, then why are the men pursuing me? And after all these years—are London gentlemen so much more desperate than Stratford gentlemen?"

Rosalind laughed. "It's not the gentlemen, silly, it's *you.* You were always so wretched to the ones in Stratford. If a man dared approach, you froze him with a look and he backed down. You were so determined not to trust them that you never gave them the chance to be nice."

A faint smile touched Helena's lips. "Funny, but Daniel said much the same thing to me once."

"Did he?" Rosalind eyed her with keen curiosity. "He seems to have said a great many interesting things to you on your trip. I've never heard you speak so much about a man in your life. Even Lord Farnsworth."

"Trust me, Daniel is ten times the man Fickle Farnsworth ever was."

"F-Fickle Farnsworth?" Rosalind sputtered. "Now I *know* you've changed. You would never have referred to his lordship so cavalierly a month ago." Rosalind searched her face. "And I suppose Daniel is the reason you've been different since you returned."

Helena blushed and ducked her head. "How am I different?"

"More comfortable with yourself. Breaking Mrs. N's rules right and left. For pity's sake, yesterday at dinner you asked for ale! Griff nearly choked on his mutton."

Helena laughed. "I did enjoy that."

"And you're more comfortable with men, too." Rosalind grinned. "You can still put a man in his place when he needs it, but you're far kinder to the ones who don't. And you finally seem able to tell which is which."

Helena's throat tightened. All these years of loneliness, of shutting herself off from people—how much of it had been due to her own blindness? And from fear that if she let them close, they'd reject her for more than her leg. She'd allowed Fickle Farnsworth's dreadful behavior to convince her she was unsuitable for marriage, then had set out to prove it by driving away every man who approached.

She had Daniel to thank for knocking the scales from her eyes. She had Daniel to thank for a great many things.

If only he would come home so she could do it.

Rosalind moved out of the alcove. "Come on. We can't hide in here avoiding people all night."

"Why not?" Helena grumbled as she followed her sister. Now that all the gentlemen seemed to want her, she found she did not want any of them. Oh, they were perfectly nice, she supposed, but compared to Daniel, they were as dull and colorless as a charcoal sketch next to a finished portrait in oils. She needed his vibrance in her life. Without Daniel, even flouting the proprieties was no fun.

As they circled the room, a young gentleman approached who looked vaguely familiar. It was only when he was upon them that she realized why. Oh, dear—it was the duke from Daniel's office, the one person who knew she had not just come up from the country a week ago. Would he recognize her?

"Lady Rosalind!" he said to her sister. "How good to see you again."

"The pleasure is mine, your grace," Rosalind replied. "But I don't believe you've met my sister. Helena, this is the Duke of Montfort."

"How do you do?" Helena mumbled as she held out her hand.

He took it, a frown knitting his brow. "Actually, I believe I *have* met your sister. I'm almost certain of it." He studied her features. "Was it at Marlborough's breakfast last month? I seem to recall that we met during the day."

"Not last month," Rosalind said. "She only arrived from the country last week."

He hesitated. Then he glanced to her cane, and his frown deepened. "But I have the strongest memory . . ." He still held her hand, and instead of relinquishing it, said, "Lady Helena, have you had the opportunity to see Rushton's conservatory yet?"

Her pulse raced fearfully. "No, I'm afraid not."

"Then you must let me show it to you. It will give us the chance to figure out why I think I know you."

She groaned inwardly. Of all the people she had to run into, must it be the one person who could put the lie to Rosalind's claims? And a rake as well, judging from what Daniel had said about him. Still, for her sisters' sakes, she would try to muddy his memory about her further.

Letting him tuck her hand into his bent elbow, she said, "Certainly, your grace. I'd be honored."

When Daniel arrived at the Rushton place, after Griff's butler had told him where Helena and the Knightons had gone, he groaned to see the crowd spilling out into the foyer. Wonderful. Just what he needed when all he wanted was to find Helena, and drag her into the garden or somewhere else private where he could kiss her senseless.

He probably shouldn't have come here anyway. A proper gentleman would have waited until the morrow to call on her. A proper gentleman wouldn't have rushed to dress himself and race over here like a besotted idiot.

But then, he wasn't a proper gentleman—and he'd certainly come to the right place for reminding him of it. Despite his clothes, he felt like a hound among the lapdogs. In the office, it never bothered him, but here . . .

He sighed. He'd best get used to it. This was Helena's world, and when they married—*if* she still wanted to, after all this—he'd be spending a great deal of time in it.

That was all right, though. The last hellish week of dealing with his troublesome uncle had taught him one thing: he wanted Helena for his wife, come what may. He loved her strength and courage, her easy acceptance of his past, and even her stubbornness. And if marrying her meant enduring balls every night of his life, he would gladly endure them.

But he wasn't certain she'd have him. Back in familiar surroundings, she might've decided she didn't want a great rascal like him after all. Being among her own kind might've reminded her of the disadvantages to marrying his sort of man, one without title or prominence, lofty name or family connections.

That fear had been a crushing weight on his chest for days. Strange how he'd felt not a whit of fear while confronting Crouch and his men, yet the thought of losing one slender woman could strike him with pure terror.

He sighed. It only got worse the longer he dallied. He squared his shoulders and set off to look for her. But it was Rosalind he found first.

As soon as he neared her, she broke into a grin. "Daniel! You're back!"

"Yes. Just arrived, in fact."

He kissed the cheek she offered, then glanced about impatiently. "Where's Helena?"

Rosalind laughed. "Why, Daniel Brennan, you ought to be ashamed of yourself—asking about my sister before I've even had the chance to talk to you."

"Forgive me," he said with a pained smile. "It's just that I'm anxious to see her."

"You could've fooled me. You were supposed to return days ago, or at least that's what she expected."

"So did I. But matters were more complicated than I'd allowed for." Crouch had delayed at every turn, refusing to leave England until he called in all his markers with people who owed him money. When the list kept growing, Daniel had finally threatened him with bodily harm and tossed him unceremoniously onto a packet boat to France. "And how is she? Is she all right? I saw Juliet briefly at Knighton House and she appeared to be fine, but she told me little about Helena."

"Helena's doing quite well, actually. We've been scurrying about, trying to make sure she suffered no loss to her reputation after you dragged her around the countryside unchaperoned." The reproof in her voice was unmistakable. "We've been attending parties and balls and the like. She's been very popular." She paused, one eyebrow lifting. "Especially with men. They flock to her like magpies. I spend all my time shooing them off."

His breath caught in his throat. "Do you?" he said hollowly. "That doesn't surprise me. Any man would be a fool not to recognize your sister's charms."

"True, but until now she's done her best to hide them. She's been different since her return. What on earth did you do to her?"

Showed her what a lovely woman she is, that's all, he thought grimly. *And now that she's discovered it, what need has she of me?* "What did *she* say I'd done to her?" he evaded.

"She wouldn't talk about it—absolutely refused to discuss you until you were back."

The pressure in his chest increased. That didn't have to

mean anything. Helena was a cautious woman, not the sort to announce an engagement until she was sure of her position. And he hadn't exactly left her with the assurance that he still intended to marry her. All the same . . .

To his chagrin, Griff joined them at that moment. "Ah, so the prodigal has finally returned."

Daniel gritted his teeth. The last thing he wanted right now was to stand here relating to Griff all that had happened, even if it did concern him. "As I was just telling your wife, I'm looking for Helena. She and I have some matters to discuss. You and I can talk later."

"Rather eager to find her, are you?" Griff smirked at him. "I seem to recall a conversation you and I had about Helena at my wedding."

Daniel groaned, remembering Griff's comments about how he should court Helena, and his saying he wouldn't want a "stiff-rumped" lass like that for a wife, even if she would have him. It had been a lie even then, and now it was painfully ironic.

Apparently judging that his arrow had hit the mark, Griff went on gleefully. "And judging from that intriguing sketch of you—"

"Sketch?"

"The one you sent with Seth. The one that shows you reclining on a bed half-dressed."

"Oh, *that* sketch." Bloody hell.

"As I was saying," Griff went on, "judging from Helena's sketch, which she refuses to discuss, I gather you've changed your opinion of her somewhat in recent days."

"You could say that," Daniel muttered, alarmed by the idea of Helena's not discussing something as damning as that sketch of him. What the devil did it mean? He had to find her, talk to her, but as he scanned the room he didn't see her at all. "Damn it, where *is* she anyway?"

Rosalind took pity on him and pointed toward an open set of doors. "She's taking a tour of the conservatory with the Duke of Montfort."

"Montfort!" Yes, he could easily imagine that randy rogue wanting to get Helena off alone. Montfort thought he could have any woman he wished—because he often did.

But he would not have Helena.

Daniel started to stalk off without a word, but Griff caught his arm, suddenly serious. "Listen to me, Daniel. You once took great umbrage at how I treated Rosalind, and with good reason. But so help me God, if you mistreat her sister—"

"I've no intention of that, believe me." He shrugged off Griff's arm, but when he saw Rosalind watching him anxiously, he tamped down his impatience. "You said something else to me at your wedding, too, how you couldn't wait for the day when you saw me in hell pining after a woman and unsure of her answer." He swallowed his pride and went on. "Well, that day has come, my friend. So you can either prolong my hell or give me the chance to fight my way out of it. Which is it to be?"

Griff broke into a grin. "Considering how you tormented me throughout my pursuit of Rosalind, the idea of prolonging your hell does sound tempting."

"Don't you *dare*, Griff Knighton," Rosalind broke in. She beamed at Daniel. "Go on, and quickly, before my fool of a husband ruins everything."

Casting her a grateful glance, Daniel hurried toward the doors she indicated. He could hear Griff protesting that he wasn't trying to ruin anything and Rosalind making some hot reply, but he didn't stay to hear what it was. The servants who were standing by directed him to the conservatory, and it took him only moments to find Helena and Montfort.

As he entered, he spotted them at the opposite end. The two of them stood gazing out through the windows overlooking the rear garden, their backs to him. The sight of Helena, so lovely in her swan-white gown, arrested him. He halted, drinking her in, wishing she didn't seem so perfectly suited to her surroundings.

Did he have the right to ask this of her, to ask her to give up all this?

Perhaps not. But he was a selfish bastard, so he'd do it anyway. Because without her, there was no point to anything.

Suddenly, Helena's soft voice wafted to him on the breeze. He stepped closer to hear her say, "Truly, your grace, you must give up this silly idea that we have met before. I would swear that tonight is the first time I've ever laid eyes on you."

"Do not play coy, madam. I have just figured out where I saw you. It was in Brennan's office a couple of weeks ago. I recognized you at once."

Helena sighed. "Oh, yes, of course. I'd forgotten about that."

"But I had not," Montfort said smoothly. "Did you truly believe I could forget so exquisite a creature?"

Daniel bristled, but he desperately wanted—needed—to hear her response, so he continued to stand back.

"Thank you for the compliment," she replied, "but I think there's something you should know about me." She glanced up at the duke. "I was at Mr. Brennan's office for a very good reason the day you saw me. You see, he is the man I intend to marry."

Her declaration shattered the weight crushing Daniel's chest. Hope flared in its place, spreading like wildfire through his limbs, flaming out of control in his heart.

Montfort snorted. "Marry Brennan? Surely you jest.

Good Lord, that would be like yoking a nag to a prime stepper."

"I beg your pardon," Helena said in her frostiest tone, "but are you comparing me to a horse?"

"I didn't mean—"

"And which am I? The nag or the prime stepper?"

Daniel smothered a laugh. The man was already in way over his head, and he didn't even know it.

"Why . . . the prime stepper, of course!"

"I assure you that my fiancé is not remotely like a nag."

So now she was calling him "fiancé," was she? It made him want to crow it to all the lapdogs in the ballroom.

She went on. "If I were so crass as to compare him to any animal, I would describe him as a lion. He's one of the finest men in all England."

Montfort was not impressed. "One of the finest—are you mad? I can understand his appealing to certain low sorts of women, but I can't believe a woman of your obvious intelligence, taste, and breeding would be so foolish as to wish to marry a coarse lout who—"

"Struggled against enormous odds to make something of himself?" she broke in. "Accomplished success despite lacking the advantages of birth, wealth, and education that your grace was given?" Her tone dripped sarcasm. "Yes, why would I be so foolish?"

Montfort shook his head. "He used to be a smuggler, for pity's sake. Did you know that?"

"Of course. I know everything about Mr. Brennan. He's my fiancé."

That word sounded better every time she said it, Daniel thought with deep satisfaction.

"*Everything?*" Montfort snorted. "Then did you know that your precious Mr. Brennan is also given to . . . shall we say . . . certain unsavory habits? He consorts with loose women. He frequents a number of places of ill repute and—"

"Not anymore," Helena said firmly. "Besides, you, of all men, can scarcely criticize him for *that*. From what he's told me, you've also been known to visit a certain Mrs. Beard's establishment from time to time."

Daniel had to bite his tongue to keep from laughing. When the lass threw propriety to the winds, she didn't do it by halves.

"M-Mrs. Beard?" Montfort sputtered. But his shock apparently gave way to something more alarming. "Well, well, Lady Helena. If you know of Mrs. Beard's, then you are far more a woman of the world than I realized. But if it's Brennan's legendary prowess in the bedchamber that interests you, I assure you there are men of your own rank who can satisfy those urges better than he."

Montfort suddenly bent to kiss her, and Daniel surged forward with a growl. But before he could reach them, the crack of Helena's hand against the duke's cheek sounded loudly in the conservatory.

"You insolent chit—you slapped me!" Montfort protested, outraged.

"If you ever try that again, your grace," she said icily, "I shall do more than slap you—I shall break my cane over your thick head."

That was Daniel's cue. "You'd best mind her warning," he growled as he approached. "The wench has a wicked swing."

Helena heard the familiar voice with joy, although her companion jumped and whirled around in horror. She turned to find Daniel standing a few feet behind her in evening cutaway and breeches, looking every bit as lordly as his grace, but more handsome by far.

"Daniel!" Her cane clattered to the floor as she practically threw herself at him. He swung her up into his arms and kissed her without restraint, though the Duke of Montfort stood stiffly by, watching them.

Her heart soared. He was here at last! And claiming her for all the world to see. After an endlessly thrilling kiss, he drew back but did not release her, holding her quite possessively in his arms.

The duke chose that moment to make his apologies. "Brennan, I do hope you realize that I did not mean to—"

"Insult Helena? Try to steal her?" Daniel glowered at the duke over Helena's head. "I s'pose I shouldn't blame you, since she's such a lovely lass. But she's *my* lovely lass, and don't you forget it. Because if I ever catch you within two feet of her again, I'll prove myself the 'coarse lout' that I am and put my fist right through your bloody jaw."

His "lovely lass." No words had ever sounded so magnificent.

Montfort's eyes narrowed, but he clearly knew better than to say anything. Rigidly dignified, he stalked past them and out of the conservatory.

"Oh, Danny," Helena whispered as soon as he was gone, "I am so glad you are back. I have missed you very much."

"I can see how much you missed me," he grumbled. "Going off alone with dukes and God knows who else. Rosalind said the men have been flocking about you like magpies, the bloody sots."

His jealousy delighted her. "If you were so concerned about it," she couldn't help teasing him, "you should not have stayed away so long." Then she sobered. "I was worried sick about you, my love."

"Were you?" He kissed her again, lingering this time as if he never wanted to stop. When he pulled back, his breath raced as rapidly as hers. "I'm sorry, love. My uncle caused me trouble at every turn, but he's gone now. With any luck, he won't bother us again."

"Well, if he tries, I'll simply shoot him," she told him quite earnestly. "Though you'll have to buy me a pistol first. And teach me how to shoot it."

He chuckled. "You seemed to be managing fine without it. But a larger cane might be in order, to beat off all the randy lords running after you now that they've recognized what I've known all along."

"Oh? And what is that?"

"That you're a treasure. That any man would be bloody fortunate to have you for his wife."

Her heart tripped in her chest. "Is that your roundabout way of proposing marriage to me again, after you so dreadfully withdrew your offer a week ago?"

His sensual grin sent wonderful shivers of anticipation down her spine. "No. Since I didn't like your answer a'tall the first time I proposed, I'm not giving you the chance to refuse me this time." His eyes glowed down at her, full of promises for the future. "I love you, lass. I gave you plenty of chances to escape me, but you didn't take them. So now we're getting married, and there's not a bloody thing you can do to stop it."

She smiled coyly up at him, her heart full to bursting with her love. "And what will an arrogant rascal like you do to ensure I comply with your wicked demands? Shackle me naked to a bed and make love to me all night long?"

His eyes gleamed. "If that's what it takes."

She wound her arms about his neck. "Then by all means, my love—let's go find a bed and a shackle."

Author's Note

For those of you wondering about Helena's mysterious illness, it's polio. The only term for it at the time was infantile paralysis, referring to polio that occurred in infancy. But it could also strike adults, although there wasn't a term for that. I discovered in my research that polio goes back at least as far as 3,000 years ago among the Egyptians. Though cases were rare until the twentieth century, they weren't unheard of. I was careful to set Helena's circumstances up so that she might fall prey to it as an adult (with no exposure to bad sanitation in her youth, where she might have built up immunity, and then sudden exposure as a grown-up). As for her struggle to regain use of her legs, there are numerous cases where victims have obtained such success, depending on the severity of their illness and its effect on their muscles. I drew on a wealth of research to depict polio's impact on Helena.

I also tapped numerous sources for my portrayal of the smugglers in Hastings. The St. Clements Caves actually exist and were indeed used by smugglers; presently a Smugglers Adventure tour takes place there. The Hawkhurst Gang was every bit as ruthless as Helena describes and did much to curtail public sympathy toward smugglers at this time. For the most part, however, smugglers were not violent. Plenty of ordinary people (yes, including clergymen) dabbled in free trading on the side and quite a few wealthy individuals subsidized their endeavors, so I had fun making Daniel straddle those two worlds.